A BULLY NAMED KARDESH

By

Marshall B. Thompson Jr.

Trafford rev. 10/12/2013

 www.trafford.com

North America & international
toll-free: 1 888 232 4444 (USA & Canada)
fax: 812 355 4082

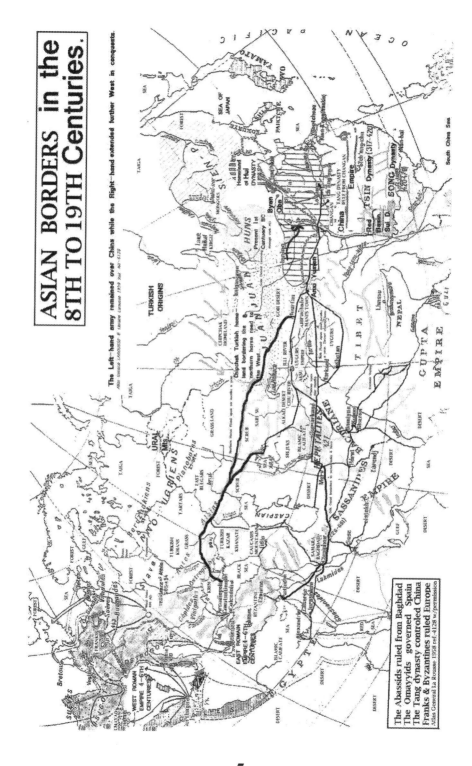

ASIAN BORDERS in the 8TH TO 19TH Centuries.

The Left–hand army remained over China while the Right–hand extended further West in conquests.

The Abassids ruled from Baghdad
The Omayyids governed Spain
The Tang dynasty controled China
Franks & Byzanfines ruled Europe
Atlas General la Rousse 1958 ref-4128 w/permission

5

TABLE OF CONTENTS

7

PS: The glossary and foreign words are *italicized* and spelled to help readers of English. They are not always spelled so in their dictionaries. MBT

AUTHOR'S OPENING

'A THREE FOLD CORD IS NOT QUICKLY BROKEN' is both a wise saying in many cultures and an ancient truth proclaiming strength in unity. But like all truth, new and old, it has to be tested periodically either directly or by close observation.

Here, I have attempted a three cord story and in braiding it together parts must necessarily appear and disappear from even the diligent readers, revealing details that enrich both the characters and the situations. As an aid: each story is printed in a different font. They have been placed in historical settings where cultural details are sometimes sketchy. Never-the-less, all have been researched as well as possible. Historic events have been bent as little as possible and while the book is fiction, it reflects a lot of truth about ancient times in Middle Asia.

A person standing on a high over-look is influenced by position and perspective. Standing twelve hundred years after the fact gives one a grand view and deep insights into the struggles of ancient peoples whose descendants still live among us. Some old problems are still with us and haunt modern politics and attitudes. Other bits of history are past and no longer form a part of our modern prejudices.

The principal strand of our story starts in an exiled leader and his restless son, Kardesh. To that story is added the invasion of clans loyal to that exiled Khan with the hostage of a young widow and baby of the old khan whose death has divided the Chipchak nation. To this, we add the expulsion of foreigners from China. There the Tang dynasty has reestablished control after its own defeat and exile. Although the three stories seem about to explode and lose contact several times they continue to form a braid that rounds out the truth about Middle Asian history in its tensions coming from east and west in dynamic interplay.

Religious interaction is projected as carefully as research and experience can make them. Although the author is personally a Christian, he has made the arguments and positions of each religious group as accurate as research and good will can make them. The author has experienced 12 years of teaching in the Middle East. This has given him a personal knowledge of the things written here.

Friendship is something so personal and deep that doctrine and custom rarely cause more than momentary disruptions. Warmth and humanity, as well as respect, are a bond too strong to be overcome by the parroting of socially acceptable formulas and views. Personal experiences of truth and unity of purpose bring an intimacy stronger than divisive prejudices. Love can include traditional enemies.

Here, then, is a word picture of history and culture in a large arena; presented as it was: warts, scars and all.

Marshall B. Thompson Jr.

9

MID-ASIA TIME LINE

At the beginning of the ninth century of the present era the empires east and west were in a state of recuperation from the previous internal struggles. Upheavals in the East with the expulsion and successful restoration of the Tang dynasty brought China into a retreat toward earlier traditions. In the far West, barbarians: Teutonic and Slavic were being converted as they settled into parts of the old Roman Empire. Byzantium was recovering from religious controversy and Islamic aggression. Islam had its own upheavals in civil wars. The first division was the Kirbala split between Shia and Sunni. War brought separation of the Umayyad dynasty still ruling Spain and the Abbassids who had departed long since to Baghdad. Both dynastic and territorial wars continued in the Indian peninsula. Khorasan had become the seat of power in this expansion against the Rajput's frontier marches beyond the Indus River. Northward the Caliphs had found their progress blocked by the formidable Turkish tribes in the grasslands of Central Asia. They could hardly hold the agricultural areas and the Turkic Uigurs resisted strongly on the east of the dividing Tien Shan or Tanra Dah range of Mountains. Everywhere, wars were perennial, but success in conquests was small. Warriors were in constant demand. However, life expectancy was low and consumption exceeded production in every sector of the world.

In all these circumstances religious affiliation was a part of the conquest structure. Yet, as always, the personal element was present to speed or retard the process. Each empire had an official language, religion, law, and ruling capital. It was dangerous to oppose the ruling dynasties and their opinions. Yet, then, as now, minorities continued to exist and practice those things dear to their hearts and traditions. They practiced such in secrecy or publicly at a high risk and material cost to their group. Their success and occasional prosperity was often penalized by the pliant majority at the behest of the ruling classes. Force, in all its human guises, was prevalent then, as now. It was often maintained even in the face of logic, compassion or need. Virtue was as rare a commodity then, personally and collectively, as it is today.

It is our purpose to explore such a world and understand its ancestry to our own situations, both in Central Asia and around the world. We are living with the results of these encounters and their ideological positions as a result of historic clashes. The resulting defeats and victories have proved to be durable in nature. The game continues, however. God has yet to lead the *finale* that brings down the curtain on uncertainty and striving; to take us home for a toasty snack and warm bed before the awakening to a new day.   MBT

MARKET RUMBLE

11

PEOPLE, PLOTS & PLACES IN CHAPTER 1

Barmani: a priest of the Manichean faith in Kokand.
Erben: exiled son of Khan Erdash, younger twin of Erden.
Erden: Chipchak Khan ruling west of the Altai Mountains.
Kardesh: the leader of a diverse gang called 'The Brothers'.
Leyla: the teenage daughter of Erben in exile in Kokand.
Sister Pakhan: a nun of the Manichean order near Kokand.
Sevman: Manichean student, a member of the street gang.
Tash: an ambitious city boy, a member of the 'Kardeshler'.
Tayze: a widowed sister of Erben's wife, sharing his exile.
 Yeet: a Kokand City gang member of many skills: like fits.

GLOSSARY:

ahbee: big brother; elder brother, term of respect for a man.
ahnie; Turkish for mother.
Apostoloi: Greek for apostles, those sent forth, missionary.
burka: Islamic woman's garment, covering all.
Dem'i-urge: God of the material, not spiritual universe
 kardesh: sibling; applied to both brothers and sisters.
lah'ley: Tulip, flower names were given to girls at birth.
lie'yuk: Worthy, if a mother dies her girl's name changes.
ley'lek: stork, an aquatic bird with long skinny legs.
ley'lak: lilac flower; shortened in names to Leyla.
sev: love; imperative; command form: "You must love."
soos: hush; shut up; be quiet.
Tan'ra: ancient creator God of the eternal blue sky.
yoke etmem: I did nothing wrong; I'm innocent.
zorba: bully; ruffian.

BARMANI'S REPROOF

The rumble started as a piercing whistle brought every boy of the gang from his assigned station. There they played games or lazily looked over the crowds of shoppers in the evening market.

A high pitched childish scream stopped every shopper near the city fountain where women drew water or washed small articles not worthy of a trip to the river. There, bordering on the market stood an unkempt child shrilling agony and agitation above the noise of a busy place in the last throes of bargaining. The market police moved toward the disturbance and a crowd of worried women and curious men formed a circle about the thrashing body of the boy. His mouth dribbled foam and his eyes were crossed and staring,

The closely jammed stalls, with their vendors and buyers, provided a maze of paths, obstacles and intersections through which a dozen children ran, deliberately upsetting displays and jostling customers. They gathered treasure and food as they ran, adding to the confusion with their own screams and ululations.

Near the back wall of the market where the empty boxes and carts stood, a tall stout figure appeared wearing a light summer burka. It covered his face and body. He piled up crates and planks to form a set of stairs against the wall.

This was the escape route toward which the crew of busy plunderers moved.

The screaming child in the circle rolled toward some of the women, who startled, fell back. Dodging around their trouser legs he disappeared down the street. Yeet's part in the action was over.

The gang with their stolen goods tucked into bags and loose coats ran in a cascade of legs up the stairs and over the wall. There the tall hooded youth stood with a long pole, stouter than a spear, in his hand. He used it to start dismantling the stairway with his pole. He encouraged them, shouting as the last few swarmed over the boxes. He left only one set of boxes as a narrow path for the last two remaining.

A tall, rat-faced boy did a victory dance atop the wall and wiggled his rear suggestively at the pursuing merchants and customers racing after their lost goods. The last boy, short but stout, dodging through an intersection was caught by a burley carter who began to rain blows on him.

The boy with the pole brought the end in a side-wise swipe to the rear of the show off and sent him over the wall to safety. The other end of the weapon plunged forward in the hand of the masked boy and caught the carter a blow on the side of the head, skewing his turban.

"Sevman," the leader shouted. "Come!" he ordered. The boy broke free and plunged on to the stairs while the blunt spear pushed the carter away by pressing against his chest.

"*Kardesh*," the frightened Sevman called extending his arms up to the commanding boy. Kardesh grabbed Sevman with one arm and heaved him over the wall. Against the growing press he dismantled the last stair with a blow and stood atop the wall, laughing and dodging the sticks and stones thrown up at him. Suddenly, fire blazed up from a pile of hay behind the wall where the children had landed. He put his pole over and vaulted out of the reach of the angry mob, into the swirl of fire and smoke, laughing wildly. He landed on the outer side of the hay stack, away from the blazing edge by the wall. He immediately started

14

raging at the laggards who had not yet disappeared. A bag with the pilfered goods rested beyond the blazing hay.

"Tash," he hissed at the rat-faced boy, who was rubbing his bottom ruefully. "You deserve a lump on the head when you waste time playing the fool. I should teach you a lesson just as we have the market today. Why are you still dragging your feet? I'm off to the widow's. *Move!*" He snatched off his *burka* and flung it down into the bag.

He hefted the bag and swung round to the limping Sevman, "What ails you now little sluggard? Will you always be the last? Have you forgotten the plan?"

The small stout boy looked up with the face of a beaten puppy full of confusion and love. "I fell wrong, outside of the hay stack." He blinked back tears. "I was delayed at the weapon's shop to get this for you." He held up a knife with a green jade carving at the butt: the head of a mountain sheep with coiled horns.

Kardesh laughed and swept the boy up to his shoulder. "It's time to leave, before it gets too hot, little benefactor." He ran as they ducked through the gate from the empty lot.

Behind them faces appeared above the wall behind the fire. "Don't let them escape!" The voices shrilled in despair.

When Kardesh had run past several streets, they turned into a narrow ally and walked to the widow's well.

There Kardesh stooped and transferred the boy to the wood frame that protected the well. He took the bag.

"Sit and drink little brother, while I stash the goods. Did you get the other things?" He held out his hands expectantly. Sevman reached under his cummerbund and jacket to produce two rings, a small jade vase and a sandalwood box for jewelry. Kardesh's strong face assumed an angry look.

Sevman stuttered, "I got the rings in one swipe and the box was on the corner of the stand."

"You were greedy and it almost got you caught." Kardesh snapped, "I told you to get three things from your assigned section of the market. We only hit those who don't pay for protection. I told you that delay is dangerous. I told you to pick them out ahead of the signal. Why do you try to go beyond our limits?" He slapped Sevman's face

15

each time he said 'told'. His voice took on a cold quiet tone. He continued cuttingly. "You got five things. Is it to brag or be the best? Maybe it's only carelessness or defiance?"

Sevman seemed to shrink. "I thought you'd like the knife. I saw it as I ran by and I hardly stopped a minute. I'll be prompt next time."

"If there is a next time; if you are the first through; if I let you work with us again you will not endanger us." He slapped the boy again on each 'if'.

Tears ran down Sevman's face; he seemed convulsed. "*Ahbee*," he groaned in agony, and kissed the hand that struck him, "Big brother, I'll obey. Forgive me, I've failed you. Please don't separate me from the brothers. I'll starve if you cast me out." He continued trying to kiss the hand, but the big boy pushed him away.

"Go hungry again, for a day, little stupid. Go to Mani your prophet. You're named for him *sev mani*, love Mani. Your Manichaean church will feed you students thin barley soup and wilted vegetables, but no meat, never meat. I hear you have a mother there or is she a sister? Get out of my sight. If you tell what you know, you'll die."

Kardesh turned his back on Sevman and walked to the far side of the well where he pushed aside a brick and lowered the stolen articles carefully to the bottom of a space between the well and brick lining. He replaced the brick and walked to the house where the window rested crookedly on its frame and slid a coin under the edge of the wood before leaving the yard.

Sevman sat watching and then, limping, exited the place and set off for the east side of the town. From his cummerbund he drew his medallion and hung the string about his neck. The bronze cupped hand seemed to hold the flame of purity which touched the dirty string and his neck with golden reflection of the setting sun. He pulled the flaps on his hat down to cover his ears. He shuffled painfully trying to hurry. He sniffed pitifully, contemplating his misery; if he were late there would be no soup.

The temple and nunnery sat on a small cultivated hill on the edge of Kokand, a town in the Fergana Valley. The fertile valley was the hub of much warfare between religious factions. Arab and Persian converts from the west supported Islam, using the highlands of Khorasan as their base. The Shamanist Kirghiz tribe from the grazing lands around Lake Baikal, above the Gobi desert pressed the Uigur Turks. The Manichean Uygurs displaced the Tang dynasty's rule. The seat of their Empire was the Tarim basin and they pressed eastward. Nestorian Christians were scattered among tribes of the north and the towns along the Silk Road toward China. Using the powers of diplomacy and arms, these empires sought to maintain their own rule over the indigenous peoples of Middle Asia, living in the lands between Iran, India and China.

Sevman slipped into the kitchen where he quickly moved to the cooking pot which rested almost empty on the dirt floor. At the bottom rested a few vegetables in the pale brown liquid. This he hurriedly transferred to a bowl. He didn't bother to eat with a spoon. He greedily drank its departing warmth, giving only a passing grind of his teeth on the tougher fibers. Hurriedly he sought bread or other food. A few crumbs and bits of bread lay on and under the table for the mice. Nothing remained on the dirty wooden plates. The hungry leave no bread. Groaning again Sevman moved hopefully toward the food storeroom which was locked. He sensed someone behind him. With a gasp, he turned back from the barred door. The tall, cadaverous form of Barmani, abbot and priest, filled the doorway. His eyes seemed to pierce Sevman's soul.

"You are late and hungry, Sevmani. Where do you wander? You go after class and do not memorize your portions for the day. You come with bruises, but seem well fed many days. You have joined the world and its causes, and leave the truth for others." He looked at the boy reproachfully. "Your mother will cry and spend her hours praying for you, rather than the apostles and missionaries. They spread the news of Mani and his prophecies as minister of the Heavenly Yesu. How can you cleave to the light if you mix it with darkness? Have you become like this present world, a hideous, impure source of evil corruption to all? We must separate ourselves. I fear you will not join the elect, but will be born into this dreadful place of trials

17

again. Worse, you will touch other lives with your own failures and contaminate them."

"Forgive me, revered Barmani." The boy went down on hands and knees and crawled toward the towering figure in the robe of fine white material. "It is true. I ask your pardon. The world is a place of suffering. The demon progenitors of this creation have touched my light and darkened me." The light, coming through the door behind Barmani, shone on the bruise under one eye.

"I see that you have suffered. Come, it is near time for vespers. Seek the light of the Blessed. Hunger is a privilege of the elect. Tonight you join with them in the denial of flesh and self indulgence. The world revels in lust and sloth, but you will learn the way of Mani and proclaim this truth to save many from the realms of darkness." The figure moved back with a motion, beckoning with all the fingers pointing downward, for Sevman to follow. The sound of music rose behind them.

"I hear and obey, oh holy one." The boy swiped his eyes and nose with his sleeve and followed meekly to the candle-lighted chapel. At the front were the symbols of a right hand, holding the flame such as he wore, and the statue of Mani in a seated Buddha-like pose, his hand pointed up to the light. The nuns stood together in a clump, singing the verses and the scholars sang along raggedly:

#1   Oh, Light of lights, come now. Shine
            In the dense darkness of our hearts.
            Open our eyes that once were blind:
            In Your Kingdom take our part.
            Warning, pleading, let us be
            Apostoloi elect to see
            Your Kingdom come: Your will in me.

#2   Creation's goals far higher
            Than the wild chaos of the start.
            Men now perfected in their souls
            Show the High One's subtle art.
            Gentle, loving, let us be

Apostoloi elect to see
Your Kingdom come: Your will in me.

#3   Dying slave feel the hate thrust
Our fleshly nature's outer rind.
Fighting for food and our heart's lust,
Lost the glories of the mind.
Planning, praying, let us be
Apostoloi elect to see
Your Kingdom come: Your will in me.

MANICHEAN HYMN

Oh, Light of lights, come now. Shine
in the dense dark – ness of our hearts.
O – pen our eyes that once were blind:
in Your king – dom take our part.
Warn – ing, plead – ing, let us be
A–pos–to–loi e–lect to see
Your kingdom come: Your >‑‑‑‑‑‑‑> Will in me.

Sevman's eyes swept in the scene, the beauty of the chapel: the bright vestment of Barmani as he bowed over the sacred books, reciting the liturgy. The fragrance of spice and sandalwood filled the confines of the room. The sacred flame glowed behind the priest. How pleasing to the eye, ear and nose, yet so difficult to live the life demanded.

To deny the flesh, repudiate its demands, control its appetites... was this not impossible? Yet, there stood the personification of such control. He was celibate, fasting, yet energetic in study and charity; a visionary, still the axis of all the communities activities.

Sevman sighed and thought of his life these past months: his rise in the esteem of others and himself, as he gave his allegiance and efforts to please Kardesh, his new leader. The demands and code of the new way of life left the old familiar ways of the congregation diminished. It was difficult, but possible to live the new life. He knew the impossibility of his maintaining the old. Head bowed, he awaited the ending of the service.

>- - - - - - -> AT THE MONASTERY > - - - - - - ->

The sister looked at Sevnan critically as he crossed her path. He smiled shyly hoping to talk, "Sister Pakhan..." he began, then paused, seeking encouragement. At the nod of her head he rushed into his prepared spiel. "I have a job in the city. I would like to leave the school. I can read and write; I know the sacred text of Mani. A job would teach me how to do things. I could be a merchant someday, travel and spread the good teachings of Mani." He hesitated and was lost. He looked into her patient face, full of suffering and weariness and could think of nothing else to say.

"You leave the true way and me, to follow the ways of your worthless father? He was a wanderer, ready to take work or sword, for any who required it: ready to force others with acts of death or darkness." Her voice grew hysterical.

"*Ahnie*, Mother, please listen..." he began.

"*Soos*, quiet. *yoke etmem*, I did nothing. It was after the conquest of the city and the nunnery. I did not seek the darkness. It was not my choice to propagate like an animal. I desired only the light and purity. The creating *Demiurge*: He has caused this; the God of Israel, full of begetting and destruction by one people over others. Approving by his blessings the deceit and tricks of his patriarchs. This was not the God and Father of the Yesu of light. He is pure and He makes me, His servant, pure." Her voice rose to a shout

20

of affirmation and then sank to a sorrowful whisper paired with tears. "You are an orphan, poor child. No father here, he moved with the army. No mother, just a Sister of Mani who loves you. I sang you the cradle song before you slept. We had such fun, you and I. Do you remember? But you grew, and we Sisters have the work of charity to do: weaving, knotting rugs, cooking and cleaning: the blessed times of song, prayers and worship. But you would leave this?" She shook her head and wiped her face with a white silk scarf. "Go into darkness, if it's your will. I will wait in the light and be pure. You'll come again. Mani will guide you." She raised her eyes to the chapel door. "I must pray now." She walked away.

> - - - - - - - > KOKAND CITY> - - - - - - - >

Tash looked around the widow's property with care. The coast was clear; none of the gang was present. It was late and the moon shone brightly as it rose above the town. The well structure was etched against the light-flooded courtyard. The widow's hut was quiet. Tash moved to the well and started trying to move the loose brick. Slowly the tight fit was loosened and it came out in his hand. He couldn't suppress a giggle of triumph.

He held the brick aloft and danced a little jig, then plunged his hand into the hole and felt about. He filled both his hands with rings and small metal objects which he poured into his sash by sucking in his stomach and pushing both hands with the goods inside. He smirked as he looked up at the moon and plunged his hand again into the hole. This time he pulled out the stolen dagger with the jade ram on the handle. He took off the sheath and felt the blade's sharpness, smacking his lips with satisfaction.

He froze: then turned his head slowly toward the widow's house. Something had moved in the shadows, a very faint scraping sound, but someone was there watching. He turned and moved toward the shadow side of the house-- nothing. Quickly he moved behind the house, hands outstretched as he fanned the air with the knife-- still nothing. He sighed with relief and returned to the well to replace the brick.

21

He fled the place to return to his corner of a deserted hut that had always been home to him. He huddled under a ragged blanket and shivered. Someone had seen him. They knew. He gripped the dagger tighter and vainly tried to sleep. The moon made slow progress across the night sky.

> - - - - - - - > EXILES LIVING IN KOKAND > - - - - - - - >

Kardesh placed his empty bowl before the hearth and rose to his feet. The father, Erben, sat stretched out on the wooden chests that lined the walls of the mud and stick plastered building. He was dressed in heavy wool pants and shirt of poor quality. As the boy moved toward the door, the man held up a callused hand. "I have heard some things I do not want to believe." The widowed aunt, Tayze and girl exchanged glances and moved to a corner of the room. The man made a motion toward the door. "This is between men." The women promptly left.

"You are young and restless, anxious to demonstrate your maturity and abilities. You cause fights and flirt with girls. But I cannot believe that you, a prince and grandson of the Khan of our tribe, would steal. We live in a golden cage," Erben the father explained, "but if God orders us to power we must be worthy."

"Your brother, Uncle Erden, the Khan, has taken the gold from our cage. Since news of your father's death, we've received no gold, nor goods. For a year you've, worked with your hands in the quarries and in brick works. We've seen no money and little food. So, will my uncle erase our names from our just claims to the heritage? It creates less resentment than a direct attack." Kardesh threw his shoulders back and stared boldly at the silent man. He raised his head proudly and stated: "We're soldiers, but the city won't hire tribesmen. With low gain I've dropped school and weapon practice. These farmers are against us. You've heard that the merchants pay for the protection I provide. I sometimes have to convince the others to enter into my care. If they come around, I return their goods little by little as I 'find' them. The food is for the kids that work with me. I buy their food and ours. I'm not ashamed." He stared defiantly as the man rose to his feet. They stood eye to eye locked in contest.

"I heard you out. Here lies your fault: you presume to make our decisions, judge my brother the Khan, and belittle your father's earnings and work. You play hooky from the church school, whose priest supplements your former instructors. He does it free for love of our tribe and allegiance to Christ. You set your gang to protect local merchants, disregarding the market police you call corrupt. You say it's to feed children. The municipality would make provision for their needs. The temples and mosques would provide help. Your love of command has caused you to organize that riffraff. You steal others goods and give a little back if they pay you. It's well your Grandfather is dead. How shamed he would be." As the boy's face dropped, his father raised his chin with his hand.

"Look at me, remember who we are. Kaya the Great, our founder, would not judge our tribe out of silence. Sanjak, your hero, would not be hasty. When word comes, we will see the truth. I love my elder brother and am loved by him. We were put in the golden cage by custom, not by enmity between brothers. The father of my father's second wife demanded it at tribal council. He bears me little love. Some say he wants to be khan in your Uncle Erden's place. There are many reasons for delayed or lost gold and news. You have been hasty and foolish." He looked at the pouted lips and flushed face before him. The boy was lighter than him, but had reached his height and was strong. His jaw was set.

"We've said enough." The father continued, "Truth lies between us now, we'll look upon it with calm tomorrow. We're not rivals. We must face these things as a family." He pointed to the door. "Think on this as you talk with Father Agaz bey at lessons," he ordered. He walked to the pot of drink with his cup. In the city they did not often use the wine skin to squirt the wine to the mouth, but the boy took the wineskin near the door. "I'll do that and we'll talk again. With your permission," he turned and departed. The old Aunt entered and resumed her duties. She spoke to the brooding man.

"It is only two years past that you came to this town. For a tribesman the life in a city is confusing, and without funds it is frustrating. Don't be too hard. He was content to learn at first. Now he wants to prove his mastery of the arts, and learning requires doing."

"He has always been headstrong and heedless, like my father who refused to recognize the dangers of a late marriage to so powerful a faction. Father liked her face, plumpness and manners. He disregarded the implications of marriage to Kaplan's daughter and all warnings from us. If only my mother could have lived a few more years." He scratched his head, bewildered and drained his cup. He filled it again. He failed to hear the scuffle.

> - - - - - - - > OUTSIDE ERBEN'S HOUSE > - - - - - - - >

"Stop, don't go," Kardesh ordered, as the girl tried to enter the hut. He grabbed her arm as she dodged. Her thin arm supported two gold bracelets. He glared at them, then at her.

She shrank back with a frightened sob saying. "What good are presents that can't be worn? A princess has the right to look her part. He already knew."

"Stupid girl!" He slapped her, back and forehand then took her shoulders and shook her. Her head snapped to and fro. A cry started, but he cut it off with his hand over her small mouth. He pulled her against him.

"How long have you worn them? In the street, or market too? You confirmed his suspicions with them. Did you say anything? If you scream I'll break your arm and marry you to the ugliest, most worthless man of the tribe and he'll beat you every time he is sober enough!"

She struggled vainly against his encircling arms and tried to breathe past the massive young hand. Suddenly she went limp and unresisting. He moved her farther from the hut and took his hand gingerly from her mouth, but left it threateningly just inches from her face. She panted quietly.

"*Zorba*: bully, you're a crude, rough boy. When will you learn to be a true prince and man? Here, take your stolen goods! They burned my flesh today. I'd rather be in rags

24

than wear your ill gotten goods." She took off the bangles, thrust them into his hand, then cautiously backed away.

"You crazy girl, you snitch on me. You snoop into my affairs, dig up secrets from my friends. I know that you and Yeet are close, whispering and giggling. You get the events from him." He clenched his fists on each side of her face. "You are skinny and ugly as the stork you're named for: *Leylek*, a stork. Like the bird, only your clothes will ever be pretty. That mother should have had to die to bear such a one as you!" He finished this with his nose in her face. Hatred and disgust filled his voice.

"What did I do? A man is responsible! One started me. I came. She had to give birth. She died for me. *Tanra* alone knows why. I'd be willing to change places with her, but it wasn't my choice." She started crying and spoke between sobs, her body shaking. "I was to be named *Lahley*, Tulip, but when she died, they named me *Lieyuk*, Worthy. City folks say *Leyla*. But you got all the kids to call me *Leylek*, because you hate me. They call you *Kardesh*, sibling, and I'm your only sister, but you don't want to be *kardesh* to me. I wish I were dead." She sank to the ground.

"I wish you were too. You big cry baby." He spun around and walked toward the gate. "I wish to *Tanra* we were still with the tribe! I wish I had my horse, my friends, and the open pastures. I hate everyone here!" He slammed the stick and cord gate, but it sagged open behind him. She looked after him, and tried to call, but he was lost in the darkness.

KARDESH WALKS OUT

PEOPLE, PLOTS & PLACES IN CHAPTER 2

Agaz bey: Nestorian minister and teacher of Kardesh.
Kardesh: a Khan's son & leader of the Kardeshler gang.
Karga: leads an attack on the Toozlu clan yurts and herds.
Kynan: older brother of Setchkin pursues her captors.
Leyla: daughter of the exiled Erben now living in Kokand.
Marium: Toozlu priest's wife comforts the widow Setchkin.
Mookades: Nestorian priest of the Chipchak Toozlu clan.
Peri hanum: an old family servant with Setchkin since birth.
Sanjak: son of Twozan bey was engaged once to Setchken.
Setchkin: young widow and baby are hostages of Twozan.
Tash: a thief of the Brothers' 'Kardeshler' treasure.
Twozan: a khan leading his part of the Chipchak tribe.
Yeet: spies a wrong doing and goes to report it.

GLOSSARY:
aslan: lion; lion colored, tawny golden hue.
aya'juk: dear little bear, cub, teddy bear.
ay'ran: a salty drink of yogurt and water.
Do'er, yah-klash'ma: stop, don't come near; stop, stay.
goon aye doon: good morning.
heidi git: go on now; go ahead now.
Kyzyl Kum: Red Sand Desert.
yalanja: liar.
yurts: round, nomadic, tent-like structures covered with thick felt.

KYNAKLAR RAID

It was a chilly, spring dawn. The band of horsemen appeared charging over the hill. They were clothed in the fog and steam of their breathing and the condensing sweat of their exertions. The hard-ridden horses poured into the small stand of *yurts,* there on a little plateau. The warriors were seeking those responsible for the care of the herd mares pastured near the yurts. Swords drawn, bows armed and fletched, they pulled to a stop. A few men faced the door of each *yurt.* Two men in the lead, carrying torches threw their fagots at the larger central yurt. Not a soul responded to the thumps and shouts. No women screamed in any *yurt.* No one came to put out the fire. Silence greeted their arrival. The torches failed to light the heavy felt and failed to find the fire-wood stacks outside the structure. The stench of scorched felt filled the air. The abandoned camp lay open to all.

"See what you can find inside," shouted the leader. "Pick up the torches. We need them to find where they have gone." He glared around angrily. The leader was a bearded man of fifty, coated and gloved for the chill. His thin, powerful frame now began to show in the increasing light.

27

"Hearths are cold, the trunks and some of the household goods are still here. Only a short march supply has been taken," shouted a tall young man from the door of the big *yurt*. Men entered and exited the yurts. Others searched for the pack animals or tracks.

"They left yesterday. The tracks are dewed over. How did they know?" shouted a tracker.

"Karga, where have they taken my sister?" the tall youth cried in anguish. He moved to mount his horse while the men stowed their weapons.

"They've gone south or west to the slave markets and the chance to become mercenaries. They're leaving their goods and herds; they must go forever." The older man stared bitterly round the camp. "We should've burned out the Toozlu, but they've forestalled us. Better we take the goods to divide. The *Aslan* mares are to foal shortly, someone must've stayed. Find them! See what they know." Men moved the horses out at a run in the increasing light. Soon shouts of discovery echoed back to the waiting men. All set out for the restive herd that showed increasing nervousness as the new horses and strangers drew near.

"*Do'er, yah-klash'ma*, stop, don't approach!" shouted Karga to his group. "Kynan, you go in with the tracker."

The tall youth moved forward smoothly with soothing croons and wind-like whistles. Downwind they approached and found two guardians. One was a man past his eighties and the other a simple boy with a hunched back. They were not Toozlu, but hired workmen. Both nodded a greeting and rode over to accommodate their new masters. They knew very little, but were content to tell it repeatedly with much exaggeration. They asked for men to relieve their long vigil. But men who have ridden all night are hungry and the herders returned to camp to hunt for food -- little remained.

"What will my father say? Our Setchkin is lost to us. How could they steal into camp and take her right from under our noses: just when we were ready to destroy the Toozlu and rule through our sister!" Kynan was distraught and stood among the bone weary kinsmen, gathered around the newly lit fire. He listed his grievances loudly. "As the old khan's widow, she has great influence on the future of the tribe, through the baby. We controlled the heir. Now the elder son will continue as Khan. He's suspicious already and will drop the Kaynaklar from the council. We'll have no weight or future." He gestured toward Karga and buried his head in his hands.

"Tears are for women. The plan's in motion, it can't be stopped at this point. If you catch the Toozlu you have our heir back. If you don't, we'll form the regency anyway, we have a child. We don't need a mother." Karga smiled evilly and then laughed at Kynan's confusion.

"B-B-B-But you discovered them gone. How can you say the child is with us still?" Karga pulled him aside. He whispered in Kynan's ear, wrapping him in his arms.

"I married off my daughter, when Setchkin married the old Khan. Both bore babies: boys only a week apart, we can say Meenay's child was taken by mistake. She'll nurse the heir, now that the mother has gone. Only the old nurses will know the difference. They can be kept quiet." He pushed Kynan away. "Now go on! You must try to catch them, but regardless, the plan continues on time."

> - - - - - - - > KOKAND NESTORIAN HOUSE > - - - - - - - >

"You're distracted tonight, my son, your mind is on other things. Would you like to share your anxieties, it's always confidential." The priest spoke gently. "Martha is in the kitchen. Priests' wives know not to eavesdrop."

Kardesh sat before Agaz bey staring at the leather page before him. The priest paused, spoke again. "Lately you're irregular in attendance on Sunday; that frequently means an uneasy conscience before God. To speak of one's sins and failures often brings relief and new strength." Agaz bey smiled slightly. "When we speak man to man, weakness to weakness, one can open one's heart." The boy pushed the page away.

"I have been working, reverend Father, no goods come from the tribe. My father strives to supply our needs by common labor, but it isn't enough. I work in the market." He looked furtively at the humbly dressed Christian leader. He discovered he could not meet the priest's eyes.

"I have heard rumors of your ah-- work in the city market. Many of the public are very angry. I've had some complaints about you. You have endangered your life and that of your family as well as the good name of the church. I beg you to consider your actions. Remember Psalm 38 'My bones have no soundness because of my sin;' and 'My wounds fester and are loathsome because of my sinful folly.' "He looked at the uncomfortable youth quizzically.

29

"You cover your extortion claiming the responsibility of protection, the very thing they're taxed for by the Council. You try to cover the ill with pretext. You exaggerate the incompetence and veniality of the market authorities. But you stir up envy and hate in many." He shook his head sadly. "These sins do not supply what you need, but will bring future disaster on all of you and perhaps on us as well. Bold sins bring anguish and punishment. To confess and abandon one's sins is to find the road of salvation. God will supply your needs if you're true to his paths and have a clean heart. Only His pardon can provide that." His tone was grieved; his appeal sincere. He tried to touch the boy's shoulder, but Kardesh shied away and rose.

"I must go now, Father, it is late. I will come on Sunday with my father and we will speak about the remedies."

"The longer one remains unrepentant and extorted goods not restored, the more damage to the soul and to many men's pathways, my son. To wait is to refuse." Agaz held out his hands in appeal, but Kardesh turned to the door and without a word he left the house. The rising moon lighted a small path for his feet.

>------> KOKAND WIDOW'S HOUSE >------>

Yeet climbed down from the flat roof of the widow's house. The outside stairs were behind the hovel where Tash had been waving his dagger. Yeet patted the handle of his curved hanjer: a razor sharp, Yemeni weapon which tucked under his sash with the curved end of the scabbard showing below. He thought it fortunate for Tash that he had not seen the stairs. Yeet had never killed, but Tash was beneath contempt and would deserve anything for stealing from the Brothers. He scratched his head, then smoothed his neat turban and murmured aloud. "Should I go tonight or sleep on it? Kardesh must handle this matter. Allah, Allah! Tash is big and mean, I would not like him at my back." Yeet shivered and looked around him. He found himself outside the entrance. "It is written, 'Justice must be prompt.' Perhaps I should tell Leyla first, she is older and my best friend. She will know what to do. For protection we could cover each other's backs." While he debated to himself he found the gate of the Kardesh house. He entered stealthily, making a bird like whistle. A small gasp caused him to stop and whisper an assurance. "Don't be afraid, it's me, Yeet." He waited till he heard a sigh of relief. Her voice was a whisper as she came out of the shadows into the moonlight.

"You have never come this late. Father must not hear." She came over and boldly took his hand. "Why?"

"Leyla, I came to see Kardesh. Did he go to the Nestorian's place?" He came close, looking up to the tall girl in awe. She knew how to read. Yeet didn't know of any other girl who could read. She was pretty in a skinny way.

"Yes, *Babam*, my daddy, wants him to continue his studies and he stays late. I, too, have some things to settle with him. What is new in the town?" She chaffed under the restrictions town living imposed on a tribal girl, raised in unrestrained freedom of movement. The introduction of the veil for women of Islam, she utterly disregarded.

Yeet gave a sigh of pleasure. He loved to talk and speculate about people and events, even when the others, the *Kardeshler*, teased and said he gossiped like a girl.

> - - - - - - - >TOOZLU CLAN ON THE SARI SU TRAIL > - - - - - - - >

Setchkin rode her golden mare at the head of the column beside Twozan bey, the leader of the south bound convoy. She noticed the spring grass had begun to grow after the frost had retreated. Going south the grass was shorter and it would disappear in the *Kyzyl Kum*, the Red Sands.

RIDING THE SARI SU

31

The trail would cross Bet Pak Dala, the Starvation Steppes. They would follow the scanty Sari Su wadi south. Then, they would find the Chu River, less shallow, but still uncertain. The trail lay between the Sea of Aral and Lake Balkhash. Farther beyond lay the desert lands won by Islamic Arab and Persian mercenaries under the Umayyad and Abbassid dynasties. These garden lands contain the Syr and Amu rivers, which supplies water for fields and cities by their steady flow.

Those who searched for the Toozlu could follow the commercial road by the mountains and villages of the east, where orchards and crops made the way pleasant. They would await news of the Toozlu appearance from the desert. All talk on the roads was of who took what, where, when.

"What do you think about our adventure?" Twozan bey shot his question at Setchkin who shrugged haughtily. She feigned indifference, but her lips pouted in a sulk. She eyed the burley leader with care before venturing an answer. He showed a friendly interest, rather than angry hostility.

"That you're fools to abandon your flocks and yurts. You offend the Kaynaklar. You lose your traditional grazing lands and if that were not enough, you steal old Erdash Khan's widow and his heir." She tossed her head proudly, then looked down to adjust the slumped, sleeping baby before her; astride the saddle as she was. Her long shalvar, baggy riding-pants, and the long split outer tunic disguised the fullness of her figure. Her round face now reflected her anger and resentment.

He spoke calmly. "The flocks grow few and thin with the dry grazing. The yurts grow old and apt to be burned by the ambitions and pride of the Kaynak. Your family plans to rule the Chipchak nation. The two sons of the Kaya family line are twins: one could start to tell his thoughts and the other would finish the sentence in perfect agreement. But Karga split them apart so each remains less than before. I've seen the purposes of your plot and have frustrated the Kaynak, though it cost us dear. Your little one will not be heir to the promise. I, Twozan, swear on my ancestors' honor."

"You're a fool to make yourself the Kaya's guard. What have the Toozlu gained for this vaunted privilege. How many hundreds of years have your family served and for what? Do you believe the legend of the thousand glory years? If so, the Khan's child has the blood of the bear in his veins. The losses suffered by our nation will be repaired," she affirmed proudly.

"Life and honor are enough for him who serves," Twozan insisted. Is the merchant with gold happier or greater? We ruled the center lands from the Tarim Basin to beyond the Ishim River. We give justice to the small peoples and the tribes within its borders..."

She interrupted to exclaim, "But now we're deprived of the Tarim irrigation farms by the Uygurs. They lost the steppes north of the Gobi to the Kirghiz, who are being pushed west by the Mongols. All are being suborned with gold and lies by the restored Tang dynasty of Changan City, in China."

"We have lost the Tarim before," Twozen continued, "over two hundred years ago to the Tang emperor Tai Zong, but we eventually got it back. The great evangelist of our faith whom the Tang called Ah Lee Ben is reputed to have said: 'God may deprive His followers of prosperity for a time to teach them humility, but he will return to bless and restore when the lesson is learned.' "

"Spare me the history lecture, Twozan. I speak of now and my son. The evangelist is long dead, as is the promise made to the Bear of the Chipchaks. I feared what you might do, so old Peri, my maid, and I took Meenay's baby and let her raise mine. It was a secret between us. Only Peri knows when and how often we changed them to fool everyone. You can ask her, she rides with the baggage. The heir can't be stolen. Your great sacrifices are in vain." She sneered and spurred her golden mount forward. As she rode, she laughed. He, too, raced.

"*Yalanja*, liar, you speak lies. You lied to my son, Sanjak, when you swore to marry him. You lie now when I have captured you and the heir. Your greed is your passion, so you sell your passion to the highest bidder, like a town whore." He reached out to take the reins, but she angrily swerved, stopped at the top of the hill, while his impetus carried him past. He pulled his horse back on its haunches and cursed. Her laughter continued unabated.

With her sleeve Setchkin cleared her eyes as the child before her, now awake and frightened, started to cry. She leaned her head over to sooth him, still in his place before her. She swung over the ayran bag from behind her shoulder and squirted a narrow stream of the sour milk into his mouth. It ran down his chin and he started to laugh, too.

"Ayajuk, little bear, you love a fast ride. Now drink your ayran and we will sing a folk song." She wiped his face and started to sing:

33

Born on the golden hills, above the plains,
Where the cool breeze blows. There is my homeland.
Wind in our faces as we go all racing along.
So, I remember: The green and silver place of our hearts.

Sing in the warming spring upon the steppe,
Where the hot sun shines, here is my homeland.
Sun on our faces as we go all pacing along.
So, I remember: My love burns brightly when I am here.

Ride where my love is found, beyond the grass,
Where great cities grow, far from my homeland,
Faces are talking and walking, all gawking away.
So, I remember: My tears mark years passing by.

SETCHKIN'S SONG

"Why do you call him *Ayajuk*? You say he is not the heir." Twozan
rode over and grimly fell into step.

"It's a pet name to confuse the jealous spirits. We called them
Takkan and *Hakkan*, 'Throne blood' and 'True blood'. Since we lived in
the same camp we had lots of fun together. This one is called Hakkan for
his blood is true. My little Takkan is in camp. This baby is not of the

Kayalar blood." She was enjoying her victory, but he reached for her wrist.

"Blood of the Kaynaklar Clan is in both babies, with who knows what other mixture? You had many suitors who asked to take you to their yurt. Did old Erdash start off a baby on the marriage night? Can it be true? Meenay married earlier but you both had full term babies. There was gossip, but Erdash khan had twins by his first wife: Erden, the present Khan; and Erben exiled to Kokand by your father. Was Erdash potent or another?"

Setchkin's face had gone pale. Her mouth hung open, stark shock showed in her eyes. Anger slowly turned her face red, and she jerked her horse around and rode back to the side of the priest and his wife. She was pouring tears. "Father, I need your protection. Twozan insults me."

The old man exchanged looks with his wife. Marium spoke tenderly to the girl, taking the baby. "Let us ride to that hill ahead and dismount to talk. My man is good for confrontation or the council, but in affairs of the heart, another woman is better. We will be safe and find comfort there." She led the way at a gallop.

"*Goon aye doon*, good morning, Mookades." A shamed Twozan rode to the side of the tribal priest. The old man scanned the tribal leader carefully, without smiling, and then spoke in a formal way with a greeting. "Christ's grace and mercy be with you. You are flustered and troubled. The esteemed guest cries out in anguish. She pours out her troubles to Marium. From where does this trouble come and where will it take you?"

"A leader must speak truth and do God's will, but this woman taunts me. She tells me she has brought Meenay's child. So, we may not have the heir. She is a devil who brought me to anger and cursing twice in the hour. She is like her father, Kaplan, the tiger." He shook with indignation and looked for some sign of softening, but found only calm logic.

"Yet, you approved your son, Sanjak's suit for the girl, when you could have pushed him toward Sevim, Erden's only child. You let him follow his whim. You would have been Setchkin's father-in-law, but you must not have wanted that. We were ready to announce the promise when Karga converted Kaplan's consent to opposition with lies. He got the ear of Erdash and filled his head with false stories about Sanjak. Even the girl could not stand against Karga. She was persuaded and married old Erdash. So the Kaynaklar Clan came to power. When Sevim

35

died in the racing accident; that door closed. However, you dissimulated and accepted everything. You let the accusations stand and didn't defend Sanjak, so he went away to bring the refugees. He wasn't present to defend himself. Erdash would have heard you gladly, he was ever fair. A union between the two strongest clans would have united our people, but you kept silent and allowed the rivalry to continue. Another woman could have contented the old Khan. Examine your spirit, what do you find there? Confess to a compassionate Yesu, He will help you and forgive." At last he smiled. The burly chief rode in silence and sighed. He remained quiet until Marium rode back with the baby. Then, he nodded and departed.

> - - - - - - - ->TOOZLU CLAN ON THE SARI SU TRAIL> - - - - - - - >
Marium looked at her husband and spoke sadly. He looked in her troubled eyes as she rocked the sleeping baby.

"What good can come of entering the lands of Islam where prejudice against Christians threatens us? At home, we could have dissimulated and stayed. Those two will destroy us all. They have lost their way. She is headstrong, scheming and in love with Sanjak." She put out a pleading hand.

"She torments Twozan's soul," he answered, "because he loves her; she knows it. He is driven by jealousy and is a rival to his son. When Sanjak returns from the East what will happen?"

Mookades shook his head sadly. "Twozan denies it even to himself, but until he faces the truth and prays, we will all suffer with them."

She lowered her voice. "She came willingly because of Sanjak, but now she fears the man who prefers to be groom above father-in-law. He's shameless. She now talks of escape. I warned her that she would miss meeting Sanjak. He's settling the refugees and will meet us in the Fergana Valley. If Erben resists the temptation of conquests and takes our part, we'll be able to return to our land."

"I think we are in the end times." He sighed, "Surely Yesu must return soon for judgment. The Tang have killed more than a thousand nuns, destroyed churches and are expelling the foreign Christians, driving them into the desert. The Han believers are being tortured, impoverished and enslaved. They are forced to return to the ancestral religions. Those who resist are beheaded. They destroy the Holy Books and cause them to blaspheme the name of Yesu." The priest sobbed convulsively.

Marium stroked his arm consolingly, tears coursed her face, but she made no sound. There came a clatter of hooves growing louder. They gasped and sought the source. A fast driven, lion colored horse appeared on the hill ahead silhouetted against the sky. The warrior raised an armed bow and shot straight up over his head. The horse reared pawing the air as the signal arrow screamed overhead trailing smoke, forming an inverted V in the sky.

SIGNAL ARROW SHRIEKS

PEOPLE, PLOTS & PLACES IN CHAPTER 3

Agaz bey: priest and healer of the Kokand Nestorians.
Tayze: tends her nephew's wounds at home.
Gerchen: leader of the Right-hand Clan of Chipchaks.
Kardesh: son of an exiled Khan and market ferret.
Leyla: despised sister of Kardesh, daughter of Khan Erben.
Setchkin: widow of Khan Erdash, abducted with her baby.
Sevman: a Manichean admirer of Kardesh, the gang leader.
Tash: takes leadership of the 'Brothers' and throws a party.
Twozan: leader of the Left-hand Clan of the Chipchaks.
Yeet: sees and reports theft and rebellion in the 'Brothers'.

GLOSSARY:

bash ooze to ney: as you command; it's on my head.
do'er: stop; stay.
ee yee: good; fine; okay.
firman: a decree by the Caliph for immediate application.
gel: come; come here.
hanjir: a narrow, sharp-pointed knife.
hoe'sh geldeniz: Welcome; happily you've arrived.
janum: dear one; my life; my soul; term of endearment.
kuz: girl.
Ne var: what's happening; what's going on; what's up?
Sari Su: Yellow Water, name of a north to south wadi.
shalvar: baggy pants with draw strings at waist and ankles.
Wigler: slang term of disrespect for the Uigur people.

GREETING THE HEIR

The lone warrior rode laughing, down toward the astonished column of tribesmen. He shouted as he rode.

"I'm Gerchen of the Right-hand Clan: those with me follow. We were told to meet near the yellow water, the *Sari Su*, hundreds of families are coming. I have signaled your presence. Where will we camp?"

"Right side of the meadow." Twozan answered with an expansive smile, waving to indicate the sunset side of the shallow stream. The spring rains had brought out the short grass, but it would not last two days of intensive grazing. Here would start a race with the summer drought to test the endurance of man and beast.

"*Hosh geldeniz*, welcome, I'm Setchkin, Khan Erdash's widow. Here to lead the columns south. Behold the Heir of the Chipchaks and the child of promise, Hakkan, my son." She held up the waking baby for Gerchen to see. The tall, laughing man dismounted and bowed so deep that his body paralleled the ground. His hands on the ground, he was in a position of complete submission. He lifted his head, stood, took the child and held him at full arm length above even the horses, laughing.

"Son of the bear, follower of the gray wolf, hero of the green and silver grasslands, ruler for a thousand years: command your servant." His exuberance frightened the baby, who looked about for his mother and cried holding out his hands. Setchken moved forward to take him.

"*Bosh ooze to nay*, Your wish is my command." He laughed and returned the baby to his mother's arms. The whole column laughed as the mother comforted her child.

Twozan watched; his face a mask. He wondered what other plots Setchkin would hatch and employ to maintain her position of authority. He sighed for the truth.

> - - - - - - - > KOKAND MARKET > - - - - - - - >

"Is this the article that the thief took?" Kardesh looked at the merchant closely. He held out a bag. The man looked into it and nodded his assent. He took the bag without further acknowledgment.

"We warned the man, he is not professional and has a family moved in from the drought area. No one will be troubled again by this one. We guarantee it, you're under our protection." The man shrugged and put the bag behind a table. He turned his back his whole rigid body expressed suppressed anger. Kardesh narrowed his eyes and froze there wondering what would happen.

"You've raised the rate so I should expect more prevention and faster service." The man's voice was like a whiplash. "You price yourselves beyond reason. Others think the same." He turned to face Kardesh and Sevman. Both drew back from his aggressive anger.

"We have not collected more or any additions since I came last week. Nothing has changed," Kardesh protested.

The man growled and put his head forward as if to bridge the distance between them.

"Your man came yesterday to assure me of fast service, but then asked for a fee for extra effort. The tall skinny one with the thin face." The friends exchanged looks. "It must have been Tash." Sevman exclaimed. Kardesh looked thoughtful.

"We'll return your money. He's mistaken to over charge you." The merchant's attitude softened just a bit.

40

"Give the silver coin back now and I'll tell you that there's much talk in the market of complaining to the magistrates. They'll carry the same sum as you collect to stimulate their greater protection and interest. So now you're warned." He took the coin without a smile and turned his back. "Get out and don't come back. You'll not get another cent out of me. Don't send any of the kardesh here, I'll beat them up. Others are looking for you to get even." He looked around and shook his fist at the boys. "Get out!"

"We have two things to see Tash about." Sevman stated as they walked through the market.

"You must have talked with Yeet, if you know that."

"I heard it three times this morning, each time with different details brought in." Sevman smiled.

"I've been thinking about this all night, Tash has a following. If he has distributed part of the collected goods, we may have to fight." Kardesh reached under his sash to touch the reassuring *hanjer*.

"Allah, Allah, I've caught you at last!" The burley carter hit Kardesh a blow across the back that knocked him forward sprawling into a stall. He kicked him in the side, driving Kardesh into a chestnut vendor's stand which sent a shower of sparks and coals into the air and littered the ground with the cooking nuts. Kardesh's scream was piercing.

MARKET FIGHT

41

The man laughed. "Hit me on the head with a pole and poke me in the chest. I'll show you how we treat dirty thieves. This city's magistrates will cut off your hand." He moved toward the prostrate boy who hobbled up on the other side of the broken stands. Kardesh was holding his arms folded with his left inside his right elbow with the right hand over his face. His teeth were gritted as he stumbled away, beginning a shambling run. Sevman ran at the pursuing carter, pushing him with all his force into the wrecked stalls. The aged, incensed owner held him. The chestnut vendor took a stout pole and clubbed the carter's head and shoulders. Cries filled the air as they danced on hot coals and nuts.

"Help, police! Fight!"

"Who pays for my nuts and cart?"

"Stop the fight."

"*Do'er,* stop, leave him alone."

"Catch the boy."

"My stand, you've ruined it!"

"The boy got away. You let him go."

"They're fighting. Police!"

"Here come the police. Make way, let them through."

Gradually the noise became less, the struggles between the owners and the carter ceased as the market police and officials intervened. Order was restored. Eye witnesses were soon interviewed. Police patrols were given a description of the two boys. The carter was detained to be fined the cost of the stands and for the disturbance. Complaints about the Kardeshler are received by the police. The authorities were dismayed to discover rivals to their rule.

Kardesh moved erratically toward home. He suffered pain, nausea and dizziness. Sevman tried to help by guiding him to a seat and screening him from curious glances while they rested. Painfully they made their way through the back streets. Kardesh, blinking tears and shaking his burned face, held his left arm with great care and he also flinched when Sevman tried to help or hold him around the body. Arriving at home he disregarded the cries of his sister and lowered himself to the bed. All he could say was directed to Sevman in panting gasps "Send for Father Agaz, tell him all that has happened. Ask him to come immediately. Tell Yeet to find the Kardeshler and see what Tash is doing." Groaning he allowed his sister to clean his face with a wet cloth and put oil on his burns. Tayze gave him ayran to drink and he soon fell into a fitful sleep.

> - - - - - - -> AT THE EMPTY MARKET LOT > - - - - - - ->

Tash was already meeting with the brothers at the Widow's house away from the market. He was facing the whole group dressed impressively in a new shirt, vest and shalvar pants.

"The carter has settled with Kardesh for me. It's a pity for I had planned to do it myself. But he has saved him a worse beating. Is there anyone here who won't work under me? Anyone want to be leader in my place? Speak now.

"I'm going to change the rules a little bit. No more of the nice guy stuff. Everyone at market will pay or suffer loss the same day. We will raise the price for our protection and our police work. We're going to celebrate with wine in our party tonight. You little guys will provide some additional fun for the membership. Be prepared to up your bare butts tonight." There was a gasp, giggling started, looks of delight and horror were reflected on different faces. There was a hiss of anger and the slight scrape of a blade drawn.

"No dirty thief is going to touch me. You stole the brother's money and now change the rules we have sworn to keep. You lord it over us, but we didn't name you leader. Now, you will lead us away from the paths of Allah. Kardesh lives and we are sworn to him." Yeet had moved before Tash with his hanjer pointed at the boy's throat. Both faces were hot with anger and apprehension. A tense circle formed about them, some showing approval, others fear.

Tash appeased, "I was only kidding. Can't you take a joke, Yeet? I wouldn't ask my buddies to do something like that. We have money, we can pay girls now. You might like that, Yeet. You like to talk to Leylek and the widow, don't you? There are lots of pretty ones in the red lantern district,

43

some your age. Think about it." He held out his hands appealingly, eyes wary, an artificial smile frozen on his face.

"I talk of wealth stolen and the right to choose. You talk of sex and sin. You'll have your choice and be damned, but we can reject you and get a share of the goods. You owe us." He turned and yelled at the others. "What's wrong with you guys? He's taken your share of the goods. Are you deaf? He took them and spent them on the new clothes. Don't you get mad?" None of the boys answered. A few looked angry, but many simply looked down at their feet. Yeet looked angrily at the spiritless group. Tash seized the opportunity to demonstrate his generosity.

"You'll all get your part at the party. I'm going to get everyone something new as a present. Besides you can have as much food and drink as you wish. Kardesh never gave you any parties or presents. He hid the stuff here at the widow's and only gave you food and clothes. He's keeping it all for himself. Going to make out like he's a khan, he thinks. The treasure belongs to all of us. We got it for us brothers. Let's go and spend it now. Follow me, we'll buy our goods." Yeet was left alone, hanjer still in hand, ignored.

TASH AT THE WELL

44

Father Agaz worked over the bare chest of Kardesh winding the strips of gauze cotton tightly about him. The boy held his already immobilized arm away from his body. His face was smeared with burn ointment a patch topped one eye.

"You have several ribs broken and the forearm..."

"It's nothing, Please, Agaz bey, talk to my father. I swear I'm through with that kind of life. I see my sin and renounce it," he sighed.

"I'm glad you've seen where your activities were taking you. You endanger your soul and body and those of your gang. Unjust gain creates resentment and hatred."

"I tried to help those kids. They were street bums and starved brats and I trained and cared for them. They ate regular and got some self respect. We protected all the merchants from thieves and shakedowns while the authorities neglected them. We had respect and the kids needed that. It was good." He groaned as he stood while Father Agaz bound the arm across the stomach.

"Physical help without spiritual instruction and change brings no recovery or improvement to the needy. They are strengthened to sin and follow their hearts. Greed, lust and pride fortify the mind against change; oppose God and truth. Then comes destruction, their sins find them out and bring punishment. You have not helped your friends."

"But Father, the church has both hospital and charity for the poor. You help the orphans and widows. Where was I so wrong?" Kardesh shook his head in confusion.

"Wrong motives, wrong attitudes, wrong road; you used poor people for personal aggrandizement, for gain and pride of place and command. You assumed that you wouldn't have to answer for what your gang did. You took away their fear of the law, without giving a fear of God and judgment. You wanted to help, but you've ruined them."

"Then what will happen now? I really do repent and will change my way of living. I'll talk to the kids and bring them to church. We'll leave all our old ways."

Agaz shook his head sadly and pressed his fingers against his lips. He stroked his beard in thought and spoke.

45

"What you start does not stop when and where you will it to. The seed sown will bear its fruit. The only hope is to pray that God will turn the evil to good. The city authorities will make inquires. The gang is becoming more arrogant, even as you did. Their service to market was, at first, well received, but small abuses crept in and envy ate up the respect. Sin leads them on a downward path."

"But God can intervene and change the situation. Isn't that what prayer is about? He can use His power, can't He?" Kardesh's puzzled face became increasingly anxious. Agaz bey's grave face moved up in the negative sign of his people.

"God's business is to save our souls and prepare us to live in His presence as part of His family and kingdom. He didn't save Yesu from His suffering, He doesn't save us from it either. We are warned that it is through suffering that we enter his kingdom. Life on earth is full of all kinds of temptation to sin and when we do, guilt brings suffering. We either repent and change our road, our life, and make restitution. Or, we refuse to change, refuse to seek God and leave our sins. Then, consequences follow: suffering, guilt, fear, and hatred hardens us. Repentance becomes harder and God seems to become an enemy to be avoided, rather than a friend who will pardon and help us. Your friends are at this juncture..."

The priest's homily was interrupted by the noisy entrance of a breathless Yeet. He gasped, staring at the bandaged body of Kardesh. He started, sighting the priest, but blurted his news.

"Tash has taken charge of the gang. They let him do it without a protest. He's taking them shopping for a party at the Widow's. They'll take everything. He is promising presents for everyone."

"That's not his stuff. It belongs to all of us and it's for support not blow outs. What's come over him?"

"Tash thinks you're out of it for good. He says you'll never be back and he's the top now. He's changing all the rules. The best things he changes for worse. He'll force everyone to pay now. The guys are scared of him. He's mean."

"There is a way that seems right to a man, but the end thereof is death." The priest intoned, solemnly.

"What can I do now? I'm out of it. I've repented of my part in the whole of it." Kardesh's face showed agony.

"But they're your guys. You trained them to work together and fight. You showed them how to trace the stolen goods and how to warn off the professionals. Without you, they'll be just gutter thieves, in and out of trouble. You started them and they're your responsibility." Yeet pleaded.

"If I went back I'd have to fight him. Not that he's very much. I can beat him with one hand," he bragged.

"You've got a good hand. I'll come into it if you tire out. Where's Sevman? He'll back us up." Yeet's faith in his captain showed in his pretty young face.

"My son, think well before you commit yourself. You do have responsibility for what you've started, but don't commit more sin trying to justify the past."

"Yes, I understand Father Agaz. I'll try to set things straight and get the guys out of this trouble. They'll listen to me." Boldly, Kardesh called to Leyla.

"Come girl, help me put on my shirt and hang my coat over my shoulders. Tell my father I'll explain everything when I return." He carefully took his arm out of the sling in preparation for the loose open shirt.

Father Agaz looked on the dress proceedings with a worried frown. He exchanged glances with Leyla. "You know that the ribs must not be allowed to take a blow or be moved by bending. A broken rib end can pierce a lung or other body organs." He looked significantly at Yeet.

"I'll see to it, Priest. He will suffer no damage. I swear it by Allah." Yeet moved his hanjer half out and back into its sheath with a click. He smirked, proudly cocked his head, then with a bow to girl and priest, departed.

"Son if you have truly repented and not just regretted the past, there will be changes of behavior and character. We wait with expectation to see these changes."

"Pray that God's will may be done and truth served in all that happens." Kardesh started for the door.

47

"Come by the hospital tomorrow morning to get the bandages adjusted and see if every thing checks out," the priest called out.

Turning to the girl the priest said, "*Janum*, you'll be the first to see any change. We have prayed for this."

> - - - - - - - > KOKAND MONASTERY > - - - - - - - >

The agitated sister, Pakhan, spoke hurriedly to Sevman, who was passing outside the temple entrance.

"Are you still here? You said you'd leave us for money."

"Well, my job is probably over, but I have to collect my part still."

"Our congregation is moving east where our religion is protected. The Caliph becomes increasingly restrictive of all, but his own. He wants our orphans to become his. Now, he forgets our treaty exemption. It's their laws they'll apply. If you wish, you can come too." She looked at Sevman lovingly.

He blushed and then bragged. "I can pay my way there. I'll go get the money now. You go with the congregation. I'll come in a few days, maybe. I have a sick friend here who needs my help."

"I would like for you to come too, Sevmani dear. I don't want to think you're alone in the darkness. I will always pray for you. Remember that." He watched her walk away to vespers.

> - - - - - - - > AT THE WIDOW'S HOUSE > - - - - - - - >

The sun was beginning to set as the gang in the widow's yard passed around the wine bags. Each took a long squirt of the liquid, holding it up high. They sometimes hit clothes or their neighbors, to the hilarity of all the boys. Some were draped with new articles of clothing and all were well fed and content. Tash swaggered among the crowd around the well. The deference shown the new leader was unreserved.

"You never got this kind of treatment from Kardesh, did you? Wait'll we start shaking down the merchants. He was always too scared to use much force." Heads bobbed happily.

"Look who's come. Sevman's here snooping. Get him guys." There was a surge of bodies toward the boy. He was caught and pushed up to the well by several.

"You joining us shrimp? You're a novice and you never got initiated. We'll do that tonight." Laughter came.

Sevman set his face and stuck out his chin stubbornly. "You're stealing the stuff that belongs to all of us. I'm not joining you, but I want my share."

Tash sneered. "We'll initiate you for the last six months you worked. If you're siding with Kardesh you'll regret it."

"I've got to have money to leave town. You owe me."

"Leaving town? Going east, back to the Wiglers? The Manichaes rule there; official religion. You can put down the others. Got relatives?" Sevman lifted his head, no.

"Your mom's Wigler, but what about the other part?" Here some of the boys capped their mouths or slapped each other on the back.

Tash leered as he continued. "You guys think that the body is all evil so it doesn't matter what happens to it as long as the spirit is freed and pure. Right? It doesn't matter about your mom or you, does it? You think pure; we'll take care of the rest." Tash looked at the boys still holding Sevman. "Drop his pants guys let's see if he's what he claims. *Ee-yee*, okay, good. Now bend him over." With that the fighting and shouting began.

MANICHEAN CHAPEL

49

PEOPLE, PLOTS & PLACES IN CHAPTER 4

Ali bey: the police chief gets pleasure from interrogation.
Karga: Kaplan's Chipchak Council agent is called the Crow.
Kynan: Prince, royal son of Kaplan and brother of Setchkin.
Mahmud bey: Imam of the central mosque of Kokand City.
Onat bey: leader and commander of the Fergana Seljuks.
Seerden: a foreign agent paid by the Kaynaklar clan.
Setchkin: abducted widow of the old Khan Erdash.
Sevman: supposed orphan at the Manichean monastery.

GLOSSARY:
Alaykum salaam: Arabic response: 'and to you be peace'.
do'er: stop; quit.
dovush: a beating; a scuffle; a fight; a brawl.
emdot: help; attention.
emma: Semitic for mother.
chabuk ol: quickly; hurry up; faster now.
kafir: pagan; unbeliever.
kardeshlerim: my brothers; my siblings.
Salaam alaykum: Arabic greeting: 'Peace be yours.'
Sari Su: yellow water; a north to south seasonal wadi.
yoke: no; not so; nothing; a general negative.
zabeeta: market police.

KYNAN PREPARES

Kynan stood feet apart yelling vigorously, as men and horses swirled about. He was in high spirits as he gave commands for a troop forming. His baggy pants and jacket were dust covered and his shaved pate was grown into a dark crew cut. His large handlebar moustache drooped on the ends, his face was a smudge of dust and sweat, but his excitement was mounting. The thump of the kitchen kettles now covered with hides to make drums, called insistently.

"*Chabuk ol*, go quickly, hurry up. Two weeks rations and a weeks grain for the horses. Three quivers of arrows for every warrior. Two bags of ayran each. *Hepsi you rue*, move it everyone, to horse, to horse." Karga bey rode into the boiling activity to dismount before Kynan.

"Nephew, welcome back from your search. We expected you to come to council to report your findings before you launch into any ill considered activity. There is safety in the experience and advice of others. You are too hasty and impetuous. Come inside this yurt, I must speak to you confidentially." He grasped the young man's shoulder and pushed.

"I found the tribe gathering in the Bet pak dala, the starvation steppes, they are following the *Sari Su* and are camped by the yellow water to move south. If we ride hard we will catch them in a week." The youth explained as he yielded reluctantly to the pressure of the older man's hands that now impelled him to the yurt. He tried to shake off the insistent grasp. "They will wait while others of their clan gather to them." His voice now held anger. He glared at Karga and the yurt residents.

"Everyone out, I will speak to the prince alone." The commanding voice of Karga emptied the Yurt of all but the two men immediately. Karga shoved the youth toward the right corner that held the icon and Nestorian cross.

"I swear I'll denounce you to the council for making these decisions from your own nearsighted will. The spring grass won't last a week for the gathering tribes. Your attack units won't have grass or grain supplement to keep them mobile. They'll outnumber you and have animals to nourish them. You'll not find good hunting on the starvation steppe. You won't even be able to bleed your horses for food. You can catch up to them, but can't carry enough for the return. What about the wounded? What if you're defeated? The Right-hand Clans have some top warriors; real heroes. Use your head!" He shook the youth.

"Kynan went limp in his Uncle's grasp. His face was slack. He moaned. "What else can I do? They have Setchkin and the baby. I must act. I've sworn to avenge them and bring them back. I'm a regent for my nephew, the Heir and child of promise. Every one expects me to pursue them. I've spoken, how can I change it now?" He shook his head in confusion. His exhaustion and nerves showed in his dejection.

"Stop and remember, we have an Heir in our yurt so the plan goes forward. They'll not hurt a hair of her head, she's too important to them. Take your troop and ride round by the Issak Kool Lake and the Chu River, where the stream meets the desert near the Syr River. There you'll find them, weak and suffering, emerging from the Bet Pak Dala Saltland. The grass will not have sufficed them either." He smiled broadly. Kynan swore, "I'll slaughter them all." His face assumed an avid, passionate look.

Karga grimaced. "Never, you must make a deal with them. They can return your sister and the baby in exchange for permanent exile. On the other hand, pardon for the clan, if Twozan will return for trial as a rebel against the Khan. Either would be profitable for us." Karga placed his hands on either side of Kynan's face and patted his cheek.

"You'll get credit as a peacemaker and reconciler of the clans, what-ever their decision." He pinched the cheek playfully. Then, he pointed to the cross.

"You must swear to obey the council's orders. It's most important. Stay here and rest from your travel for an hour. I'll send in some food and finish the preparations for the tribe. Then, you must ride."

The sulky youth sat angrily. "I don't like peace, I like war! All this effort for peace; peace makes no heroes, wins no victories, goods, or promotions. It leaves men untested and restless. Peace is dull routine! War is exciting and profitable; full of challenges and opportunities."

"If the Toozlu flee or fight you'll have all the war you can handle. But they're a Chipchak clan of the Golden Lion Horse Tribes. They will talk and search for an accommodation first. It's their strength and weakness. This Christian good will and mercy always demands opportunity to make a settlement. It may even entice Twozan into our grasp. He knows himself innocent and will presume to prove it." He started to chuckle broadly and Kynan joined him.

> - - - - - - - >KOKAND CENTRAL MOSQUE > - - - - - - - >

Ali the new chief of police stood before the council. His turban was neat, his beard trimmed and his whole uniform impressive. His report was flawless. The spokesman and imam of the central mosque thanked him and made a gesture of dismissal. He turned to the other members of the advisory group. A neat little man of about fifty, he spoke carefully in measured Arabic with admixtures of Persian.

"We should not present the details to the Caliph until the matter is concluded, and more information is gathered. We must set in motion a plan to capture these little devils. Those with families we can warn and fine. The others must be imprisoned or apprenticed, put to work where they will benefit the community. This could not have happened except through the slackness and corruption in the *zabeeta*. Our new chief, Ali bey, has already made many changes and some men will be punished."

"Mahmud bey, Your pardon, I speak as an appointed agent of the Seljuk tribes who live in the meadows and mountains. We maintain with our army the frontier of the north. We are unhappy that many of the tribesmen who work in the city, especially in the police, are discriminated against. Ali bey has kept all Arab and most of the Persian police. Turks are discharged and falsely accused of being Manichaean." He stuttered indignantly at this point. His speech was in Turkish though it had many words of Arabic and Persian intermixed. He continued. "The town's people confuse us with the Uigur enemies that have remained in the valley under treaty. Many suspect our loyalty. Some of our people feel that we should move west, away from this frontier area to escape these suspicions. We converted to Islam, but we have always had from ancient times, teachers from among 'the people of the Book'. Many of our clans were Christian. We now all follow Islam. Our practice and understanding may lack the perfection that some insist on, but we are loyal and sincere. We are in control of the area of the two rivers for the Caliph. We support the decisions of the religious Imams and enforce justice. We enforce all the *firman* decrees of the Caliph. But we are treated as the bottom of a prestige ladder: Arab, Persian and lastly Turk. This is in contradiction to the Koran. We're the warriors who protect your lands. In 200 years you haven't taken possession of the old Turkish homeland. You need us to hold them from our frontier. Do not, in this new zeal for the exile of all Manicheans and justice for market criminals, prejudice our future by preferring one people over others."

The city Imam received the complaint and resumed his speech. "We treasure the words of wisdom of our friend Onat bey. He is invited to both supervise the withdrawal of alien people and to interview the gang members we will arrest tonight. We know the principal areas where the gang meets. They are children, but lawbreakers will be punished. Regardless of family excuses, the Sharia must be upheld."

> - - - - - - - >TOOZLU ON THE SARI SU TRAIL > - - - - - - - >

"*Do'er*, stop, don't let them go! Hold back the cattle and horses. Take the horses to water after the kitchen people have their supply. Use your whips. Don't let the cattle rush the water. They'll muck it up. Keep more distance between the herds. Keep the herd away in the dry land. Don't let them on the meadow. The horses get the tallest grass and the cows finish it." Twozan rode among the noisy herds shouting. He shook his fist in frustration as the cattle tried to rush the water and the huge Kangals ran forward biting noses and barking. It made a great uproar. The mounted men rode among them shouting. Finally, when the cause seemed lost, one man seized a bell cow and slaughtered her there. Wiping her blood with a kerchief, he then rode to the forefront waving it like a red flag on his sword's end. The smell of blood turned the first rank and others followed. Fear drove them from their goal.

As order was restored, Twozan returned to the remains of the column. The advanced guard continued beyond the kitchen. Each clan camped apart to eat.

"You did nothing but brood all day. Now you rave and shout about the use of water." Setchkin teased impudently.

"We don't have enough grass or water. Even the wild varmints will suffer lack this year." He clicked his tongue.

"You've handled the march well enough, but you made a grave mistake with the clans and should be ashamed of your decision to run." Setchkin smirked and tossed her head. She took the lead passing in front of Twozan.

He gazed at her and shrugged, refusing to be baited. However, he couldn't resist a chance to retaliate. "You make your mistakes, too, but like all women you point the finger at others."

She drew back as if struck. "Its men who are all the same: full of lust, pretext and pride. I came with the hope of a frank talk, but I see little chance of success." She started to rein her golden horse away.

"Wait, let's talk. You are right. I'm brooding over our situation. The grass is both short and scanty. We are sweeping every thing bare as we pass. We will start losing stock in another few days. We can't stop even for an extra day, they are fouling the water and there isn't enough."

"This was foreseeable and predicted. But you took the risk and pay the forfeit. You can still ride us out of here by abandoning the stock." She had dropped her hostile manner.

He eyed her thoughtfully, at least she didn't say, 'I told you so'.

"If we ride out we will die on the roads. The tiger and his cub will be waiting for their little kitty." He tried to pinch her cheek, but she dodged.

"Why did you change your mind about my betrothal to Sanjak?" She spoke suddenly, all sincerity.

"Would you believe me if I told you that I had reasons that concerned your own good and happiness?" He sighed.

"I promise a fair hearing, I can't say beforehand what I'll believe." They exchanged glances then, she turned away.

"Sanjak was unsettled. I sought to avoid a bad marriage for you, and future troubles with the strongest clan in the tribe." He sighed again, deeply.

"How was he unsettled, I felt he loved me. He said so enough." It was her time to sigh and wipe tears.

"He continued to watch other girls closely. He regularly visited a few. I thought him frivolous, not ready. He was all impatience to visit the

Tang lands when he heard of the persecutions and expulsions. He was anxious to be a hero, but not a husband. He would have broken it off himself, were it not for the weight of the Kaynaklar. He was always self calculating and prudent about his future."

"And you're not? You were going to promote Sevim, Khan Erden's daughter. You sent him away when I needed him."

"Sevim was always there, but I let him follow his fancy and he was fickle. I'd no idea they would promise you to old Khan Erdash. I'd intended to save, not hurt you, but then it was too late." He turned round to see the following riders wreathed in travel dust. He continued. "I'm telling the truth. I thought I was right. But you were hurt. Forgive, if you can." They passed the men hauling water for the kitchen, protecting a small pool for the people. They rode past in silence, then, he turned and called back to the workers.

"Watch that the animals don't contaminate all the pools. Dam the stream in several places wherever there is current. Let the water accumulate."

> - - - - - - -> KOKAND CENTRAL JAIL > - - - - - - ->

"Where are the prisoners from your raid, Captain?" Onat bey asked, looking around the dark cell.

Ali bey pointed to a miserable bundle sobbing in the corner of the room. Onat bey, the Seljuk commander stood staring sourly at the dejected boy.

"Only one? You're sure you have all the gang now, Ali bey? I can see why the market was terrorized. No doubt this is the remarkable leader who caught the criminals and was paid for returned merchandise. Take him into service. He's more effective than your own. You might make him an onbasha, a corporal to start." He laughed in derision. Ali squirmed and shot a resentful glare at the smiling visitor.

"They were forewarned. My men got there in the dark and all were gone but this one. But he'll serve my needs. He'll be a mine of information. I'll work it all out. I'll squeeze him dry." Ali posed dramatically; walked to the wall and took down a thin metal rod which he flexed in his hand. He continued pacing the room and patting his palm with the instrument. Then he switched the air making it whistle. The sobbing stopped and an awed silence followed. The trembling boy's eyes bugged and his mouth fell open.

56

"I've heard of your methods. I'd prefer to question the boy and get the parents to tell what they know first. Punishment as a routine is not profitable. Let the parents do it when they learn that they pay a fine."

Onat bey sat on the floor near the child and started to talk. "I'm Onat bey; sent to help. What's your name?"

The child whispered: "Sevmani."

"You bear a prophet's name. Truth is required from you. Isn't that your teaching? Come, no man fears the truth."

Nevertheless, his fearful eyes studied the man, then he nodded; yes.

"Why didn't you run away with the others? You must have had time, all the rest got clean away."

The kindly tone brought tears again to Sevman's eyes and he cleaned his face with his sleeve and shook his head. His voice was low. "I was hurt and can't run. They beat and abused me, they're mad at me. I wanted my share now; to leave the city. They refused. I only woke up when the police came."

Onat passed him a pillow and the boy arranged it behind his back and sat gingerly on the edge of it. He winced when he moved. Onat watched with narrowed eyes as he assessed the nature and extent of the injuries.

He smiled reassuringly. "They don't like you now. You don't like them. It'll be no breach of honor to tell what you know about them. Who is the leader?" Onat leaned on an elbow to see into the boy's face.

"Tash, the big rat faced guy, is the boss now." He looked at the closeness of Onat's face and faltered.

"Yes, go on. Tash is boss. Who was boss before?"

"The guy was hurt and had to quit. Tash took his place." Sevman looked studiously at the marble floor.

"What was the name of the old leader?" The response was silence. "Did other boys dropout with you?" Quiet continued.

Ali interrupted loudly whipping the steel rod in his direction. "We know how to persuade the guilty." Sevman cringed, but did not speak. Onat jerked up his head, no, and made a patting motion with his hand. He resumed his trail. "How many boys are there?"

57

Sevman shrugged. "It changes, but about two dozen are usual. There were twenty tonight." He noticed blood on the back of his hand and sucked it silently.

Onat leaned closer. "You'll give us their names. All those who beat you, you remember every one of them. Tell us how their faces look and how big they are." Onat sat back with satisfaction. He smiled at Ali bey and motioned with his head.

Ali turned. "Call the scribe." He spoke sharply to his man, who immediately left. He narrowly watched the Seljuk leader, critically pursing his lips.

The scribe was prompt and prepared. The list grew apace under the skilled questions of Onat. At length the volunteered information ran dry. No reference was made to leaders or gang dropouts again.

"I suggest you send out your men and net a few of these riffraff, then you'll have all the names and facts you need. What one won't give, others will supply." Onat stood.

"You've had your visit with the police and seen our prisoner. The council should be content that the matter is under control. The judge will soon have the guilty to fine or sentence. You've had your way with the questioning. Are there any other requests?" Ali was cool, correct and courteous.

"No, I have other duties: the Manicheans. Also there are rumors along the trade roads. Something big is happening near both the frontiers. There are movements of large numbers of people both from the North and the Far East. I need to find the causes of these movements: if they be more than rumors. We depart at dawn. I'm done here. Thank you. *Allah ismar ladik*, God wills it, farewell."

"*Gouley gouley*, Go happily." Ali bey stood his tallest. Onat nodded and left. Ali stared long after him. Gradually he allowed the anger in his heart to appear on his face. He turned to the child who sat watching. He spoke. "Now you'll tell me all you know and withhold nothing. Otherwise you'll suffer a *dovush*, a beating."

Ali looked at the scribe, still sitting. He hissed. "Be prepared to write every word he says." He turned to his man. He snarled with a grim smile. "Hold the kid's feet up above his head." He reached over for the thin rod. He again tested its flexibility.

"You say your name is Sevmani, I say you're *kafir*, a Manichean idolater. You follow the false religion of Mani the mad Persian prophet. You're fleeing to the Wiglers, the enemy of Islam and our Abbassid Caliph. I'll show you how we treat heathen."

Sevman cried out shrilly. "No, please, I told everything you needed. What more?"

"I want the names of your leader and his companions who left when Tash took over." He whipped out.

"Ay–e–e--e, don't. Help. *Kardeshim*, my brothers. Help me, someone please help me." A wet red welt appeared on the sole of both feet.

Sevman struggled and jerked, throwing the attendant off balance. Screams filled the air as Ali bey continued to thrash the boy.

"Come, help shut off this vermin's screeching." The secretary entered into the struggle. He grasped Sevman by the throat to silence him; with the attendant holding the ankles, they stretched Sevman on the floor. Ali lashed out at the thrashing figure and caught the choking boy across the knees. There was a crack and the splash of blood. The noise suddenly stopped with his collapse into a coma. It was followed by silence. Ali, arms folded, stood gloating.

SEVMAN INTEROGATED

59

PEOPLE, PLOTS & PLACES IN CHAPTER 5

Valiman the Hun: officer trying to aid refugees from China.
Bowzhun: a rich Baghdad family hiding during expulsions.
Chinese officer: in charge of confiscating foreign assets.
Jon: a serving boy attends the Bowzhun family interests.
Kahya: a servant of the Bowzhun family in Tang China.
Koolair: a child of an Arab family in China's capital city.
Maril: an unmarried daughter of the Bowzhun merchant.
Nooryouz: an Umayyad ambassador's granddaughter.
Sanjak: helps refugees who are being expelled by the Tang.
Yusuf: father of the Bowzhun family in business in China.

GLOSSARY:
ah'ma: Chinese for mother.
bulbul: a nightingale.
dwai: correct, certainly, Chinese affirmative.
kowtowing: kneeling; bowing humbly.
noor: light; bright.
tutu: Chinese for officer.
youz: face; surface.
yurue: walk; move out.

FIRST IMPRESSIONS

Sanjak felt a thrill of joy course through his veins. In China, he was important! He was aide to Valiman, the key leader in the evacuation of condemned foreign families and the evasion of the Tang emperor's confiscation decrees. They stood against injustice. He was Joshua to the Moses of an exodus from the lands of the oppressing Pharaoh.

All in Changan City felt the expulsion orders and the activities of the police. Fear hid the movement of all who understood the intent of the throne. All Nestorians, Buddhists, and Manicheans, were interdicted. Foreigners were being expelled and the Han people would have to renounce alien religions or suffer jail, enslavement or death.

Since all goods were forfeit, the trick for the refugees was to get out with their goods intact. Money was required for travel and a future reestablishment in the homeland. Those remaining would withdraw to friendly border areas and try to wait out the decree's application and eventual end of Tang madness.

Sanjak entered the Bowzhun's empty house with boldness, he had hidden the family. The Muslims of Baghdad had a treaty of exemption with the Tang. This Baghdad family was Christian and not protected by it. Only a married sister was lacking to complete the family's withdrawal. Sanjak waited for the old servant, who was out selling goods at the market. Yahya would guide him to the new hiding place.

Within the house, all was quiet and he sat in the garden to wait. It was spring, the birds flew around him, some sang. In the silence, between sounds, he clearly heard singing. Nearby, a sweet child-like voice sang of longings and needs.

> - - - - - - - > CHANGAN ARMY CENTER > - - - - - - - >

"*Dwai Tutu*, correct, commander, the Bowzhun servant is selling metal objects in the market to the artisans and bowl makers. I saw him. You must move quickly or the money will be lost." The informer waved his folded hands before his face in obsequious salute; *kowtowing.*

The captain turned to his lieutenant with a satisfied smirk. "Take two companies and occupy the Bowzhun estate. Bring in all the aliens who wear the white turbans. Punish anyone who aids them. Destroy those who resist. Don't forget, a few women would improve life here." The lieutenant sucked air through his teeth, bowed deeply, pleased with the assignment. "We rid our land of the foreign exploiters, and remain enriched." The lieutenant left.

"*Tutu*, where is my reward?" The informer queried.

"Come tomorrow when we know the full value of your new information. The roaches run for cover."

Outside the door, Jon, a gangling youth, watched the forming of the troop, the departure of the informer, and then he ambled away. He was two streets from the military post when he started to run.

> - - - - - - - > CHANGAN ARAB HOUSEHOLD > - - - - - - - >

Nooryouz sat in the corner of the room. Tears still moistened her cheek as she recalled the words of her old father. 'I have treated you like a son, taught you to read, and postponed your marriage. But the time has come to consummate it. The man is no older than I, and is both honorable and rich. We have need of an alliance with one whom the Abbassids trust. Our family came to represent the Umayyad. It is a bad time for foreigners in the Celestial kingdom. We need both his riches and standing or we will suffer the fate of others in Changan City.'

She sat meditating her future: one week till the auspicious day. The shrunken, angry, demanding old man who had come to the house twice before was to take her away forever. She felt a shudder, but if it were necessary to save her father's house and their estrangement from the ruling Abbassids in distant Baghdad: why not? Was this not the will of Allah? It would save them from the expulsions that others outside the treaty with Baghdad would suffer. Jews were exempt because they did not proselytize; Muslims because of the approved commerce treaty. She decided she ought to be happy, but the tears continued to flow. She looked at the orchard in the patio. There, the plum tree bloomed. She quietly went to stand close, breathe in its sweet perfume and sing.

62

PLUM TREE SONG

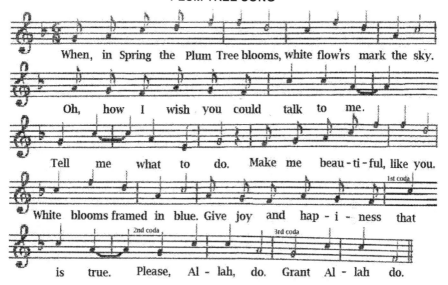

When, in Spring the Plum Tree blooms, white flow'rs mark the sky.

Oh, how I wish you could talk to me.

Tell me what to do. Make me beau-ti-ful, like you.

White blooms framed in blue. Give joy and hap-i-ness that

(1st coda)

(2nd coda) *(3rd coda)*

is true. Please, Al-lah, do. Grant Al-lah do.

1

When, in spring the plum tree blooms,
White flowers mark the sky.
Oh, how I wish you could talk to me.
Tell me what to do.
Make me beautiful, like you,
White blooms framed in blue.
Give joy and happiness that is true.
Please, Allah, do.

#2

When at night the bulbul sings,
Allah, my heart cries.
Oh, how his song makes my heart to ring,
Tells me love is right.
Make me beautiful like you,
Sing songs in the night.
Joy will give happiness that is true.
Please, Allah, do.

#3

As dawn comes the pale moon fades,
Morning star appears.
Guiding me onward where fears will fade,
Love will soon appear.
Make me beautiful like you,
Guide me to the light.
Great joy and happiness come from You.
Grant, Allah, do.

It was to be an auspicious day. Why didn't she share her news with her secret friend? Maril had not whistled near the garden wall for a week. Nooryouz had tried twice in the hour of rest to whistle her up, but without success. She sighed. She stopped the flow of tears to listen to the talk of the servants.

Old Ma Ling was bemoaning the turmoil in the city. Part of the Ma clan had remained Nestorian when her part of the clan had converted to Islam. So, her talk was angry. "They would not run such risk if they had regarded the clan elder Ma Tsung. Now we who embraced Islam are all safe, but those who continued in error, as Christians, are harassed and destroyed." The others were accustomed to her harangues and knew the pride of the Ma Clan. They made sympathetic clucking sounds as they continued about their business casually.

Nooryouz thought again of her friend Maril, whose family was Nestorian. Her father would never speak of them -- for him they did not exist. But she had no other with whom to play, being the last of an old aristocrat's litter. The baby Koolair, by the new concubine was suspect, she arrived precisely 9 months after the purchase date from the Syrian trader. The baby was now weaned, two years old and running, usually to Nooryouz since the mother remained ill and in bed most of the day. She caught up the child and walked to the back garden. Behind the large plum tree in a jumble of wild bamboo and brambles she paused to whistle, like a bird near a nest. There was no answer. Cautiously she stepped to the wall and pulled out a brick that slid freely out of the design. Then another brick higher up also was slid out far enough to make easy stair steps up to the high top. She pushed other bricks out making a socket hole in the wall to form stairs down the opposite side. A bamboo pole served to push each step back in its place and cover the signs of an exit. Now she could comfortably descend with the child in her arms. All the Bowzhun servants knew of the girls' games with the baby, so she pushed boldly forward to see why her friend had been silent for a week.

> - - - - - - - > AT THE BOWZHUN HOUSE > - - - - - - - >

Sanjak heard the whisper of bamboo and grass from the far corner of the garden. A child's giggle and coo came to his ear. Startled he stood, turned and with shock beheld the form of a mother and child. They seemed to come straight from a heavenly world of perfection and beauty. He stared incredulously, noting the youth and loveliness of the girl, and cool assurance of the child, who held out welcoming arms.

"Oh, Holy Virgin!" Slowly without breaking eye contact Sanjak sank to his knees, face flushed, hands open before him, pleading mercy.

Nooryouz stood, startled, ready to flee. She had never been this near a boy. A warrior? Perhaps the angel Gabriel? A friend of the prophet? Their eyes locked, she felt naked and blushed scarlet. She was in home dress: flimsy vest and trousers, no veils or burnoose to cover her. She lifted an arm to cover her hair and realized that she was unshaven. All body hair would be removed before the wedding, the day before its consummation. She sank to her knees in humiliation releasing the child.

Koolair stood stretching out her arms. This was a game she loved to play with Maril and Nooryouz. She would run rapidly from one to the other. But now, here was another who knew the game and waited. Bubbling with laughter, she ran up to the figure now with hands on the ground, and hugging his neck planted a wet kiss on the cheek. Turning, she started to run back.

Sanjak was murmuring, "Lady, forgive me; Lord, forgive me." when the wet kiss and laughing voice brought him to himself. "Yesu! Praises be..." His voice caught in his throat.

Koolair was out of reach and planted a kiss on Nooryouz's hot face. They clung together. Nooryouz smiled at the child's enthusiasm and summoned her courage for a timid question to the beautiful youth.

"Who are you, My Lord? Where is my dear Maril?"

He wiped his eyes and stood. "Sanjak of the Chipchak Nation. Maril is safe. We must go where she is when the servant comes." He noticed the earrings on the child and saw through the flimsy robe that she was a girl. "She's a little beauty. What's her name?" He approached and held out his hand to help her stand.

"Koolair. We ..." A sharp whistle came from the street and a tall boy came running in, opening the gateway door.

"Kahya is here, but the police follow. Someone told. Quick, they'll come here." Sanjak caught Nooryouz's arm in a grip of steel, forcing her to her feet and toward the gate.

"I can't go out without covering. I can't leave my home." She spoke in fear and haste. He caught up his travel cloak on the bench and spread it over her head and the child in her arms. As she caught the edge to secure it he propelled her toward the door with his arm behind her.

"Trust me, our lives depend on it!" Down a side ally they darted. The boy, Jon, directed the servant to follow them and waited until the first of an army squad appeared. Then he ran off in another direction to lead the pursuit away.

> - - - - - - - > ARMED OCCUPATION > - - - - - - >

"Well, the birds have flown," the Tang lieutenant observed, "but we have the cage and wealth in hand. Search the Bowzhun grounds and buildings for evidence of help or destination. It is forbidden to save or sell the properties: death to all who resist the royal decrees."

The Tang lieutenant made a cursory sweep of the house and sent the men to search for buried treasure in the yard. One returned grinning. "*Tutu*, honored one, come and see." The brick step-work over the wall was clear evidence of an escape route. One of the soldiers passed over to the top and jumped down, and others followed. A scream from the house announced their detection by the servants. An old Arab warrior and a few old retainers came out of the house armed with swords. They fell upon the intruding soldiers. However, more troops swarmed over the wall. The fight was short. It ended quickly in a victory as the soldiers overran the defense. Then looting began.

> ------- >IN THE CHANGAN SLUMS > ------- >

The house where the Bowzhun family had taken refuge was in a warren of alleys and one room shacks not too far from the river. Considered too dangerous to patrol, the authorities depended on the reports of paid informers and close watch over the market places to check the possible plots and crimes perpetuated from this slum. It was no surprise to the police when persecuted families took refuge in their grim shanties, but they would be eventually detected and caught. Their dress, language, money and manners would betray them with the help of the thieves, prostitutes and pimps that occupied the same district. No rewards were offered. A modest share of the victim's assets was enough to keep the tips and betrayals regular and the police active.

Sanjak was relieved to get Nooryouz to the family and was gratified when Maril came joyously forward to kiss her and take the little girl up. The whole family acted surprised.

"You probably didn't expect to see your sister again, but I went back to see." He said proudly to Maril.

"This is not her sister this is Nooryouz, a neighbor. My older daughter is married and not at our house. It was her we were worried about. You are mistaken in bringing this girl. Her family has diplomatic immunity: they are Muslim." The father, Yusuf bey, shook his head indignantly.

"I had news for Maril and I came through the back. I didn't know you had left. This man didn't take time to listen. Father will be furious, they have announced the propitious day for my wedding. The groom will have the police out." Nooryouz made a face at the mention of the groom and made a kind of whiney as if she couldn't decide whether to cry or giggle. The cloak had fallen revealingly.

"Maril, take your friend inside to get her properly clothed." Yusuf indicated a cloth hung to divide the room.

Sanjak stood mouth open and eyes staring wildly. He sank to the nearest bench and shook his head as if to settle his brains. He put both hands to his chin and asked. "Would you explain this again, in detail?"

> - - - - - - ->AT THE BOWZHUN HIDING PLACE > - - - - - - ->
Maril and Nooryouz clung sleepily together and the child Koolair slept beside them. Kahya, the chief steward and servant of the Bowzhun family consulted with Sanjak in low whispers, as if the walls had ears. Yusuf was on family errands seeking news and money for travel.

"Jon went to both houses. The surviving servants are being interrogated. The Abbassid agent has offered rewards for the return of this girl, Nooryouz, his bride. The mother of the child has vanished. She was from a northern tribe and may have returned to them, if the soldiers didn't get her." The old servant reported, shook his head, sighed and continued urgently. "It is an affair of face because of the treaty. The lieutenant is in disgrace for the attack on the house. They will search thoroughly. We can't attach her to the deportee column, all will be watching."

Sanjak nodded, "We can't leave her. She says she won't marry the agent now that her father's dead. She has no other family. This city's not safe. What can we do with her?"

She stirred. "They're watching for a girl. If I dressed like a boy they wouldn't notice me." Both men stared at her, shock on their faces. Sanjak jerked his head up indignantly.

She said, "I used to play I was a boy. I'm good at it. I put my hair into the turban and wear a stiff vest of brocade. Boys have all the fun, so I practiced. I used to watch them from our balcony window. I even slipped out a few times. I learned the street words the donkey boys use." She stood legs apart in Turkish trousers and quilted jacket and horrified them with a string of strong, lewd phrases: "Damn it, *+*+^*! Move, you mother of bastards. Move your ass or I'll ram my quirt up your tail and clean out your bloated brown belly, *+#*!+*."

"Enough, please, save it for the road." A shocked Sanjak looked incredulous, but somehow happy with his transformed Madonna.

Kahya looked disapproving, but finally shrugged. "Jon has worked on the road as a donkey boy. He can show her the work. It's safe only if she's willing to cut her hair and dirty her face." He watched her reaction.

"How long will I have to do it?" She asked Sanjak.

"Perhaps a year or more, beyond the Tang borders surely."

She wrinkled her nose smiling wryly. "If I married old grim-bitter it might last ten times that. A donkey is better company."

67

"I've permission to send out a caravan of the expellees. They will accompany a drove of animals exported to the Uigur Nation. Their agent Manly, got a bargain, and will supervise the breeding stock and herders. It's a large group. Our refugees haven't the resources to remain here all summer. I've been in touch with my relatives north of the walls and they promise some food and protection on the trip west. I want you to be in charge." Valiman the Hun, worked in the midst of scribes at tables with papers. He wore Chinese court robes and not the required white turban of the merchant class. He moved and spoke like a ruler of armies.

"I thought I would stay and help here. I am only just learning the Han language. There is so much to do yet," Sanjak objected. "I haven't any experience moving exiles."

"These families can't wait. I have relatives and old friends in government who warn of increasing danger. We must keep the detention camps as empty as possible for the sake of those yet to be processed. When people are too crowded they die. Your people understand this and lead a nomadic life. You have experience that is invaluable. I have prayed and meditated on this. You must go." His voice was firm, but he smiled at the disappointed youth.

"My lord, how can I desert these needy people? We have many still hiding in the slums," Sanjak protested.

"Just my point, my friends will see that the lists are open for adding names at your pleasure. Those now hidden cannot remain long undetected. We can move them now if we seize the moment. I believe Yesu would have us proceed boldly. God and people favor confident action."

"I understand, Lord Valiman, but I regret leaving your service. There is so much to learn from a leader like you. I don't know enough." He fumbled to a halt.

"Yesu will teach you. Don't be discouraged. You'll be useful in this and not as safe as you might think. It's actually quite an achievement to arrive safely." He patted Sanjak's arm. "You have a young muleteer to get safely away. Besides the anti-foreign leaders are questioning your presence in Changan. They know little of your people and are suspicious of all the northern tribesmen. We have too frequently invaded and ruled. Our blood permeates north China and they fear us with good reason."

A saffron robed Tangut Buddhist monk sat impassive in quiet meditation in a corner; while the Hunnish priest recited scripture from memory to a small group gathered about him. It was John's gospel. 'In the beginning was the Word, and the Word was with God and the Word was God.' Two tiny children clung to the mother near the door, both were crying, 'ah ma! ah ma!'

68

Sanjak stood nearby at the prison gate by the guards, talking to a prison authority, who was examining his writ of permission and looking disdainful at the same time.

Sanjak was conscious of a Chinese man hanging on a *Tau* cross behind him outside the gate. They stood beside the post and below its top cross bar. The man was still alive. Sanjak could not look at him.

"Yes, you have permission to extract foreigners who give bond of immediate exit. There are widows and children not on the list which you can have for a bit more silver. We have more than we can feed here in detention. The sooner they are cleared out of our land the better. We have no need of barbarians here."

Sanjak sighed. "We are raising the money as quickly as possible, but there are legal tangles with the confiscation orders."

"Your goods were acquired from our culture, made by our artisans, where could you find its equal? It was bought with money gained at our expense. You have no right to any of your goods. Buy your people out with wealth from your own lands."

Sanjak suppressed his rising anger. "Our lands are far away and our sweat and efforts provided our goods which you take."

"Our sovereign rules under heaven. We are to be freed from foreign innovation that corrupts our civilization. Your tortured God has no place among us. Those who follow him must go his way." He pointed to the hanging Chinese figure on the cross. "In the past is all art and perfection, the golden ages past must ever be our example." A small movement of the head indicated the interview was terminated. The guards shifted position slightly. Sanjak left avoiding the post. He flinched as a droplet of blood stained his hand.

> - - - - - - - >IN THE CHANGAN MARKET > - - - - - - - >

Jon grinned whimsically. Just imagine teaching a girl how to work like a pack boy. He giggled a little, but hid his face so his companion Noor, for that is how he had shortened her name, couldn't see it. The kid was doing alright with grime darkened skin and clothes. Jon was old enough to be interested in girls, but still held the boyish prejudices and humor. She did not always know how to respond to remarks the other market people made, but her Han Chinese was good. She learned fast, he admitted reluctantly. He had made contracts and hunted up work for them to do, so she would make him some money for the trip and learn how to be a working boy: two good things at one time.

"We're at the end of the day and we'll walk slowly by market's edge. A man who is all men's friend will appear to preach to the crowd. Ma Ping Hai, is one great God man. People fear his prophetic words. Yesu's strong spirit calls to their hearts. You'll see it all, soon now."

69

"I see a man near the wall. He is shouting at the people and they are moving toward him." Noor was moving toward the man.

"Wait! Stay close! If the police come, some people will fight them. We'll stay at the edge. We'll hear it all, but be safe."

"People of Changan, peace be to you of good heart and right actions. God rules in Heaven and sends good words to men of earth. God loves men and gives freedom to act, to choose, to live a good life or evil. God pays to all good for good, bad for bad. Yesu came to make a good offer to all. Yesu suffered for your bad acts, you must accept God's good act for you and worship Yesu. You will find peace of soul now and a place in God's heavenly garden when life ends. If you fight against God, you will lose. He will take away your peace and unity. Your souls will burn with his anger. Your land will suffer division and weakness, not just during your lifetime, but also for your grandchildren's grandchildren. God proclaims it will be for 'times, a time and half a time'. Some of you burn and loot houses. You will suffer for this bad action against those who worship Yesu. It is not God's will." The whole market listened, silent, no business was going on. The fearless Nestorian preacher continued.

"The Tang dynasty has been justly called great in the past. They have ruled and united the people for great achievements, but now the restored Tang want to destroy all your ancestors chose, and all you can choose. No man can retreat into the past to undo the present. Think carefully. Is it right for one man to judge Heaven? Can any man on earth say: mine only is the right way -- all must obey? Only one, who came from heaven, could say such a thing. Yesu, God's son and Living Word, is 'God with us', living His life as a man. He suffered rejection and death for our sin and unbelief. See what happened to those who rejected him. They are scattered. You too will be victim to those who hate you. You will be divided among yourselves. You will not be one people again, until foreign armies make you whole. Hear me! In Daniel's book is understanding: 'a time, times and half a time' in hundreds of years for your punishment. Hear God's warning! Repent now that you may live and prosper..."

Three companies of soldiers charged in from different gates to part the awed crowd, driving quickly toward the lone speaker. The market crowd screamed objections to the troops. Shrieks and catcalls echoed. Rocks began to fly. People shouted, "Stop them;" "Let him finish;" "Sacrilege;" "Infidels!"

Bodies blocked, feet tripped and hands grabbed at the soldiers who tried to push past, and through the mass of listeners. Blood flowed along the path opened in the crowd. The speaker had vanished and many others were running away.

Jon yelled, "*Yurue*, move it. Let's get out of here." Outside they met more troops moving toward the gates, but the soldiers were too busy to notice two dirty boys running with their donkeys.

> - - - - - - - >AT THE EXIT GATE OF CHANGAN> - - - - - - >

The city guards stood arrogantly before the gate of the Royal City of Changan, while the captain of the imperial guard examined the party of foreigners seeking to pass. As he read the expulsion lists and departure dates for all outsiders, he scanned their long faces and high, thin noses with displeasure. His lackeys examined their packed goods which had been laid out in detail. They now were being hastily repacked by the disgruntled muleteers and servants. A self-important inspector demanded. "These silk garments are too fine for export. All this must remain behind."

As he spoke the donkey boy, waving a piece of script, interrupted indignantly. "Here is the exporter's receipt given to my master. The second bundle's contents are old clothes. Why do you paw through everything?"

The man pushed the frail, dirty faced donkey boy aside contemptuously and moved forward to strike again. "Dirty Syrian bastard, go home to your kennels." Immediately the flat-faced Jon picked up a large rock and heaved it at the offending speaker, who screamed protests. But Jon had his Syrian friend in tow and had taken the bridle of a loaded mule to lead past the gate. They were out in an instant and refused to stop, while the man threatened, and the guards laughed. Gradually, all the party followed in their steps. Another band of exiles were expelled westward, to live or die in the struggle to reach home.

DONKEY BOYS

71

THE PEOPLE, PLOTS & PLACES IN CHAPTER 6

Barmani: Abbot of the exiled Kokand Manicheans.
Derk: agent of the Caliph in Kokand with special powers.
Gerchen: a leader of the Right hand horde performs for all.
Harun: an old police official of Kokand and family friend.
Jon: The donkey boy irritates Sanjak, but proves a friend.
Manish: herds sheep and plays a pipe for entertainment.
Mother: Yeet's blind mother works knotting rugs.
Sanjak: leads the refugees west out of China toward safety.
Setchkin: makes adjustments in her situation as a hostage.
Sevman: is recovering from a tortuous interrogation in jail.
Twozan: finds his leadership challenged by circumstances.
Yeet: confirms his purpose and finds friends for his help.
Yemen'li Hasan: Yeet's dead father, a soldier from Yemen.

GLOSSARY:
afair reen': congratulations; bravo; well done.
Alaycum Salaam: a response to a greeting: peace to you.
Allah bera ket ver sin: may God bless you.
ahblam: my older sister; the title usually holds respect.
Allah ismar'ladik: I must leave: God wills my departure.
Derk eder'sin: Do you understand? Do you comprehend?
emma: Arabic for mother.
hiyer: no; not at all.
kapa chininee: shut up; shut your mouth.
koorsura bahk'ma: forgive my mistakes; overlook my error.
Papaz: a priest; Christian minister; preacher.
Salaam alaycum: a greeting: peace to you.
soos: hush; be quiet; calm down.
Wigler: slang, for Uigur a Manichaean Turkish nation.
yo: slang for no; general negative.
yu rue: walk; move it; get going.

MOTHER'S LOOM

"*Salaam alaycum*, peace to you, mother of heroes." Yeet stood at the darkened door of his mother's room.

"*Alaycum Salaam*, child of daydreams. At long last you remember your mother, ungrateful scamp."

"*Emma*, mother, how goes your rug? Does it grow wonderfully now that it is past the half?" He entered the room. The loom occupied the center and only an aisle separated it from her bed and stove. He peered at the carpet whose rich colors were obscure in the dark. The design was hardly discernible. The mother did not pause... not one moment did she lose control of her strings and knots. Her face turned toward Yeet and she leaned toward his voice. "Well impudent one, do I get a kiss? Or have you become too much of a man to remember? When your father lived you had kisses for everyone. Come let me feel how you have grown." As the boy kissed her cheek she stopped long enough to put one arm around him and after a squeeze felt his head, face and chest. She patted Yeet and resumed her work of rapidly knotting the rug. She talked for he was silent.

"How goes your work? You have not brought me nuts or fruit to entice my agreement with your pretexts and games? You used to entertain me with all the exciting things about city life, but now you forget and neglect me."

"You have no need of my eyes now mother. So, I use them elsewhere. You have food enough by your work. If I bring you overmuch, the other girls steal your tidbits."

"Such a one were you in your father's time. You were always a monkey, into everything. Wheedling whatever you wanted from your doting dad. But now you've left off your apprenticed work with the jeweler and want to be a man."

"I have to make my own way since the shop burned." He thought a moment. "I have a friend detained by the police last night. We got there too late to help. Our leader doesn't dare go. I need to find out his sentence or fine. I want to know. How can I inquire at the jail without suspicion or trouble?" Yeet put his hand on his mother's cheek and turned her head to his, facing her into the light. Her nimble hands continued working while the sightless eyes stared.

"Your father had many friends there. Find one and talk Arabic to him. Fat Harun would be a good man to see. Confide in him. He'll help when you tell him who you are."

"*Emma*, Mother you are wise. Allah gives you light. I must go at once and do as you say." Yeet kissed the cheek before him again, and ran from the room.

>- - - - - - - ->ERBEN'S HOUSE, KOKAND> - - - - - - ->

Kardesh, bandaged and drawn, stood with head hung before the presence of Erben, his father. The two women sat timidly in the corner. The man seemed calmly to stand like a towering angel pointing the way out of the garden. This was no drunken man cornered by his problems.

"The police will be seeking your gang, if what I hear is correct. It matters little that the boy who replaced you has erred. They'll hunt you as well. They'll make an example of all of you; especially to cover any negligence on their own part. We must leave Kokand." He lifted his hand. "*Hiyer*, no, no protest. I have an offer of work in a quarry. It is far

74

enough away that I assume the police won't come out of their jurisdiction. It's an open life there and you can drive a cart and get a wage. You'll not be bored with excessive study. I have scriptures from father Agaz. We will study them at night. You need spiritual instruction. You'll work and pray as you heal. You can drive a horse, others will load the cart. We'll leave tonight. Leyla and your aunt Tayze have trunks and packs to prepare. You'll go bring in the cart and horses. Bring Yeet and come by moonlight. Go now."

> - - - - - - - > ON THE SILK ROAD > - - - - - - - >

The first night, after all the excitement of the first day's journey, the exiles found little hospitality at the government-contracted inn. The food was inferior and the service reluctant. The owner intended to gain as much as possible from the hated foreign expellees. He cheated them and always demanded more for any extra service. Only Sanjak's newly formed militia kept looters away from the refugees.

Sanjak, after an evening of arguments and threats, looked for Nooryouz, and found her in the stable sitting on the straw. She was yawning, but still attentive as Jon explained how to repair a bit of leather harness. Since she already knew sewing and braiding, Jon found that her only problem was the strength to push the large bone needles through the leather. They had found a large, smooth, palm-sized, concave stone to do the job. Their success brought laughter.

"How'd you know so much about horses and their gear, Noor? I never thought girls were smart." He looked up self-consciously and seeing Sanjak, Jon apologized. "*Koorsura bahk ma*, excuse me, I forgot. She's a boy for the trip." He looked around to see if any others had overheard him. Sanjak stood there struggling with a new feeling. Jealousy was not a familiar sensation.

"Don't forget again or I'll have the hide whipped off your bottom." He expressed it with unwanted anger. Both found the statement funny and went into gales of laughter.

"*Soos, kapa chinnin nee*, Hush, shut your mouth! We must be careful, our lives depend on it." He stood still, suddenly indecisive, the problem of the sleeping arrangement had struck home. Their giggles ceased. Sanjak plunged ahead. "The inn is out to cheat us and the government, so I think I'll sleep here, with both of you in the stable. Let's find a dry corner and some clean hay." Manish played his pipe softly by the corral. The Manichae herder slept outside with the animals. They all slept dressed.

> - - - - - - - >AT THE KOKAND JAIL > - - - - - - - >

75

Yeet rested, leaning against a wall, while watching the police department's door as men entered and left. It was after the Gunesh prayer time early in the morning. He slyly listened to those loitering just off duty or waiting to go on for the day. Most spoke Arabic or Persian. Yeet waited until the last duty officer came out. He was fat, old and balding; talking and laughing with a younger man. Yeet ran out and pulled on the back of his vest.

"Uncle Harun! Uncle Harun, Mother sent me. Yemenli Hasan is my father. You remember, don't you?"

The old man turned and looked puzzled. He scratched his head. "Who are you boy? Of course, I remember Yemenli Hasan and his wife. Did he have a son?"

Yeet smiled. "My name is Yeet. Mother works in the municipal rug factory. Ahblam, my elder sister, works there too; what else can a poor girl do? Mother sent me." The man waited now.

"Yeet: brave young man? What can I do for you?" He scanned the thin youth carefully, measuring with his eyes.

"There's a family friend here. He was detained last night. I need to know if they will release him or if he has a fine to pay. I know his family." Yeet ran out of words.

"What's his name?" Harun looked suspicious.

"His name's Sevman." Yeet's anxiety increased.

Harun nodded his assent, slowly still studying the boy. "Ali Bey has questioned the boy. Wait three days till they have captured the gang. Then send his father. His family's Manichae; They'll be fined." Harun glared at him.

"His mother's worried. I'll tell her."

"Why would a good Muslim befriend a Wigler?"

"Mother was a Christian until she married, she often says all religions contain some truths about God."

"We must never dilute the truth revealed to us. Your sister must never marry an unbeliever. You must keep company with believers. Fight all enemies of our faith."

"But there is a saying of the Prophet, that the Christian is a close friend of man and God," Yeet protested.

"You misquote, there are other verses that annul it. You have failed to memorize the Koran as you should."

"The Arabic is not such as men speak, Harun Bey."

"Would God's language be like that used by men?"

"But both Manichae and Nestorians lead good lives."

"The times of darkness terminated with the coming of the last Prophet, Mohammed, may he rest in peace. The people of the book had but dim light, now it is noon."

"I work with Sevman. We carry shopper's market baskets. We also help unload the merchant's carts."

"Were you robbing in the market?"

Yeet's eyes grew. "I have never stolen. I run errands for merchants, they know me. Ask them."

Harun hawked, spat, and nodded, then knowingly asked. "Do you sometimes have a fit near the fountain? An attack of madness?" Yeet trembled and didn't have an answer.

"You should be apprenticed; Idle loitering with worthless hang-abouts, for a penny here and there, is bad. I loved your father and the child I bounced on my knee. Take care you don't disgrace them. I'll see your mother about apprentice work with a coppersmith I know. Would you like it?"

"I've never thought of doing that." He could breathe again. He looked at Harun, who, now, was smiling. "*Allah beri ket versin*, God bless you Sir. If God wills it; may it be so. When will you know?"

Harun made a sour face. "This week there's a gang to find. After the second Friday I'll see the man and tell your mother. Meanwhile, keep out of trouble and away from the market. Understand?"

"*Allah ismar ladik*, farewell Uncle Harun. Your word is water on a summer day. I'll tell mother today." Yeet kissed Harun's hand, said salaam, put his hand to his chest, bowed and quickly stepped away. After the corner he ran.

> - - - - - - - >ON THE SARI SU TRAIL > - - - - - - - >

Gerchen stood facing the audience across the fire that reflected off his strong features. In the middle front of the concourse of people sat Twozan with the priest, Mookades, and his wife, Marium. Setchkin, and Peri the nurse for the baby, sat behind the priest. The loud talk tapered off as more eyes swung to take in the imposing figure of the warrior. He bowed gracefully, held open his hands and recited emotionally, his deep bass voice booming.

1. Kaya east and Kaya west; Kaya comes around.
   The hero's great persistent faith has faced the tiger down.

2. Kaya north and Kaya south; Kaya finds a way.
   The bear's both wise and wary, he wins without delay.

3. Kaya first and Kaya last; Kaya's on the trek.
   The dragon slayer harries them, the Huns fall to their wreck.

4. Kaya weak and Kaya strong; Kaya wins a wife.
   He fights the white bear of the north. He wins, but saves its life.

5. Kaya comes and Kaya goes; Kaya never stays.
   The river rafter lives with wounds that hindered all his ways.

6. Kaya starts and Kaya ends; Kaya plans the way.
   The greatness of his purpose wise shapes lives until our day.

7. Kaya lives and Kaya wins; Kaya makes it home.
   The 'child of promise' found the way wherever he had roamed.

8. Kaya fast and Kaya slow; Kaya wins the city.
   The yoke he bore was not in vain, he lived though men did pity.

9. Kaya first and Kaya last; Kaya lives forever.
   A thousand years his family reigns for Yesu's love ends never."

GERCHEN RECITES

78

A rumble of approval sounded in hundreds of throats. While several voices called for a story. Gerchen's reputation was known in all the tribe. He immediately launched into a dramatic presentation of the dragon hunt. Behind him two figures rose, one, a warrior with bow; the other was a man with a dragon like head worn over his own. They assumed a position of opposition and moved as Gerchen spoke. Silently they wheeled and menaced each other.

Twozan felt the breath of Setchkin on his neck as she gasped in admiration. He glanced back and saw her rapt face and enlarged eyes focused on the speaker. Gerchen was describing the fiery breath of the great beast. The actor with his hands before his face held out a round shield and ran forward with his sword. The monster quivered and bellowed striking again at the attacking figure. Gerchen's voice boomed out in victory as the dragon writhed and died.

Suddenly the area behind the story teller shifted with the entrance of armed men who commence a dance with swords drawn which they clashed against their shields as they whirled and jumped.   The girl gasped and leaned forward watching the retreating figure of Gerchen. Twozan could not take his eyes from her face. Her beauty held him captive. Suddenly her face flushed as she became aware of his fixed gaze, their eyes caught and held for a bare instant. Her face froze and she pulled back to her seat, while he closed his eyes and his lips moved with some silent, secret message that only Tanra could hear.

> - - - - - - - > KOKAND WIDOW'S HOUSE> - - - - - - - >

Yeet had waited the required time of three days. He returned with the cart used to transport Kardesh and family to the quarry. He had kept it one day beyond the agreement to bring out Sevman. He stood near the deserted widow's house tossing his knife at a post near the well. Sometimes it stuck. He sang softly this little song while practicing:

#1   I wonder why boys are so bold and so brash.
          I wonder why girls are so shy.
           I try to see through the things that folks do.
           I question always and I sigh.

Chorus: I wish that I knew what God is up to.
          I wonder always, wonder why?

#2

I wonder why markets price high then go low.
I wonder at much thrown away.
I seek answers, why? So many lie!
I search for the truth and I cry.

Chorus:

#3

I wonder why money is so hard to keep;
That both food and sleep do not last.
The good that I do won't last the day through;
I'll try, pray and seek to be true.

Chorus:

#4

The world is a wonderful place to live through;
With sights, tastes and smells to enjoy.
Such wonders in store, surprises galore;
Yet friends will find troubles and more.

Chorus:

I WONDER ALWAYS

80

"*Afair reen*, congratulations, truly spoken." The voice came from behind Yeet causing him to spin around. "You must make a smoother throw and calculate the turn of the blade, If you intend to master the dagger." The voice was Turkish, but smooth, fine as silk and steel. A slender man near thirty stood at the gate watching. He didn't smile, but his voice was friendly, compelling. Walking forward he took the knife from the post and hefted it.

"I'm Derk, *derk edersin*, understand?"

Yeet's laugh was loud and spontaneous. He felt a sudden warmth toward the clever man. He was well dressed, but travel worn and dusty.

"How did you get a name like that?"

"My mother always wanted to know if I understood what she was talking about. She used it so much that I thought it was my name. I would point to myself when she said it and repeat it. So, Derk stuck. Understand?" Both laughed and Derk turned to face the post. He smoothly sent the knife into the center of the post at chest height.

"The trick is in getting the timing of the blade right. Then you can find the distance easily. Come take your turn. Slowly, watch the turn of the blade."

Yeet stuck it. "I see what you mean. Thanks, My name is Yeet."

"I'm Derk from the Chipchak people of the north. Have you ever heard of us?"

Yeet stuck out his chest. "Of course, my friend is from there. He just moved away ..." Yeet's voice ran down as he recalled the secret.

But Derk seemed to pay no attention. He put his foot up on the waiting cart and puckered his lips. "What's this for?"

Yeet rushed to the new subject. "I've a sick friend who'll be released today. I'm to pick him up this morning. My uncle has arranged it all."

"Where do you meet him?"

Yeet paused then answered. "He's at the municipal jail. He's been detained. He may need help, Uncle says. I'm to bring this cart."

The man eyed him. "He may indeed, if he has been questioned. Perhaps I should come to help just in case. I'm going that way." His look was thoughtful. Yeet nervously clicked his tongue to start the horse. He tried to act innocent, but the man knew something.

> - - - - - - -> IN THE KOKAND JAIL > - - - - - - ->

Sevman sat on the stone floor and stared at the dungeon's mud brick wall. His eyes were wild and hair a tangle. Flies buzzed busily round his swollen feet and knee. A guard announced his freedom and that a friend waited outside. He still sat staring, unable to take it in. Then an old fat man came to the door and stood looking at him for a time. The man left and all was quiet.

He could feel the pain, pressure and corruption of his rotten flesh. 'We're dirt and dung' he thought. 'The light must be freed from this body of bondage and pain.' He sighed and tried to move, but his hands, too, were swollen and tender though not so cut up as his feet. The fat man returned with another two men who picked up the child roughly by knees and shoulders and despite his screams, carried him out to a waiting cart. The men were grim and showed disgust in the dirty task. The boy smelled of urine and feces.

"Mother sent willow bark tea, drink some now." Yeet insisted. He was embarrassed by the attention he was drawing as he had the men put Sevman down on the thin covering of hay and felt material on the cart bottom. He put the gourd to the boy's mouth and tipped it up. Sevman swallowed spewing the medicine and gasping. He was forced to take more after every breath.

"Enough, young man, He's survived one ordeal, he may not take another." Derk clicked his tongue and urged the horse to go. Yeet was busy kissing the hand of Harun and agreeing to last minute instructions about his future.

"Wait, Derk bey, we must go to the hospital first. He'll have to be washed and the wounds cleaned." He stared and shuddered as he looked at the flyblown wounds on his feet. Sevman had fallen back with his arms over his face.

82

He groaned as the cart jolted forward. The hospital lay at the Manichaean Temple on the hilltop outside town.

"You said that Sevman's father couldn't come to pay the fine. Yet you paid in his name. How'd you get it, boy?"

"From mother, she keeps my earnings."

"Earnings from what? Have you other family?"

"I keep busy and am paid. I've mother and elder sister. They work at the rug factory, I live in town. I must return the cart now, it's overdue." He hurried the animal.

"Why? Where's it been?" Yeet took the horse's halter strap and ran beside it. The cart rattled on faster.

"Out around. Thanks for your help, Derk Bey. No need for you to come out of town. Barmani the doctor will take charge."

Derk stood in the dust cloud and watched the running boy out of sight. Then he turned back toward the police station.

Derk showed his identity badge. It was known by all the army and police services in the empire. He received instant and courteous attention, while all the information sought was provided. They would have passed him to Ali Bey, but he stopped their efforts with one decisive move of chin and head. He leaned confidentially forward to whisper, "You have neither seen nor heard of me or my questions. It's between us only." They nodded secretively as he walked out.

A KEEN TEACHER

83

PEOPLE, PACES & PLOTS in CHAPTER 7

Agaz bey: harried administrator of Fergana Valley Hospital.
Ali bey: continues his interrogations of the guilty.
Barmani: prepares his community for exile to the East.
Erben: bereft of homeland fund works in a quarry.
Gerchen: finds himself in disagreement with everyone.
Joseph: a novice pries, working at the Nestorian Hospital.
Kardesh: heals and hides, hauling stones in the quarry.
Karga: member of the Chipchak Council and Kaynak clan.
Leyla: finds new hostility in the place of safety.
Mother: bids her son, Yeet, goodbye.
 Seerden: a secret agent of the Chipchaks.
Setchkin: becomes an arbiter between rival leaders.
Sevman: needs time to heal and help to hide.
Tash: becomes important as a source of information.
Tayze: moves with the family to a quarry outside the valley.
The Widow: must hide because the gang used her property.
Twozan: finds conflicts with the right hand clan's leader.
Yeet: helps friends and evades enemies.

GLOSSARY:
barish: peace; quiet down.
 chador: an Islamic woman's 'head to toe' public dress.
do'er: stop; hold; cease.
 emma: Arabic for mother.
git dish ar rah: go outside; get out.
git shim dee: go now; get out this minute.
 hoe sh bol duke: happily we've arrived;
hoe sh gel diniz: happily you've come; welcome.
kafir: Arabic for heathen; unbeliever; pagan.
shalvar: Turkish baggy pants; women's bright prints.
yo: a negative, used with a click of tongue & toss of head.
yoke: nothing; not at all; no.

PARABLE OF THE BIRDS

"Why did you bring this wounded child to us? We are departing the city; the government is confiscating our buildings for a stable and army depot." Barmani looked with anger at Yeet. He turned to Sevman and said harshly. "'Be sure your sins will find you out.' I've warned you repeatedly about your lack of discipline and your choices. You turned your back on the light and sought ease in the world. Now see your condition. The evil creator of this world has you in his power. Your clay returns to the dust, but where will your spirit go without the light?" Sevman groaned and held out a swollen hand. His voice was faint, breathless and dry.

"Forgive, oh elect Barmani, I have sinned against the light. I repent and beg your mercy." He cried out weakly.

Yeet spoke up. "Oh, *Papaz*, I only just got him out. Please give food and water and I'll go on to the other hospital. I'd forgotten the deportation order. I'm sorry. It's the will of Allah."

"It's the will of a despotic ruler who forgets Umayyad generosity and the injunctions of the Koran for 'People of the Book'." Barmani stopped and looked around carefully. No one heard. He looked at the boys again and sighed. He motioned toward a vine covered building.

"The well's there, draw water. I'll send one of the sisters with bread. You must do all; I have other things to attend to before the decree of exile sends us into the unknown. Put him in the temple annex till the heat has passed, Wash his feet and hands. I'll stop by later. Stay and talk to him, we all need friends and hope, to live. I'll do what I can, when there's time."

> - - - - - - - > PURSUIT ARRIVES AT THESYR RIVER > - - - - - - - >

Karga, the tribesman, called the tall outsider, a Muslim Turk, over and walked toward the horse line. There the horses were feeding on hay piled in the center of a circle. They were alone in the area, away from yurts and gatherings of men.

"I've arranged for you to be in the advance group. After the business with Twozan is finished, you must get to Kokand. We protect Khan Erden's right to rule, without fear of his brother Erben. We'll let the bird and the fledgling fly and die. Leave the daughter in the cage. We'll have uses for one with bear blood. You understand your duty, Seerden?"

"I act on your instructions. I will not fail. Be confident. He'll fly far and be lost out of sight. If not, I'm still the best knife-man in Khorasan." He patted his dagger sheath and smiled slightly. Karga lifted his head sharply in disagreement.

"Yoke, none of that, Erben stood too close to his twin. No violence. Both our lives would end too. His end must be in flight or accident, nothing else."

The man nodded subserviently, "But what of the young prince, Kynan? What is my role with him? He doesn't know me."

Karga patted the air. "Just keep him in your sights. Win his trust. Make peace with the Toozlu. Don't let him kill off all the whole clan."

Seerden's words came slowly. "That may not be possible."

"Ride out, I'll follow with more men. What we do is for the tribe. Tanra will help, He loves the bear's kin."

> - - - - - - - > WHITE MARBLE QUARRY > - - - - - - - >

The mountain side is split, exposing the rock. The slope is covered with fragments. The exposed side does not stop, but descends to a pit. Below is a chaos of rocks and slabs, in the center of which lies the shallow waters of a lake, born of hidden springs beneath the jumble of rock. The quarry is famous for its beautiful granite and marble. Also the water has a strange quality. Whispered to have magical effects, it is dreaded by all. Those who work here drink of the upper springs. The bitter water in the bottom of the pit leaves its white residue around the edges. Above the denuded mountain tops of the quarry, spots of green can be seen high and far off. The desert occupies the foothills and smaller mountains. Only as one climbs to the plateau does grass and then trees appear. This too is left behind as the high cold desert of the world's roof is reached.

Here in the quarry, work the stone masons, men who deal with the hard and intractable flesh of the mountains. Who become like those elements with which they work: rough, intractable. Yet, like the rocks, they too have their fracture points. With the abrasives that make up polish, stones and men come to shine out their inner life of character where all can see it. Here, came the wounded Kardesh to hide and recover. His warrior father, the exiled younger twin, Erben, came to find work denied him in the city. Tayze, his sister-in-law, kept house and the timid Leyla made up the rest of the family.

The work was all simplicity; cut rock and haul it. Each part of the process was carefully supervised by the expert masons. Tools and workers were equally appreciated and cared for. Locked tool-sheds for the first and simple two room mud-brick houses with an outside shed for a kitchen for the second. The commissary provided daily fresh food: bread, flour, meat and cane sugar. The bazaar continued to be Sunday, even after Islamic occupation, and also one day at midweek there were fruits and vegetables of the season. Cloth and hand craft of various kinds were sold.

To the place came men who built of stone or who contracted to build. Polished slabs were available for those who wished to face a floor or wall below the tile roofs. Rich men and powerful, who kept up the prosperity of the quarry, came to choose their material. With these the master mason wined, dined and drove hard bargains. The satisfied customer always knew exactly what he had. The masters would not lie about quality. But there were spoiled blocks that men could buy and perhaps bilk some unsuspecting dupe. Stone is as complex as the earth and the men who work it.

Here Erben, prince of the Chipchak nation, worked, driving wedges and splitting stone. Kardesh, the heir, drove a wagon hauling stone. They ranked lowest of the low in a proud community, but they earned their keep and their bodies and souls could heal and grow.

> - - - - - - - > KOKAND MONASTERY > - - - - - - - >

Barmani stood up and rolled his shoulders and sighed heavily. He called Yeet in from the outside where he had been leaning against the wall trying to control a heaving stomach. The wounds had been bandaged.

"Let him rest now and take him to the Christian hospital later. They will attend him though he is not of their faith. I have removed the maggots and straightened the breaks somewhat, but I don't think he'll walk again."

Yeet stared at the sleeping child through his tears. "When will he wake? How do we feed him?"

The ascetic shrugged, and cleaned his hands in water with ashes a third time. He spoke grimly.

"Great corruption produces more of the same. The knees and feet will form pustules for days or weeks. Pray that he will have the strength to overcome it. Feed him watery broth and eggs. I suppose you will have to use bone to heal bone." He made a face at the thought of using bone based soups. He sighed again and moved away. "The sisters will come and move him to the cart."

> - - - - - - - > CHILDREN'S DETENTION > - - - - - - - >

Ali bey walked the line of chained children. Some cried, ignoring any presence. Others stared sullenly at his feet. Ali smirked with satisfaction. He stopped before Tash and stirred him with his foot. The boy's whining voice showed his submission. *"Yo, nothin' more, I told you everything."*

"The treasure is gone. Did you move it?"

"Yo, now when could I have? Ask the widow."

"She's gone, so have the others, the one you call Kardesh. Their house is empty. Where would they go?"

The boy shrugged. "Far away." His voice held hope for his envied brother. "A long way from here."

"I'll have him and his stolen goods. You must know where." He watched with serpent intensity as the boy slowly moved his head up in a negative gesture. "Only his inner circle would know. Sevman or Yeet might know."

Ali's head snapped back in surprise. "Yeet? But he's the one you said never stole. I didn't arrest him. He just hung out with the gang. He has good recommendations among our people. He's a criminal?"

"Is there a law against havin' fits? Or havin' bad friends? Yeet's a nice little guy, but he don't know much about the under side."

"What he does know, I'll get it out of him tonight."

> - - - - - - - > KOKAND NESTORIAN HOSPITAL > - - - - - - - >

"Yeet glanced over his shoulder nervously, nobody noticed the lumbering cart or the unconscious boy lying in the back. He shivered and hurried the horses. The Christian chapel lay inside a walled property almost lost to view from outside. The caliphate had decreed a modest role for all the people of the book. Christians and Jews within the empire were socially on the bottom. However, both communities continued to produce outstanding individuals to serve even in the Government in key positions.

The hospital gate lay open, past a newly built mosque, placed to defend patients from temptation to convert. Yeet negotiated the entrance and was directed to the shed where Father Agaz sat talking to a staff member, a grave faced, novice priest, too young to grow a moustache.

"*Hoe sh gel din is*, a happy welcome, how was the road?" The younger man was eager to meet the cart.

"*Hoe sh bul duke*, Happily I've arrived. The road was good, but my friend is bad. He needs care."

"That's why we're here. Christ healed the sick and his disciples are to do the same." The novice was eager.

"Brother Joseph, This child has been attended. His feet and knees have been bandaged professionally. He wears the medallion of the Manichae. Why is he here?" Both men looked severely at Yeet, who responded hurriedly.

The Revered Barmani has been ordered to leave the Fergana Valley for the Tarim Basin, the land of the Uigurs. He sent over Sevman after tending to his wounds. He said you'd accept him because you're merciful." The men looked at each other.

89

"The cheek of that heretic! After he humiliated me publicly! He argued the matter of Augustine's past history and his sainthood in the western church. Now he sends me his heretic patients. He reserves his medical attentions to the rich and powerful only. He has no time for the poor and lowly," said Father Agaz, eyes blazing. Yeet stared open mouthed.

Joseph grinned. "Conversion changes people," he confided to Yeet. "Augustine was a Manichae and Neo-Platonist reprobate before his conversion. He had rebelled against his Mother's Christian faith. He returned to faith, not because of family pressure, as Manichaeans' claim."

Yeet's face was blank; He understood little of what Joseph had said. Only one part brought light. Someone had returned to his mother's Christian faith. That was unheard of in Kokand.

"I, too, have heard of the exile of the Barmani people." Joseph said, trying to pacify his priest. "It is gossip that the Caliph will try to force all to convert or be exiled."

Father Agaz's face darkened, he breathed deeply. "Though we face the same dangers, we don't serve the same master; neither will there be the same reward. How many of our churches did this heresy split? Mani claimed to be the manifestation of the Holy Spirit. But he is dead and our Savior is alive: resurrected." Father Agaz pointed up, his face aglow, as he finished his outburst. He then motioned the cart in. Joseph turned to Yeet with a welcoming smile. "Go to the second building. We will tend to him there."

Yeet held up two gold coins to Father Agaz, who stared in surprise at the bounty, and then, at the youth.

"My friend has money," Yeet stated, "so take good care of him. I'll return after my journey and settle up."

"Where did you get that kind of money?" He took the coins, bit tentatively on the edge. Exchanging looks with his novice, he put his hand on the cart, detaining it.

"He was preparing to go with Barmani and had raised the sum from those who owed him. He cannot travel now, so I give it to you for his healing." He clicked his tongue at the horses and the cart moved forward pulling the priest off balance for a moment.

Joseph called after him. "How was he injured?" But the boy was moving rapidly to the second building where an attendant drew near.

"I have another call to make before the sun is high, I must travel, but you will care for my dear friend. I will award you a gift, if you are attentive." Yeet pressed a copper coin into the surprised attendant's hand. Together they carried the unconscious boy into the building. The cart rattled out of the yard a few moments later.

> - - - - - - - > FERGANA VALLEY > - - - - - - - >

The widow sat on the patient donkey, dejectedly wiping dust from her moist cheeks. Her bloodshot eyes peered from above her veil. It served more as a filter for the dust than a covering for an aging woman. Her meager belongings were piled on the following donkey, bundled into two packs. Her husband had relations in the hills beyond the fertile valley, but she preferred not to live in constant obligation to them. She had learned to carry a lighter work load in town. Now, she had no choice. The cause of her present distress was not her fault. Hers was not the guilt. She had tried to help those children, but they had gotten into trouble. Now, no one would shove coins into the crack under her window for their use of her well and property. Allah had decreed, and none could change it. Fate had written it on her forehead. She must go to the country: live and work there. She wished she were dead. Now the tears began to flow. Life would be hard again.

> - - - - - - - > KOKAND RUG FACTORY> - - - - - - - >

"I must return the cart, Mother, then I will travel and work away for a while. If Uncle Harun seeks me, tell him I'll find apprenticeship elsewhere and not to worry, I have taken his words to heart. My friend, Sevman, is in good hands at hospital. I hope all will be well for you and him. Sevman will come see you when he heals. He knows where you are. I'll be with friends and you mustn't worry about me. I'll get word to you some way. It won't be that long and I have money with me for all my needs. If others seek me

91

you must decide what to tell them." Mother stopped knotting. She reached over and placed a hand over Yeet's mouth. She laughed softly and spoke reprovingly.

"Young men are not supposed to be loquacious. You speak overmuch." She stroked the cheeks and kissed both. "You know I'll miss your visits, news and extras, but you have chosen your way. I'll care for your things and pray, waiting for your safe return." She turned to her loom again.

"Mother, do you still pray to Yesu? When you married and became Muslim did you stop praying to Him?"

"You have been thinking again? Such a prying mind: snooping into secrets might scandalize the stuffy and unimaginative." She laughed warmly. Yeet joined her.

"Does one drop fifteen years of habits and belief because one lives with a husband? No. New becomes mixed with old. Yesu, Isa they call him, is a prophet of miracles. When life presses hard who would not wish for a miracle? If I don't dare call him Son of God, I can say Word of God without reproach or danger. What man is not father to his word? Did God ever exist without His Word? The gospels say the Word took flesh and dwelled among us. Emmanuel came to show us God and save us from evil. Remember, these words are between us only. Go in peace and worry no more. I'll keep your many secrets and you mine. He will help you."

"Oh *Emma*, you are wise, Allah gives you light." Yeet's arms were about the mother's neck.

She sniffed. "Go scoundrel! You always go out for adventure and gain. *Git dish arah*, leave before I get angry."

> - - - - - - - > WHITE MARBLE QUARRY > - - - - - - - >

The cart had moved steadily up among the mountains, the valley lay completely out of sight. Leyla had watched as they climbed up and over the hills and down into dryer lower land, again and again.

Everyone was silent and morose, only Yeet would talk much with her. Then he had left them at the settlement to return the cart. How she wished she had gone with him. The quarry seemed deserted and desolate compared to the excitement of town. She had grown used to its activities and now missed them. The humble working people, their neighbors, seemed like aliens.

"Here comes the new girl!" The other girls fluttered around like disturbed blackbirds, all were topped by black *chadors*. Their *shalvar* trousers, scarcely showing below the *chadors*, reflected their natural love of color. Some got their water pots from a near door. All trooped down to the memorial fountain where the stones controlled the rush of water from the mountain side. There they formed a line blocking access to the water. Ignoring her greeting, they filled their pots while Leyla waited in embarrassment, trying to think of something more to say. The girls shot hostile glances at her, then, they mocked her.

"Why doesn't she wear a *chador*, is she an idolater?"

"She may be a--you know what--one of those sinners."

"Infidels are shameless and show their faces."

"Look how skinny she is, no one would want her."

"Not even as a fourth wife."

They laughed, twittering and snickering with each remark. One gave her a push with her shoulder. Another pushed her into the others. She dropped her pitcher and it was kicked into the drainage ditch. They all laughed.

Leyla screeched, and grabbed one, pulling off the *chador* and ripping the blouse. She pushed her into another. She whirled to pull another black cloth. With this they ran screaming. Leyla shouted Turkish insults after them. Then, crying, she retrieved and washed and filled the pitcher.

She knew she couldn't tell her brother. He no longer tormented her, but he was so quiet she wished he would say something, anything. But she dare not complain. Her father had taken to drink again. He would sometimes sing songs, but they were strange. He repeatedly sang one that puzzled her. It was about birds:

#1   Sing songs of freedom, life in the wild;
              When you're a bird in a cage life is mild.
              Sing of alertness, life on the loose;
              Beware and don't put your head in the noose.

Sing songs of free-dom, life in the wild.

When you're a bird in a cage life is wild.

sing of a-lert-ness, life on the loose!

Be-ware and don't put your head in the noose.

#2   Birds are protected, while in the cage;
Outside there's freedom for hunters to rage.
Swift draws the huntsman, arrows fly too;
Roll and evade if you want to get through.

#3   Cages are boring, sing out for change;
Where life, death and danger are all in your range.
Thrill with the striving, it will be past;
Cage life is friendly with longer to last.

#4   Sing in your safety, sing in your cage.
Show joy in each moment and trust in your sage.
Chance shapes our choices: that, or God's will.
Changes are permanent, for good or ill.

> - - - - - - - >SARI SU TRAIL> - - - - - - - >

A fire-eyed Gerchen rode to the head of the column. His anger expressed in the way he used his horse. He made the nervous animal rear before Twozan and Setchkin, who were deep in a heated debate about camp priorities. His demand cut in. "Why are we going west today? We must go east toward the mountains and grass. We are losing several animals a day: we need to get to better pasture soon. You impoverish us by choosing the dry route."

Twozan grimaced, "You can decide between poverty, death, west or east. Choose the dry, but safe road or the abundant green road to war and death at the hands of the combined clans of the Chipchak Tribal Confederation. The Tiger will have the Khan's troops ready on the Syr River to the east. There's no other way for a nation as large as ours to move south."

Gerchen jerked up his head. "Yo, but our stock dies. Why should we fear a fight? I would take Kaplan's head."

Twozan lifted his chin. "You would have to take down a wall of your own friends and cousins to reach him. War comrades would die. You brought too much stock. You were told to come for a quick escape not a leisurely migration." Both men glared.

"Peace, warriors, listen, let us agree," pleaded Setchkin. "The way is hard, but it leads to safety. We must increase the consumption of meat for we may lack both strength and fit stock when we reach the Syr River. The weaker animals must die now, before they lose their weight and flesh. We must dry the meat for the long journey." She looked from one to the other solemnly.

"There's not grass enough for even one day's delay. I say let's go east. If the Tiger eats us, we die bravely." Gerchen rattled his sword.

"We're in the area of salt and alkali lakes where the Chu and Sari Su Rivers joined before. We can stop early, slaughter in the evening and dip the meat in the water to let it salt and dry white. Some can be saddle cured while still continuing our journey. We'll send the stock ahead and catch them easily. In this heat it will cure in a day. We women will do it. However, we'll need some help to manage it. It's hard work." She smiled and fluttered her eyes at them. "Gerchen Bey, you'll get us some help won't you?" He nodded confidently until she added: "Would you really take my father's head?"

He looked at her warily. He tried to smile, but failing, stuttered. "I meant I'm a better warrior and could best him."

"What a pity there's not a better way to show superiority. Must men always die to demonstrate it?"

STEPPE FLOWERS

95

PEOPLE, PLACES AND PLOTS IN CHAPTER 8

Ayshe: daughter of a farmer changes a mother for a patron.
Derk bey: an agent of the Caliph comes to protect Erben.
Gerchen: finds himself an opportunity for warfare.
Mother: is interrogated about her son, Yeet.
Onat bey: seeks information at the frontier.
Sanjak: leads the refugees toward their homelands.
Setchkin: faces leering men and helpless people need her.
Sevman: needs time to heal and take his medication.
Tayze: moves with the family to a quarry outside the valley.
Twozan: believes conflict with the farmers is necessary.
Yeet: makes new friends and enemies as he tries to help.

GLOSSARY:
do'er: stop; hold; cease.
e lai ri ay: forward; go on; go ahead.
git shim dee: go now; get out this minute.
hal e nay bock: look at the state of it; see it now; just look.
kafir: Arabic for heathen; unbeliever; pagan.
pie'dash: partners; sharing equally.
who juze: charge; forward; have at them.

BURNING OUT GOPHERS

The whine and thud of arrows interrupted the talk between Setchkin and Gerchin. Ahead of them, behind a low hill, smoke started rising. Gerchen broke into a gallop.

The fire blazed from a wattle building of reed and brush held together by a dried layer of mud, before the blazing building stood a group of angry armed tribesmen. They were looking down at the body of the farmer. Before the house, lay an acre or more of plowed earth. The topsoil had a thin cover of yellow brown grass, with developed heads of wheat. Other huts were seen along the horizon. Broken ground with white spots of alkali were among them. In the distance several men were shouting and waving farming tools as weapons.

"*Who juze*, charge, death to the gophers." The voice of Gerchen brought the men to attention. Two women broke from the house and scurried around back to lose themselves in the low bushes.

The riders raised their bows and one sent an arrow close behind them. The older woman fell screaming, a strangled cry that indicated a pierced lung. The younger stopped to help drag the other to shelter.

"*Doer*, stop, you'll not make war on women. I won't have it."
Unnoticed Setchkin had ridden up behind Gerchen. Her voice pierced
the tension. Her face was angry red. "Go have your war elsewhere, leave
the women alone. They are under my protection."

Gerchen shouted again. "*E lai ri ay*, forward men, burn them out! Kill
the farmers!" He reined back and gave Setchken an arrogant smirk.
"Leave the women for later." The troops thus led the captain.

"You want to play rough, my hero?" She said it softly to the back of
the departing band. She rode to the edge of the brush, where she could
hear the sound of ragged breathing. She sat quietly for a time. Distant
shouts and yells came from the other huts, fire crackled.

"I offer you food and protection. If you remain out after dark you
know what they will do to you. You've no where to run that horses can't
run faster and farther. I've a lovely baby that will comfort your heart. I'm
sorry that one of you is injured. If you live, come to me. I'm Princess
Setchkin. Repeat the name: it's your password to safety in the camp."
She turned her horse and slowly rode away. In the distance near a high
bit of ground she saw Twozan and rode toward him.

Twozan stared at the fields broken by bare earth and worn paths.
Tears found their way down his rugged face. He dismounted to go and
sit on a rock outcropping above the fields. He sat morosely gazing at the
area leading down to a small lake, now made smaller by the heat and
drought.

Setchkin rode up and sat watching intrigued. Finally she dismounted
and made her way to his side. She tentatively touched his shoulder.
When he remained in thought, she spoke. "Why do you grieve? Are you
ill? You can't be tender toward these moles. Their agonies and trials
wouldn't affect you. Can you explain?" She touched his forehead for
fever. He brushed her hand away, absently.

"My father brought me here once. All was a meadow full of flowers
as far as you could see. It was my first trip to the cities of the south. I
was twelve. We stayed an extra day because of the beauty." He raised
his voice shouting. "*Hal e nay bock*, Look at it now. It's ruined! It is over-
watered by the ditches; leaching on the surface, bringing up the salt and
alkali from below. Plowing ruins the thin coat of grass and gets a few
years of poor crops. Now it is fit for nothing. In twenty years it'll still be
worth nothing. They'll move on and do it again and again."

> - - - - - - - >SYR RIVER CROSSING > - - - - - - - >

98

"*Git shim dee*, go now," the bleeding mother urged. "The woman will protect..." Her voice failed and she coughed helplessly.

The girl shook her head firmly, "Not till you can come with me. They are *kafirs*, unbelievers. What is their word worth?" Anger filled her. "They'll not leave us in peace."

The dark eyes fixed pleadingly on the girl, once again the woman rallied. "Ayshe, go..." The coughing and blood came again and she quivered and went limp in the girl's arms.

Ayshe stared, surprised, she shook her. "Mother, Mother wake up!" But there was no answer. She pulled her mother over to some low bushes and laid her feet toward the south-west, pointed to Mecca, so she would face the city on the day of resurrection. She dug the grave with her hands, piled sand above, and covered it with stones.

"Princess Setchkin calls for me." Ayshe shouted at an inquisitive horseman who came to see the girl walk out of the brush an hour before sunset. He eyed her suspiciously and then pointed down toward the little pond with his whip. She walked in that direction and did not speak, although he followed her closely. He tried to intimidate her with the nearness and antics of his straw-colored horse. Her face was cold and angry. She arrived dry-eyed and hostile at the Princess' yurt. There sat several weeping mothers, with children from the farm village. There were some orphans too.

As she arrived Setchkin came from her tent. "Girl, care for these little ones. They must be fed and settled for the night. Old Peri will show you where. Do as she says. You sleep with them to be safe." She spoke coolly and turned away. No inquiry was made about the wounded mother.

> - - - - - - - > YELLOW RIVER ORDOS > - - - - - - - >

The Buddhist monk stood in his saffron robes in the midst of tribal soldiers. He addressed the commander confidently. "Yes, *Tutu*, it is as you have heard. The landowners and their emperor possess themselves of our metal images and treasures. We who are foreign-born are expelled. So I am again in the *Ordos* land inside the Yellow River's loop, where the tribes still rule."

"Welcome home." said the waiting Yuzbasha. "Why should they destroy commerce and religions? Both of these multiply wealth and promote tranquility. Contrary stories come to our ears. Our Khan does not apply the emperor's decrees."

"The return to Taoism opens the door to raid all sources of wealth. The temples of all faiths serve in place of the money lender to keep coins in reserve for the prudent families. Who else can they trust? But we are jailed because of envy. We are robbed by the 'Son of Heaven'." The monk made the statement with angry pride.

"We hear that they excessively tax and discriminate against local and foreign merchants, they must wear the white turbans and are treated with contempt. This must destroy prosperity." The commander paused mouth open. Another voice cut in to answer.

"It's the old land-owning families that pressure for restrictions. They lose able workers to enterprise and the newly rich are usurping social positions. So, merchants are prohibited from land purchases for these reasons." Sanjak joined the group, bowing low to the commander, who acknowledged his salute.

The monk bowed also and spoke. "Our able leader has come to add wisdom to our words. He lives beyond Kansu, our land at the foot of the great mountains, where our kin the Tibetans live. Beyond even the land of the Uigurs. Speak freely. He's not of the Turks of the Gobi, who provide troops for the emperor's needs."

"Welcome to our land, all your needs will be met. Though many think of us as a part of the Tang patrimony, we have a measure of autonomy from the people of Han." The commander bowed his welcome.

The monk then boasted." We who wear the saffron robe chose to be distinct along with our followers. But it is our own choice not an emperor's imposition."

Sanjak took up the theme. "Each religion wears its symbols, but the doctrines are given flesh and bone by the way its followers live and obey the rules of that faith."

The monk spoke bitterly. "Our doctrines are corrupted by the authorities to back their own interests. Our doctrine of retribution is changed to a doctrine of submission to the government. Your rebirth will be as your personal and moral life deserve, not as government and citizenship dictate."

Sanjak frowned. "Better to have salvation in one lifetime than to be responsible for successive lives with their failures."

"Opportunity is offered repeatedly for those who wish to better their soul's condition." the monk objected. Tension grew.

"God purifies the soul's condition through the sacrifice and offered blood of Yesu, who was 'God with us'." Sanjak stated.

"Gentlemen, you both have done meritorious acts in conducting the caravan of persecuted ones to our border. While you're here take the opportunity of rest and preparation for your future activities and travels."

The commander then called one of his lieutenants. "Guide the exiles to the prepared ground beyond the city. Make sure all their needs are met. They are allowed visits from those of their faith, but they must remain in the camp." The commander turned to Sanjak continuing. "You understand that since we are such close neighbors, and are always under tribute to the emperor, that we

100

cannot allow any other people, besides citizens, to remain here for commerce. By the end of summer you should be beyond Kansu Province. There those who wish to discard the white turban and the black with a white shoe may do so. You may wear what your custom demands." He bowed deeply, dismissing Sanjak. He turned to talk with the monk.

> - - - - - - ->SYR RIVER INN > - - - - - - ->

"You must have some idea of the size of the force. The border is so close here. You must give us that and the location of their camp if you expect the reward I offered."

"Onat bey, one doesn't make specific inquiries of soldiers or armed messengers. It's not healthy! There must be above two companies and they are in the mountains, hidden in some valley. They send their scouts west down the Chu River and around Lake Balkash and the Illi River to the villages. They search for a clan of the Chipchaks, the Toozlu, on the run, I'd guess. They ask questions, but don't answer any. Besides that, there are still Uigur irregulars that visit some villages. We have armed men on every hand." The old caravan veteran watched Onat bey's head move.

"So, the tribe turns on its-self? Dynastic war! Old Erdash leaves the heirs to fight? Who is the Binbasha?"

"I heard the name of Kynan only once, but he is a son of the Tiger, Kaplan, father-in-law of the dead Khan."

"Which of the twins are the Toozlu favoring, Erden Khan or the younger Erben?"

The caravan master, now turned innkeeper, cocked his head and smiled, his shrug was eloquent. "We've had neither sign nor sound that there is any other clan movement. There are refugees in the Uigur capital and caravans out of the east, but nothing from the west."

"You disappoint me, old friend, I expected better information. But don't relax your vigil, I want news."

"I have one bit that may interest you. I know a dangerous man when I see one and such a man, Seerden, has passed here. He stayed the night, going to Kokand from the north. Suave, sly, self-assured and fast, would you like a full description?"

101

Onat bey smiled at the innkeeper. "You saved the best for last, I should have known."

> - - - - - - - > WHITE MARBLE QUARRY > - - - - - - - >

The loaded cart creaked up the quarry slope painfully, while Yeet called encouragement to the oxen and applied the whip. Kardesh walked dutifully behind, adding his weight and strength each time the wheels emerged from a pothole. The flat slabs of thin marble-facing swayed with the motion of the cart. Paid by the load delivered, they worked from first light to the edge of night to augment their gain.

The first weeks they had lived to work, eat and sleep with little earnings, but as strength, health and experience increased so did the earnings. Social life was limited to the two family rooms, with Yeet sleeping on the flat roof. The neighbors considered them *kafirs*, unbelievers, and ignored them. Still the rooms could ring with merriment and wit. This life included songs and rests with little local contact, except between the producer and the contractor. Breakage and repairs were deducted, deliveries and work rewarded, but nothing was saved.

Leyla and Tayze had begun to make friends among the neighbor ladies. Christian or animist, most were hill people who came to work for the copper coins. They were living in the poor, crowded and transient part of the camp that clung to the broken mountainside. The substantial homes of the overseers and masters were higher on the hills, under the protection of noonday shade from the mountain and a few watered trees. These owners found fellowship and worship among themselves, in the marbled mosque. Each knew the others worth and station. The temporary help were free to come to worship and learn the true faith in humility. The big Turk, with his large son who wore the eye patch and his arm in a sling, were but one pair more of the multitude of workers.

> - - - - - - - > KOKAND HOSPITAL > - - - - - - - >

Sevman moaned and tossed on the wool stuffed mattress, a thin palette laid on a mud brick shelf built into the wall of the hospital building. He no longer floated above the passing aids, doctors and visitors. He had listened with interest to the pitying 'tsk' 'tsk' and shrugs. He didn't even hurt. He would join the light. He was redeemed from the clay and evil, but he couldn't fly up to the sun and the heavenly Yesu didn't visit him any more. He was overcome from time to time by heaviness and found himself again in his body to rave and cry with pain. It would be better to die. In his next life he would become one of the elect and sin no more. Then he could become a part of the light and no longer suffer. Yesu would say 'Well done, good and faithful servant. Enter into the joy of your Lord.' Then the dream would shatter with renewed agony. The aides or doctors would give him an opiate and change the bandages while he slept or drifted about in a lovely place. He looked forward to the ease from pain and the golden dreams. Slowly his body healed. When the crisis had passed food became a pleasant preoccupation. His shrunken frame craved nourishment. Although health and strength gradually returned to his body, Sevman's soul languished.

> - - - - - - - > KOKAND RUG FACTORY > - - - - - - - >

"You know the purpose of my visit? It's to save your Yeet's life, nothing less." Derk stood at the entrance to the small work room taking in the loom, bed and meager goods in the narrow space between. The place was littered with her personal belongings in disarray. Ali bey's police had searched clumsily, but thoroughly no doubt.

"I tell you again, I don't know where Yeet is or where Yeet proposed to go. I only know Yeet was leaving town. He said goodbye and left." The woman's defiant voice filled the room while her hands continued knotting the rug. "Another beating won't get you more than the truth. If you don't have sense enough to recognize it, Allah have mercy on fools."

Derk looked at the healing bruise on her face and cursed the clumsy police and their sadistic chief. "Truth is all I seek and reward is yours for telling all. I'm a friend of Yeet. He told you of his knife throwing teacher? We met only the day before he took Sevman to the hospital. I helped load the poor child on the cart." He waited while the

103

woman thought over his statement. Her continued silence underlined distrust. He tried again. "Yeet said he has a sister working here with you. The manager said she left over a year ago. Where is she now?" Derk noticed the ceaseless tying stopped for an instant.

The woman's voice was cautious. "She died shortly after leaving work. Yeet said she was buried among the nameless poor." Her voice was tight.

"What was her name?" His voice held compassion.

"Fatima," her voice was a trembling whisper.

"Your husband's favorite, I understand from Harun. He knew her as a baby. Life has been hard for you since then."

Her fingers did not pause, but she pursed her lips. "God tries our souls to reveal our faith and character. He keeps us day by day. We have value for Him."

"You didn't go to the funeral? Only Yeet?"

"I didn't see her, but I know she's dead. Nothing is left of her. I only have Yeet now." Her voice was definite.

"Strange, Yeet speaks of her existence." He paused.

"Yeet has a vivid imagination and may need the sense of an older sister's presence to guide and console."

"As a friend I would like to speak to him"

"He has gone. You will have to find Kardesh and his treasure alone. My Yeet is out of it now" She smiled.

"I look not for petty treasure, but to save lives. The feared *Bowzkurt*, the Gray Wolf, is after Yeet to find his friend's father, a Chipchak Khan's twin." He peered closely.

"But Yeet didn't say where. Yeet said, 'Wait till Sevman comes to see you.' After that Yeet will come here." Her hands stopped their work and covered her face.

"He said nothing about the kind of work or country where he'll be? No hint or joke?" Derk's face worked.

She wiped her eyes with her sleeves and frowned thoughtfully. "I said to stay safe, and Yeet scoffed that hauling stone was both safe and dull."

He sighed now. "Well it's better than nothing. I brought you back the silver coin the police took. You may need it."

"You will keep in touch then? You said you were a friend." He smiled, and pressed the coin into her palm.

104

"*Pie'dash*, partners, I will share with you and you with me for the good of Yeet and the Khan's twin."

>- - - - - - - > KOKAND HOSPITAL >- - - - - - - >

After two months, the doctors deprived Sevman of his opiate release and damned him to the hell of pain and loss. He begged all who passed by with real tears and promises of rewards, gold and silver for his relief. No one believed it. No narcotics: bitter willow bark tea was all they would give him. No one in Kokand remembered him. His community had moved to the Tarim Basin. His thin voice was only a whisper and it tired people to listen to his pleas. His voice, like his feet, never recovered its normal use. At the end of summer, he still dragged himself around the room and out to the garden area. He was required to help with hospital work and it was found that he could garden effectively without standing. He lay in despair among the vegetables and fruits of the orchard. He cried there musing on a black future. No one visited him from the city. Only the novice would occasionally sit with him and gossip of hospital life. The *Kardeshler* Brotherhood no longer existed.

RUINED LAND

105

PEOPLE, PLOTS & PLACES IN CHAPTER 9

Ayshe: has become a prisoner incorporated into the tribe.
Barmani: is welcomed to the Uigur Khanate and promoted.
Emperor: Khan of the Uigur people welcomes exiles.
Jon & Manish: herd Manly's sheep on Uigur lands.
Kynan: leads an army to recover his abducted sister.
Nooryouz: a refugee with suitors anxious to possess her.
Onat: a Turkish Seljuk leader protects the northern border.
Sanjak: must lead refugees out of China before winter.
Seerden: a secret agent of the Gray Wolf Society.
Setchkin: finds herself as a protector of non-combatants

GLOSSARY:
Bash ooze two nay: I'll do it right away; as you ordered.
bowzkurt: the Gray Wolf; a secret political society.
Bosh ver: nonsense; nothing to it; it's empty; no meaning.
ek'mek: bread.
gel shimdi: come now; let's go.
kumiss: fermented mares' milk; a clear alcoholic beverage.
oo'lak: boy; son; serving boy.
pie dahsh': partners

KYNAN WAITS

Kynan, seated on a stone bench against the wall of a Caravansary let out a roar of frustration. "*Oolak*, boy, more lion's milk! We grow thirsty waiting for your service. Bring *kumiss*, in heaven's name!"

"Here friend, my pitcher is full. Let's share and enjoy the blessings of the mare to the best of mankind." The stranger poured out a large portion of clear fermented liquid into Kynan's beaker. Then he added a dash of water from another pitcher. The mix became cloudy.

Kynan laughed loudly and waved it. "Look, from milk to milk again! All power be to the horse of the Golden Stallion Tribe, provider of milk, blood, meat, hide, and best of all *kumiss*, to power the mind. Glory be to the horses and their riders!" He drank while looking over the stranger.

"I fail to find your name, friend. How much have I drunk tonight? Are you one of the mercenaries? What tribe?" He laughed in a friendly way but continued to scrutinize the stranger to the best of his ability.

"I'm but a man of the border, increasing the gain of the merchants since my prices are less than that of the bazaar. My father was of the Seljuks, my mother was too beautiful not to be carried off." Both men laughed knowingly and drank again.

Kynan began to warm to the man. "I'm bored here on the front lines. I wish we could visit the cities of the south without problems with the Caliph's men."

"Mercenaries come and go at will. I can get you anywhere you might wish to go. Onat knows all the borders. It's how I make my living. Name the place."

"Onat, I have spent the summer at my father's command. We sit and send out eyes to watch, but without action. My relatives have returned to the yurts, but I am planted like a tree. Only the mercenaries remain with me. They are always drunk and disorderly." He shuddered and licked his lips. He lifted the beaker for a new draft of lion's milk, wiping his mouth with his sleeve. "I wish to visit Perikanda and Kokand. How long would it take to get there and back?"

Onat smiled wisely. "Take two weeks for traveling there. Take time to see things. Then, come back in the fall to prepare for winter or action. Would that please you? Would your enemy's position and condition change critically in two months?"

Kynan shook his head. "We wait to see how they survive the heat and drought on the Bet Pak Dala and the drying of the Sari Su and the Chu Rivers. I'm forced to wait until they are crippled by adversity and then offer peace." His face reflected disgust at such a fate.

Onat paused. "Is it then a matter of family honor? Surely they're not an enemy tribe to be punished. Why press into farming country?"

Kynan pursed his lips and drank to the bottom of the beaker. He rose unsteadily and left with only a phrase. "I'll let you know when it's time to travel."

>- - - - - - ->SYR RIVER SOUTH ROAD > - - - - - - ->

Seerden wiped his weapon carefully. Disregarding the Tiger's full instructions, he obeyed contrary orders from a more powerful patron. That was part of the delight of his work: to have several pay sources and to collect his dues before the contrary results were known. Life was never boring. He looked at the message bundle of wool market cloth with smug satisfaction. A chip of white marble, a looped noose of horse hair from the special lion horses of the Kayah clan of the Chipchak nation, a bit of gray hair from a dog or wolf, a stub of a candle of bees wax, and ten gold coins, were the obvious articles in the bundle. A tiny feather rested under the hair with a thin broken bamboo slat from a cage, birdlime marked the strut. The message: 'the bird has broken out of the cage, fled by night to a quarry. An important man of the Chipchak is to be killed by order of the Gray Wolf secret society.' The down payment was included. "Too clever: take a totem of Turkish origin, connect a legend with ruthless power and top secrecy." He

108

stopped and looked about. To penetrate this mystery would be both dangerous and profitable. Many nations would pay well for the identity of the leader. Perhaps it was a death sentence to work for such. The watchers would be watched as surely as the prey. Perhaps the executioner executed! His senses were sharpening. He, Seerden, would find the trail. Who could tell where it would lead?

> - - - - - - - > SILK ROAD CAMPING >- - - - - - >

Summer's end in Kansu was torture. The sun beat down without mercy. The monsoon rains came so seldom and so sparsely that it accomplished little for the vegetation. The increase in humidity caused the sand and dust to stick like paint to their perspiring bodies. Water was in short supply. Quarrels and fighting developed among the travelers. Children cried and got lost, wives nagged and gossiped, men argued, everyone criticized everything. Divisions caused distrust. Subversion undermined all Sanjak's authority and directions.

Evidence of Tang control had diminished to the west and local military leaders ruled capriciously. Garrisons were restricted to the towns. Refugees were ignored or exploited for goods and cash.

Nooryouz in baggy cotton pants, blouse and vest, now rode a donkey instead of driving it. But she stayed near the string of animals that Jon drove and their speech together still held the salt and brimstone that they had used before her transformation back to a girl. Nooryouz had a small tent now and Sanjak and Jon slept outside it near the corral. It was there that men sought the leader with their complaints, accusations and insinuations. All his advice fell on deaf ears.

"We'll soon be safely across the border. We must continue to press forward. If we slacken for the laggards, we'll be compelled to winter in Kansu where the law may yet be applied. Only in the Tarim basin is there freedom." Sanjak repeated this insistently on every occasion. But the number of those falling behind or waiting on the sick grew as pressure from the throne was distant and seemed less insistent. Weariness increased among the travelers as the leadership became more frazzled and less sure. "Everyone go back to your wagons, food must be ready and you've had a long day. No more talk today."

"*Gel shimdy*, come now Sanjak bey, the food is ready. You have not eaten since morning." Nooryouz insisted. Gradually the tent area was cleared as Sanjak sat on the ground near the fire.   The desert nights were tranquil, but guards were posted for protection against thieves. Jon excused himself and left for his turn watching the pastured stock. He was working with Manish, herding the flocks Manly had bought. They were destined for the Tarim Basin.

109

Sanjak finished the bowl and took up a drinking horn for ayran. Nooryouz cleaned the bowl with sand and a small rinse of water. Then she cleaned the cooking pot.

"The ayran and yogurt have a strange taste. Why?"

"Jon's goat freshened with the kid. We added her milk to the mixture. The grazing is sparse and bitter here."

"What will the kid drink?"

She laughed then. "What you drank, mixed, but we will use his meat within the month if the grazing gets less."

He sighed. "We are always on the edge of some disaster."

"But you always save us and get us through, Allah be praised."

He leaned forward holding his hands open. "Yes, you get me through, Nooryouz." He stood as she backed modestly away. He reached out and caught her by the shoulders. She stood wide eyed and open mouthed. He took her stance for consent and after kissing her, reached under her blouse. She jerked away and slapping his hand down, whirled toward the tent. He stopped, startled and ashamed.

She hissed. "Who taught you to behave like this to a girl you haven't spoken for." She stood before the tent door, angry.

"Gratitude, I thought would teach you to love. I was promised once and the lady didn't want to wait for me. I hoped you would want me now. I thought you knew I chose only you."

She searched his face for truth and found it. She decided to probe deeper. "She, no doubt, thought you would choose only her. Now you say you choose another: me. Where is the truth for both? You would have me be the second wife?" She waited.

"I was yours from our meeting in the garden. I never married the lady. My father opposed it. He thought me unfaithful to her, and broke it off. It was to be an arranged political marriage. Her family became unhappy, so she was given to the Khan, a political arrangement that profited them greatly." His face twisted.

She touched his cheek. "Were you unfaithful to your promised one? Did you seek love elsewhere?" She was hesitant.

His answer was bold. "I was called home from my studies at the hermitage for the engagement ceremonies. My best friend at school has a family a day's ride away. I visited them overnight. The sister was like the brother, a gem of rare qualities. She was good and pure, of a religious frame of mind. I liked her and the family, so I went frequently to share my doubts. My father suspected the worst and worked against me. I returned to the hermitage, but they questioned me. Because of rumors and gossip about my relations with my intended, they disciplined me. They turned me out. When Setchken married the Khan I left for China."

She was now standing as close as possible and he bent to kiss her. She sighed. "Tell me of your love. Convince me, I want to believe you, but I lack experience. I'm afraid."

He took her hand, smiled and softly sang this melody; a
traditional pledge of love:

SANJAK'S SERENADE

Full moon shines high a-bove my head; I feel
your pre - - sence, i sense your per - - fume,
taste your sweet lips. I hear your name, o-
ver and o-ver a-gain for you hold my heart.
I love you, I kiss you, I've missed you.
Oh, come. I speak the truth. Oh, hear the song
of my soul You hold my heart. Yes, you do.

#1   Full moon shines high above my head.
I feel your presence.
I sense your perfume, taste your sweet lips.
I hear your name, over and over again,
for you hold my heart.
I love you, I kiss you. I've missed you.
Oh come. I speak the truth,
Oh, hear the song of my soul.
You hold my heart. Yes, you do.

#2   In my dreams I hear your voice so clear.
We sing our love song, poignant with melodies,
Sweet with our love.
Hear the refrain, over and over again,
For you hold my heart.

111

I'll feed you. I'll heed you. I'll need you always.
We'll thank God too, in everything that we do.
You hold my heart. Yes, you do.

They embraced and she breathed in his ear softly. "I'd be willing to be even your fourth wife, if you would know the truth." They entered the tent together.

> - - - - - - - > SARI SU TRAIL >- - - - - - - >

"Ayshe, wake up you lazy heathen and tend that crying baby. You're useless with the children." Setchkin spanked the girl on the bottom hard enough to wake and send her sulkily from the palette to the baby who lay on the floor among pillows. Setchkin held up her quirt menacingly. "We only worked two days drying the meat. I worked as hard as any of you. Even the children helped. I'll beat you if you neglect them."

Ayshe stood up wearily, her face pasty and drawn. Her voice was shrill. "I'm not well, I can't eat the food." She paused. "If we only had bread or vegetables." Her hand went to her throat and she swallowed with difficulty.

"*Ekmek*, bread? That dry stuff you farmers bake? You eat those seeds with it: lentil or beans? But we have meat, three kinds, plus wild birds. We are no longer just a horse tribe, we have cattle now. We collect wild plants to cook with our meat. Cheese, milk, ayran or yogurt make our diet one of the richest on earth. Fresh blood to mix with any of them. Saddle cured fresh meat when there's no time to cook. Who would want the sticky rice that looks like little white worms? Or the dark bread with little seeds? Ugh, how do you get it down?" Setchken shuddered.

"The milk makes me sick, I get cramps. I can only eat the bulgur. Muslims are prohibited to eat some of those things. The saddle-cured meats are raw. I can't drink anything except water and it tastes like alkali. I get hot and tired in the afternoons, Peri sent me to bed. I want bread or lentils all the time!"

Setchken lectured her. "Wheat is expensive. We buy it from the west. Buckwheat and rye can also be found, but the black bread is as heavy and unappealing as the clods that grow it. It produces no burst of energy like milk or dried meat. Saddle cured meats are fresh not raw. The heat of the horse and pressure of the rider cures it. If you don't like the fresh taste, put onion tops or other leaves with them for flavor. A half day's ride will make any kind of meat good for travel rations."

Ayshe did not answer, but let her head droop listlessly. Setchken gave her a shake and push. "Get the children bedded down for the night. Tomorrow we leave the desert and visit villages of the Syr River. We'll

112

trade meat and hides for your kind of food. You can eat your fill. We'll cross the border into Dar al Islam in peace. You can talk your Sogdian Persian dialect and make friends, but don't try to run away. We're your clan now, when we move, you'll move too. Only death will part us."

> - - - - - - - > SILK ROAD CAMPING >- - - - - - - >

Sanjak did not return to the tent for two days. He had ridden ahead to contact the border troops of the Uigurs. However, they refused to deal with the caravan or give any permission of passage before interviewing the people. His failure sharpened his need of Nooryouz. He smiled at her eagerness to listen and satisfied himself with talk of his travel to the border. He ate her prepared food with gusto. "I have done nothing but talk and eat since arrival so tell me: how is our caravan? What has happened around here?"

She smiled thinly and shook her head. "We travel and eat. The animals grow thinner, the people longer of face. Many are angry for one reason or another. There are quarrels among the families." She sighed and turned away as she cleared off the vessels on the cloth spread on the floor. Her face showed strain.

"What have you and Jon been doing for feeding the animals? Are there any new meadows or pasture?" He smiled indulgently.

"We don't talk now. He does all the driving with some of the other boys." Her face showed resentment.

"Then tell me of the ladies. How go the households: Those who expect or have babies." He knew she loved to talk of them.

Her face clouded with emotion. "They won't talk to me. Only Koolair and Maril remain friends. Her father says I'm a fallen woman and the women shun me. The men make jokes and stare at me. I hear noises outside the tent at night."

He stared open mouthed. "But Jon sleeps outside. He protects you. They are curious and impudent, not dangerous."

She started to cry. "Jon has not slept here since you moved into the tent. I am completely alone. Your priest says I have sinned and God will punish me." She buried her face in her hands.

He reached out and brought her close. "The sin is mine and the punishment should be mine. My need was so great that I didn't think of the price you would have to pay. We can be married."

She shook her head. "The priest says we must be of the same faith to have the blessing of God. The Muslims say I can't marry an unbeliever. The Manichae say I have fallen into creation's errors and that demon's lusts hold my heart in captivity. The Shaman suggests spells of magic and sacrifices to bring good fortune and take away evil. I don't know what to think. I have lost my friends and you went without telling me." She was near hysteria and trembling now.

113

"It seemed necessary to go on ahead. Some men encouraged me to warn the guard before the main body approach the Uigur frontier. They've no love for the Tang and are very suspicious of everyone." He stroked her hand.

"You could've told me. You left without a word."

"You must've heard it from others," he insisted.

"It's not the same. You should've told me."

"Damnation, I don't have time to clear everything I need to do. Too many people's lives depend on prompt action. I didn't know that I'd go when I left you." She began to cry. He softened his voice. "You know I love you. I'll always come back to you."

She continued crying and shaking her head. "Then you're not mine. You belong to the caravan. I have the loan of you while we rest. Like the angel I thought you to be. You go away and appear when God permits."

"Don't talk nonsense. I'm always yours. Things will change. I'll tell everyone in the Caravan you're my wife."

"They won't believe you without a wedding."

"I'll find someone who'll marry us. I'll make them. You belong to me now." His voice was angry.

"I'm happy to be your concubine. It's what people expect of a girl without family. But I won't be what they call me now. A concubine knows where her master has gone."

"Don't start that again! I can't always know ahead of time."

She, too, was now red faced and angry. "You can send a donkey boy or child to come and tell me what to expect. Then they'll know I belong to you. Otherwise, I'm the woman who entertains a man for a night and then has no idea where he goes or when they'll meet again. I won't live like a whore. Not even for you."

"You're my wife. I'll never leave you," he shouted.

"Treat me like a wife and everyone will believe you. Ignore me except after dark and others will expect the same privilege. The trouble is only beginning," she shouted.

"You're impossible," he shouted and left the tent. Later on he returned and was admitted. They cried and loved until dawn.

> - - - - - - - > TARIM BASIN > - - - - - - - >

Barmani, immaculate in white, lay before the divan of authority, as the Khan of the Uigur nation addressed him. Scribes and nobles attended the meeting silently.

"Your travels have been long and arduous, most serene Barmani. You have prevailed in a manner worthy of the Apostle Paul or the Prophet Mani for whom you are well named. You are most welcome with all the faithful who have accompanied you." The khan extended his open hands to all. "Come, rise, with those of your flock who have

114

accompanied you here. Share with us now your wisdom." He lowered his hands.

"Blessed be the Father of Lights who has allowed us to see this day in your presence. May Yesu, the one who brings to everyone truth and salvation, grace your kingdom with blessings of peace and prosperity. May you direct your people by the rules of Mani, the prophet and Holy Spirit of our God." Barmani continued in a quiet voice, "Many of our community remained at the border to recover their strength from our summer's exertions. Some, alas, were left along the hard road of our travels. May Tanra rest their souls beneath His throne of light." All the assembly voiced a soft 'Amen.'

"News of your expulsion and journey preceded your safe arrival here. Your example will encourage others to flee rather than convert to the doctrines of Islam's false prophet. We have designated lands near the border for your community. There is much work for you with those who suffer a like fate. You will have special jurisdiction and hold authority over refugees, but you will have to provide the food and cloth from your industry. Our resources go to resist the power of the Kirghiz from Lake Baikal area. They press us on the north-east, spurred by Tang ingratitude." There was a general long hiss of breath from the listeners at these words. They knew the rage of their hearts against an unscrupulous friend turned enemy: the Tang rulers.

SILK ROAD CAMPING

115

PEOPLE, PLOTS & PLACES IN CHAPTER 10

Atilla: merchant leaving Changan returning to Kokand.
Barmani: rules the monastery at Aksu and helps refugees.
Captain: escorts refugees to Aksu for a winter stay.
Hussein: a rough friend of Umer, ready for anything.
Jon: loses out, but makes a close friend for the long trip.
Kardesh: gets a new challenge in his quarry home.
Kynan: loses his victory, but gets a trip to the city.
Manish: journeys with the refugees as herder.
Maril: keeps the Bowzhun families' fire going for guests.
Mert: a merchant refugee from Changan, fond of drinks.
Onat: secures the northern border for his tribe and Caliph.
Sanjak: duty comes before pleasure, and pride before a fall.
Twozan: finds himself in trouble with an enemy.
Umer: The master's son presumes on his father's position.
Yeet: finds that doing what is right is hard.

GLOSSARY:
binbasha: general; commander of a thousand men.
Bosh ver: nonsense; it's not important.
bowz'kurt: the Gray Wolf; a secret society with an aim.
do'er: stop; hold; stay.
Em'dot: help; emergency; look here.
hanjer: a narrow, pointed knife used in stitching leather.
hitch: not at all; never.
high'van lar: animals; beasts.
Hoo joos: charge; forward; have at 'em.
kor'kak beery oh: he's a coward; he's scared.
onbasha: corporal; head of ten soldiers.
yuzbasha: officer: head of a hundred men.

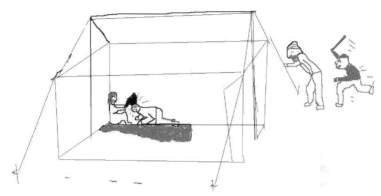

DEALING WITH DRUNKS

Nooryouz woke from her sleep with a start. Someone was shouting outside her tent.

"Come on girl untie this flap or I'll break it. We have to talk." The slurred voice demanded again.

"She's not going to entertain the likes of you, Mert," teased another voice. "She gets paid by the Turk. You don't have big money like he does." Muffled laughter followed.

"Shut your mouth Atilla. I jus' wanna talk, no harm in 'at is dere? I jus' wanna see the pretty gal up close." The front of the tent heaved with his weight as he pushed again.

"Hey Noor, come on open dis t'ing. I wanna see yu bad. I got a pretty present here fer yu. Come look." The tie gave way before him. Atilla laughed again.

"*Emdot*, help!" Her voice carried over the camp ground. The big man had fallen to his knees beside her. She pushed up against the back of the tent. A short heavy set man filled the doorway. The big man fumbled swinging his hand before him helplessly. Noor pulled her feet up beneath her chin and tried to pull up the tent edge. She felt for her knife, but everything was tumbled about.

"Well, you got 'er now. So talk if that what you came for. I'll hold the present if you like. It'll keep," Atilla commented.

"I can't see 'er. Where's she gone?" complained the drunk. "She's slipped out."

Atilla walked around the outside falling over the pegs. "Nuthin' out here, Mert. Have another go, she yelled in there."

Slowly, still on his knees, Mert extended his hands upward and then down just above the ground. Just as he touched her she hit him with her iron cooking pot, kept in a corner, safe from robbery. She darted for the entrance just as Atilla drew near. She screamed

117

again as he caught at her. Then she was pushed to one side as a figure fell on Atilla bearing him into the tent and on the ground. The tent pole gave way and collapsed the tent. Inside figures thrashed as more people arrived from around the camp. Some reached through the opened door and pulled out those inside one by one. An angry Jon was the first pulled out followed by Atilla and Mert. The drunks were pulled away and turned over to their relatives to pacify and bed down. Tomorrow there would be fines.

"I'll put up the tent." Jon murmured, and a few helped get the pole straight and the sides setup. He started to move away, but Nooryouz grabbed his sleeve and held him.

"Oh Jon, I owe you so much." she sobbed. He shrugged. and tried to free his arm. She hung on.

"Please, let's be friends again. I need your friendship Jon. I'm sorry I let things change. It's my fault, but it's too late to remedy. I know you are displeased, but I need you Jon. How can I live without you and Maril? You are my family." She laid her head on his shoulder. He stood stiffly, embarrassed and awkward. She still clung to his sleeve. He sighed and tried to find words. The camp was quiet. He finally sat in the open door while she sobbed herself to sleep on her pallet behind him.

The first light of morning was near. It brought Jon awake and he stood facing east. Nooryouz knew what he would do. It was time for the morning song: half-Christian hymn, half-Hunnish sun worship. It contained the longing for warmth characteristic of cold lands avid for the comfort of sunshine.

He punctuated the music with a clear bell while Manish piped.

#1   First light creeps in to stay;
    Night turns into day.
    Bright increasing, moonlight ceasing,
    Darkness hiding in the caves.
    Let there be light! The Sun is born.
    Our hearts are full of joy and grace.
    God gives us this day, sing and play.

#2   We see with open eyes;
    Sunlight blues the skies.
    Rainbows rising, waters shining,
    Shadows sliding back of trees.
    Fire lights the sky! The sun is born.
    Our eyes are full, bright colors trace.
    God gives us this place, with good grace.

#3   Gray dawn, the rain may stay;
    Lost, we search our way.
    Wayward choosing, gaining, losing,

118

Feet now slipping down death's road.
God with us be! The Son is born.
Our souls seek light; we fear the night.
God brings us bright day, thank and pray.

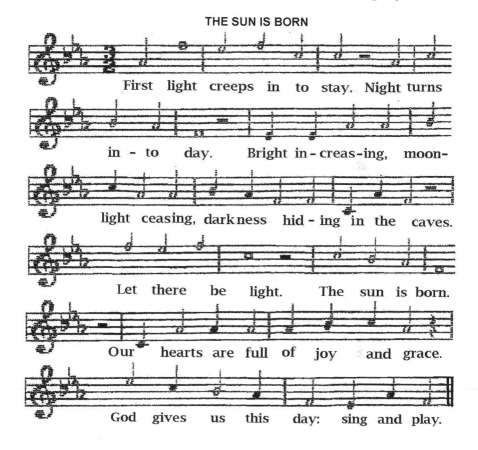

THE SUN IS BORN

First light creeps in to stay. Night turns in - to day. Bright in - creas-ing, moon-light ceasing, dark ness hid - ing in the caves. Let there be light. The sun is born. Our hearts are full of joy and grace. God gives us this day: sing and play.

Animal noises gave the loud amen to the song. Manish and Jon ran to let them pour out of the corrals.

> - - - - - - - > WHITE MARBLE QUARRY > - - - - - - - >

Umer, the master's son was avoiding the foreman who was teaching him the work. He had used his father's preoccupation with a delivery, and deserted the shop. He was enjoying the cool of morning with a friend, playing backgammon and drinking barley beer. They were on the second round when Umer left the game and walked to the entrance of the tea house. Stretching idly he spoke out of his boredom.

"There's a new girl in the workers' quarter. Turk, not plump enough, but not bad. She's cute enough to be worth a personal investigation." His friend nodded knowingly.

"I know, I spotted her, too. She's open faced, but her dad's got warrior gear in the house. The boy with the eye-patch looks like he's been in a fight. They're Chipchak."

Umer shook his head impatiently and interrupted. "You're timid and reluctant to venture, Hussein. I already know her name, Leyla. She's meek enough to be a push over." He smiled confidently and twisted his mustache.

"I hear she drove off a pack of snide bitches at the fountain. They are jealous of girls who show their face. Mother said her language was shocking," Hussein laughed.

"I like spice, watch me," Umer smirked boldly. "Let's go over and test the brother now. We can use the cash, and we'll see what's behind the eye patch."

> - - - - - - - > WHITE MARBLE QUARRY >- - - - - - - >

Yeet was impatient to leave the bazaar, but Kardesh was exchanging jokes with the contractor. The cool fall season meant fruit and plenty in the land. It was time to bring Sevman out of the city. How could they do so without bringing danger to Kardesh and the Khan's brother? There would be spies or followers. He might meet friends who would ask questions. Yeet was not proficient in lies, they would know something was wrong. He stared at his feet. It was as chancy to come back directly as it was to go to the city in the first place. They had to bring Sevman here.

"What's wrong friend, why so distressed?" Kardesh had come out unperceived. He studied his slender friend.

"*Hitch*, nothing, I'm okay. I was tired waiting." A thread of irritation entered his voice. He frowned.

"Nothing comes across very heavy. I'm glad it's nothing serious, it might take me another summer to get over whatever you might inflict on me." Kardesh laughed and pounded Yeet's shoulder playfully. Yeet slid sideways to evade the hand and found himself blushing darkly. He could think of nothing to say and so walked hurriedly ahead. While Kardesh, his laughter dried, stared after the retreating form. Behind him he heard the sound of contemptuous laughter.

"*Kor cock beery oh*, He's a coward. The kid took off when he saw us coming." Hussein was anxious to impress his friends. "He left the stupid Turk here to get initiated."

"I'll tell him about our exclusive society. We protect you summer workers that stay on. No theft, or damage to your cart and animals." Umer took up the theme. "We insure your safety on the job or off. Besides we have pull in the master's office we can influence the amount of work you're given for good or bad. Depending on how much you pay." They laughed in an easy but intimidating way, forming a barricade before him.

"So? How much and how often?" Kardesh folded his arms on his chest and moved his head back so his nose was up and he looked through his narrowed eye at the three dandies before him. He spoke in a gentle low voice, smiling as if he had found friends. They became uneasy. His voice said one thing his body another. One of the boys whistled and two boys playing backgammon looked up and nodded. They left their board and walked toward them, leisurely chatting.

"We don't take crap from workers." Hussein put his hand on Kardesh's shoulder angrily. Kardesh covered the hand with his own and, still smiling, squeezed till Hussein was pale and protesting. He let the hand drop. The other boys joined the ring around Kardesh.

"No, you take money, that's okay, but I asked the conditions. Who collects and what's his commission?"

The bristling silence was broken by a sound 'thunk' on the willow tree beside the fountain. A sharp *hanjer* had driven deeply into the soft trunk. Yeet stood with a second knife in hand; ready to throw. He was grim and angry.

"Don't Yeet, I can take care of this." Kardesh smiled confidently and turned to his opposition. "My friend Yeet is hot-blooded like his Yemenli father. So I won't repeat your thoughts expressed earlier." He watched closely.

The gang was suddenly unsure of what to do.

Umer stuttered, "C-come have tea with us. We'll talk things over." They had suddenly become earnest, and

121

watched carefully as Yeet walked to the tree and pulled out the dagger with some effort. He left without a word or even a glance at the boys. The gang relaxed and looked at each other. They needed time.

"You would make a valuable addition to our group. You could collect for us and take your share." Umer said slyly.

> - - - - - - - > SILK ROAD >- - - - - - - >

"Nooryouz, where are you?" Sanjak drew up before the tent noted its tied door and dead fire in the hearth. He looked at the corral where the animals were being driven in for the night and rode over to call again. He saw Jon. "Is Noor around here?"

Jon pointed with his chin. Sanjak rode toward the camp. He saw her there helping Maril while Koolair clung to her neck. As he rode toward them he spotted the cooking pan there on the fire. She had moved!

"I came to tell you of my return to the border with an advanced group tomorrow. I knew you would want to know." He pulled his horse to a halt before her. She stood motionless. Koolair stared at his face then held out her hands to him. He took her and settled her on the horse. "You're staying here tonight? With the family?"

She hung her head then looked at Maril. "Nooryouz is afraid to stay alone now. You'll leave early, better go to bed early."

He looked from Maril to Noor and shook his head uncertainly. He spoke hesitantly. "I understand that two men were fined for drunken brawling last night. The camp captain settled it. I have to go there for a report still. I'm sure you'll be safe here till we arrive at the Uigur capital. Manly, the drovers' chief, has gone ahead to arrange it all. We can be married there. My duties will be over."

"I ... We won't have to be alone anymore?" she questioned. He nodded, kissed Koolair and handed her down to the girls. He rode reluctantly off into the increasing darkness.

> - - - - - - - >THE UIGUR EAST BORDER >- - - - - - - >

Sanjak tried again squinting into the glare and wind. Most of the column of mounted men had drawn up behind him. The loud squealing axles of carts and wagons could be heard approaching. Women in pants and children in long quilted coats came running. The guards had sent word back to the commander of the garrison who came with the full contingent of armed men. The Uigurs were accustomed to the sight of carts, camels and merchandise, but not families and household goods. They were suspicious.

"We're refugees from the Tang Empire, we return to our tribes of origin in the West. We've Uigurs as well as Chipchak, Seljuk, Persian, and others with us. We've pass papers from the trade representatives of our merchants. Most here are those merchant or

122

artisan families who lived in approved centers appointed by the Tang government."

"I regret that we have no instructions regarding the passage of unauthorized families. Those who are Uigurs, registered merchants authorized to reside here and others that are Manichae can be admitted. However, such a vast number of aliens would be unacceptable. Not even to pass to the other frontier. Food alone will be hard to come by for so many."

"We've shared the journey and our expenses, we'll all cross together. Those who have a right to stay will do that. The rest will exit to the west. The Uigur merchants in our column will guarantee us. We've all agreed. They're willing to post bond for our passage. You can send a detachment with us to guarantee good order," Sanjak pleaded.

"I'll agree to send notice to the capital and beg instructions. But have you valuables that can be left here as guarantee?" The commander kept a stern face as befitting a man in control, but his palm itched to inspect the goods.

"It'll take too long and we're out of food now, the desert crossing has wasted our herds. The Tang forces confiscated much of the goods and properties. Manichaean nuns were killed in the capitol, Changan, and all foreign temples closed. Especially Manichaean, Nestorian and Buddhist are being killed and exiled. Only Muslims and Jews are safe, their lives and goods are respected." Sanjak insisted.

"Long ago when we held the Baikal steppes, we helped restore the Tangs to power," complained the commander. "Thus they have repaid us. They helped the Kirghiz to displace us from that good land and when we took refuge in China and the Tarim Basin they destroyed our religion and harried our people." The Captain looked along the line of carts and the swelling crowd of people which clearly outnumbered his garrison. "Come spend the night near the water and we'll send some provisions for your food. I'll advise the Emperor of your coming journey to the capitol. We have pigeons to speed the matter. I'm sure a sum left here as guarantee would suffice to speed your peaceful passage." The commander smiled and gestured broadly. In this way it was arranged.

> - - - - - - - >NORTH SIDE OF THE SYR RIVER FRONTIER >- - - - - - - >

Kynan sat in the shade of the willow grove, beside the Syr River. His lieutenant rode up to report. "*Binbasha*, the scouts have spotted the out-riders of the tribe, the main body is just visible behind them."

"They will walk into the trap," Kynan gloated. "Now we'll test these renegades and teach them a lesson. I'll have my sister back and the heir. My father will make me war chief of the united tribe."

123

"Kynan bey, We're inside the Caliphate border, I would recommend the posting of rearguard and to keep a troop in the rear as reserve and reinforcements. We have no idea of the placement of the border patrols of the Seljuks."

"*Bosh ver, Yuzbasha*, nonsense, lieutenant. They have no idea we're trespassing, only their smugglers even know we're close. A squad with Onbasha Tamol can be our reserve. We'll sweep up this trash and be gone before the village behind us can get notice to the authorities. The Caliphate never advances beyond the cultivators and merchants. Beyond this valley there is no boundary. In every desert from here to Baghdad there's no control beyond what local sheiks and Khans permit. The Abbassid Empire rots at its core, how much more in its branches. Proceed as ordered."

Yuzbasha Erol bowed his head. "*Bash ooze two nay*, on your command, *Binbasha*, We await your signal." He rode away into the horseshoe shaped ambush as a cloud of dust formed on the northwest horizon. Kynan lifted the bag to his lips for a new draft of lion's milk, wiping his mouth with his sleeve.

> - - - - - - - > SYR RIVER FORD >- - - - - - - >

Twozan sat at rest on his golden horse seated facing backward watching the spread of his columns and their animals in an extended fan. He and the household of Setchken formed the handle. He was uneasy: they had breached the border, but no delegation or even border guards awaited them. How could the Caliphate government be so careless? The Kaynaklar had failed to pursue or negotiate. How could they be so inept? All his men were on battle alert. Something was going to happen he could feel the hair rise on his arms. He spun on the saddle to face the head of the march and shouted a command to his alert staff and waiting guards.

"Put the animals ahead, they'll smell the water soon. Signal the drovers. We're ready now." Two flags were displayed and waved on spear tip. The drovers took the herds forward at a run. They shouted their encouragement and the dust of their coming rose and spread on the wind. The red cloud moved before them masking the advance. The uneven line of approaching animals moved between the groups of warriors and families, each at its own pace like dark thunder clouds between mountains. The horse herds were running skittishly ahead. The cattle bawled as they ambled forward, while men shouted and dogs barked urging them on. Eagerly they ran for water. Ahead other eyes observed their run.

"*High van lar*, Animals, they're driving the animals forward. Stop them!" Kynan leaped from his carefully prepared ambush shouting above the rumble of the advancing herds. "Shoot now! Take out the warriors quickly before the dust hides them." The wind borne dust already obscured the charging figures and herds. The scattered volley of arrows from his startled mercenaries were deflected by the shields and armor of the Chipchaks who followed the drovers and herds. A few animals and men fell, but the torrent of animal flesh isolated the clumps of scattered enemy. They lost cohesion.

"*Hoo joose*, charge the hidden cowards!" Kynan screamed.

Gerchen and his captains with bent bows, charged the dismounted archers. On contact, they drew swords for the close work of hand to hand fighting. No mercy was shown and no prisoners were taken in Kynan's resisting troops.

Two companies of mercenaries retreated immediately and fled on horse beyond the deserted village. They were willing to serve, but not die for money. The drovers and their herds stopped beside the village and watered at the ford. The exhausted animals, quivering nervously, vented their fear in noise and milling about. Twozan rallied his reserves to keep the animals moving and protect them. Gerchen's men finished mopping up. They came up in small groups bringing the loot of armor and weapons with them.

"I'm ready for pursuit now. Give me some of your men and I'll track them down. Not one will escape!" Gerchen shouted excitedly as he rode up to Twozan, holding an extra sword.

"My men are needed for defense and herding. We must move quickly, it's not safe here." Twozan and his men were driving the animals south across the river, through the fields, and into the desert, using their nervous energy in activity. The herd having drunk their fill swam the water reluctantly.

"We can finish them off. They're on the run," Gerchen insisted.

"Let them live to tell of our escape and victory. They'll picture us bigger and better to justify their losses."

"It's weakness to show mercy now when we could finish them." Gerchen's face was dark with anger.

"It is folly to linger on the border where new troops may arrive while we're scattered. Get your men back here and across the river. Form a line between us and the south bank. Cover our rear."

PEOPLE, PLOTS & PLACES IN CHAPTER 11

Agaz bey: the hospital administrator is under surveillance.
Derk: continues his efforts to find the persons he needs.
Emperor of Uigurs: suspects outsiders and expects gifts.
Fatima: Yeet's sister appears for a dangerous mission.
Gerchen: seeks occasions for friction and domination.
Joseph: the novice is learning humble hospital service.
Kynan: defeated and foe escaped, he remains a prisoner.
Leyla: alone, gets attention from the contractor's son.
Mother: worries about Yeet, because of his pursuers.
Nooryouz: has a week of honeymoon luxury before trouble.
Onat: succeeds with his ventures and enjoys his triumph.
Sanjak: finds a week of rest, yet menace in the situation.
Seerden: has information about his prey passed to him.
Sevman: finds his illness a trial and the alternatives worse.
Tash: now spies on old comrades for his new master.
Twozan: meets angry criticism with calm logic.
Yeet: now finds life grim as dangers increase.

GLOSSARY:
Ahman, kadun:Drat it, woman; an expression of frustration.
bayan: lady; madam; a term of respect.
Bosh ver: never mind; it's nothing; pay no attention.
bosh ooze two nay: as you command; just as you say.
Dish arah ya git: get out; go outside.
Jinn: an evil spirit of great power in Islamic cultures.

FATIMA DEPARTS

The summer had wrought transformations in all the Kaya family who had healed and browned and in Yeet who had grown taller. He matched Leyla who looked less thin and tall to him now; she was starting to round out. The desert heat was mitigated by the work under the cliffs in the shade. The altitude kept the dry, thin air moving. Kardesh was now able to do some of the lifting of the slabs and blocks that they transported to a central area for customers.

Yeet could leave now. He had promised Sevman to return for him. A shipment of marble was prepared for the city and Yeet was chosen to dispatch it. The Kaya family made no objections. They knew the police wanted Kardesh. They also knew Yeet had friends in the police and was not in danger. He was the logical person to contact Sevman who must be well by now. Leyla cried in secret for her dear friend and gossip who would leave them, but the others were happy.

Yeet came in with a grim, stern face. In vain Leyla tried to engage him in conversation or at least in a fond farewell. His response was reserved and negative. Erben was at work and Tayze out. Yeet picked up a bit of food

Leyla had wrapped for the trip and took up a small bundle near the door as he left. He started the cart and was off down the road. She waved till he was a dot on the horizon.

She sensed someone watching her. She had felt this before. That boy Umer had taken to watching her as she worked. He was somewhere near, but she didn't want to meet his eyes. Leyla continued to stare at the road long after Yeet was out of sight. She prayed for a safe trip and a soon return. She knew her brother was again involved in something bad. What would happen next?

> - - - - - - - > SYR RIVER CROSSING >- - - - - - - >

"Form your companies you cowards. You won't be paid for running away! You're supposed to be professionals, show it now! Stop and reform!" Kynan was livid with rage. A bleeding slash trickled blood over his face and shirt. "*Do'er*, Stop, reform here." One *onbasha* raised a standard and mounted a small hill to be seen. Some of the riders moved toward him. Others continued to flee. But then another voice cut across the valley from the western hills.

"*Do'er*, stop, you're surrounded. Surrender in the name of the Caliph." Onat Bey, in red coat and white shalvar and turban, rode forward with his troops in six deep files. The companies formed a half circle around the village. The Caliphate had turned out the army.

"Go to hell! Back across the river everyone. Back!"

It was too late, they were scattered and too far away to hear any commands and past the discipline of obeying. Those who surrendered were taken away chained. Those who ran were chased, shot down and stripped. Hungry scavengers gathered where they fell. The work went on for several hours. Onat bey wished to free some of his men for pursuit, but the Toozlu were well to the south by that time. They were lost from sight, hidden under a blanket of dust as the evening breezes began, blotting out the horizon. There would be wounded and weary stock. Onat bey turned to his adjutant, "Find me a squad fresh enough to send after them," he demanded.

> - - - - - - - > KOKAND CITY >- - - - - - - >

Seerden sat in the warm Kokand City Inn room at the end of summer staring at the message bundle. He had visited every quarry and stone mason around the Fergana Valley. High mountains with cool water had been a welcome relief from the lowland heat. But all his traveling

128

had brought him no closer to his assigned prey. He sat in Kokand examining his evidence and waiting for some comment from his contact or a clue. He broke the bamboo strut and polished the white stone. He wrapped the long horsehair around his finger. He pulled the gray wolf hair apart and held it to the light.

Suddenly he grunted and picked off a hair from the underside of the mass. He scrutinized it, and then murmured to himself, "Their spying eye is at the quarry with the prince. They haven't been outside to get any message to my guide. This bundle must be the original sent to my contact and he added the wolf hair and money as a message to me. The woman's hair is accidental from the spy or the contact. It got mixed with the fur." He held the light gray hair up to the light, gloating. He still had the desert and mountains to the west to search. Too much time had passed. He waited for a guide to the family's hiding place. The boy, Yeet, should be seeking his friend soon. A well placed eye would have the details for him.

> - - - - - - - ->ROAD TO SYR RIVER BARRACKS >- - - - - - - >

Onat bey rode beside Kynan, his prisoner. Behind them among the guards rode the mercenary force in chains.

"You'll have your wish fulfilled, commander. You'll see the cities of the south. You'll even have an imperial escort and my company without payment." Onat laughed for joy as his horse capered, sharing his rider's mood.

Kynan shouted in frustration. "You came to me with lies and pretexts. You made a fool of me, deceived me for information."

Onat quipped. "When drink won't loosen men's lips, boredom will. A wise man bides his time." Onat laughed again.

"Why did you let the others escape? Why attack us first? Did they bribe you?" Kynan's confusion was complete.

"Nomads have right of passage in our lands. You were a band of armed men; an army within our borders, a challenge to the Caliph's dominion. You attacked the

129

nomads traveling with families and animals near the village. The nomads fought, the villagers fled, they were in danger of pillage. You are clearly striving to destroy our property."

"They're Chipchak warriors who hold my sister and her child hostage. We sought to free her." His anger showed in his red face.

"We have courts in our cities. You can have her back if your cause is just. It's too late to pursue them. They'll be investigated later. I promise to make it a personal matter." Onat bey smiled as he left his prisoner with his guard and galloped back to his captain.

"Have the men stop at the next village for the night. Tomorrow, leave those with slight wounds behind to heal. They can follow when the burial detail and seriously wounded men catch up. I'm pressing ahead to the inn on the main road with their leader. There's reward for all of us in this."

"What about the nomads, Binbasha? If some of the mercenaries convert and join us, shall I pursue them?"

"*Bosh ver*, nonsense, Yuzbasha. If you can spare three men, dress them like villagers and send them with produce to skirt the group and go to the nearest town. Report and return skirting the tribe again. Don't get too close. I don't want to lose men. They'll be angry and suspicious, but they'll have more contacts to the south, like it or not. But no fighting yet, it's better to run from them for now."

"*Bosh ooze two nay*, as you order Sir." The captain cheerfully replied touching his forehead.

"But not you, my fine Yuzbasha. I forbid you to join the three. You must stay and persuade the mercenaries and get them to the inn within ten days." Onat bey rode away chuckling at the Captain's sour expression.

> - - - - - - - > KOKAND RUG FACTORY >- - - - - - - >

Yeet was tired after his long trip, so he slept at the rented place and went to the rug factory to freshen up and rest before seeing Sevman. Before he entered his mother's room she had detected him.

"Come, my darling, give me a kiss. God caused you to remember me after the long hot summer." She reached out.

"Allah has given me his sun and air with blessings. The work was rough but honest." Yeet leaned down to kiss.

"I reach for your head and find shoulders. How strong you have grown." She felt the length of his tall thin body, back to front, top to bottom. She sighed and patted his chest approvingly.

He smiled affectionately. "The food and the work are simple, my friends are good and now Sevman will join us to speed his recovery."

"He will speed your death. The Kaya family is being searched out. There's an agent of the government here, Derk, who seeks you for questioning as well as the local police chief. Treasure and politics merge in Kardesh. I fear your involvement. Your uncle Harun sent word to remain hidden."

"Allah calls for bravery and loyalty in all His people. Kardesh has fed and protected me, I owe him."

"Sevman has not visited me. He's reported ill still. He's watched. They'll trace him to Kardesh."

"Then we'll lead them elsewhere." He shrugged.

"Sevman's people have immigrated to the Uigur country. He could join the exiles." She was hopeful.

"His heart has long since departed his community. It would be worse than torture to return him." He paused. "It might be better to let my sister contact him. She can visit the hospital without suspicion. They can arrange an escape by night."

His mother drew away. "I see no lessening of danger in such a move. I told Derk, the Caliph's agent, that Fatima is dead. He believed and won't check further I hope. I would die of mortification if he knew the truth. Things have changed. It'll be perilous. What if they catch you?"

He smiled. "I'll arrange everything. No one will suspect any tricks. We'll get him out in the blink of an eye."

"The presence of the Gray Wolf has been detected. He is on a hunt. I've been warned that he's on the trail. He has eyes everywhere. If he scents you he'll move in for the kill."

131

Yeet stared at her as she stopped knotting. "We must leave no trail. I'll move tomorrow. Thank you, Mother. I'll be careful. I won't stay at the rented place. Don't worry." He kissed her frown.

> - - - - - - - > KOKAND WIDOW'S HOUSE >- - - - - - - >

"I'm sure someone was at the house during the night, on the roof. It was after dark and there was no moon till early morning." The old neighbor woman's voice quavered.

Derk looked the woman over carefully. "You're sure it wasn't some beggar or itinerant?"

"Since the widow left no one has dared to come on the property, everyone knows it's forbidden. The police pass every day. The whole yard and house have been dug and prodded for hiding places of the treasure. I'm sure they took it with them or perhaps the widow took it. She left without a word of farewell, even though I was a faithful neighbor for five years." She shook her head in sorrowful disbelief.

"Did you visit the property to confirm your suspicions? You must have some proof of an intruder," he asked.

Her voice became low and confidential. She looked at the door. "The old bucket was damp the rope coiled in a new manner. I found tracks in the dust behind the house going to the roof. I think someone slept there." She stated.

"One person or two?" His eyes gleamed eagerly.

"Only one. I found dung in a corner, the wall was stained - a boy? There were a few crumbs, and a body impression on the roof. No one else stayed there." She smiled brightly, waiting expectantly.

"There was nothing else? No earth moved or dug?" She shook her head, adjusting the veil and cover.

"Only what you've heard. You promised a reward if I were vigilant. It's still early morning." She nodded wisely.

"Why didn't you send for me, immediately? You knew how important it is. I might have caught him." He sighed.

"I wasn't sure at first. Then I was afraid. A false alarm might anger you." She smiled apologetically, eyes sad.

"Nonsense, here's a silver coin. I'll give another one if we catch him. Keep watching the house. It must be our

132

secret." He patted her hand. She nodded knowingly. "When you find the person, let me know. I'm curious to know more. Promise you'll tell me." She got up with a sigh. He stood and turned to leave the house. "I'll go across the lane and look at the property now. No need for you to come. I know what to look for."

She accompanied him to the door fixed in the wall surrounding her meager property. The brass door knocker, a hand of Fatima, rested at chest level and the small door way was hardly the height of a man. He stooped to exit, just catching sight of a cloth bundle resting at the base of a fruit tree. It seemed to have been thrown there after he came in. She pushed the door shut behind him just as he turned to say his farewell. He touched the knocker, he heard muffled sounds, she seemed to be running. He knocked again.

"Bayan?" She didn't answer. He heard a distant sound behind the gate. She must be in the house. Derk looked at the mid-morning sun and across at the property entrance.

In the entrance he could see a narrow fresh footprint, small size. It was superimposed over the old woman's wandering steps, the larger prints. Forgetful of further investigation he started running toward the rug factory.

> - - - - - - - > UIGUR PALACE QUARTERS >- - - - - - - >

Sanjak sat on the divan staring at the floral patterned tiles that covered the walls. His face was solemn and preoccupied. Beside him were several pages of inventory listings. He sighed deeply and glanced at the pages. Behind him, a pale slender girl in brocaded silk approached. Seeing his lack of alertness, Nooryouz softly crept up and whispered,.

"It's a statue of the hero of the great rescue, meditating his next move, anxious to save the refugees from the vengeance of the Emperor. Would that it were alive to receive the thanks of his adoring public, or even such a one as I."

He turned his head, all smiles, to see her beauty. "Nooryouz, you imp, sneaking up and startling people. We've been here five days and no audience yet. I begin to worry."

She folded her hands on her breast, shook her head and puckered her lips, eyes twinkling. "Poor man, if he has no caravan to supervise, trips to make, people to council, goods to pack or distribute; he goes mad, staring at the wall and sighing for more activity." She laughed and without giving him a chance to speak, continued. "Sanjak dear, you never told me about the delights of a stop in a state rest house. We are well rewarded after our long journey and sacrifices." She blew gently on his ear. Causing him to laugh, spin and try to catch her, but she evaded him. He pursued her laughing, caught and kissed her.

"What are you holding in your hand?" He tried to see behind her. She resisted and spun away. Laughing, she held up a small zither triumphantly. "Look, the first I've seen in months. Now I'll play you something nice, something special." Nooryouz's bright little face shone with eager anticipation and she laughed as she strummed her zither. She picked the familiar love song with precise, swift fingers and sang softly:

NOORYOUZ' SERENADE

#1   Full moon shines high above my head.
                       I feel your presence. I sense your perfume,
                       Taste your sweet lips.
                       I hear your name, over and over again.

134

For you hold my heart.
I love you, I kiss you. I miss you, Oh come.
You must believe, Oh, hear the song of my soul.
You hold my heart. Yes, you do.

#2   In dreams I hear your voice so clear
We sing our love song. Poignant with mem'ries,
Sweet with our love.
Hear the refrain, over and over again,
For you hold my heart.
I'll feed you. I'll heed you. I'll need you always.
We'll thank God too, in everything that we do.
You hold my heart. Yes you do.

> - - - - - - - > KOKAND RUG FACTORY > - - - - - - - >

"Ahman kadan, darn it woman, I had to bribe the factory guards and girls to get in to see you. Why should you be ill today? You promised to help me save Yeet. I know he's in town, you must have seen him. Where is he? What will he do?" Derk yelled, staring at the yellow faced woman lying in bed.

"I had a seizure; a Jinn must have taken me, this morning after Yeet left. I told Yeet all you said to, he understands the danger. He remembers your help and all you taught him. He'll not go back to his summer's work."

"But you were supposed to tell me...but never mind, will he go to the hospital?" He stared at her. "Look me in the eye and tell me the truth." She nodded meekly.

"He won't go himself. It's too dangerous, but when Sevman is out they'll hide till it's safe to go back to Kardesh. He says they'll not go to Barmani in Tarim, Sevman doesn't want to return." Her eyes pleaded for belief and help.

"Swear by Yesu that you tell me the truth." She wrung her hands and pleaded. "He knows I tell the truth. Don't let the Gray Wolf get my precious." Tears appeared.

"Did he sleep at the widow's place last night?"

"He traveled part of the night, I think and came here first, at dawn. Then he left for town and the hospital. I took sick at mid-morning. The doctor came immediately. He's paid by the factory..."

135

Derk looked distraught. He broke in. "Who'll Yeet send to the hospital?" She looked up startled and mouth open seemed unable to talk. She blurted. "Fatima will go." Then she burst into tears. "I'm so ashamed, now you'll find out." She sobbed loudly.

"It's near noon, I must go to the hospital now, but I'll return this afternoon. We need to clear some things up." He left hurriedly.

> - - - - - - ->TOOZLU CLAN BEYOND THE SYR FORD >- - - - - - ->

"Keep those herds together we'll move all night. No camp and a cold supper for all. They may come after us." Twozan rode up and down the column repeating the orders.

At the end rode Gerchen sullen and aloof with his group of angry, complaining warriors. Their voices rose to a buzz like angry bees in a distant swarm as Twozan drew near. He eyed the men and they came up like wasps from a disturbed nest. Each hissed his anger and defiance.

"We're to run all night with our tail between our legs?" Dramatic gestures accompanied the words.

"Why did you yield before the enemy's attack?"

"Why choose the road to dishonor?" Each named fault echoed with angry men's growls. Twozan coolly sat on his lion-colored horse and listened impassively. Someone half-drew and slammed a sword in its scabbard. Horses whinnied restlessly.

"What dishonor in protecting tribe, family and herds? What yielding when we kill two for one and the enemy can't pursue? A beat dog runs for home, we advance in a strange land." Twozan's voice was calm, cold and logical.

"How you twist the truth! We travel all night, eat cold food and dodge an enemy, which you say can't pursue." Gerchen rode up to face Twozan, throwing the words in his face. "You didn't wet your sword. You rode away with her."

"Your men were the heroes. Why should I waste time in an attack you would order and perform so well? Do you think I didn't know what you'd do? I had to protect the hostage and flocks. Let each man enjoy doing his part."

"Then the victory's mine. I should've ordered the men to finish the job." The men were quiet now, listening.

"Tanra gave us the victory. We entered an ambush scattered and unprepared. Still we defeated them. Yet you cry out for more blood?"

Then, Twozan's voice became warm and friendly. "Rather we should have offered Tanra prayers of praise and thanksgiving."

"There is no glory in small victories. We could have had them all." Gerchen was not appeased.

Twozan laughed. "I can't believe you failed to notice the Abbassid troops west of the village. I could see their regiments in black cloaks, flying black standards. They moved on the fleeing mercenaries. They must have taken them all without trouble."

"We could have beaten the Abbassids while they were scattered."

"Would you have attacked the side that gives refuge and protects nomads?"

"Yes, all who raise the sword against us. We have bested them for two hundred years."

Setchken had ridden up unobserved. "In our territory, not in theirs." She interposed, tartly.

"Besides, they now use Turks as the mainstay of their army," Twozan argued, "Even their commanders. We may be meeting one soon. They'll come to investigate us. We need their friendship for passage."

Gerchen grimaced. "They'll try to convert us from Tanra to Allah and take away our favorite foods and drinks. They have even more rules and restrictions than Christians do."

Twozan shrugged laughing. "External rules or internal rules, neither is easy. More important is which is true."

Setchkin interrupted here. "The truth is that the herds and main body are well ahead of us and the rear guard has come to hear your talk. I have sick children and many responsibilities ahead and I hope I'm not alone there. You have families too. Goodnight warriors, may you live to fight again." She spurred her bright mare in a dash forward and the body of men followed slowly, talking among themselves.

> - - - - - - - > KOKAND HOSPITAL >- - - - - - - >

Fatima descended the cart inside the hospital gate an hour before noon. She was fastidiously dressed in shalvar and coat with a thin chador covering all. Even with all the cover, the careful attire and youth showed through. Her beauty was evident with touches of extravagance. The hospital staff stopped its normal routine to stare. She, a woman, contrary to custom, had driven the cart in, and alone! She enjoyed the sensation she made.

"How may we serve you Bayan?" Father Agaz spoke over her head being careful not to look directly at her.

"My brother Yeet has a friend here. He sends me to inquire as to his health." Her voice was soft and whispery.

"Yes, I remember your brother. He brought Sevman, the lame one, in the spring. He has healed and works in the garden." He motioned toward the back of the property.

"Shall I fetch him for you Bayan ...?" Joseph paused significantly, waiting for the name. Father Agaz nodded his approval.

"Fatima. My brother couldn't come. He will meet us. Please bring Sevman now." She stood calm and dignified while the staff moved into action.

"My brother left you gold, Reverend, in payment. Do I owe you more?" She inquired softly. He paused considering.

"He has worked for food, but there is the opium and other medicines owed. A small silver coin should suffice." He spoke apologetically. "He got the habit for a while, but he's cured now. The desire will still be in him. You must guard him. Keep him busy and among friends. He broods over his loss and is withdrawn and morose. We can't cheer him up."

"I will tell my brother all you say. He has sent a small gold coin as payment and contribution for your work in honor of Yesu. May His blessings be yours." She held out the coin and dropped it into the priest's open palm.

Sevman was brought up on a small hand pulled vegetable cart. The boy got out with help, but he could not walk erect; he crept like an old man with bent knees and a foot was turned in.

"Sevman, Yeet will meet you soon, but you must come with me. I'm Fatima his sister. I have heard all about you. You will drive the cart. We must hurry." He was astonished as they placed him in the cart with the reins.

Fatima sat behind griping the sides as he drove off. She started to laugh wildly and unrestrained as Sevman whipped up the horses driving on the heat-cleared street like a charioteer in a race. Dust blotted out the cart to the watching priest.

Behind them one of the mesmerized staff uttered a cry of alarm, and started after the cart. Then realizing its headway he turned and ran back toward the mosque. Father Agaz frowned. He motioned Joseph to follow the man. A secret agent had reacted to the escape too late.

> - - - - - - - >KOKAND MANICHEAN MONASTERY> - - - - - - - >

The figure was among the rocks on the hill outside Kokand, beside the confiscated property of the Manicheans.

"They should come soon. I'm sure this is the day. I feel it." Tash had told himself the same thing all week.

Tash munched the stolen bread and wondered at the negligent way the local army unit occupied the buildings within the walls. During the summer the gardens had shrunk in size and the weeds appeared. The previously clean buildings were stained with dust, dirt and filth. The chapel housed the horses. The men occupied the nuns' rooms and the well house door was open to the sun and wind. The hospital was foul-smelling and full of flies. The door sagged open, one leather hinge was torn.

The waning heat of autumn brought the smell of ripening grapes from the vineyard. A number of soldiers lazed or napped under the vines enjoying the fruit. The gate guards were among them. Who would want to trespass on a cavalry unit? Why bother guarding the gate?

In the distance a cart came quickly on. The horses were dusty and sweating, but walked briskly. The occupants were laughing and talking animatedly. Suddenly they quieted. They came to the gate and passed through it unobserved toward the rocks where the figure of Tash had now hidden.

> - - - - - - - > KOKAND JAIL > - - - - - - - >

"All of you let the boy escape. The woman drove off with him. The hospital was the easiest assignment you could have, you scavenger dogs. You ought to have moved when the woman spoke his name. How could you let that Wigler pig get away, you donkey bastards." Ali bey was in a rage and his agents cowered.

One plucked up his courage. "Ali bey, you required secrecy. The Christian Father was not to know of our surveillance. To reveal our informant would lead to his discharge and ..."

Ali's glare silenced him. "You could see into the grounds from the mosque. You're supposed to be alert for messages or visitors when the hospital is open. She drove the cart right in! No, you have failed and will be sent out to village assignments for a year at reduced wages."

"But Ali bey, what about the pursuit? They must have easily caught them..." The spokesman started and broke off.

"*Soos*, silence, get out! All of you! I don't want to see any of you here again!" They left eagerly.

> - - - - - - - > UIGUR PALACE >- - - - - - >

Sanjak bowed deeply on his hands and knees before the great Emperor of the Uigurs. He, like those in power farther east, followed the strict protocol and ceremonies of absolute rulers. So, Sanjak remained thus prostrate until his name at last was called. Then he sat back on his heels, knees still on the floor. He found himself staring into two pair of arrogantly intrusive eyes; the Emperor and his first minister. Their faces were like masks of marble, rigidly still, but lines of cruelty and dissipation were etched there.

"You bring criminals escaping the Tang justice: deviant religious groups and bearers of illicit treasure robbed from temples and churches. We have communication from our agents. We have watched your movements. The news of your coming has preceded your caravan. You bribed your way into our kingdom. Those who pretend resident rights have paid you to deliver them to our city. Why have you done this?" The minister accused.

"My Lords, you have been badly informed. Have you spoken to the merchants who we delivered from confiscation and ruin by the Tang? Who are your enemies, sires? Are they the Turks of the North or the Han Emperor in the East? Those Tang whom your people, the Uigurs, helped to return to their lost throne are showing gratitude in a strange way. I have saved many of your people as well as my own." He watched their expressions.

Hot anger escaped the Emperor's control. "The Kirghiz are Turks of the north, they hold our ancient lands and capital. The Seljuk oppose our moves west in the hire of Islam. The southern people: Ghazinevy, are a bastard mix of fighting mountain clans and Turk renegades. Why should we trust a barbarian Turk?" Their faces were implacable; Sanjak saw no hint of regard or leniency.

"You will have received offers of reward from Changan. They believe that many of the refugees have treasure. They regret our expulsion. The Uigur merchants are very rich, but they are your people. Their riches are part of your strength. Will you give that to the Tang? As for the others they go farther west. We paid the required border deposit. It's part of your treasure. You leave us as impoverished beggars if you hold us here. What merit can that win for you before the Yesu of light?"

"It would not be honorable to have you return east to Changan, but we must have a fee. The food you are using must be paid for. We can't provide any free. You have some young men and women in your caravan that could be sold to gain the passage money you need. We would do the business transaction for you, give them to us." Their greed showed.

"These youth are our guards, without them we'd be pillaged by the weakest robbers in your kingdom."

"Give up the girls then. There is a handful of beauties and one's like a princess. We want her." Their expressions changed and the tone had become cordial, wheedling.

"Nooryouz is my wife. She is granddaughter to a former Umayyad ambassador sent after the battle of Talas. The family became merchants when the Muslim Empire became Abbassid and the grandfather replaced. They have lived with the Han people for over a hundred years. The other girls are spoken for or married. You can't take them. Why should refugees pay? Yesu requires mercy for the needy."

"Go then, we'll consult the council and see if your rulers will ransom you." The tone was cold, final.

COURT INTERVIEW

141

PEOPLE, PLOTS & PLACES IN CHAPTER 12

Ali bey: wants to find the treasure and people get hurt.
Ayshe: finds life hard, food sickening, duties exhausting.
Barmani: passed a busy summer at Aksu and prospers.
Dahkool: Mountain Rose serves Uigur palace ladies.
Jon: the East Hun moved into Manish's home to free Noor.
Kemeer: shows his skill as a wrestler to win, yet loses.
Kynan: taken to prison by Onat bey at the Kokand base.
Manish: has a cousin in the palace who can contact Noor.
Marium: the priest's wife is a pleasant help at all times.
Nooryouz: enjoyed the Uigur capital, but can't leave.
Onat: brings a prisoner and gets reports from Tash.
Sanjak: changes from leader to prisoner and exile.
Setchkin: finds much to think about in the land of Islam.
Tash: reports his findings and is rewarded.
Twozan: encounters yet more problems in leadership.

GLOSSARY:
Allah Shukoor: thank God; praises be; said in relief.
Aye yup: scandalous; shameful; brazen.
de kot: attention; precaution; take care.
Dish arah ya git: get out of here; leave; go outside.
em dat: emergency; help; I need you.
esharp: a scarf for covering the head; a sign of modesty.
esh tut: take a partner; hold a companion; an equal.
hoo juze: charge; have at them; let's get them.
hoe'sh geldin iz: happily you've come; glad to see you.
hoe'sh bul duke: happily we found you; glad to be here.
pesh ami barak: stop following me; quit it.
soos: hush; quiet; don't talk.

SANJAK'S ARREST

"Nooryouz, where are you?" Sanjak rushed through the state guest house calling. The guards were not present at the gate. Inside there were no servants. The house so full and attended when he had left was empty. Her meager supply of clothes were also gone. While he called and searched a troop of special guard marched up to the main door. Two held bows at ready, while the others advanced.

"*Dekot*, attention, Sanjak Bey." The Yuzbasha called out his name as a soldier moved to each side and took his arm. He screamed and fought, but he was surrounded by the whole troop and subdued with truncheons and chains.

The captain addressed the prostrate, body. "I'm to escort you and the refugees to the western border. The Emperor has shown mercy and heard your plea." Sanjak groaned and muttered her name, shaking his head.

"Don't worry about the woman. The granddaughter of an Umayyad ambassador has a better destiny. The Abbassid usurpers would not receive her with honor. Here she has a great future. The Emperor will see to an appropriate match." The prisoner started thrashing, calling, but was held.

"The Uigur merchants, who came in the caravan, have a good opinion of you. They have financed your food and all expenses. You can't escape. I have your horse here. We will immediately leave , but be warned: a return to the capital is forbidden. It would cost your life."

> - - - - - - - > SOUTH OF THE SYR RIVER   >- - - - - - - >

Ayshe took the empty skin and started to the water hole. A man on horseback came from behind the tent and rode slowly behind her. She

143

glanced at him. It was the man who followed her the day she had walked into the camp. She had seen him every day following her with his eyes. She felt him now, every nerve felt him. She knew his name was Kemeer, he was a champion wrestler. He had lost his wife with the coughing disease the year before. His mother kept the Yurt and the children for him.

At the spring she filled her skin bottle and nervously turned to face him. She put her hands on her hips and frowned, forcing her voice to hardness. "Have you no duties, that you must follow me? *Pesh ami barak*, Stop following me!"

A smile of contentment spread on his face. Her Chipchak was improving, and he liked her spirit. "My yurt needs water, it's a woman's job, but I have no woman, my mother tires." He swung a skin bottle off the back of his horse. He followed, lightly moving his strong frame down. He confidently towered over her.

"You think me a slave. You treat all of us like your animals: cattle in your fields to breed and kill as you please." Her voice was cold.

He laughed and shrugged. "Farmers don't realize how smart and decent animals are. They have much to teach us. Life with the herd is freedom not slavery. Your people keep only a few, isolated, kept from the herd. They are enclosed in huts by night, on ropes by day, away from the crops. You hold them in contempt."

"What would a herd animal teach me?" she sneered.

"When the young heifers come into heat they crowd into a circle facing the bull, cavorting and bawling to get his attention. When he reacts to their scent and actions they turn and walk away slowly with their tail slightly raised. The herd is enlarged, needs are meet."

"*Aye yup*, shameless, vulgar man!" She stormed at him and turning she grabbed up the skin and lifting it to her shoulder moved away. Her body swayed under the burden. His laugh followed her as he filled his own water skin. Then his voice cut her into a run.

"Aren't you lifting the tail just a bit now?"

> - - - - - - - > CAMP BEYOND THE SYR RIVER > - - - - - - - >
"Why waste a day here at this spring?" Kemeer asked Twozan irritably. But the tribal leader was tranquil.

"We're between villages and water is precious. We must slaughter and dry the excess stock and give the healthy ones a chance to recover. Your mother needs time to recover. The old need rest like the children."

Kemeer nodded sighing: "Rest for the women and children, sport for the men. We need to show our skills."

Twozan laughed and pounded Kemeer's back. "You need a rival as much as a wife. I hear the Right-hand Clans have a first rate wrestling champion. I'll bet my gold on you. Will you fight tonight?"

Kemeer smiled proudly. "I'll be the first to strike and the last to stand. Just show me the man and let us begin."

> - - - - - - - >UIGUR CAPITOL>- - - - - - - >

Jon watched the guards escorting the westerners away from the city. Sanjak was in chains and irrational. The Uigurs were polite, but firm, only the recognized Manichaean merchants and workers could remain. One of the herders was a poor Manichae, Manish. Jon was invited to his family hut. The soldiers paid no attention to young drovers. But all other travelers were hustled on their way. Jon made plans.

"Noor will need a message from us. Sanjak needs one too. We'll send a message to Yusuf Bey. He's in the caravan, but will not be guarded as strictly. He'll find a way to get it to him."

Manish nodded agreement. "I've a friend who writes Uigur."

Jon gave the negative head rise. He thought a moment. Yusuf bey reads Syriac, and Chinese ideographs. We need one of those. I'm Hunnish, but I never learned to write it." Jon shook his head in perplexity.

"We can find a scribe for any language near the law courts." Manish asserted.

"But could we trust one of them?"

"How could we get even a whispered message to either of them, and how could they be sure it was your word and not a deception?"

Jon shook his clenched fist. "I'll use a sign or personal item to confirm the message. Hide something special in a bag. We can send one to Sanjak through Yusuf bey."

Manish dropped his reserve, grinning. "You can get a bag to Noor by this relative of mine, a girl with a divided lip. She was sold to the palace. Dahkool has freedom to visit the kitchen and gardens. It'll be easy to get news through by her."

Jon smiled back. "I've just the things to send each of them."

> - - - - - - - > AKSU VALLEY MONASTERY >- - - - - - - >

Father Barmani retired to the roof of the convent building. He had begun a fast two days before, the first since his departure from Kokand. He sat meditating on the changes since they began their travels. He remembered the struggles on the road, how hard the passage of the mountains had been, even in summer. Now the emperor of the Uigurs had assigned him a temple with garden

145

grounds on the lower hills near Aksu, a town and caravansary. Troops were stationed here. Here caravans prepared to cross the high mountains to the Caliph's domains. It was a vital strategic center from which his influence would spread. It was right that heaven should so reward his faithful ones, himself, Barmani, among them. He could anticipate the growth of his buildings and followers as he continued to set the example of living in the light for those in darkness.

He reviewed in his mind the arrival of his exhausted band; living on the charity of the villages. The captain of the guards had immediately dispatched notice to the capitol. The court had made the assignment of the old convent where a few refugees and nuns had a camp. Under his enthusiastic guidance the property and grounds had been repaired and pruned for winter. Food would be short, but a quick garden had been planted to take advantage of the last warm days. Now the moment of rest, prayer and purification had come, he knelt.

"Blessed be Mani, bearer of the truth of Yesu. Blessed be the Lord of light who guides his people to a land of refuge. Thrice blessed be the teachings that free us from the power of the demiurge. The God of the Hebrews created this world of death and corruption. I pray for the prosperity of our community and nation. I pray for Sevmani left behind in the Fergana Valley. May he be healed of his afflictions and freed from the deceitfulness of riches. Let him return to the light; to the feet of Yesu in repentance. Heal his doubts. Though his body be weakened and destroyed let his soul be free of the bondage of rebirth and corruption. Let him return and remain in the light forever. I ask this in the name and resurrection power of Yesu." Barmani fell silent, but continued kneeling before the image of Mani, whose right hand held the burning flame.

> - - - - - - -> CAMP SOUTH OF THE SYR RIVER >- - - - - - ->

The men were stripped for combat. Each wore only a belted loincloth that held them in tightly. Both were powerful men who looked fat, but were all muscle. Those muscles now drew tight with power as they strained against each other. Fierce frowns marred their normally placid looks.

Twozan sat on a kind of couch that was placed on the rugs that marked the outer edge of the field of conflict. Three sides were filled with excited men and one with a dense crowd of women and smaller children. Setchkin sat near Twozan's divan, Ayshe, Marium and warriors' wives crowded behind her. All twittered with excitement. Children darted screeching through the crowd. Ayshe was all eyes. This was a new experience for her.

146

Each man made several throws. They were well matched, but to win the shoulders must touch ground for a count of three. Both struggled to hold the other down, but without success. Then Kemeer slipping in got a hold on the opponent's leg lifting it and twisting the foot up. He threw his weight in a body block. The Right Hand's famous champion was thrown off balance and fell on his back. His breath was expelled by the force of the fall and the impact of his opponent's body, The champion gasped and pushed in vain. Kemeer's weight and determination held him.

The roar of the crowd approved the surprise. Gerchen was up screaming at his champion to escape the oppressive bulk of Kemeer.

The arbitrator was counting. While the women shrilled ululating victory cries, except Ayshe who stood hypnotized. The third count sent the men into a frenzy of shouting. Gerchen was screaming curses, livid with rage.

The men hoisted the bulky Kemeer, still stripped, to their shoulders and balanced him with supporting arms and hands. They paraded around the camp to finally stop before the kumiss bags of fermented mare's milk, set out for the celebration.

> - - - - - - - >UIGUR PALACE HAREM >- - - - - - - >

"The gardener has sent you flowers madam." Dahkool, a slave, displayed the mass of late fall chrysanthemum flowers in a kitchen pot. My friend outside the wall sent these. He begs your pardon for using the old kitchen pot to hold them. He had nothing else to gather them in." She placed them at Nooryouz feet.

"The flowers are lovely. The pot is poor work from the east like we used in the caravan. Take it back to the giver and say I'll not have it inside the wall again."

HAREM PRISONERS

147

Nooryouz haughtily turned her back on the girl and the flowers. "Come fix my hair and tell me the latest gossip from the kitchen." She reclined on the divan with her head on the edge, hair trailing the floor.

"There's much speculation about you, my lady, outside the walls. People view you kindly. Boys who sleep at tent doors wonder how you bide."

Nooryouz stretched lazily. "I dream of friends and my travels. Life is good inside the wall, for winter comes. Flowers will return in the spring. Jon...quills will come early then, I know."

"You are watched closely, lady, even by a few of your friends from the caravan." The slight serving girl with the harelip worked whispering as she leaned over the now seated Nooryouz braiding her hair and arranging the coils in the Uigur fashion.

Nooryouz nodded agreement. She held up the polished bronze mirror frowning. She whispered. "Some are ready to leave life and love in the caravan for the luxury of court. Ease and beauty now deceive their minds. I cannot include them in my plans. Since you bear messages you want freedom too, we are together, Dahkool. I must be angry now, forgive me." She shook her head impatiently, pulled the pins from the arrangement and walked away disdainfully as the braids fell below her shoulders. She went to another servant whom she knew to be making reports to the eunuchs. She spoke loudly and scornfully. Dahkool looked shocked an instant and then composed her face. She sadly took up the pot of flowers and walked toward the kitchen.

"The ugly one hasn't the touch. You try it." The smiling servant bowed, smirking triumphantly as she set to work.

> - - - - - - - > KOKAND ARMY BASE > - - - - - - - >

Onat bey took his prisoner to the Kokand army barracks. He had no intention of turning him over to the police. As he rode through the main gate, he saw Tash leaning against the opposite wall obviously waiting. He slowed and stared hard at the tall, gangling youth. He lowered his head just a bit and leaned over and spoke to the guard. Then he continued on to the command building while Tash moved past the gate and followed in a casual, nonchalant way. Before the building Onat drew up and waited. Kynan, the prisoner, sighed, but said nothing.

"I waited for the little dogs at the old Manichae building," Tash reported. "Yeet met him there and they went east for a day then, south for another day. After that they went through the hills southwest into the desert. They

148

took the road to the Black Hills Quarry. No one else uses that road, so I left to get back as soon as possible."

Onat bey nodded approvingly. "I understand a girl took him from the hospital. What happened to her?"

"She went into a deserted building behind the hill and stayed there. Yeet took Sevman on almost immediately. So I followed them." Tash paused thoughtfully and continued. "I hope you get Kardesh and his dad. They'll have hid the treasure. But I'll keep searching here. I have sharp eyes."

"There are many treasures that can't be held in the hand, or even weighed." Onat smiled at the boy. "You're too young to know that yet." He took a silver coin out of his sash and handed it to him, dismissing him immediately. "Your quarters await you, Kynan Bey. Follow me."

> - - - - - - - > TOOZLU CAMP > - - - - - - - >

"Ashe, the children cry. Get to them girl. Can't you hear them?" Setchkin called as she came out of the tent with the baby on her hip and walked to the next tent entrance. There Ayshe lay groaning and moving her arms restlessly. She shielded her face from the flame of the torch Setchken held over her head. Her face was drawn and had turned a pale yellow hue.

"We rode all night after drying the meat, but you had all this night to rest. What'll we do with you? You're too delicate for travel hardship." Setchkin looked her disgust at her maid.

"She's too ill to help. Let her alone. I'll take care of the children." The priest's wife had come up behind her. Setchken whirled to see the kindly face of Marium.

"You spoil the girl, besides you don't know their language and they know only ten words of Chipchak."

"Your baby knows even less, yet I manage with him. There is God's love language that all understand." Marium pointed. "Go to bed girl, and you too, noble lady. Tomorrow will be no less strenuous. I'll take the baby so you can sleep." She took the child from the annoyed, unresisting Setchken. She went into the children's tent and walked to the whimpering children. One looked very pale and still. She started a slumber song patting and singing. She sat on a rug with legs extended and laid the baby on top of her legs, his head against her feet. She rocked him from side to side. These were her words.

149

#1
Slumber umber, sing and play.
First light comes and then the day.
Sleep is good, awake is better.
Love of sleep is like a fetter.

#2
Slumber umber sleep away,
Night is now and then comes day
Dark is good, but light is better.
Tiredness comes like changing weather.

#3
Slumber umber, grow by play,
Stretch your soul to mind each day
Dreams delight, they rest you better.
Quiet sleep will heal all matters.

Slumber Song

Slum - ber um - ber sing and play.
First light comes and then the day.
Sleep is good, a - wake is bet - ter.
Love of sleep is like a fet - ter.

>- - - - - - -> UIGUR MONASTERY, AKSU >- - - - - - ->
"*Hoe sh gel deniz*, a happy welcome." Father Barmani bowed
slightly and smiled. Yusuf bey, now in charge of the refugee
column, bowed respectfully, ignoring the Uigur soldiers, escorting
him.
"*Hoe sh bold duke*, Happily we find you. Unfortunately, we may
have arrived too late to travel over the Mountains of God to the
West."
"It's a hard journey, I came from there many months ago. It's a
troubled land. How sad that you must depart..." Barmani saw the
impatient frown on the Lieutenant's face and broke off his

condolences. "Enough talk, your men must be exhausted. You have pressed on from the Capitol and need rest before facing the mountains." He motioned toward the open gate behind him. "Come we have food prepared awaiting your arrival." Barmani stepped aside and others led the men and animals forward.

The Lieutenant stood beside him as the carts and mules moved into the grounds. A small company of horses rode past with a chained, dazed man riding in the midst of the soldiers. He looked to neither side and seemed to be unaware of what went on around him. The lieutenant stared at the passing man and spit on the ground. "What fools men are to give their hearts." He growled to his austere companion. "Women go where face and fortune carry them. Men should take what's offered them and be glad. My parents got me one I can keep. It's sensible, she expects children, not love."

Barmani looked contempt at the speaker. "The world was created through lust by demon powers. You reflect their nature and passion." He drew himself up proudly. "To become light in this dark world, you must free yourself from the powers of violence and lusts. The elect liberate themselves from the present world. All followers of Mani should do the same." He turned and entered the gate, leaving the commander alone to murmur his response.

"You fill fun's place with an ascetic's pride and snobbery, poor fool!" Concluded the lieutenant bitterly to the air, "but you'll never know what you miss." He spat again and turned to enter the monastery grounds.

> - - - - - - - >TOOZLU CAMP BETWEEN THE RIVERS >- - - - - - >

The funeral was brief following the proscribed pattern: death in the night, discovery in the morning, interment in the afternoon. The farmer's child was thin and shriveled; he had not liked the new food. The herders thought he had come to them ill. Only the priest and the farming children came with Ayshe and Setchkin. The service was a mix. One by one each had their part. The farmer children led by Ayshe repeated some Muslim prayers. The priest prayed for rest for the soul of an innocent. Setchkin put some dried flowers on the grave. Then she herded the children to the camp. Only Ayshe, pale and sickly, remained beside the grave.

The last light flickered in the west and the camps fires reflected on the hills. A horse came slowly out of the brush toward the grave. She looked up startled. Kemeer sat calmly watching her quizzically. He said nothing. She drew herself up and tried to look dignified. She tried to stare him down, but he just sat unsmiling waiting.

"Why do you come around here? You aren't wanted. The child meant nothing to you. Go away," she wept.

"It's late. The name of the Princess Setchkin won't get you past the skulkers and shadow dwellers. Those who sleep by day and rove by night will be out of their caves seeking prey. We've doubled guards. Villagers too, come to spy on us and take an animal or two." His voice was soft.

"You might lose a slave?" She queried sharply, drawing her *esharp,* scarf over her head.

"*Esh tut,* take a partner, gain a friend." He followed her walk toward the camp. The horse almost touched her back. She thought of the first night she had walked into camp. Her loss stung her heart. She stumbled.

"You could ride if you wished." She ignored him. He rode beside her and reaching down pulled her up to sit behind him. She shrieked, but clung to his back when she almost fell. He smoothly moved his great, lion horse from walk to a lope, eating away at the distance to camp.

Suddenly two figures rose from the hip-high brush before them. One held a club, the other a sword. Some ten feet behind them another two figures rose, they showed no weapons. No one spoke, but all stood at ready.

"Tanram, Tanram!" Kemeer muttered under his breath. He drew his sword and swerved his horse right, away from the first two men. They stood transfixed, for a full second, before starting to close the distance. As Kemeer pounded past them, the man with the club threw it at the back of the rider. Ayshe, hunched and clinging with all her might, felt the wind whistle above her and Kemeer's grunt as the weapon struck a glancing blow on his head and left shoulder. Then the men were behind them now. Two more remained blocking them from the camp.

"*Ahman, Tahnrum,*" Kemeer's scream shocked her as he rose on his stirrups and tried to stop his galloping steed. His body bent double and swept her off the back of the horse. A small stunted tree to the left snapped in two and the top came flying toward them. The taut rope whipped around, wrapping itself about their stunned forms. The horse had passed under the rope and he continued to run toward the camp. Ayshe had fallen clear of Kemeer, but found herself in agony, unable to get her breath. Weaponless and shocked, she did not see the men close in on Kemeer. "*Yesu gel,* God help me," she heard him cry. Then she heard the clash of iron.

The man who threw the club leaned over her, a knife in hand. He darted the knife toward her throat. She screamed and pushed his hand away. "Please, don't kill me," she cried in the village dialect.

The man slowly lowered his knife. "You're a village girl? We thought you were tribal. Are you their slave?" He scanned her face in the dusk. "Come, you can cook for us. We need a woman."

A scream of pain distracted the talker. Turning he saw the swordsman fall, his neck pouring blood. The two backup men had closed in with spears and shields. One pushed a shield at Kemeer. The pointed boss bore in the shoulder, while the other thrust at Kemeer's side. He fell. They roared, gloating in triumph.

"Foxes in the calves' pen, get them men!" The sound of galloping horses came vibrating through ground and air. "*Hoo juze*, charge. Kill the bandits!"

"Run! We have a cave under the hill." Her captor gestured toward a looming prominence. He grabbed her wrist and pulled her up into a shambling run. The two men had picked up some of the rider's gear and were running away. As they came near one flung a provision bag at her companion and continued to run. He caught the bag and dropped her arm as they continued to the edge of the brush where the action started.

Then, she stopped running and looked back. Kemeer had not moved. The riders from the camp were drawing near him. Uncertainty gripped her heart.

KEMEER'S FALL

153

PEOPLE, PLOTS & PLACES IN CHAPTER 13

Ali bey: learns of his enemies' plans to attack the Toozlu.
Ayshe: has to make a life shaping, vital choice.
Dahkool: keeps busy making plans to escape the harem.
Erden: angered that the help sent to his brother is lost.
Jon: is present to help in the harem escape.
Kaplan: the tiger faults the khan's twin; blames the Toozlu.
Karga: finds fault with the neighbor's security and police.
Kynan: prisoners have time to think and plan escapes.
Manish: a Manichae donkey boy helps Jon's refugees.
Maril: wants to escape the harem to go home to Baghdad.
Mother: gets many visits, one from a Gray Wolf for truth.
Nooryouz: runs a risk for her husband's unborn child.
Seslee: unable to face danger for the freedom she craves.
Tash: reports on his master's plans to his rival.

GLOSSARY

bana yetish: Help me; Give me a hand.
ba rak: Leave me alone; stop it; quit.
de kot: be careful; attention.
do'er: stop; don't go.
em'dot: help.
heidi kuz: Hi girl. Hello girls. Come on girl.
Kim'oh: Who's there? Who is it?
Ne var: What is it? What's wrong? How are things?
Ne'rede? : Where?
Tanram: my God; Sometimes repeated as a war cry.
Yesu gel: God help us! Come, Jesus.
u kar ah da: up above; up there.

MATTRESS REFILLS

"*Kim oh*, who's there? Don't play tricks, I know you're there at the door way. Answer me." Her voice grew more agitated, but her hands continued to knot the rug. Exasperated with the lack of response, she railed at the presence, her voice piercing and angry.

"You are not Yeet or my supplier, they respect my limitations. You are not a thoughtless child, I can tell by the sound of the boards and your breath." She paused. The breath had become a quiet pant like that of a dog. Then her hands paused, a whimper rose to her lips. "Like the sound of a wolf!" She breathed urgently, "What business have you with the likes of me?" she waited.

"Tell me where to find Fatima." A whisperer panted a reply.

She held her head in her hands. "She rents the corner house with the blue door, in the red lantern district above the market fountain. When she works... she's gone a lot, they tell me. She travels... please don't hurt her, she is too daring... she knows no shame." She paused to listen. The panting had ceased.

The presence had somehow lessened. With a shuddering sigh she turned to the loom, her hands resumed tying knots and her lips moved in silent prayer. 'Praise Yesu, I've passed from death to life. Will he return?'

> - - - - - - - > UIGUR PALACE HAREM>- - - - - - - >

The circle planning the escape was small and select: Only a few of the most trustworthy and determined shared a part in the attempt. One was Dahkool, the servant who could contact the workers, guards and kitchen people. Nooryouz was the mover and energy behind the effort. Her friend, Maril, was from back home in Changan. They included the enthusiastic Seslee, who was parted from her exiled family. She was the most likely to betray the plans by body language and the changes of attitude. Because of the heightened excitement she conveyed, security was increased. The doleful, sad captive had suddenly been transformed. Guards were alerted and doubled.

Jon, the donkey boy, had remained working in the city with Manish, waiting to contact his friend, Noor. They all waited in vain for instructions from Sanjak. After a month Nooryouz could wait no longer. A palace midwife physician would terminate any detected fetus. She could, with friends help, fake one or two pretended periods. But too many risks were involved to permit a long wait. Urgency was required.

> - - - - - - - > UIGUR PALACE COURT YARD >- - - - - - - >

The mattress men were working diligently with several guards watching with interest. The harp like bow was held against the arm and a string was vibrated with a small mallet as the wool was moved into contact with the string. The lumps of matted wool seemed to dissolve into lustrous piles of fiber, softened for winter comfort in the newly restuffed mattresses and divans. Eunuchs carried the mattresses out of the side gate to the corner near the rose garden. Dahkool and another servant carried out the round ottomans to empty and stuff again, piling them at random near the wall.

The working men tried to strike up a conversation with the servant girls, but were ignored.

"*Haydi Kuz, Ne var*? Hi girl, how are things?" The girls worked with their noses in the air although Dahkool did giggle once and cast a second glance at a young guard.

The working men exchanged looks. The mattress workers smirked as the girls left and started teasing comments among themselves.

"Must be nice sitting around guarding a gate, entertaining the ladies, eating palace food."

"Wish I had the family connections to get a job here in the palace."

"I'd like to get a shot at the new girls."

"Easy work!"

While the young talked, one old workman sat stuffing the divans. He smiled slyly as his hand felt a small bag with metal coins hidden in the inside corner of the leather cover. The day had come. The last payment was in his hands. All was ready. Soon he'd retire for a very comfortable winter.

> - - - - - - - BETWEEN THE RIVERS >- - - - - - - >

Ayshe strained her eyes to see through the dust and dark. As she paused surveying the landscape, a rough hand grabbed her neck and the wounded spear man pulled her aside.

"*Bana yetish*, help me. That devil cut my spear shaft and drove his sword through my shield. I'm wounded." He leaned upon her, panting, his shoulder bled profusely. She came round in his powerful arm and pushed a part of her head scarf in the wound and ripped part of it to bind the wound. He kept his grip on her neck and pushed her.

"We must go to the cave. Come, we need help." He put his good shoulder on hers and staggered forward. She bore the weight and steadied his progress. In time they arrived at the cave. The other three were there huddled together waiting. The man she met first came forward to take her arm. He pushed the wounded man back toward the wall.

"I caught her first. She belongs to me. I may let you have her sometimes, but I'll call the shots." He glared at the other men. They glared back as tension rose.

"You are the donkey who decided to attack some tribesmen. If we hit farmers going to market, you get their goods. Get them going home you get money and other supplies. Tribesmen give wounds."

CAVE DWELLERS

157

"I'm in charge here. You've prospered with me."

"We were routed out of our mountain top because of your over-confidence. You left a trail," the wounded man said. His rope hauling companion shouted out an accusation: "We lost two men and our old cook to the police last month."

"Ali bey beheaded our men."

"The woman lost her hand. You've lost your nerve."

The youngest spoke timidly. "We huddle in the cave and go hungry. I wanted to steal sheep, but you insisted on attacking the burial party."

"They wore gold, they have horses. We'd lost ours with the fort. It was a natural target." He still held her arm and she grimaced from the pressure. She took off her thin gold bracelet given by the wrestler on his victory, threw it to the man who had blocked their path. She spat, "I was a slave. That's all my riches. Take it! You waited too late to strike. You got a slave and a warrior," she laughed bitterly. They listened stunned as she continued. "You missed the princess. She wears enough gold to make you rich. But they would have killed all of you. I've seen them fight. They killed my mother... all my village." She shuddered, sobbed convulsively and then she cried. He let go her arm and tried to put a comforting arm about her.

"You're one of us now. We won't always live in a cave. It takes time to get back on our feet. Here take back your bracelet we'll win more." He grabbed the thin circlet from his companion and pushed it roughly on her arm, patting her.

She wriggled out of his grasp and pushed him away. "You all need food and rest. You said you needed a cook. What do you have to cook?" Ayshe walked toward some bags hung against the wall. The wounded man kicked a bag nearby and indicated a recessed, draped wall with his chin. "Flour here, meat hanging in the cool room, metal pans and oil near the fire."

She moved around to each place. "I'll cook after I clean that wound and change the bandage. We'll use oil on the cloth so it won't stiffen or stick." Three men nodded agreement. Only one made a face.

> - - - - - - - > KOKAND ARMY CITADEL >- - - - - - - >

Kynan stood at the upper window, watching the change of the guard carefully. He could not see all the posts of course, but he was astute enough to presume and estimate the distances. He rehearsed in his mind the layout of the city, although he had only seen the main thoroughfares

158

leading to the citadel. He was thankful that he was not confined to the prison whose entrance he could see. Life there was miserable indeed. Yet to be confined in this upper room was agony. There was too much time to think. He was appalled by the large number of blunders, bad choices and, he had to say it, sins, he had committed. These all weighed heavily upon him. He ate the prison fare day after day with distaste and longed for the foods of home. He put a mark for each day on the wall, watching the lines fill the open spaces.

Accustomed to freedom and command he was now reduced to confinement and obedience. He knew that there was a chance that he would be ransomed or held hostage to some ploy of the Caliph's government against his people. Unused to discipline or self-control he became gradually a very different person. His hidden, inner man now controlled and used the fleshly outer man as a tool. He simplified his actions and aims. Cunningly he sharpened himself to observe everything on his daily exercise outside. His room became a gymnasium for practice to strengthen his body for escape.

He even resumed the rites of his church as a shield against the Islamic day: the calls to prayer, external demands of Sharia and the temptations to surrender his soul for favors. He observed daily Matins and Vespers and demanded and got the visits of the city priest. He began to memorize the Scripture portions, supplied by Father Agaz. They gave hope and inspired confidence. He became careful in every thing he did and said. The changes were noticeable and for his captors worrisome. He was at the window every time for any activity on the post. As he waited, he watched, planned and learned patience.

> - - - - - - - > KOKAND CITY DISTRICT >- - - - - - - >
A red lantern stood lit at the entrance to the house. Inside it was a labyrinth of paths and rooms built of mud bricks. They filled in the area where in wealthier houses a garden or patio would stand. There was little that spoke of prosperity in the warren of rooms. These hidden chambers were connected to maze-like paths from which women

would appear along the way to implore a customer. Children were evident everywhere and played in the wider intersections of paths. A few scanned those who passed with interest, but the younger were intent on games. A few old men loitered near the entrance and offered home brew for those who wished to brace themselves before seeking sex. Questions could be asked, names and directions obtained. Music quavered on the air as some were entertained. The themes were the eternal songs of glory, love and happiness; none of which seemed very fitting to the surroundings. But hearts yearnings must be sung.

The heavily muffled man that entered brought respectful attention. Well-to-do men rarely wanted to be identified. Laborers and the poor in general did not care who might observe their needs. They paid as they could. However, abundance brought the greedy attention of all; money buys so many things that comfort body, mind and heart. Some rich use such occasions to show off, but more wish not to be seen.

"Fatima, you say? Which one? We have several you know. The young daughter of the Prophet, may he rest in peace, has many who bear her name. She is one to be envied by all mothers; bearing to the noble Ali the two famous sons Hassan and Hussein, may they rest in peace. The blessed and only daughter, the favorite of the prophet, may he rest in peace." He slowed his patter; the man's eyes burned him. He stopped.

"She's very young, from the rug factory where her mother still works. She has a young brother who hangs about the market. He must come here," the voice demanded. The men exchanged glances and a gruff old man spoke from the corner.

"She's in the rented section. Not a regular like the others; no pimp or madam, but safe. They are a family of dagger throwers, - Yemeni. Gone a lot, too." All the men nodded in agreement.

"Show me her room." The talkative man recovered his nerve and tongue, so he led the way quickly through the garden and up an inner stairway to a walk around on the second floor. He passed several doors before he stopped

160

at the corner room and indicated the door which bore a metal frame. The door faced the wooden walk rather than the garden and the one window was over the garden patio, inaccessible.

"She must pay well for so secure a room," commented the visitor. "Does she have outside windows?"

The nervous guide spoke too quickly. "A garden balcony and a window with flower boxes. She must do well for she paid ahead of time. Six months now, but she entertains no customers here. I know her brother has been seen entering from the balcony so perhaps others do too."

"You're sure she's away now?"

The man shrugged, "At least two months now. She was going to visit a sick friend at the hospice. She was in and out that day. The brother climbed in the night before. They were up all night. She is open and friendly, but the brother is sly and silent."

"Who holds the key to the door? I have a gold piece for the key. I must see her rooms."

The man snickered and shook his head, ingratiating. He smiled and put a hand up. "There are no other keys, but I have a ladder for the same price. The inner window is of bladder in winter."

"The coin for a ladder, but a gossip gets the knife. Understand? She's escaped, but you've no place to go," the voice growled.

A sickly smile of agreement was returned.

> - - - - - - - > BETWEEN THE RIVERS >- - - - - - - >

Late-fall in middle Asia is dry and cold, but Ayshe preferred the cold to the dangers in the cave. After cooking the meal, and leaving the men to eat, she went out to gather wood. She ran at a measured pace toward the distant sound of corralled animals. Where the animals slept there would be warmth and herders. She was known now by all the tribe and that was her guarantee of respect and safety. She heard the sound of a shout behind her. The bandits knew their danger and were searching. Hoping she was lost, but fearing she would betray them. They too, moved toward the camp.

She decided to move to one side of the camp and to make contact from the opposite side. She knew the herders were alert, especially after the attack on the wrestler, Kemeer. They might detect the bandits and attack. She had escaped, but would she survive? Where could she find safety? She could be hurt in a melee in this darkness. She paused for breath and listened carefully. She heard nothing and trembled with cold, waiting as her teeth chattered and hair stood up on her arms. The black about her seemed filled with enemies.

>------- > CHIPCHAK HOMELAND >------- >

Erden, Khan of the Chipchak nation, sat at council and wore an angry, stern look. The large yurt was filled with men wearing their best, seated on rugs woven of silk and wool. The Khan sat on a raised divan. To each side, the chief advisers, close friends and relatives were seated on the packed and padded chests that circled the inside of the yurt.

"My brother was sent in exile for his and my protection. The golden cage is to save an heir without endangering either the ruler or his family. Plots to change dynasties or replace one leader with another are discouraged by distance. Why has my brother had to work for his keep? Have I no warriors to protect my convoys to supply all his needs?" He looked at Karga the commander of the horde.

"Know, oh great Khan, that all shipments are safe on our side of the border. They are lost within the Caliph's lands where our troops cannot enter. We have hired the local gendarmes, but they meet a superior force. It's claimed that the Gray Wolf Society is forcing a breach between us and the Caliphate..."

The Khan roared out his ire. "This damned society of traitors will be rooted out. I'll have this wolf's pelt for a doormat."

Kaplan the tiger spoke. "Beloved leader, we will search out his men and find the source of these threats to our tranquility. But, meanwhile, there are choices and problems. You know my son Kynan was lost in a skirmish with the Caliph's Seljuk troops. His sister, your father's widow was abducted with her child. The Toozlular, led by Twozan bey, have taken refuge across the border. We fear his plans include your brother and his family. Erben has left Kokand and is hiding. His plans are unknown." He paused cautiously.

"My brother, Erben went away to work and to move his son from a difficult city situation. I know my brother. He plans no mischief, his loyalty is strong. If there is trouble we must look elsewhere. Who is pocketing my money sent to relieve my dear ones?" He stared hard at Karga who shrugged.

"Police, the government or army are likely enough suspects. It can't be bandits. They can't command large numbers of well armed men. The Caliph can't be seeking war, he has enough trouble at home. He may not know what is happening. Local dynasties are assuming increasing control. Islam is losing its drive."

The Khan grimaced at his commander, then laughed. He leaned forward in a humorous bantering way. "They control the southern commercial routes, all agriculture: fruits and grains, plus the population for tax and troops. Perhaps they wish to relax and enjoy the fruits of victory. What profit can they find in losing battles to nomadic herders? This alone is reason enough to leave us to ourselves."

His expression became sad as he thought deeply. "No, the danger here in the north is seduction to luxury and the power of a ruthless system of new traditions that will steal away our freedom. Our *yasa*, traditional laws, lost to their rigid Sharia. Our merciful Yesu, lost for their stern prophet. Our *Injil* of truth and grace from Tanra lost for their Koran of contradictions. Our freedom lost to their enslavement." Silence followed, none dared answer their Khan's observations.

>- - - - - - >BETWEEN THE RIVERS >- - - - - - >

Ayshe stooped and finding a rock flung it with all her strength at the cluster of tents. Then she followed that with another and yet another. The result was like disturbing a wasp nest. Armed warriors on horses were thundering off in several directions while armed women with bows moved into the brush behind the tents to guard the camp while brush was added to dwindled fires, to blaze in hot brightness. As light moved into the darkness around her Ayshe could cry out.

"Princess Setchkin, it's me, Ayshe. I've escaped the bandits, I've come home." As she stumbled into camp she started to cry from relief and to hug the children and women. She moved toward Kemeer's yurt. The mother would need help or consolation. She must find out.

In the distance a cry of pain, then of mortal terror sounded. A horseman whooped and sent an ululating cry of victory which all others answered in kind. The human hounds were forming a loose pack in pursuit of the 'foxes'. The other women came out of the brush and greeted Ayshe warmly.

"We're eager to hear your story Ayshe. Tell us about what happened." And she told it almost the way it happened. She didn't notice how naturally the Turkish words came to her. But she did know how much she enjoyed telling it.

"Ali bey, Onat, my master, has taken troops to march on the Toozlu. They are moving west. He hopes to surprise them and make them agree to serve the Caliph. That would give them mountain grazing above Samara, north of Baghdad," Tash said.

"I wondered why he left them about so long. How will he get them there? He can't trust them without an escort. The Caliph won't permit an army to move without his special permission." Ali bey dug in his cloth belt for a small money bag and gave a coin.

"He's got some Arabs and camels. I reckon they're going to keep everyone honest." The boy peeped at the coin in his hand.

"Did he speak of his purpose? Why send more Turks to the Caliph? He has a palace full of Khorasan slaves now."

"He never speaks his mind. He did say the camels would keep the tribe close together and on guard."

"Any attempt to outrun them in the desert would be suicide. Chipchaks won't like a spying eye and will move quickly to avoid living long with them. But can Onat bey trust the Arabs? They're suspicious of the Seljuks." The boy shrugged and put the coin away.

It was after the autumn sunset and just before moon rise, a pale light illuminated outlines and edges. Nooryouz stared at the barely discernable target 10 yards below, next to the wall. Dahkool had drugged her friend the guard of the kitchen gate. The old mattress man had left his goods out for use. Jon helped her arrange four old wine skins now inflated with air and to pile the newly cleaned wool on top and around them. It would not be as soft a cushion as they had wanted.

Those who were restricted to the Harem on the top floor had managed an exit to the top of the wall. Maril, after a kiss from two veiled figures, walked to the edge and jumped over. There was a muffled thump and the body seemed to bounce back above the target, then a softer bump. Two figures were now leaning over Maril, working to prop her up. They could hear her breathing heavily to get her breath back.

Now the three figures moved away and two returned and motioned for another jumper. Seslee stood rooted, staring down. Nooryouz whispered in her ear and eased her forward. She balked. Nooryouz pushed her suddenly and a screaming girl thrashed her way down to a resounding thump. She bounced to the edge and slid off in a cloud of wool fibers. The sound of crying and moans came up from below. Two figures ran to pull her up.

The challenge of the tower guard came from behind her as she stood on the rim. Nooryouz felt faint, the target seemed to swim before her eyes. The guard's call was answered from a dozen posts. Figures below began to move away toward the trees. Only one stayed. Nooryouz remained frozen on the lip of the wall. The sound of running steps echoed. Capture was imminent. If she were caught she would lose the baby.

"Oh Yesu, God of my husband, protect our child. Allah, Help me." She leaned forward. Wind rushed about her body as she fell. Fear gripped her heart. Suddenly everything went black, then, she felt herself floating.

HAREM ESCAP

PEOPLE, PLOTS & PLACES IN CHAPTER 14

Agaz bey: wakened by a fugitive, gives advice and money.
Barmani: passes a winter of scarcity with refugees.
Esther: gets a message from a lost daughter.
Dahkool: escapes the harem with friends.
Jon: directs the escape and gets messages of hope out.
Koolair: is learning to visit with friends, but finds trouble.
Kynan: escaping, finds his greatest needs met on the way.
Maniette: the nine-year-old Uigur girl works in the kitchen.
Manly: sends notices to the escapees' families.
Maril: must remain hidden to find her way to Baghdad.
Nooryouz: manages to join her friends and escape.
Sanjak: finds news and reason to have faith in Yesu.
Seslee: learns to face boring routine to win freedom.
Traveler: seeks food from a boy, but finds something else.
Yusuf: learns that his daughter is free.

GLOSSARY
effendim: term of respect; my lord; sir.
Fergana horse: a famous black and white breed.
Hyer ola kuz: Hi girls. How are you girls?
hyer olmaz: No, it can't be. It's not so.
imsak: the pre-dawn prayer every morning.
iftar: first meal after dark during the month of Ramadan.
Kim oh: Who's there? Who is it?
Maniette: to be (like) Mani; a girl's name.
moobahrek: blessed; holy; sacred; bountiful.
Ney oh lure: Please. What does it matter? Why not?
Ne var? : What's happening? What is it?
Sah ol: To your health; Thank you; I'm grateful.
shalvar: steppe pants; baggy trousers.
Yardim et! : Help me! Give me a hand.
yatsa: evening prayer a few hours alter dark.
zurna: a small recorder-like, reed, musical instrument.

UNDER THE BRIDGE

Nooryouz seemed to float on endlessly, then, she came to herself suddenly and was bewildered. On the wall-top just above and to the right, a guard was running toward her. He was looking down at the inflated skins. She, too, looked and saw a figure limply lying on them. Someone started pulling the body away, over the piled wool. Another figure brought a mule from the woods and ran to help Jon. Yes, Jon and Dahkool were pulling up the limp form and laid it across a cushion saddled on the mule's back. It was a smallish woman in dark woolen clothes. Then she recognized it! Herself! She stared in astonishment. "*Hyer oldmaz*, oh no, impossible, I can't be dead!"

She screamed as the guard drew back an arm and threw his spear at the target below. It passed through her shoulder and she felt nothing. One of the inflated skins made a sad small noise as the spear pierced it. The two figures and the loaded mule began to run. The guard took off his bow and bent it to catch the string. Now he took an arrow from the quiver, but the figures had reached the woods as he sent the arrow after them.

Noor found she could move only by will, not by effort. She willed to find her body. She longed to know what was happening to her friends. She now began to float toward the woods, her speed increased as she found herself passing through the trees. But no one heard her calling. She prayed.

"I tell you she's dead. We must leave her here. They'll give her a royal burial, any burial is better than we can give. Seslee is hurt bad and Maril is still shaky." Dahkool's voice was all panic and shrill.

Jon contested firmly, as they continued to run driving three mules. "We don't have time to be sure, could be shock or a head blow left her limp and cold. She landed flat on her back, but you can't tell what it did to her. We'll wait and see. We must be to the bridge before the horsemen arrive."

Nooryouz could see a bridge just ahead. Looking back at the castle she could see the main gate opening to release a party of mounted guards. Jon led the mules down a rocky side trail to a place of refuge under the bridge. It passed over very little water, but bridged the two high sides over the crevice. She willed to go under the bridge and was just beside the stone parapet when the pursuit rode by. They didn't see her, neither did her friends as she came near.

"Allah, please let me live." She waited, nothing happened. Her friends had lifted her body off the mule.

Jon took her hand and pleaded, "*Ney oh lure*, please wake up Noor." His voice trembled, "Yesu, make her wake up!"

Dahkool started pushing on Noor's diaphragm to make her breathe. Maril prayed, and held Seslee who was starting to moan and cry.

Watching the retreating horse-guards a new thought came to her. The baby! It must be very tiny and would need her now. Also the troop of horses would come back and trace their trail. She was responsible for the escape. They were in danger because of her. They needed her. They must move!

"*Yesu gel, yardum et*! Lord help me! She had heard the words from Sanjak in time of distress. She began to drift closer to her crying friends, she wanted to cry too, but couldn't. They loved her, even Seslee and Dahkool, who were new friends. Manly and the leather master were waiting for them.

"Look she's breathing," shouted the serving girl. Violent coughing shook her body. Nooryouz perspective had changed in an instant. She was confused and weak, but struggled to sit up. Questions poured at her.

"Are you hurt?"

"How do you feel?"

"Don't move yet."

"We must go now," Jon overruled. "Part of the troop will backtrack for signs of us. Get her to the mule. No, put her on in

168

front of me. I'll hold her up. Now, mount up everybody." He led the way up the drying creek bed, around a turn in its course.

> - - - - - - - > KOKAND CITY JAIL > - - - - - - - >

Ali bey stared down at the thin gawky boy before him. He smirked with satisfaction as Tash flinched.

"I see you do recall our meetings. Now, I have had news of your travels and spying for a certain commander who has just left hastily for the south. He is too far away to help you, if he remembers you at all. We must talk about your travels. Tell me all about it." He smiled mockingly.

"I've done nothing wrong. There's no law against watching people. I watched some people who were thought suspicious. I'm not ashamed of it." He spoke it out like a litany, well thought out, ready on his tongue.

"But of course, nothing wrong with spying and snitching. The ones you watch would be delighted, if they but knew who you report to." Ali Bey laughed with ironic delight. "I already know, so you won't give away anything. I repeat, tell me about your travels, now." He leaned forward.

"I spent a couple of days out of sight at the mosque garden. When they made their escape I got on to it and kept about a mile away. The girl brought Sevman to Yeet and disappeared. I followed Sevman so I don't know where she went. Yeet took off with two horses. Where does he get money for horses? All I've got is a donkey." His resentment flared.

"So you lost the trail? They ran off and left you; went to a well-used road and you lost the tracks." Ali bey turned away, fretted and pursed his lips. Out of the side of his eye he caught a momentary lift of Tash's lip. A backhand brought blood to the boy's face. Ali bey's face was livid. "But you're not telling all. You're playing games with me. That's not healthy." He pushed the boy away. "You're bleeding Tash. Do you enjoy it? I do. We can get some more from another hole. Seven places in the head alone where you can draw lots of red ink. Each hand has five excellent places for pain and blood. There are 16 joints in one hand alone, painful, but not much beautiful color. Think Tash, do you want to feel some of my games? I love to play, don't you?" He caught one of Tash's uplifted hands

169

and twisted a finger. The lad screamed, moving to relieve the pressure, this brought their faces inches apart. Ali bey whispered, "Tell me." His face held a pleased, playful look.

"The horses had mining stuff you could see, Picks, bars, lanterns, food and other stuff in the packs. I saw all that before they lost me." He pleaded, tears mixed in his blood. "Please *Effendim*, My Lord, it's the truth and all I know."

Ali only grinned and continued the pressure. "Let's hear you plead. Be eloquent, move me to pity." His soft laugh was drowned by the boy's scream.

"*Yo, yapma*, don't, please, forgive me. You'll learn everything I know. Spare me. My master will see the damage and ask questions. He is astute and will know. Please don't, I've told it all. I have nothing left but your mercy, Lord."

Reluctantly Ali bey released the finger. He gently kissed the boy's bleeding cheek and cleaned his own lips with his tongue. His eyes shone and he cleared his throat.

"Yes, I believe you, but when you do another trip for your master you will report to me before and after. Who will know? I have rewards, too, to offer. You won't always eat quince when you deal with me. I've a sweet side. I love boys," he smiled. From his cummerbund, he took a soft white cloth and tenderly blotted the blood from Tash's face.

> - - - - - - -> AKSU VALLEY MONASTERY > - - - - - - ->
Barmani stared at the late winter landscape. The Uigur expulsion of all Westerners: Christian and Muslim, was still pending, waiting for the mountains to clear of snow and gale winds. The present group was only the first of more to come in the spring. Food was limited and the guests restless. The lieutenant was slovenly and self-indulgent; as free with insults and slights as he was with drink and escapades in the nearby villages. The remaining caravan had formed their own defense security and kept a roster of duties and work to aid the struggling community. Barmani sighed. He had honor as a servant of the state. He intended to exercise his full authority to keep control.

Only Sanjak kept to himself, self-absorbed and morose. His daily light and moment of joy was the visit of Koolair who still continued with the Bowzhun family. After the year of traveling she had grown close to a nine-year-old kitchen girl who besides being like a loving big sister was very confident and verbose. They went everywhere together. The little girl, Maniette, was always ready to retell all news and gossip. She was bubbling with suppressed excitement as she brought Koolair and came to visit Sanjak. The guards too found in her visit a diversion.

"*Hyer ola kuz*, hi there girls, what's new?" they asked smiling. Koolair flounced in the new velvet *shalvar* and coat the nuns had found and made for her. Maniette had a made over dress of Maril's from the Bozhun family. Both girls were pleased: each knew she was pretty.

"Sa*h ol*, health to you brave ones. I know what your commander may not know yet. I must tell Sanjak first," Maniette announced.

The soldiers open the door wide permitting their entrance.

"No secrets little one tell us all together," a guard insisted.

"There's fresh news from the capitol. Horse-guards are searching the country side near the capitol. Everyone thinks harem girls escaped from the castle. Many search hoping for rewards. The chief eunuch is imprisoned with the kitchen gate guard. People talk of inflated skins and teased wool piles in the garden grounds. They jumped four lengths from the top of the wall. They ran away with mules, rode up a cliff and were lost. Some say an Umayyad princess is loose," she whispered, wide eyed. Her hands trembled in her lap.

"So? How did such news arrive? In the cold no caravans have passed. How can news come from the kitchen and not from our commander? You come here with lies," one guard grumbled. His face brought menacingly close to the girl. Koolair looked startled and started to cry.

"No, no! Two poor farmers arrived last evening from the Capitol," Maniette explained. "Barmani e*ffendi* allowed them to sleep in the stable. They say the city guards are detaining all passing travelers. Even beggars are searched and questioned." Her eyes were wide with excitement. The guards stared open mouthed.

Sanjak said in a strained voice. "The princess is Nooryouz, a friend of the Bowzhuns. Anybody escaping is a long way from here! They can have food for only a few days. Winter cold will freeze them..." Sanjak's tearful voice broke.

The big soldier slapped his own thigh loudly. "They'll be caught before the week is out. You should not listen to idle talk of bored kitchen help and lying farmers."

The other one stormed, "You can't come here again, foolish girl, until our lieutenant authorizes it. You must not come to spread gossip." The big guard quickly got the children out of the room. Sanjak sat as if he were doused in cold water, eyes wide, unseeing.

Hours had passed. The morning light was still some hours away. Sanjak stood, draped in his quilted bedding, at the small slit window that was equipped more for aiming arrows than for viewing. He wore the look of shock still, but resolve and steel had entered his soul. He spoke musing.

"How thin my faith has grown. How quickly I gave up all hope, when evil men had their way. They blew me away and laughed, mocking me and I gave up in despair. How contemptible and stupid I let myself become. Oh Tanra! Forgive me for being so weak and blind! Forgive me. Grant me strength and wisdom for these trials."

He sadly sang, softly, not to wake the guards outside. But his love song had new verses added:

#1   Full moon shines high above my head.
     I feel your presence.
     I sense your perfume, taste your sweet lips.
     I hear your name, over and over again,
     For you hold my heart.
     I love you, I kiss you. I've missed you.
     Oh come. I speak the truth,
     Oh, hear the song of my soul.
     You hold my heart. Yes, you do.

LAST SERENADE

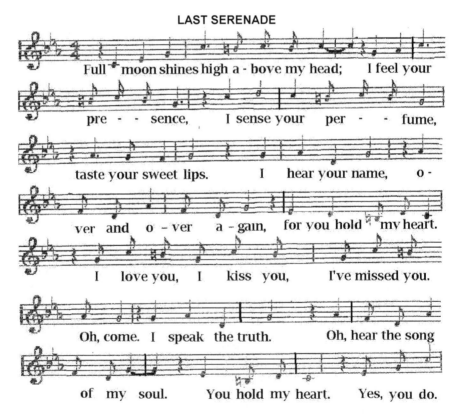

#2   Bright stars shine high above the world.
      I seek your face now, replete with memories,
      Sugar and gall.
      I see my blame, over and over again.
      For you hold my heart.
      I love you, I'd kiss you. I miss you,
      Oh come. You know it too.
      Oh, feel the tears of my soul,
      You hold my heart. Yes, you do.

#3   The portrait of your form so dear
      I hold within me. I press my heart near,
      Vision aflame.
      I feel the pain, over and over again.
      For you hold my heart.
      I love you. I'd kiss you. I wish you were here.
      You know it's true.
      Oh, feel the depth of my love.
      You hold my heart. Yes, you do.

>- - - - - - - > KOKAND ARMY CITADEL >- - - - - - - >

Kynan stared in disbelief, the late spring guard detail was again two men short. For some reason they had clearly eliminated two posts in the night detail. The Ramadan daily fast had begun, yet troops were poised for travel and units were departing. Fewer guards would mean that only one patrolled area was visible to the guards at one period of his five minute walk from one post to the other. There would be a three minute interval when that area would be usable. He stayed up all night timing the posting of each guard in relation to the others and to the last, outer wall. To arrive at, and pass that wall was his necessary goal.

The guards in the outer perimeter walked in opposite directions so they could meet and talk a moment with a guard in a tower. Then they reversed to walk toward each other and meet half way between the towers. Four hours is a long time and the desire to talk to each other grew. Walking gives time to think of jokes or comments for the next opportunity to speak again. Boredom produces careless observation. They had to eat at night for 28 days and guard duty took four hours out of the feast. The time for escape had arrived: Kynan was ready.

He was served a meal after *Yatsa* prayers, two hours after sunset. Another meal came an hour before *Imsak*, when drummers walked up and down the streets to wake the sleepers for the last meal, two hours before dawn. It was still an hour before the muezzin would call the *Imsak*, pre-dawn prayer when fasting began. He ate hungrily and carried in a pouch most of the remainder of bread he had hoarded the past three days. He left through the place in the roof he had been weakening. He carried a stout pole with hand and foot holds cut into its side. It was especially prepared for mounting and descending the outer wall.

Army people were up, sleepily eating and drinking, bundled against the chill, occupied in the preparations for a day of fasting.

Kynan replaced the roof tiles carefully. The dishes would remain till late morning clean-up, everything became slack as the fast dragged on. His departure would be discovered much later, when he'd be hidden or disguised. He knew the place and timing of each sentry, how long to stop, and where to hurry, on his route out. He would cross the wall without detection.

His plans worked out, he was smoothly successful.

Following the road he found a wealthy house. He entered boldly and helped himself to clothes hung in the armoire while the family slept. He continued, dressed as a merchant, to the hospital hospice and entering found the people asleep.

Only Father Agaz was awake preparing for mass. His shock was great. "You have escaped? Why do you come here? They will come searching for you. You must leave."

"Have you news of Erben? Do you have horses available?" He whispered stern faced and demanding.

"You endanger our heads. We're already in bad grace here with the escape of the boy, Kardesh. How'll we explain the escape of an army prisoner? The Prince is still free. They left before the search. There're no horses here. Take this money and go before the people wake." He pressed Fatma's gold coin in Kynan's hand. The priest's pale face and pleading eyes persuaded him. As he hastened out, the sleep filled eyes of neighbors watched him bemused.

174

Later, on the street, he met a pair of drummers. One held a dancing bear on a chain with a ring in its nose. They would wake the sleeping town for the pre-dawn meal, before the fast that came with the light. They eyed him, but said nothing.

> - - - - - - - > KOKAND WIDOW'S PROPERTY > - - - - - - - >

Kynan watched the house with care. It had a deserted, abandoned air. The gate hung just slightly open, so he ventured in. He moved it enough to make a slight sound, but no voice, human or animal challenged his advance. He found the old, obviously abandoned house near the market. Within its walls it had a well so he wouldn't lack for water. It was overgrown with weeds and he found, behind the house, the stairs to the roof where he could continue to hide. The drummers were now making their rounds of the town waking people for the pre-dawn meal, *imsak*, after which they would abstain from food and water all day. He would not be able to move until after *Yatsa*, the evening prayer at the mosque and the *Iftar* meal were over. Even then the people would be socializing and on the street.

He settled himself on the roof in a corner where the parapet and higher trees would shade and hide his presence. The lights were being lit in all the nearby houses and the smell of cooking was in the air. Kynan got out the food he had brought and ate. After his exertions, he fell asleep before the dawn, and didn't waken until night.

> - - - - - - - > ESCAPING THE CITY > - - - - - - - >

Kynan, stood listening, the social visiting and sharing of special dishes of the evening meals was going on. He hurried down the street, apparently a guest late for his *iftar* meal that had now commenced with beating of the kettle drums signaling the end of day light. The twilight was fading as he gained the southern edge of the city. He could see beyond the scattering of village dwellings the rougher rise of the land. He needed equipment: a horse, food and water for the trip into the dry, unknown southern lands. He scanned the surroundings with a predatory eye.

Passing through the orchards and irrigated fields he saw ahead the lights of several houses. From one house came the sounds of loud laughter and music. The beat of a dance throbbed in the night air. First hunger had been satisfied and now the banquet leisurely proceeded with entertainment. Women were present supervising the serving of the courses. The house was not large, but several families of relatives had come together for the last days of the fast and feast. Three girls had been hired to dance together for the admiration of the men. All, young and old, watched attentively, despite the good-natured criticism and contempt of the women of the family. They would sometimes mimic some action of the performers. This produced ample humor and guffaws, lost in the blare of music of the shrill *zurna*, lute, and drum.

Kynan observed the exterior of the house and the stables. There would be a nice selection of horses. There was a scattering of family boys who were near the kitchen door enjoying choice leftovers and held-back morsels. The animals were long since bedded down and resting. The trick would be to get one or more out before the men retired for a few hours to awake again before dawn for the last meal of the night. Enough local alcohol had enlivened the scene to make the men voluble and women giggling. To get in and out now seemed the most prudent move. He slouched toward the stable like a man sleepy after the first big meal after a long thirsty spring day. In the dark, no one took notice. Inside he stopped and gasped. They had a dark Fergana horse with a brilliant white face, socks and rump. He sighed; it was too noticeable to take. H e chose a gray.

He had the horses ready: one saddled for himself and a pack animal ready to travel. One of the men came in pulling a woman, his arms occupied, He failed to notice Kynan approaching. It was the woman who came laughing and protesting who yelled. She threw up her arms and pointed. "*Kim oh*? Who's that?" The man turned, peering stupidly. Kynan gave him a left backhand across the temple. He grabbed the woman and tried in vain to stifle her screams. He wheeled her about and let her body hit the wall. She fell breathless while he led the horses out into the night. Several men and women were looking out of the kitchen, but he mounted, and rode away before they could investigate. The music continued as he came to the road and ran the horses away toward the hills.

> - - - - - - - > UIGUR MOUNTAIN PASTURE > - - - - - - - >

The cold mountain wind whistled over the ridge where the huge flock of sheep grazed in the eddy of a wind shadow. Just out on the edge of the herd, two young men hunch over eating a bit of cheese and dried mutton. Scattered around the thousands of sheep were other pairs of herders similarly occupied. A few, young or old, had scraggly beards or moustaches, but most were young and had boy's cheeks. Tangled hair warmed their necks.

All were dressed in baggy pants, a long calf-length coat whose sleeves covered the hands and boots that disappeared under the coat. All this was topped by a deep crowned small brimmed hat and a long cloak stiff enough to stand in wind, rain or snow.

The morning drive was about to begin. The sparse grass, winter dried on the stem, caused daily movement to new pasture. Even then the sheep thinned in winter and after the lambs were dropped, fattened on spring and summer grass in the high mountains. Westward below the snowline through the foothills, but above the irrigated fruit farms they moved. They avoided the villages: farmers and grazers had differing interests and contrary views. Why meet or talk?

The sheep were rested and hungry so they moved well; running from one clump of dried grass to another. Those behind pressing on those ahead, who stopped to gather several bites of grass. A line of eager replacements take the lead, to stop in their turn. The lead shepherd guided the flock and drovers by hand signals and colored flags. It was a familiar yearly drive. The merchants, travelers and soldiers on the road below rarely took note of them. Grazer boys were dirty and ignorant, full of songs and jokes, paid in food and clothes with no money or family. But they saw the country: hour by hour, day by day, east to west, valleys to mountain peaks in all their seasons. They knew their country as few others could.

Manly, the flock master, spoke to Jon who stood with a small wrapped package in his hand. "This is the message you wished to send? It contains only the personal item, no words?"

"It should be safe. Just to let them know she is free and give hope."

"I have a man to take it. He knows the monastery in the Aksu area. He has served my family for many years. You can trust him to get it safely through to them."

> - - - - - - - > AKSU MONASTERY > - - - - - - - >

Father Barmani sat before the altar. The temple was empty for all were busy with communal duties. He discovered to his chagrin

177

that his meditations were distracted, his mind turning repeatedly to affairs of the refugees. He was annoyed that the Nestorian Christians continued to meet together each Sunday. Some were observing Matins and Vespers as families. Attempts to interest or win families with favors failed. He found himself ignored as the Lieutenant took more interest and command in the affairs of his charges. A few of the animists had shown interest and attended the Temple of Mani. He sighed and again tried to focus his mind on the light. Mani guided him, he must stay facing the light. God's reality was there.

Across the courtyard Sanjak kept vigil by his window slit. His mind was on Nooryouz and he let his memories retrace the well-worn paths of intimacy. He hummed their song and unseeing stared out at the winter scene. Behind him the jailers sat, one was asleep, the other was lost in memory like his prisoner, thinking thoughts of home and family.

Koolair sat with little Maniette and the kitchen help, glad to do little chores for a small bite or sip of some goody shared by the nuns and scullions of the community. She was the best fed of the refugees and she consciously worked to keep her status. She was developing the manners of a coquette and an actress. Maniette was her best friend and she learned to speak Uigur-Turkish.

Maril's mother, Esther, stared at the small object placed in her hand by the rough hill man. He seemed to be from one of the mountain tribes of the north, but he was touched by the *Jinn*. His words were broken and spaced with giggles. It was the green jade earrings that she was wearing, that had stopped his eating at the kitchen door of the community hall. The indigent and hungry travelers came there in hope of leftovers, always made available to the needy.

The wild hill man pointed to the jade earrings Esther wore. Nodding vigorously he had produced the jade pendant, part of a set. She recognized the heirloom, a present to Maril from the family. He held it to his ear, nodding vigorously. He pointed at the earrings again. His giggles now sounded like the bleating of sheep and he pointed east outside the building. Yusuf drew near and reaching, took the pendant from his wife's hand and stared at it closely. He seemed stunned by his examination. The piece was snatched from his hand and the little man, full of angry sounds, went and placed the pendant in Esther's hand again. He took her free hand and pressed it to his forehead. Then fearful, he pushed to the door and was gone. Those who pursued him thought he went over the rear wall into the hills.

The refugees had so many versions of what happened that the truth was never verified to the authorities of the community and the pendant was never seen or heard of again. Esther and Yusuf continued to be leaders and encouragers among the exiles.

The shepherds walked behind their portion of the flock. Each kept to the several hundred animals before them and each with rocks and shouts moved their part of the herd. It was a wave of life covering the side of the mountain. The boys were slender each carried bundles on back and front. One limped. The other had a baby spring lamb on his arm and a larger one in the bundle on his back. They did not talk or sit to rest, but continued to press the hungry flock forward, eating their way through the country.

A traveler stopped his horse on his mountain journey to ask directions. "*Hyer ola olum*, how are you my boy? Where can I find food here about? I'm running short." The boy with the two bundles pointed down the slope with his chin. The valley road with its traffic was just in sight.

The man made an ugly face. "I'd lose half a day to go back there. Have you no food? I'll pay." He studied the child's small delicate, but dirty face. The chin and head lifted in the expressive negative of the tribes people. Ahead a ewe was birthing a lamb and the shepherd moved forward to collect the baby, but it did not move. He thrust the orphan in his arms under the mother and wiped some of the veil material over the face and body. He pushed it toward the mother's nose and picked up the dead lamb. With a knife he started to skin the tiny thing. He cut off the tiny tail and bound it to the wool of the orphan, the skin he tucked in his bag that hung over his stomach like a hump. The ewe was suspicious, but soon let the lamb nurse. The shepherd held up the meat of the stillborn to the man, offering it.

"I'm Muslim, Allah forbid that I should eat such." The shepherd took out the skin and wrapped the body in it and put it away in a bundle. He moved the bundle from his back. The noise of the animals grew. He began to walk away throwing stones at the lingering strays. The traveler found this disconcerting. It was rude and ignorant. Annoyed he shouted at the retreating figure.

"If you learn to talk you can gain money by serving the merchants at the caravansaries. They pay for a pretty boy who's mannerly." As he wheeled his horse and climbed away, he thought he heard a baby cry.

He failed to notice that a rough old dwarf-like tribesman had been running towards them while he talked. Now he turned away. The shepherd had moved into the flock and had the back bundle pressed against his chest. The noises had quieted.

STEPPE FLOWERS

179

PEOPLE, PLOTS & PLACES IN CHAPTER 15

Atilla: back from China finds life, wife and home boring.
Ayshe: is now part of the tribe and enjoys marriage.
Gerchen: surrenders to offers of easy money.
Jon: does a shepherd's work, but challenges a benefactor.
Kerim of the East Bulgars: an old name covers a bold man.
Kemeer: rushes to defend the tribe.
Kynan: takes on a new name for his Ramadan escape.
Manish: must guide his friends over the border.
Manly: must cover his family's actions and return home.
Maril: must escape westward to be united with her family.
Nooryuz: must cross the border to save her baby's life.
Onat: decides to remove the threat of the Toozlu grazers.
Seslee: would like Manly to go on west with them.
Twozan: wins a draw with his opposition and gains peace.

GLOSSARY:
ark a dash: friend; comrade; one who covers your back.
bayram: festival; holiday.
Bock shimdi: Look now! Look at that! See there?
De kot' eden: Attention; Be careful; Notice please.
Effendim: my Lord; my master; (if something is not heard.)
Higher ola oulum: Hey there my boy; How's it going son?
Hoe sh geldin: welcome; your coming is welcome.
Iz aniz le: With your permission; May I? (To enter or leave.)
Kalk, yabonjee var: Get up, foreigners; Up, strangers here.
Sheker By'ram: Sugar Festival, the three days after the fast.

DEFIANT SONGS

Kynan traveled by night. He moved steadily west toward the desert. He was now armed and supplied. He had five horses for regular shifts of mount and packing. Spring weather made travel easier.

Kynan stopped abruptly, to his left a man riding a horse appeared on the ridge. The rider was drunk and singing to himself or to the world at large. Head back he howled his melody at the dawn. He didn't guide the horse with bit or bridle, but let him pick his own way home. The horse moved at a casual unhurried walk. The singer had been breaking the prohibition of intoxication while keeping the religious fast. Now he was telling his neighbors that he was happy and didn't care what they thought. He wanted them to know that even drunk he was smarter then they were.

#1   Ke ke ti key, te te ko toe,
           Life wears a hard bit and riches are slow.
           De de pi die, pe pe da pay,
           You'll owe the courts by the end of the day.
           Give me more money, and a wife that stays.
           I'll sing a sweet song, If you will but play.

#2 Ji ji ga jay, ga ga ji goy,
Love is a pleasure when hearts fill with joy.
Fi fi ba foy, ba ba fi bay,
Don't borrow credit if misers won't pay.
Keep all your money and children at play,
I'll sing or keep silent if you will but stay.

ATILLA'S REFRAIN

Kynan realized that there must be a well-traveled path there. He had been looking for a place to hide for the day. He remained still and observant while the rider continued. He looked toward the horizon, hoping for a light or other signs of habitation, but there were none. What now? Ramadan fast was almost over. The new moon would be born in another day and its sighting would begin the *Fitr Festival* or *Sheker Bayram*, the signal for a return to the normal patterns of food and drink by day. Visits to friends and family would put people on the road, increasing the danger of detection. The search by military and police would intensify. He could make more time by night, but he had to travel blind without any knowledge of enemy movement or what would wait for him on the road. Dare he make human contact? He had to get to his goal. This wandering man was evidently close to home.

"*Effendim*, pardon sir, may I join you?" Kynan with his stock and goods rode up to the singing man. He lifted a bag in hand as he drew close enough for good eye contact in the early light of dawn.

"Here is *kumiss*, a traveler's drink. Will you join me?"

The rider had stopped trying to sing, but continued forward as the horse did not stop. "*Hoesh geldin*, welcome, come here if you'll share. Atilla'll share too," the man replied, "all the way home."

Kynan reached the horse's bridle and stopped it. The drunken man peered toward Kynan, but couldn't make out this man who would ride with him. It was still too dark. Atilla shrugged, the horse walked on, and he started to sing again; the same refrain.

> - - - - - - - > DESERT SPRINGS NEAR THE AMU RIVER >- - - - - - - >

Onat bey sat resplendent in his red coat which came to his boot tops. They had traveled much of the night, the last night of Ramadan. Now they would surprise the Toozlu tribe by descending from the hills where the water springs fresh from its sources. Desert plains spread before him. Where could the tribe run? He occupied the best refuge for defense. They could only flee from his advance. His forces outnumbered the tribe three to one. His eye, in the growing light, caught the movement of the camel corps sent to occupy the area where the spring flows into the wadi and put themselves on the west bank of the stream near the camp. The Arabs would hold the water and be a gate to attack the heart of the camp. Two Seljuk pincers would advance from the sides of the hills to enclose the yurts, while his horsemen would pour into the sleeping camp. The enemy was not Muslim and would not be eating their last pre-dawn meal as his own troops had. Only tribal sentries, if posted, would be prepared for any swift action.

The increasing dawn light announced the arrival of the sun and Onat Bey waved a small square banner to start the movement. At that moment a rider plunged, shouting, into the camp. It erupted into action. Call to arms sounded as men and women ran out of the yurts armed and mounted their horses. The approaching pincers rode abreast at a trot, expecting a sleeping camp. They found a hornet's nest.

> - - - - - - > AT ATILLA'S HOUSE > - - - - - - >

"We have drunk the morning through good friend, but I have no stomach to face the day. In three days my wife will return from her visit with her mother. Words and worry will return to plague my life. She commands in my absence and will also in my presence" Kynan smiled companionably at his new friend Atilla. They had talked, drunk and occasionally slept since their meeting just at dawn. Skepticism and raillery were the order of the day; interrupted by songs of love and drollery.

"*Ark a dash* Atilla, friend, your name speaks of bravery, victory and wisdom. Come with me to the West. Let your fair lady administer your lands and men. All is routine, even a woman is adequate, especially one who is sharp and shrewish." Kynan laughed and embraced his new friend.

"You may laugh. I have to live with her," Atilla winced.

"The point is you don't have to put up with her. I offer you the chance to travel and see the world: to see the great capitol of the empire. Your losses can be recouped, you may become richer. Khorasan has become the key to the kingdom. Turkish servants run the Caliphate."

Atilla sighed. "By Allah, you are a persuasive man. My wife and child will gain a good life here. My going would increase their share. I've little taste for the country life and prudish neighbors." He grasped Kynan's hand and stood unsteadily. "Ah, to see Baghdad!" They clung together as Atilla continued. "I know you are a Turk and probably a Christian too, but I gained a respect for your people in their dealings with the Tang rulers in China. It's a privilege to go

184

with you as friend and companion. Then he reached out clumsily for him to fill his goblet as they embraced. "Good, we'll drink on it."

>- - - - - - -> OASIS CAMP OF THE TOOZLU >- - - - - - ->>

"*Kalk, yabonji var*, Wake up, strangers are coming, everyone up and out, troops are here." The sentinels' alarms cut through the circled yurts like a knife as the men rode to the chief yurt to report to the commander. Twozan bey was already out, stringing his bow and slinging two quivers of arrows behind his shoulder. Sliding his scabbard under his belt, he gave his full attention to one sentinel, while the others went from yurt to yurt rousing the camp.

"A troop comes, the same dress as the frontier force we saw. The ones we outran. They are crossing the wadi, up near the source." The sentinel ran out of breath. He was the only person not moving.

"How many do you estimate? What else did you see?"

"I think two hundred. Perhaps others follow. Twenty lancers with camels are with them, I've heard of them. They speak the language of Allah and can pass deserts without water."

Twozan shushed the man and motioned him away. He cried, "I'm riding to the herds, we must drive them to the wadi and put them between us. They will screen us with the desert dust. Let the men go to the lookout. I'll meet you."

The Chipchak camp was stirring like a stomped ant nest. Men were arming. Women and children were shouting and running to their assigned places. Gerchen rode, yelling war cries, to gather his men.

Ayshe ran to a horseman following him with a full water bag. "Take the water, husband, this is desert land." She touched his hand and they exchanged glances. "I'll pray," she promised, her love and agony reflected in her eyes.

"Take the hunting bow," Kemeer said. "Remember our practice together. Use it to defend the yurt. Save the child you wait for."

"Go with God," she replied, trembling.

"Stay with God", he answered, spurring his horse.

> - - - - - - -> COUNTER ATTACK > - - - - - - ->

Several piercing screams were all that was needed to awake the herd and animate the bunch. The thirsty, upset animals were off at a run. Stretching their rested muscles they plunged down to the wadi bed, just into the right wing of the pincer. The troops had to give way before the

185

mad rush of the mob of frenzied animals. Some soldiers were carried with it or downed. Many were trampled.

At the same time the 'Right hand' of the tribe sent their animals from the high bank back toward the east mountain and water source. This movement blocked and confused the waiting men of the center, only those of the left pincer arrived in camp. But the camp and yurts were also filling with straying, confused animals. The stampede had quickly ended. Hunger had reasserted itself, but pasture was far away from the camp. From among the wandering, bawling mobs arrows came from men, women and even children who dodged among the animals. They fired at unexpected intervals and shifting places. Accuracy was minimal, confusion maximal, but inevitably all the tribe was pressed toward the hills and seepage springs.

Camels have an advantage of height, but lances are of little use when herds of animals pressed around them. The Chipchaks appeared to shoot an arrow and then disappeared behind the milling animals. The animals rushed for their morning drink pressing the camels back. No right minded Arab stands between a thirsty herd and their water. The camel corps retired, rapidly moving up the mountain slope.

By this time there was no line of contact between enemies. There was a field of animals and a kind of guerilla warfare with some of the tribesmen on horseback firing arrows as they pressed their way among the nervous animals. Troops and tribesmen were scattered, cursing and calling, all moving toward the higher ground where Onat bey sat resplendent in his red coat and white turban. The tide surged forward.

> - - - - - - - > TRIBE ENCAMPMENT BATTLE > - - - - - - - >

A look of resigned exasperation wrote a clear end to the situation as Onat bey called out the order to retire. His signal man waved the appropriate colored flag and the troops turned to push their way back to their starting position.

The scattered center line quickly formed up behind Onat bey. Seeing the confusion he had the trumpet sound.

"*Dekot edin*, attention: listen carefully. You're in the Caliph's lands and I'm his representative. I offer you peace and the chance to serve and win land and wealth. Stop your fighting. I'll keep my men back." The arrows continued.

"Twozan bey, the fight is profitless let's have a truce.

I promise peace in the prophet's name. Let us talk. I'll withdraw my men and remain here with only the camel corps. You come with your council and guards." An Arab fell, arrows continued.

"I can't stand by and watch you kill my men. Take your herds and withdraw. I'll come later. You can't escape. You are too deep in our lands to escape us."

The women and children started back toward the yurts. The herdsmen started moving the animals from the spring water. The warriors drew together in a defensive formation just in bow-shot. Gerchen whipped his horse toward Onat Bey to send an arrow whirring at the white turban. Onat Bey lifted his left hand with a small target shield on his wrist and deflected it nicely.

"I'll give you two horses equal to the one you ride, if you will but serve the Caliph. We need intrepid warriors in Khorasan. Come, make peace. Become rich!"

Gerchen stopped. Twozan's voice carried clear and hard. "We will talk later. Now, withdraw your troops and go with your camels far beyond the springs, our cattle hate their smell. Our women will not be looked upon by the Arabs. Go higher up." Twozan's voice carried clear and hard.

"I understand you. We will withdraw." He ordered the signal be given and listened to the Arab complaints. They had anticipated herds and women for their part in a victory. A failure could cost a commander's head. He knew they would bend ears with their disappointment. Failure in battle showed Allah's disapproval. He should cover his back!

"You of the camel corps must move back to Yuzbasha Uthman in the center. I will keep my guard and staff with me. They intend no attack, but will remain on the defensive."

He dismounted to face the Arab leader who had dropped his reins and left his camel kneeling.

"Your attack failed because you waited for the pincers. The center should have advanced and left the pincers to contain the escapees." The Arab was angry and excited. His hands moved and face contorted.

Onat bey froze, "They would have fled down river in the midst of the flocks. They might have fired the yurts and our horses would panic. Everything depended on surprise. Your corps lagged."

"I would have led a successful charge. You failed. Allah has deserted you: You son of a Turk." He spit out the words and drew his dagger.

Onat's left hand shield took both point and hand aside. His open right hand hit the Arab's chin in an upward blow and he collapsed. Onat called his men. "*Dekot*, attention! Have the Camel corps retire with Tuchman's troops. Take their commander on his camel."

The Arabs were staring like baleful serpents poised to strike. His guards had already drawn their swords. The tension held.

"Yesu, what has happened here?" Twozan spoke from his horse as it started to shy from the strange scents.

Gerchen laughed and replied from his mount as he rode near. "We are not alone in distrusting Arabs."

The dark faces turned to appraise the nearing enemy. One hissed a word: "*Infidel*." Hatred burned in the sound.

> - - - - - - - > ATILLA'S HOUSE IN THE AMU VALLEY > - - - - - - - >

"Atilla bey how have you become so detached from your land and family? Have you been bored for years and finally grown to the point of breaking?"

Atilla roared with laughter and pounded his friend Kynan on the back. "Remember I told you, Kerim bey. I had carried horses to sell in the Tang lands. It is that trip that planted the craving to see new places. The refugees I returned with were kept by the Wigars, but as a Muslem, I came straight here. I've only been home about eight months. I was bored from the third day. I always crave excitement. If I can't find it, I make it. Even the trials of the return made staying here dull. No dirty, hungry journeys are half as tedious as comfortable life, fattening like an animal for slaughter." He shook his head as if to wake up.

Kynan looked at his companion with admiration. "You never cease to amaze me. I took you for a farmer. Then I thought you were a herder: finally a merchant. Now I

188

discover you are an adventurer. Each better than the last, now we are travel mates and brothers." Kynan poured drinks.

"We must leave tomorrow. She'll come by evening, but today is still ours. Here eat some more, we can enjoy food day or night while the Sheker Bayram lasts. No more fasting all day, Kerim bey." Atilla lifted the cup in salute.

Kynan drained his and filled them again. Thankfully he smiled. His new name was accepted without pause. "Tomorrow, we welcome the start of a new adventure."

> - - - - - - - > IN THE TANRA DAH MOUNTAINS > - - - - - - - >

A group of herders stood and sat about Manly, the leader of the drive. He explained their situation and position to them.

"We could go north toward Ining in the Illi River country. That's the road to grazing country, where Hun and Turk tribes roam. Those of you who were with the refugees will want to go there," Manly stated judicially.

The girls nodded eagerly. "You'll come with us, won't you?" inquired Seslee, she smiled beguilingly. She was always careful to station herself where Manly could see and sometimes work with her in the drive. Even with shepherds' clothes she looked fetching.

"I can take the herds there in summer, but will have to turn back before fall. I have to be back near the capitol for the fall slaughter. The palace is the best market for our wool and meat. I'll have to replace you so I'll have to visit the local village now to hire shepherds," Manly replied. While the others expressed concern, Seslee pouted.

"I know no other work, it was my father's. The herds are ours. I can't join refugees and leave Mani's country." He touched her dirty face tenderly. "The idea is tempting, but you'll find a welcome wherever you go."

"And you'll find the axe if anyone learns of this. Border crossings are tricky. How'll you explain your loss to the locals?" Jon inquired. "Shepherds don't disappear."

"They owe me for past favors and they love their own. Why should they care about refugees? Besides, shepherds do disappear when they desert. It happens," Manly responded.

"What if they should learn of the reward? Greed moves even neighbors," Nooryouz stated. She nuzzled the baby.

"I'll wait until you're gone. They won't have noticed you closely." Manly shrugged, "Except Seslee, who can't help being noticed." They all laughed. She grinned impudently.

189

"Why do you do this wonderful thing for us? How can we repay you?" She fluttered her eyes and moistened her lips. She arched her back, raising her face to see his eyes.

"*Babam*, my father ordered it. I knew Jon first, then when my family agreed, I helped your friends. I helped Jon to bring you to the flocks and disguise you. Now as summer advances your chance to escape has come. When we reach the alpine grass you must go. I'll return to my family. The touched one will teach the new boys, just as he did you."

"Will you forget me then? I could be your wife and lover. Why can't you go with us?" She held his face between her hands. The man blushed now, and turning, lowered her hands.

"I told you. My father decided. Besides, my family has decided on a girl. I'll send Manish with you; he is little, but knows the trails." He tried to walk away, but Jon grabbed him by the shoulders. There was a brief struggle. Sighing Manly stood still.

"Why does your father hate the royal house? What is the reason?" Jon questioned.

"First my aunt and then my sister were taken to the harem to marry princes, but were taken as concubines instead. There was pretext of finding some flaw in them and a slight on our genealogy. Father has never forgiven the insult. He will see the Emperor and royal house destroyed." He flung the words and broke free of Jon's grip. "You were salve for his pride. But you are also a sword above our heads. Enough! Go with the Prophet Mani's guidance," Manly concluded, and walked hastily away.

> - - - - - - - > DESERT TRUCE > - - - - - - - >

"You have dubious allies, Onat bey. I would not turn my back on them." Twozan commented while watching the angry camel corps retire with their unconscious commander. They shot resentful glances behind them aimed at the commander and conferees.

Onat Ignored it. "You've been in our territory for months now. You need to define your condition. Ours is the land of Islam. The right to bear arms is attached to that allegiance. People of the book who are native to the land are permitted to live here, but not outsiders. They're not allowed to stay or immigrate here. You must become converts within the year or be enslaved. I think you're aware of the laws here. Most of the tribes find the change easy. Many find it profitable for the Caliph needs personal and palace guards that are free of the political rivalries and loyal to him only." He awaited their response.

190

"We flee for our lives. We're grazers," Twozan affirmed, "and not used to the village hours and prayers. Our beliefs and practices harm no one. They're old and predate your beliefs. Why make hypocrites of us?"

Onat bey studied the faces before him. "The Caliph is the shadow of Allah on the earth. He balances three peoples and many interests in the different lands around the five seas of the world's center. Allah is to be exalted, as his prophet Mohammed, may he rest in peace, declared. Accept the prophet and his message and you'll be taught the five pillars of Islam and our festivals."

Gerchen spoke quickly. "What matters an oath? If we think differently we'll practice each what we will. We are a free people."

"A khan or *binbasha* is bound by his word, friend" replied Onat.

"All men believe we are judged by our declarations before Tanra. I will have to call all our people to decide this thing," Twozan declared.

"I grant you this: three days time. You must remain at the springs. If you run I'll send the Arabs after you. They're great trackers. The camels can go two weeks without water. You know what they'll want to do. I want better things for your tribe. Remember, I am also a Turk." He turned and left.

The two leaders stared at each other. Finally, Gerchen turned to his horse and mounting saluted the air. "Tanra will have to give us three days grass where one exists. We are in the lion's mouth now."

Twozan stood watching. "Tanra will see the weakness of our hearts which brought the need of Yesu's death. Resist the lion, for only then will he flee." He reached a hand into a seep spring's tiny pool and brought it to his mouth. He continues to muse. "Will we stand when riches lie before us? What is a truth that is both present now and in the future, yet unseen, compared to offered riches seen and felt today?"

PEOPLE, PLOTS AND PLACES IN CHAPTER 16

Ahmed the carter; facing a steep path found death.
Tayze: confidently continues to meet the family needs.
Doctor: a Jewish physician cares for the quarry workers.
Erben: more problems on his hands than rope burns.
Hussein: a gang member, ever ready to show strength.
Kardesh: rescued, but finds revenge brings poor rewards.
Leyla: exposed to constant danger in the quarry village.
Seerden: finds his man and prepares an accident.
The Warden: makes a rescue that penalizes the village.
Umer: plans for his own satisfaction, but fails every time.
Umer's Father: a rich man confronts a rebellious son.

GLOSSARY:

do'er, barak onu: stop it; leave him alone; don't; leave off.
Jinnn charp tun mu: did a Jinn touch you; are you crazy?
soos, kuzum: quiet, daughter; silence, my girl; hush, girl.
gubertajam: I'll slaughter you; I'll butcher you.
Kaya-lar: name of the Chipchak founder's royal family.
yapma: don't do it; don't be like that; don't.
yoke / yo: no; nothing; not so; none.

QUARRY CLIMB

"Hi pretty girl, lucky I found you alone." Umer leaned in the door way, confidently smirking. Leyla looked up and squealed. She backed away from the advancing boy.

"Umer, what are you doing here? You can't come in here. My father and Kardesh are due home now. You must go."

"They have a late job, an urgent delivery of facing material. It's cooler by night. We can have a cool time here. I brought a bottle of something nice for us to have."

"Tayze is visiting next door I'll call her if you stay here." She had moved round the central fire place and was trying to move toward the door when he backed to the door and tried to catch her. She moved back behind the fire.

"Your Aunt is helping as midwife along with your neighbor lady. They were in too big a hurry to stop by."

"You know I've been watching you ever since you got here. I'm crazy about you. I know you like me. I can tell by the way you look when you see me staring." He was smiling confidently and held out the small skin bottle.

"*Dish arah ya git*, Get out. My expression had nothing to do with you as a person. I don't like you, you soft dandy.

I won't drink anything with you. I'll scream and the whole neighborhood will hear. Get out now." She confronted him face to face in her anger. He reached into his belt.

"You can die screaming, no one will catch me in the twilight. No one knows I'm here. Don't be a fool." He waved the knife under her nose and grabbed her arm when she tried to distance herself. He swung her around and laid his knife arm across her chest and his hand held the knife near her neck. She struggled a moment making some squealing sounds but she did not scream or get free of the hold. He tore at her blouse with one hand keeping the knife at her throat.

> - - - - - - -> MARBLE QUARRY CLIMB >- - - - - - ->

"We're on the last climb with the final load of marble facing. Soon we'll be home the richer." Thus Erben encouraged his two work companions. They sat resting on a wide shelf of rock beside the steep path that led out of the quarried depths. Beside the two men were thick backpacks with stout straps of leather to fit around the shoulders. Each held its quota of polished marble, faced two by two to save the polished surface. It was all Kardesh could do to haul packets to load on their cart at the bottom of the hill. He pushed and put a wood block behind the wheel as the donkey strained. Once the pack was on his father's back Erben seemed to carry the burden with ease. Ahmed, his older companion, however, seemed to strain and pant in the spring chill, demanding more rest time.

The man who was contracting the load, a stranger from the city, complained nervously about the loss of time. "I'll have to travel all night to make an inn before dawn." He growled. "There are Turks loose in the wild lands, between the rivers, threatening everybody. Who knows where they'll be by the time I get home?"

The porters only grinned at his discomfort. "Okay, let's go." Erben grunted and his companions rose slowly to load the packs, each helping to lift the slabs into position. Again the purchaser led the way. The trail over the lip of the quarry edge was pure rock, sanded for traction, but very steep. Here the city buyer, Seerden, sprinted ahead up the slope and panting on the top of the trail, removed a large flask from his pack. He emptied its contents over the surface of the trail. Then he vanished into the night.

The three men stared up in stupefied silence as they advanced, then Erben felt his foot slide. He crashed face first onto the rock, felt the oil spread beneath him.

"Stop, oil..." he cried as he felt his body swivel under the load of rock. Beside him Ahmed screamed and the sound moved away and down. Behind him he heard a crash of rock and the sound of running feet. Erben reached up and caught an overhanging bush. The marble jerked his shoulders cruelly. He slipped off one side of the harness, twisting. The branches on the bush broke off. He continued sliding on his side, down the path. He grabbed again, the rocks' weight now held him on his back. His hands stung and burned as he caught the wild growth and his velocity slowed. He heard the crash of stone and sudden silence below him. He knew his friend, Ahmed the carter, had died.

His leather pack caught on some uneven foothold. His eyes and mouth were filled with plant trash and blood, but his feet thrashed over air. The rocky edge pressed into his flesh below his buttocks. Blood oozed from scratches and cuts on his face and arms.

"Babam, Father, my father," Kardesh called frantically. Erben felt the oil spreading under his bottom.

"Barak, leave, get a rope. Don't risk coming here. The oil is spreading. Leave the cart blocked. Get help." In the distance from the work shed and village dwellings voices of inquiry and alarm were raised. All knew the sound of a death fall.

Erben shifted his weight to get a new hold on some branches over the path. He felt the stone pack start to slide again. He cried out, "Yesu gel, Lord help me." He twisted up and caught a larger branch, but the weight of the marble dragged him on, the branch broke. He tried to remove the harness but it was twisted. His feet were now above him thrashing on the oily path. He found his knife and slashed blindly for the shoulder strap. He cut leather, twine and flesh as pain swept through him and the marble sheets slip out from beneath him and plunged down the cliffside.

His head had no support but his back was touching broken stones on the platform where they had rested earlier. Reaching out his hand Erben found a pack of marble fallen off Kardesh's cart. It had dropped as he backed the donkey down the path. Erben's hip rested on it. He wondered if it had stopped his slide. The sound of his pack hitting bottom stimulated him to try to get up. More people were calling excitedly, some were lighting torches.

"*Dekot*, Be careful, there's oil on the path. It's on the top part. Ahmed fell. My pack just went over. Thank God I got free in time." The stunned listeners echoed "*Allah shukoor*."

One tearful voice however, began the lament for the dead.

> - - - - - - - ->ERBEN'S QUARRY HOUSE >- - - - - - - >

Umer laughed with satisfaction. He kept his knife at Leyla's throat, but was busy with his free hand.

"You know, I really like you, but like it or not you better go along with my plans." He jerked her around toward the broad mud brick bench that ran along the inside of the house. She rolled her tearful eyes up at him and hatred burned from them. She struggled as he forced her down. He stood gloating in the gathering dusk. He leaned across her and yanked at her baggy shalvar. He froze at an loud distraction.

A scream pierced the tension of the room, suspending all motion and interupting every thought and intent. There followed a thud of rock and body followed by meaningful silence; then came a delayed cascade, a second rock fall. All about, from the houses people were running and crying out.

Umer cursed and let Leyla go as footsteps came running to the doorway. A woman's voice shouted. "Someone's fallen. Ahmed was with your father on a late load. It must be one of them." Leyla jumped for the door and ran wildly into the street before the houses. Her clothes were in disarray, but the woman thought she was dressing as she ran. No one could catch up with her.

> - - - - - - - > QUARRY ROADSIDE >- - - - - - - >

Kardesh stopped the cart. He was halfway down the trail and he could see people running toward him.

"*Eepler*, ropes! Bring rope to get him off the hill. There's oil on the path. He's stuck there: can't go up or down."

"He blinked and swayed. He shook his head and passed his hand over his eyes clearing them. One of the men ran up to him and thrust a coil of rope into his hands.

"Throw this rope to him from the path. I'll try to get above and secure one end to a rock or tree so he can be pulled over the oil. With two ropes we can keep him on the road, avoid a fall." The man turned and ran, with another companion, to the start of a trail that took a rougher, higher climb to the rim. As they climbed they continued shouting encouragement to Kardesh.

"Come on boy, we'll be there before you get started. Move on now, we'll save him." They were moving with the confidence of experience up the rough, narrow track used only for pedestrian traffic.

More people came running up the path, others gathered at the foot of the cliff around the body of Ahmed. The crying started again. Leyla pushed through the crowd.

"What's wrong with the girl? Someone stop her."

ERBEN'S RESCUE

197

Several men reached out, but she dodged. They warned her. "*Dekot*, be careful! There are broken slabs on the path." Unheeding, she ran on pursued by Kardesh. In spite of all shouted advice she did not pause. He ran behind, reached out to grab at her.

"*Barack*, let go me, I want daddy. I hate your friends; that slimy Umer. You always hated me." She pulled at her vest, held in his grasp and hit out with both hands. He grabbed an arm and struggling, held on. "Let go my clothes! Don't twist my arm! You're hurting me again! You're just like Umer!" She jerked forward and slipped on an oily slick. Screaming she fell down on her knees and slithered forward on her face, spread eagle.

Kardesh hung on by arm and clothes pulling her back toward the high side of the path. He tried to calm her. "No, don't struggle. I won't let you fall."

"Daddy, help! Kardesh is hurting me. He sent Umer."

"Leyla, *nay var*, what is it? Wait, I'm coming." Erben slipped as he tried to hold the strap of the remaining pack of rock with one hand while he reached for the dangling rope. The men above had tied the rope to a rock and a scrub tree. "Wait Leyla, it's bad here. I'm coming down. Stand clear below." He tried to pull himself upright with the rope, but slipped, oil splashed on his hands, rope and face. He slithered, his feet tripped on the pack of stone and he fell off the edge of the path. The rope burned into his hands as he tried to stop his fall. The knot at the end of the rope saved him a full body length below the path. The blood from his skinned palms ran down his arms to his face and body. Screams of terror accompanied his misstep. Most of the spectators were frozen in time and space.

"*Babam*, hold on, I have a rope." Kardesh with one gigantic effort pulled his sister from the ground and pushed her before him down the path. He stopped and looked back at his father now dangling beside the cliff face. His body was silhouetted against the whiteness of the steep drop.

"You wait at the bottom, don't try to follow me." Kardesh yelled at Leyla with his final push, to where others held her. Then he turned and climbed the trail above to the rope and men. There, above the dangling victim, gasping for breath he arrived and thrust the extra length of rope into the hand of the workers. They had already started untying the rope, looped around the rock, to knot it on the extension.

"Keep it looped around the body of the little tree, two turns, hold tight. We can't let him jerk or we may lose him. Now, ease it out slow and steady. No stops," the older man ordered. The three men worked smoothly and the rope moved steadily down. Near the end of the length of rope the slack and cheers announced the end of the journey. A bleeding, exhausted man was received below and hoisted to the viewers' shoulders in triumph. Those above dropped the rope and ran down the slope to join the jubilant crowd.

> - - - - - - - > ERBEN'S QUARRY HOUSE > - - - - - - - >

It took a long time to see an end of the visitors at the *Kayalar* house. People circulated between Ahmed's wake and the bed of the exhausted, rope-burned, Erben. All the familiar words of condolences were repeated frequently at both ends of the line. Leyla and her aunt served tea to all and received the gifts of cooked food from the women just as the daughters of Ahmed did in their house. The whole community of White Marble, from the humblest quarry men to the agents and entrepreneurs, made their social calls dressed in their best. Men were valued by their skill as well as riches. So all were welcome and enjoyed the food and drink provided.

Kardesh, excited and verbal, told the story over repeatedly. No one seemed to tire of it. The men who brought the rope came in for their part of the action. Only Leyla's part was not spoken of; it would bring shame.

The burial would occur in 24 hours as prescribed in Islam. The casket would be carried on the shoulders of his fellow workers. Erben, the Christian, would be expected to bear his part in the afternoon service. The grave would be oriented south-west toward Mecca. Accident victims got special treatment at the quarry; no one would work that day.

Leyla's hysteria was taken for nerves and every one was helpful. Tayze was experienced in soothing Leyla.

All seemed well until a group of youth entered and spoke to Kardesh and praised Erben's escape. Although they were prompt to leave without eating; Leyla saw the hated face of Umer among them. She burst out crying to the consternation of all. Kardesh drew near, perplexed by the outbreak. He shook her. *"Ne var?* What's wrong? *Jinn charp tun mu?* Did a *Jinn* drive you crazy? Why are you howling like that?"

She hit him. "You brought him here. He's your friend. He'll try again. I won't let him. I'll kill myself first," she yelled.

"Calm down. What are you talking about? Try what?"

"Why've you always hated me? I didn't mean to kill mother. I didn't know. You wish I'd never been born. Oh Tanra, why do I live like this? Why take mother? Why didn't I die too?" Women friends and neighbors took firm hold of her and carried her into a side room. There, the worried and suspicious women pried and worked on her, until she told all.

> - - - - - - - > QUARRY CONTRACTOR'S HOUSE > - - - - - - - >

Umer stood, sullenly defiant, before his angry father who stood facing the boy. His face was hidden in shadow and his bruises bled as the father fingered the thick cane in his hands. Both men were breathing hard.

"I will not forget what you have done to dishonor our family. And you will not forget it either. Had you told us you wanted a concubine or wife, wouldn't we have gotten one? Especially one we could approve of: a clean, chaste girl from our own people. What have we denied you? Nothing! I started as a simple quarryman like all the others. I'm the son of a Farsi farmer. By diligence and hard work I brought us to where we are today. You have certainly profited by it. You seek to force yourself on a worker's daughter now. A Chipchak barbarian's child! Not even a Muslim! All the neighbors will talk now and drag up our family history. Authorities will change their tone and grow cold and difficult. I let you choose your path and this is my reward.

200

See how your mother cries?" The wailing of the women was loudly heard.

"I didn't intend ..." The boy started to reply, but the cane lashed out and his cry pierced the air as he fell.

"I've heard of your activities in our quarry market and now this. You were arrogant in assuming you could do anything you liked because of my standing. Now you will start as I started. I'm sending you to my brother in the mountains. His quarry is small and poor. There you will work for your food without any privileges. If you do well we'll reconsider the matter in two or three years. You leave tomorrow. Stay out of my sight. I don't want to see you again until there is news of a change." The father threw down the cane and left.

>- - - - - - > QUARRY LAKESIDE > - - - - - - - >

Umer sat behind the rock in a bit of shade. The village knew now and there was no peace there. The boys snickered at his ineptitude and failure. The girls snubbed him and some giggled when he passed them at the fountain. The adults gave him angry stares. He couldn't meet their gaze. He had no desire to go to his uncle's quarry, but he couldn't imagine what else to do. Some of his gang had seen him go down to the Bitter Lake, but they left him alone.

The gang watched Kardesh surreptitiously as he went about looking at the places that Umer had habitually been found. He ventured a question to some who he knew were not partial to Umer. Their heads moved upward in the negative gesture. However, near the fountain, one of the girls made a subtle gesture with her eyes and head as she passed with her jar of water lifting it to her veiled head. His eyes followed the direction and fell upon the colored waters below the little village. He made a slow turn on his heel, left the square and deliberately made his way down to the shore. He stared at the water a moment then turned to find four young men behind him.

Hussein called out. *"Gel*, come Umer, you have a visitor." They smiled grimly and came closer.

201

"What foolishness has brought you here?" one sneered. "Perhaps he wants to collect for us again."

"Will he pay what he owes from the last collections?"

Umer's angry voice cut in from behind them. "He will pay now! You came to seek me out? Here I am! What do you want?" He pushed past his friends.

"*Gibertijam*, I'll slaughter you." Kardesh exclaimed as, head down, he took Umer in the stomach with his shoulder and they fell to the rocky shore. Kardesh straddled him and banged Umer's head on the rocks. Then he picked up a large stone. As he poised it he was hit from behind by two bodies and carried to the stony floor. His head was pounded against the rocks. Umer, helped up by a companion staggered over and pushed the bullies to one side. He clumsily knelt beside Kardesh while his friends held Kardesh down. He picked up a pointed stone and started to hit Kardesh in the face with a short downward chop. Kardesh twisted and thrashed around as the bullies held his arms and feet. He screamed as the rock hit his eyes and nose. Blood splashed and stained them both.

Villagers hurried to the edge of the hill to look down at the lake and the fighting boys. Eventually three of the larger men started down the path toward the fight. The village warden shook his baton and shouted. "*Do'er, barak onu*, stop, leave him. You and your families are responsible for any damage you do."

The gang looked up. Umer got up and with the help of the others threw Kardesh into the stagnant waters. Then they ran, down the beach and up the hill away from the village.

"Quick, the Turk will drown. Help me here. Leave the boys, we know their families." The warden was wading out gingerly into the strange waters. Distastefully, the two men joined him. He lifted the boy's head above the water and shook his head at the sight. The others lifted from the armpits. They turned to the shore. Kardesh coughed blood.

"Let's get out of this poison. Go up to the fountain overflow. We'll wash off there." The warden bent to pick up the feet. The men puffed up the hill their breath a cloud.

"*Allah*! That damned water is starting to burn me. Let's get into the fountain and wash," complained one.

"*Yoke*, no, you'll contaminate the water supply. Go to the overflow. There's enough water there," commanded the warden.

"This poor devil will have a wreck of a face now, if he lives." They dropped the body in the trickle of the fountain overflow. They slapped water over their arms and legs. Villagers drew near ogling and shuddering at the sight of blood and raw gashes in the face of the foreigner.

"I don't think they broke his head, but they tried and time will tell." The warden washed the boy's face with a cloth as the deep cuts oozed blood. One eye socket seemed collapsed. Kardesh remained in a stupor. He moaned and coughed occasionally. Blood trickled from his mouth.

"Let's get him home. Hassan, you go call the doctor to meet us at the house. Some of these foreign families have the devil's bad luck." Bystanders nodded agreement.

FIGHT AT BITTER LAKE

203

PEOPLE, PLOTS & PLACES IN CHAPTER 17

Ahmed: a member of the Umer gang who wants an easy life.
Tayze: is left with all the responsibility of caring for the sick.
Binbasha: the Uigur general is reproved for his investigation.
Doctor: continues his attention in a grim case.
Hussein: decides to go to another quarry and takes a new name.
Kardesh: lies wounded in the quarry, while others leave.
Khan of the Uigurs: still waits for the return of the harem escapees.
Leyla: dazed by all that has happened needs a change.
Nooryouz: has a baby boy, Sanjer, to care for.
Sevman: finds little satisfaction in life, but will serve friends in need.
Umer: decides to go to Samarkand and join the army.
Uigur lieutenant: leads the refugees to the western frontier.
Yeet: brings Sevman to help and be helped by the Kaya family.

GLOSSARY
arka dash: friend; comrade; back-coverer.
babam: daddy; my father.
bosh ooze two nay: I will comply; I will obey; yes, Sir.
chesh'me: a spring or ornamental fountain with a stone facing.
Dar al Islam: The Land of Islam: a contrast to Dar al Harb a land of war.
de kot': careful; attention.
din' lee: listen; hear this.
Hyer ola olum : A greeting - How are you boy?
hazer ol: get ready; be prepared.
kappa chin ini: shut up; shut your mouth;
koor sura bock ma: forgive my mistake; excuse me.
ooyan, kalk kuzum: wake up, get up daughter; up my girl.
tayze: maternal aunt ; mother's sister.

Funeral visitors

Piercing screams echoed again and again through the small house. Leyla stood petrified, staring at the form on the stretcher, the battered face and broken teeth. Tayze came up behind her and put a hand on her shoulder.

"*Soos Kuzum*, Hush daughter help me get the bed ready." She tried to move Leyla gently to one side so the men could pass. Her hands were brushed aside.

"*Yo*, no, not here, not here." She pushed past the people crowding the door and ran out, away from the houses up into the mountain. Blank astonishment registered on every face. Daughters of Islam are not permitted such displays of public rejection. Several men of the accompanying group stopped outside the door. It might be an unacceptable thing to enter an unclean house of a foreign unbeliever. They expressed their sympathy from the doorway.

"*Iz aniz le*, with your permission." The Jewish doctor asked as he moved meekly through the crowd at the door. People gave way reluctantly, the doctor was an anomaly. His skill and knowledge not his politics and religion kept him in his remunerative position. Like all minorities of the time, status could be maintained only by excellence.

"Bring the light closer to his face, I must see." The doctor almost let a sigh escape. He probed the face gently and wiped away the blood. He examined the broken teeth and lifted the lids to observe the eyes. He shook his head. Tayze moaned softly, letting the light tremble.

"I will sew two of the cuts. The others are best left covered as they are now. One eye is destroyed. The other might recover in part... or totally. We will do the best we can. Time will tell." He cleaned the blood from his hands in a basin and then took out a roll of clean horsetail hair. He threaded the needle.

"His throat and face wounds are irritated by the bitter water. They were washed away before serious damage, but it may affect the remaining eye and throat. He needs rest and broth. Take this powder. Use it when he's restless. He must sleep. Tie his hands where he can't reach his face. The powder that covers a fingernail is enough for two hours sleep. Use it sparingly." He cleared his throat and murmured quietly.

"Now we must close the cuts. Do you have vinegar? Good, bring it. I'll come tomorrow, but don't worry the Muktar will pay the bills. There'll be fines and complaints against the youth who did this savage thing." He puckered his lips and set to work on the gashes.

> - - - - - - - > ROAD TO THE QUARRY > - - - - - - - >

Yeet pointed with his whip and laughingly shouted. "*Bock shim de*, look now, there's the quarry mountain. We'll be home tomorrow. We'll surprise Kardesh. He'll have given up on seeing us this spring."

Sevman, seated beside his friend, holding the reins of the donkey, looked up with sad eyes. His face had lost the little boy look of wonder and had taken on the sharper lines of suffering and knowledge. Maturity had its price. Lines of worry etched his pale face. His eyes squinted against the afternoon sun. He was perspiring. Yeet broke the silence at the crest of the hill. "I'll walk on the down hill, I need to run some."

Sevman nodded as Yeet slid off the side of the little cart. Yeet's whip came down and the donkey trotted forward, but slowed in the steep decent. Yeet ambled along.

206

"You say he has changed? The work has brought good to all of them?" Sevman's voice held doubt.

"They're browning and vigorous working here in the desert. It is a happier place than Kokand."

Sevman grimaced. "If you carry the darkness with you, any place can become dark. Only those who have found the light can be sure of it anywhere." Sevman's forced gravel voice was sad. He looked at his crooked legs. His expression was tearful.

"*Yapma*, don't Sevman, They're hoping to see you. They sent me to collect you, but we were watched so it was better to work at that mine for a while. You got your strength back and you liked driving the carts with the ore."

"Darkness to darkness, no one could see my feet and legs. My voice was just something easily identified. It didn't go with a thin, pale, bony face."

Yeet became angry. "You whine and complain because we freed you and helped you get a job. You don't show gratitude or pleasure to friends. You just feel sorry for yourself. You make me sick. I thought you'd be a great companion again, but you aren't. You love only yourself, and none of us."

"I do love you, but I'm not someone people can love. I see myself as marred beyond being lovable. I look at my self and wish I were dead." He rode, shoulders bent, unseeing.

"Allah let you live, why should you refuse or regret his gifts? Enjoy while you can, life is short. We will be in the village tomorrow. You'll see how happy they'll be. They've waited a long time."

Sevman did not answer and Yeet burned off his hot anger plunging down the hill at a run. He sought the *cheshm*i, the stone enclosed fountain to bathe, his face and arms in its coolness. He helped Sevman to dismount and to drink and bathe. Yeet played, splashing water and Sevman laughed.

> - - - - - - - > ERBEN'S QUARRY HUT > - - - - - - - >

"Is he conscious yet?" The doctor paused at the door. The tired face that confronted him moved her head up in a negative nod. She moved as if numbed. Behind her Leyla sat on the floor grinding wheat with a millstone by hand. Her face, too, was set and her eyes wide and fixed.

"Someone is with him at all times. Yesterday, after you left, he was feverish and restless. Today he sleeps." They entered the room where the father sat by the bed made up on the mud-brick platform, his hands were bandaged. Erben's face had a set determined look. It was the expression of decision. He stood as the doctor approached the bed. The doctor examined his patient.

"The stitches have held. The blood still oozes, so we must get liquid into him. Otherwise he will dry up and die."

"How is that possible, Doctor? He will drown if we pour water in his mouth," Tayze objected.

"Put a wet cloth on his eyes with a corner in his mouth. He'll swallow spontaneously and it keeps his mouth moist. He'll be clean and watered," the doctor chuckled. He turned to Erben. "Let's see those hands. Are you keeping them oiled and exercising them? Hands are delicate they can stiffen and thicken."

Erben smiled. "They are stiff and the skin is tender and painful to touch, but I'm doing all you said."

"Yes, you are healing nicely. But you may lack strength to work in the quarry." He shook his head.

"If I can hold reins and guide a horse I'll be alright. I'm leaving here and going west. I have news: some of my people are there."

"The boy will need more time and care. It would kill him or do permanent damage if he were moved now."

"The boy can stay with Tayze and the neighbors. I must take Leyla and go. She'll break if I keep her here longer."

"I understand and agree. She has been through too much. I'll find some helpers for Tayze." Their eyes held, full of respect.

> - - - - - - - > OUTSIDE WHITE MARBLE QUARRY > - - - - - - - >

"Okay Umer, we're hunted, out in the country with no food and little money. What now?" Hussein stood over him.

"*Kapa chinini*, shut up, let me think. We have two choices besides going back to the village." He looked up.

"You know we can't go back. What are these choices? They better be good," growled Hussein. The other listeners agreed.

"We could go to my uncle's quarry and work, cutting and hauling. Uncle would feed us and we would live as workers, till my father buys my pardon."

One boy, Ahmed, cursed and stomped angrily. He shook his fist at Umer, shouting: "Remember, you promised to take us out of quarry slavery. We were going to be rich and important. We shook people down and prospered. Now we're fugitives on the run," Ahmed wept.

"You blame me for all of it, but you wanted it. I got you what you wanted. I can still get you what you want."

"You guaranteed the results, you failed. We'll go to the quarry and slave for a new start," said Hussein. One of the boys agreed.

Umer's face turned red and twisted. He jumped up shouting. "You can go to the quarry if you like. I'll be a hussar. I'm going west to Samarkand City and join the army. I have a cousin in the lancers. He'd welcome me. He asked me to come see him."

"Not me, I've a brother in the troops. He's told me about guard duty and patrols. I'm not joining anything with that stuff." Hussein shouted excitedly. He continued hotly. "I've done quarry work, I've watched my father, brothers and uncles do the work. It's hard, but honorable."

"You didn't want to do it before. You'll be as poor as the rest of your family. As a soldier you can win loot and get rewards and recognition for bravery and victories."

"If you're a murderer, they'll still execute you! A change of name and quiet work, one might escape detection."

"Hussein, you stupid ass, we didn't kill him. We bashed him up, but we didn't kill him." Umer was now hysterical.

"I'm going to the quarry. Will your uncle help? He knows you?"

Umer turned his back to regain control. "How should I know? I don't remember him. My father said he would send notice of my coming, but I'm not going. All you who want to go into the lancers with me, come on. I'm going now. The rest of you can go to hell."

There was a moment of silence. Then the group divided. Hussein stood with one of his neighbor friends watching the others walk away.

"Do you think Umer's uncle will receive us?"

"Of course, I'm Umer now and you can be Hussein!"

> - - - - - - - > TANRA DAH MOUNTAIN PASTURES > - - - - - - - >

Warm days came more frequently with occasional spring rains which desert and mountains rapidly absorbed. The green started in the desert and crept up toward the mountains.

The migratory herds had arrived at the western-most frontier of the Uigur lands. The desert, low country contained farms and orchards supported by irrigation. The herds had moved up to the highest mountains where all borders ran. The Baghdad Caliph's empire lay to the west, but the occupants were largely Persian and Turk. The herds could not pass the border guards; they would return east following the mountain trails.

Nooryouz smiled down at the tiny baby slung to her stomach. How quickly one could forget the awkwardness of pregnancy and shepherding in the desert and hills, eating little while craving more, and chasing the animals from the crops of the farmers. When troops or outsiders came she hid among the animals wearing the shapeless costume of all shepherds. Who could know she was not an ignorant boy?

She had watched so many ewes give birth that it bore no fear for her. Seslee and Maril cared for her needs that spring while Jon and Manly kept watch, stirring the sheep to bleat when her cries grew loud.

She was filled with joy and fear. A boy would be killed if she were captured; only a girl would be spared. The birth of Sanjer confirmed her determination; she must be free for her son. She must cross the border in the mountains.

> - - - - - - - > WHITE MARBLE QUARRY > - - - - - - - >

It was late at night when they reached the quarry. All the houses were dark, the village slept. Yeet clapped his hands before the door of the mining hut. There was no response. After numerous attempts, the boys got out blankets and bunked out by a protected south wall to await the dawn. They huddled close for the desert mountains are cold even in summer. They awoke shivering when the sun shone on their faces. The door opened and Tayze's shout of surprise triggered them. They rose and greeted her excitedly.

210

"*Goon aye doon Tayze*, Good morning, Auntie. We've come to see you. Kardesh will be glad to have our help at work."

"Kardesh is ill and sleeps. We have no time for visits. I must fetch water and cook. Don't you know what happened? Go away." She caught up a bucket to draw water.

"I'll go to the *cheshme* for water." Yeet took the bucket from the worried woman's hand and ran toward the community fountain. Sevman looked at the weary face. "I can build a fire and tend the pots. Let me help you. I can help watch Kardesh if he needs it."

She relaxed. "You two were always better than the others. Yes, come in. I need all the help I can get." She turned away.

Sevman could tell she was crying. He dragged himself to the door. 'God blesses the helper and helped', he thought. 'It's a way of sharing light.' He struggled into the kitchen and sat on the floor feeding the fire and was waiting to receive the water Yeet brought. Then Yeet went again for more water.

She spoke again, *"Koo sura bakma*, forgive my fault. I was over-burdened. Erben and Leyla left yesterday and the neighbors have done little to help. The doctor asked them to help, but they must work. I take the brunt of it."

"Kardesh is our elder brother, we must make him well again. We'll share the work together."

> - - - - - - - > UIGUR PALACE > - - - - - - - >

"You have had six months, yet the harem remains empty of three candidates, missing from their place. A serving girl who corrupted our guard has not been punished nor the missing retrieved. You, too, have been difficult to find these last months."

The Emperor of all Uigurs glared at his general. The general lay prostrate before his Lord. In his spring robes of wool and silk, he lay on the marble floor with hand outstretched in an appeal to be heard. The gesture was ignored. The Emperor went on.

"You are son of my father's brother, but royalty implies responsibility as well as opportunity. It must never be confused with privileged permanence. I expect more information than how the escape was arranged. I want news and a prompt return of the

211

kidnapped. I want to know where they are and when you will bring them back. I want instigators punished. No one steals my jewels. I had great matches planned for the Umayyad and her attendant." The general's outstretched palm trembled.

The emperor went on. "I know the roads have been blocked and all baggage and travelers searched. I know the capitol and the villages in all the kingdom have been searched house by house. I know that all borders have been reinforced. Patrols are constant. Guards are quadrupled in numbers and now include the best trackers of the nation. Your spies are watching every suspect. Money is offered for information. Hundreds have responded, but all prove trivial and inconclusive or fantasy and fabricated lies. You see, I know your report by memory. I've heard it enough. It sickens me!" The general's trembling hand was raised again.

"Cousin, you may speak, but without new facts you will signify the end of my patience and your life."

"My Lord, glorious in the light of Mani; news comes by pigeon from the west. A complaint from a traveler crossing the Mountains of God, made to the Prefect of the Illi Valley. He met shepherds moving the herds up for spring grazing. One refused to talk or sell him food. He was angered and feels the person was a woman and not a boy. He claims to have heard a baby cry, but admits the spring lambs were loudly calling, too. Later he thought he saw a pregnant woman silhouetted on the crest. He was sure it was not a bag or lamb. He swore it on oath."

The Emperor sat and contemplated the prone figure and averted face of the man. He sighed and stood.

"You have sent mounted men to investigate and I will have to wait until the man is interviewed further, and the shepherds visited. You have nothing more to add? No other news? Get up, the oath I swore to my uncle still holds. You again prolong your life." The Emperor turned to leave.

"My Lord, There is a young man, son of a prominent family, who obtains herds near the Tang Kingdom." He rose.

"Am I supposed to know this lad or his family?"

"The little brother of the Lady Pahky is a nephew of the Lady Bahil. The family now seeks a marriage for him. He has come of age. He took herds over the border, sold them and bought breeding stock. I have learned he may have returned to Tufan driving the refugee's animals."

The Emperor turned, faced his general, hands and mouth open, astonished. "He would know the refugees? Be their friend? Did it take six months to learn this? Where is Manly now?" The imperial hands were on his hips.

"Driving the family herds west according to the overseer, My Lord. The merchants who were rescued by the Chipchak, Sanjak, are scattered and reluctant to talk about their hardships in

212

traveling. We're sure of only one drover with them. A poor boy named Manish." He gestured apologetically.

"And where is this poor boy? Whose herds does he drive? He knew the refugees; does he know the location of three of them, who were once ours?"

"We don't know yet, My Lord. The family of Manish have moved to their village and we are interviewing their neighbors now. There was a Hun living with them for a while. We hadn't registered the tribal people here, so we didn't know of it. I think they ought to be registered too."

"You didn't think of it! Now you come up with it? The family of Manly has not been happy with the royal house. Whatever the outcome we must pacify them. They have much widespread influence. I shall have to offer one of the princesses, unless, of course, he has helped the escaping ones. Perhaps we could eliminate their influence, if you have proof."

"I have sent a squad directly to the summer camp grounds where the herds should be arriving soon. They carry messenger pigeons. We will know in a week."

"Do not fail me cousin, your career and head depend on it. Also, we should get rid of the refugees. They must be released to cross the border now and we'll see if that draws the missing ones into action. Send spies after them into the Caliphate. We'll learn how the Seljuks treat them."

The man bowed low. "*Bosh ooze two nay*, I obey, my Lord. May your light shine upon your people." The general backed out the door. "The blessing of the prophet Mani be with you."

A GENERAL'S REPORT

213

PEOPLE, PLOTS & PLACES IN CHAPTER 18

Ahmed: begs for food on the way to Sarmakand.
Tayze: left with work and in spite of selling secrets, has no money.
Bolben: a horse master and smuggler, looking for love and wealth.
Derk: gets information about Fatima from the Rug factory owner.
Erben: Has heard about the Toozlu presence and goes to meet them.
Gerchen: exiled by a tribal division seeks glory for his clan.
Jon: seeks a guide over the mountains to freedom.
Kardesh: unconscious still, suffers the injuries of his fight.
Kemeer: has strong opinions and has converted to Islam.
Leyla: seeks to escape Umer and the quarry, but trouble follows her.
Mahmut: third of Umer's group going to Samarkand for the army.
Manish: hopes to lead his harem escapees to safety, but they wash up.
Marian: the priest's wife offers advice to all.
Mookades: the priest has advice for the unheeding.
Seerden: has a failure to rectify and an identity to find for wealth.
Seslee: is interested in escape and a husband.
Setchkin: is free to decide what she will do.
Sevman: devotes himself to his mentor's needs for health.
Twozan: refuses to convert to Islam, so he must go home.
Umer: makes trouble and hurts people wherever he appears.
Uigur Lieutenant: leads refugees to the border for a price.
Widow: now lives in the country with her hoard of coins.
Yeet: provides money and friendship for Erben's family.
Yusuf: objects to giving valuables into the lieutenant's care.

Glossary:

beer air beer air: one by one; successively.
jan o var: wild monster; beast.
kardeshim: my brother, my sister, or my sibling.
kuz zum sackeen ol: calm down daughter; relax girl.
ooyan kalk: wake up; get up.
sod a kot: a portion of a Muslim's income set aside for charity.
ser sery: bum; hobo; drifter; worthless person.
soos: hush; silence; quiet.
Tanra overim: I praise God; praise to the creator.

QUARRY BEGGERS

"Have you no *sadakat*, offering for the poor? Good lady, see our need." Ahmed stood by the door of the mud farm hut where his clapping had brought a stern faced old woman. Behind her a great kangal hound gave a warning growl.

"*Ser sery*, vagabond, up early or have you walked all night? I knew your kind in Kokand, thieves in from scrounging the market. If it weren't for the Kardesh I'd still be in my little house there." Ahmed and his friend were dirty and had slept in their clothes. She made a face and looked inside. "I've a bite of bread and early figs left from last night. You can't expect much from a poor widow exiled in these thorn-lands." They smiled voicing their thanks. She closed the door and returned to pass out a broken bowl with the food. They wolfed down the contents and passed it back.

"Allah bless you, helper of the poor," they said in chorus.

She nodded, peering out the cracked door. She watched them move away. When out of sight she slipped out the door leaving the dog.

"You guard the house. I'll check the apricots." She latched the door and stared around and went to a gnarled old oak tree. She examined the ground around the tree. Then stared up and patted a swollen knot in the bowl of the trunk. She smiled and nodded in satisfaction and went to the stairs at the back of the hut. Above on the roof were the drying trays of fruit. She started to climb painfully. She heard a slight sound and began to turn, a boy with an angry mouth slipped a cord over her head. She called and reached the boy's face clawing furrows down the cheek and chin. But he tightened the noose and the knots dug into her throat. Her falling weight brought intolerable pain. Inside the hut the dog threw himself against the door in a fury of barks and growls, but the latch held. Umer hissed. From the bushes his two companions joined him.

Ahmed whispered urgently. "Why did you kill her? How can we get to her goods? The dog is mean and we've no way to get rid of him. You can't fight a kangal with knives." Umer ignored him as he rolled the body over and exposed her face. With a shudder he searched.

"Allah what a face, better hidden. Damn, her purse is flat as her breasts." He straightened up angrily.

"Umer, what's she done to you? Your face is all blood." Ahmed moved a hand to touch him. Umer slapped down the hand. He lifted his stained face in pride.

"She has hidden money. I saw her hiding place when she came out the door. It's that tree; either under or in it." He walked to the tree and examined it closely.

"You're crazy. What kind of money would an old widow woman have?" Doubt filled his friends' faces.

"I don't know, but I'll find it." Umer drew a knife.

> - - - - - - - > AKSU MONASTERY > - - - - - - - >

"Now listen well. You will prepare for the journey out of our territory. We will move south and west and we'll leave you in the mountains to continue your travels to the Abbassid lands. I command you to put your valuables on animals that will be escorted by the guards. We will keep them at the rear of the column for safety." The lieutenant was sober and well dressed. Everyone knew orders had arrived the day before.

Yusuf motioned to speak. He was nervous and worried. "Our valuables are few. Our families must have food where we are going. You can't expect us to give everything to go on a few beasts that'll be the aim of every bandit in the mountains. We'll need the guards ahead to prevent an ambush."

The *yuzbasha* held up a commanding hand. "*Do'er*, stop, I know the road and you don't. I know best how to protect my charges, you don't. Leave this matter to me. All jewelry and coins will be bundled with family names attached. Everything will be orderly. I take full responsibility." His face held calm arrogance and contempt.

The consternation on the faces of his listeners was universal. The silence was transformed in a roar of objections. This time the *yuzbasha* turned his head to shout. "*Hazur ol*, ready." The soldiers strung their bows and notched arrows to draw. Silence fell again.

"Be ready to travel tomorrow at dawn. I will brook no delays. Have your valuables bagged and marked. Any found hiding valuables will be left here and sold into slavery or executed." He made a gesture of dismissal and rode away. The soldiers disarmed their weapons after the crowd had broken up and left. Each family worried over how much they dare hide and carry. What would they surrender to the bag? At what risk?

> - - - - - - - > ERBEN IN THE AMU VALLEY > - - - - - - - >

"*Ooyan, kalk kuzum*; wake, get up girl. It's time." Erben leaned over the form of his daughter Leyla. He blew a stray curl to one side. Then picking up a stem of dry grass, tickled her chin. To wake a person too abruptly might endanger the person by the loss of their wandering soul. He smiled as she stirred, opening her eyes.

"Ah, you're back with us. How were your dreams? Where did you travel?" He went back to the camp fire where food was cooking.

She sat up. "I ran. Something was chasing me. I climbed a hill and saw a river or lake below me. I scrambled down, but it reached for me and I jumped. I floated into a cloud that hid me and seemed to fly over the waters, but it pursued me still."

"I'm the wind which will bear you up and away. Soon we'll join members of our tribe. I've heard rumors and now, I know where they are. You'll be with people who love and honor you." He sat cross-legged, fists on hips, a Khan again.

"Our people? They have come? Where are they?" An expression of joy crossed her face. She came to the fire.

"Yes, ours. We go to them now. In only a few days we'll find them. They are in the west." He nodded assurance.

> - - - - - - - > SEERDEN'S HOUSE IN KOKAND > - - - - - - - >

The wolf's message read like an allegory. 'Your attempt to down the eagle failed, but the bird flies to escape with the chick. The fledgling is hurt beyond repair. The news source is now useless. Move to intercept the eagle and bring him down. Remember to preserve the chick. Ignore the wounded fledgling. The eagle's flight will be toward his nest, now in the west. In this hunt you must be the archer. Set on him before the falconer nets him.'

The enigmatic message, written in flowing Arabic, summed the movement of weeks and held clues that added to the whole. Seerden studied it carefully. Slowly a smile lit his face as he nodded thoughtfully, so close now, yes, so very close. Reward upon rewards awaited him. But first he must find and terminate Erben and also encounter the final clue that would give him tremendous power, the identity of the Gray Wolf.

> - - - - - - - > ERBEN IN THE AMU VALLEY > - - - - - - - >

"Father we have ridden all morning and I'm thirsty. Let's stop at this house beside the road and test their well." Leyla brought her sturdy pony to a halt in the open yard before the country hut. She dismounted with a jump.

"You've done well. I'm pleased you've not forgotten your skills. You are still a Chipchak born to the horse." He looked round the farm. Within the hut came the excited whine and barking of a great dog. He heard the buzz of flies behind the house. The earth around one of the old oaks was dug with earth tossed about and a hole cut in the bole exposing a nest of animal or bird. His body became tense as the horse paced impatiently. Her pony tossed her head and whinnied.

"Come quickly dear. Something evil has happened here. We're outsiders and must leave lest we be blamed."
She had drained a gourd of water and was drawing more to offer him. She walked to his horse and lifted the gourd.

"Drink, father, it's good water." He accepted it and took the contents in a great gulp. Rising on stirrups he tossed it beyond the well and his horse erupted into a gallop.

Leyla shrugged and mounted, racing to catch him. The pony ran to exhaustion. But still Erben outpaced her. At the top of a high hill she saw him waiting, she called. "Mercy father, you're too well mounted for us. Wait there." She rode her tired mount up the hill only to find he had descended to a shady grove in the valley. Dismounting she led her animal down. The heat was strong on them.

"Psst! Umer, look who's coming after the mad man. Isn't that your little bare-face? The girl you were crazy about?"

Umer quickly parted the branches to look back. He made a rasping sound, sucking the air in shock.

"Do you suppose they know? She doesn't look afraid, even if the old guy is acting crazy." Mahmud commented as she walked by, sweaty but collected.

Ahmed peeped out and commented, "No, but she's dressed like the tribes. I like civilized girls. But look at Umer, he's in a trance."

"Allah, his heart is in his face. He's drawing his knife. Stop him!" Both boys grabbed Umer as he pushed aside the branches to plunge out on the path. The widow's donkey chose this moment to bray and pass water. They pulled him back into the brush while he fought them. Leyla took a dive for the saddle and hugging the pony's neck was gone in a burst of speed. Ahmed yelped as the knife grazed his arm. He kicked Umer in the stomach knocking him to the ground.

Damn you *janovar*, monster. You won't endanger us with more deaths. We'll take half the coins and go. You keep the donkey. I don't want any of that old woman's goods." Ahmed examined his scratch carefully.

"You want the part that got her killed, you cowards. That girl's the cause of our troubles. I'm going to get her." Umer's angry words burned the air as he rushed on. "If you're afraid of the mad man and that little bitch, you can go, but you'll not take anything from me. I got it, I'll keep it and you can go to hell." His waving knife emphasized the words.

They watched him carefully. "We're in this together, Umer, but we can't stop to follow someone. We have to get away before local folks start to search for us." Mahmud was apologetic. Ahmed turned sulky and moved over toward the donkey to untie its halter. He was afraid to go alone, but he would never trust Umer again.

"I follow the girl. They're strangers here too; suspect just as we are. Who but us knows what happened at that house this morning?"

> - - - - - - - > WHITE MARBLE QUARRY > - - - - - - - >

"*Kardeshim*, my brother, I await your orders. " Sevman sat beside the primitive bed in dog-like devotion for his master and friend to speak. He was not impatient. He changed the cool damp cloth over the dark bruises and stitches. The patient groaned feverishly. Sevman put the corner of a sopping wet cloth in Kardesh's mouth leaving it until it shared its water with the hot dry mouth. Then he dipped the cloth again, tirelessly. Tayze and Yeet worked in the kitchen.

"*Tanra overim*, praise God that you have come. How was the city?" She paused awkwardly. Smoothed her wrinkled brow and sighed. "You left the bundle I gave you?"

"At the neighbor's house, yes, but the colored rag was not flown the next day. I slept in a house nearby. I left that afternoon."
The woman paused to wipe her eyes.

"So, no bag, no answer?" Her face was tragic.

"A man came to check where I used to sleep, but I had moved to another place and he didn't find me. I knew that the lady was either compromised or helpless. So I went ahead."

"He promised to pay: simple information for cash." She sighed deeply and turned her face away to the wall.

Yeet waited on Tayze sympathetically. She reached up and brought down a packet. Opening it she emptied a purse of a few coins. She counted and gave them to Yeet.

"It will buy lentils, leaks and bread for tomorrow. After that we'll depend on neighbor's charity."

"I got a little money from the city and from the mines where we worked this winter. We'll get through."

> - - - - - - - > IN THE TANRA DAH MOUNTAINS > - - - - - - - >

"You've been across the border before, Manish?" Dahkool asked their young guide. They led the rest of the party by several lengths. Manish looked back at those who followed. He was free of his work as herder. New boys had replaced them with the herd. He and Dahkool were of a close enough age to have an understanding; so he spoke in a voice of conspirators.

"Only as far as the crest, I've not been over the plateau or down the Illy river valley where all the villages lie. They're not sheep country. Horses abound in the heights above the rivers, but the plateau is too dry and cold even for camels." She thought of the great two humped beasts used in the China trade and wondered at so dangerous a land.

"Why then risk so high a pass? Why should merchants go that way?" He looked in wonder at so thoughtless a query, but answered her question softly, because she was a friend.

"It's the shortest way to the cities where they must sell their goods. Farmers can't afford luxury goods; the taxes being what they are. Only land owners and government people can buy them. Don't worry. We will go through grazing country that only smugglers use, to come out on the north side. The merchants' roads are filled with soldiers and customs officials. We'd never get through there. Officers are few in the high grazing country."

He stopped and sniffed the air. "There's a new smell here, I don't know it."

She laughed shrilly and held out her clean little hand. "We washed with perfumed soap I brought. We smelled like sheep before, now we're clean." He hadn't noticed that her face and hands were clean, hair trimmed and clothes mended.

They were walking below the crest of a cool meadow when Manish dropped to the ground pulling Dahkool with him. High above a herd of horses had passed over the crest and were descending on the meadow above them. Manish whistled to the rest of his group and motioned them to earth. The voice of the herder was heard singing loudly.

#1   Hi ho he, fattened, healthy be.
            Grow in strength, beauty and all speed.
            Follow me! Stallions, mares agree:
            Distant China your colts will see.

221

#2   Su sa so, learn much as you grow.
        You will know, all the paces show.
        If you play, never heed your way
        You will pay, master's hunger stay.

#3   Wi wa wu, eat the whole day through.
        You will grow, swift as winds that blow.
        If your head will match your heart
        You'll be winning from the start.

BOLBEN'S HERDING SONG

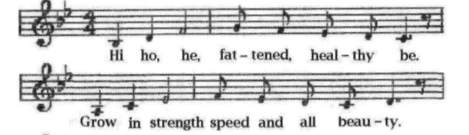

Hi ho, he, fat-tened, heal-thy be.

Grow in strength speed and all beau-ty.

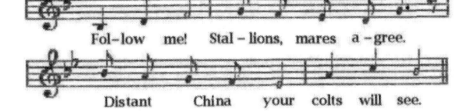

Fol-low me! Stal-lions, mares a-gree.

Distant China your colts will see.

The singer stopped abruptly as the horses shied and in a moment had armed his bow and strung an arrow urging his horse into a run. Manish jumped to his feet with his hands high above his head and at the same instant yelled.

"Bolben, look who visits you." Manish stood still and motioned to the others to get up and do the same. They complied nervously. The horseman rode a wide circle about them searching the ground and horizon. He drew up to Manish.

"Heaven help the straying sheep. Their little brother is on their trail. What news Manish? Why so many shepherds without sheep?" The two boys grinned at each other. Then Manish reached inside his jacket for a metal disk with symbols and two kinds of writing on each face.

"My master sends his sign. We seek to cross over. He has found new workers and will come to pay his debts to your chief."

Bolben stared carefully at Jon, then at the slight form of the other shepherds. He shook his head.

"Welcome to the land of the Ust Yayla People. You think these can make it? Better they stay and marry here." He smirked at Seslee. She looked down and petted the lamb she carried in a sling. Then she put him down to eat the grass. Bolben hid his eyes and gestured dramatically.

"She puts sheep on the pastures of the Heavenly Mountains! Where can the horses go if the sheep take all?"

"You're a great friend of the sheep men, indeed, of all the men in the high country."

Bolben raised his nose. "But my tribe think me mad. Go over the pass and down the valley. This area is clear. But the next mountain has extra troops so keep you eyes open. There's food at the hut up the right fork. Expect me tonight." With another look at Seslee he spurred after the wandering herd. Manish shouted his farewell. Seslee tittered, but the others looked shocked. How easily he had penetrated their disguises.

> - - - - - - - > ERBEN IN THE AMU VALLEY > - - - - - - - >

"S*ackeen ol, kuzum,* calm down daughter. Hush now dear. Tell me," Erben insisted, "what's wrong?" Leyla clung to the horse, crying and shaking. He held the bridle and calmed the animal, but not the girl. When he touched her shoulder to comfort, she reacted by screaming.

Finally he pulled her from the saddle and shook her. His face was grim, his order clear. "You are the daughter of a khan, Princess Leyla. you will control yourself and tell me what is wrong." His words struck some cord and she stared wildly at him. Then she embraced him respectfully almost dutifully.

Clearing her face with one long sleeve, she bowed before him and quivered while speaking in a thin hysterical voice. "Umer burst out of the brush beside the road as I walked by. I jumped on my horse and raced away." He passed the pony's reins back to her.

"From here just up the road? Wait here, I'll check for the scoundrel." He swung onto the saddle and left in a rush.

"Don't leave me!" But he was gone. Dust sifted by. Looking about she scrambled to mount her nervous horse. She rode out to the road to see him ride to a near cluster of brush. There he dismounted and walked slowly forward.

She could not remain behind and rode slowly back. She caught up just where Umer had appeared. Erben had found the place where the brush was broken. He studied

223

the tracks. She rode up to observe his actions. He followed the track back on foot, but stopped when he saw their direction.

"They're three, gone back into that limestone ridge. It's a perfect place for ambush. They've no mounts, only a donkey. We'll out distance them easily." He turned back to mount. Together they started down the road again.

He reached over to squeeze her trembling hands, he spoke reassuringly. "They're exiles from the quarry. Nothing but evil will come in their future. I know what must have happened at that house. Avengers will be hot on their trail. A clan of our tribe await us in the west. With them we'll be safe. Fear nothing, leave Umer and his gang to Tanra." He took the reins from her hand to lead. The gallop cooled her anxiety.

> - - - - - - - > WHITE MARBLE QUARRY > - - - - - - - >

"I'm here Kardesh. Hold on. Yeet's here too. We're all together again." Sevman held a hand and leaned over the pallet to whisper in his ear. Yeet came in with a bowl of lentil soup which he set down on the bed. He put his hands on his hips in exasperation and looked down at the two boys. "Look at the two of you. He can't eat, you won't eat and both are getting thinner. No, don't give me any nonsense about fasting so the light will shine brighter."

"But it does Yeet. Prophet Mani says so. The elect choose the way of asceticism." Sevman's face was open.

"You're not elect. You're not well. You're not considerate. You make yourself unfit to help in the daily work. You make us bear the hardships." Yeet was shouting.

"You save food." Sevman giggled at his joke. "Don't be angry. I'll eat your lentils. I'm not elect, but I wish I were." He reached over and took the bowl. He paused, sighed and started eating slowly. Yeet sat by Kardesh's head and put his hands on either side of his face. He whispered. "*Ooyan, kalk*, wake up, get up. You've slept long enough, big brother. *Aman Allah, Allah, Yesu gel*, God help us. Things go badly. Please, hear me. We need your help." He took his hands away and wiped his sleeve across his face. The boys exchanged looks. Then a long unbroken silence followed.

224

Kardesh's breathing changed pace and he sighed. First his eye lashes fluttered, then his head stirred. He stared up at Yeet and then at Sevman. His lips moved but no sound came. Both boys sat with their mouths open unable to move. Kardesh was awake!

> - - - - - - - > KOKAND RUG FACTORY > - - - - - - - >

Derk stood in the rug factory talking with the manager. a cultured Persian whose gestures and words were eloquent. The prosperity of his enterprise was shown by his jeweled hands, ears and silk robes over shalvar pants.

"Orphans and widows are our main support in the general work. Most work with cotton or wool, but we have our specialists in linen or silk. The lady you asked about knots rugs combining silk and wool of the finest quality, so we quite spoil her with privileges. Fatima, too, was an excellent worker. My word, she had the keenest eye for detail and subtle shifts of color and texture. Her rugs were of unusual tightness, you understand? It had a very high number of threads per thumb measure and resistance to fraying. I've not had another like her."

"How long was she with you?"

The owner responded. "She came with her mother after the death of the Yemeni. He was army first, then police. When he died their association buried him, but the support for a widow with children is insufficient. Fatima must have been about seven and she learned so fast, in five years she became proficient. Some children show that kind of talent, while others don't," he shrugged.

"What did she die of? Was she sickly?" Derk pressed as the conversation moved to urgent points.

"I was traveling for contracts and sales to the northlands. I have customers even among the tribes. I understand it was due to a fire in her room. The body was badly burned. She was buried the next day."

Derk pursed his lips. "When did you meet her brother Yeet?"

"Once with the mother while she was working. He explained that he was apprenticed to a goldsmith and jeweler and had this day free. After the funeral when I

225

returned I saw him once again. He showed me a silver ring he had made. It was fine work. I asked him to make me a ring. Here it is, see the woven gold cables around the jade stone. I understand that the jeweler died and he was serving in the market the next year."

"Were the children much alike?" Derk insisted.

"Family resemblance, sure, but he was taller, darker, and louder. He was a determined, but cheerful type, not like timid little Fatima, shy and tongue-tied. My loss was great. There was an unlimited market for her work." He sighed.

> - - - - - - - > REFUGEES LEAVE AKSU > - - - - - - - >

"This is your last stop in Uigur-land. The desert plain before you marks the border with the Abbassid Muslim Caliphate. Down from the plateau is the army station. They will admit you there. Don't linger on the crossing, people die there." The lieutenant smiled slyly. "Caravan goods have been picked up along the trail from travelers who didn't survive. Travel light and fast. Now go forward." He pointed ahead as the assembling crowd fell into line, took up their goods and began to move forward. The lieutenant led the line of refugees for the first several miles. Their treasure came behind with a special guard. Sanjak was brought to the head of the column and the guards withdrew. Koolair accompanied Yusuf and family. The people pressed forward eagerly. No one noticed when the guards and treasures fell back and vanished.

> - - - - - - - > SEEPAGE SPRING NEAR THE AMU RIVER > - - - - - - - >

A strange, out of season rain fell that night. The meeting was held in the largest yurt which bulged with the press of men and women in attendance. A large lamp lit from one side of the assembly. Most sat shoulder to shoulder.

"Why not accept the offer of their officer. We can become guards for the caliph. We'll keep our beliefs and customs as we wish. They won't know what we do," Gerchen argued angrily.

ONAT'S OFFER

Twozan stood shaking his head. "You deceive yourself, in their lands we'll be watched and they'll require us to conform in every important way, at least outside the tribe."

Gerchen pushed Twozan. "No, we won't change under threats. We're men." Everyone was now shouting and gesturing. Many stood pushing angrily.

Father Mookades pushed between the men as he shouted at Gerchen. Another pushed in to add his shouts to the others. None sat to listen. The volume was at full.

"We're free people. We keep our ways. We may change a little, but we will continue to be ourselves."

"The khan has not come to take up our cause. He's hiding now. I'll return with those who'll go." The noise became louder and more emotional. Twozan held up his hands, but few noticed until he blew out the lamp and shouted.

"Wait, let everyone voice his opinion. Otherwise all talk and no one hears what is being said." Twozan's shout filled and quieted the turbulent yurt's interior.

"*Beer air beer air*, one by one, yes that's good." The noise increased in a tone of agreement.

Kemeer spoke up. "*Soos*, hush everyone. Let the speaker be heard." Many called out for quiet and the crowd hushed. The lamp was lit again.

Setchkin spoke in a high piercing voice. "What of me? Am I free to return to my father's yurt? I can vouch for your rascality, penury and rudeness. My father will rejoice on my return, but I can't guarantee that for any of you."

There was an uncomfortable silence at Princess Setchkin's statement. What of the mother and child? Abduction had hardened the Kaynaklar's pursuit, but would her return soften it? To send her to the Caliph would condemn them forever.

The priest, Father Mookades, spoke to rally those who would wish to return. He meant to pave the way of reconciliation. "Our family is pledged to Yesu. We cannot demote the living Word of God to become followers of a lesser prophet. Our Tanra is a unity, not a singularity. Besides, all prophets are traced from Isaac, not Ishmael. The child of promise, the thousand year rule by the Kaya family is from Tanra."

"My wife is Muslim." Kemeer began. "She says it is easy to convert. You have to repeat the pledge to Allah and Muhammad, the one they use in their call to prayer, and you are accepted at once. No confirmation, baptism, waiting, or even catechism. Utter simplicity. No saint's days to

227

keep and only one fast each year from dark to dark for one moon. They make a party of it every night." Kemeer the wrestler's answer pleased some. There were nods of agreement.

Marian the priest's wife spoke her mind. "Among Christians we have the Blessed Virgin as a model and example for women, but in Islam what woman can take her place? Females are not only deprived of worshiping one of their own, but also of possessing one husband alone. They take many wives." Some men hid their grins, snickers and nudges at this point.

Gerchen motioned for quiet and spoke. "We are offered gold and goods to do work we love. We can and will believe and practice what we like. I say take the oath and serve the Caliph. Because any oath I take will be for that end only. We move west."

Twozan countered. "I have the most to lose by going back to the Khan. Death will await me. But I'll die in faith and repentance. Erben has ignored us. I've failed you. We've sacrificed so much for so little. But I'll not accept the offer. I'm willing to lose anything except Yesu."

Gerchen grunted, "The warriors will want to go with me. You and the priest can go home with the princess. She's a fickle bitch, but she might get you off, if she doesn't kill you first."

> - - - - - - - > TOOZLU DIVISION > - - - - - - - >
"The desert blooms, Tanra has sent rain." Setchkin's face shone with joy as she looked out over the hills.

Twozan said gloomily. "Perhaps the devil celebrates the dividing of the clan: the breaking of friendships, the failure of our hopes for the future of the tribe."

"Beauty is from Tanra, the devil can't create such things. I'm going home whole and with my child. You men will make your politics, but they're a small part of this world. Plans never work out like you want them to. Tanra still rules over all. Friendships that are breakable aren't real." She looked at him and laughed shaking her head mockingly. "You lost; I won!"

"You laugh at us and the misfortunes we suffer. Now you're free to go as you will." Scorn was in his voice. "Our resistance has saved you from capture and the harem of an Arab Prince."

"Consider how fortunate you are to return to our land." she retorted saucily, "You won't have to travel with the camels. Besides, working for a Sultan must be dull. Rich, powerful men are difficult; they expect to be obeyed, catered too, and spoiled. They are often slow to pay or even stingy." She gave him a side glance and continued. "I think we should return to the north together. Better we all go as a group to look out for each other's interests."

He averted his face which moved convulsively. "You jest and laugh at me. Why would you wish to travel with your captors? The sight of us must make you sad. Tanra has delivered us to our enemies."

She touched him. "I'm sympathetic. But you fail to see that while Tanra has frustrated your actions, he has answered my prayers. I return to my family. Yesu *boo yuke ter*. Jesus is wonderful. Tanra is great."

"Yes, you have your way, but what will you do with the children and mothers you harbor?"

She shrugged, smiling. "They choose. Most were Muslim before, those who practice it still are. Some learned our language and how to herd. They can stay or return to farming: a worse slavery than me. People choose their fate and blame it on Tanra."

She sniffed. The air carried a scent of perfume. She closed her eyes. The day was too beautiful to waste on grief or spend with sorrow, so she walked away. She stopped at the last yurt and stood looking for a long time. She whispered, "Now that I'm free what will I do?"

SUDDEN FRIGHT

PEOPLE, PLOTS & PLACES IN CHAPTER 19

Abdul: his assassination attempt is only partly successful.
Aslan bey: salutes his commander's success too soon.
Atilla bey: longs for adventure and action, but is sent away.
Bolben: agrees to help the fugitives, but his price is high.
Dahkool: tries to protect the escapees and get a horse.
Derk: is an agent in distress for lack of early information.
Erben: tries to take his daughter to the safety of the tribe.
Jon: continues to conduct his group despite mistakes.
Kerim of the East Bulgars: provides a cover to hide Kynan.
Kynan: attempts to play the mercenary from a Bulgar tribe.
Leyla: nervous and anxious to move on as fast as possible.
Manish: leads his escapees toward the passes to the west.
Maril: has a limp from her fall. but keeps up with the others.
Mother: gets family news from Dirk bey at the rug factory.
Murat: the youth pulled down by two hunting hounds.
Nooryuz: has a baby to protect and move toward freedom.
Onat: feels victorious in his diplomacy; others don't agree.
Orhan: escorts Atilla and friend to search for the strangers.
Sanjak: leads his refugees into the Abbassid territory.
Tewfik: Sheriff of west Kokand seeks a murderer.
Tracker: a man of long expertise in tracking people.
Twozan: must return to his enemies with his hostages.

GLOSSARY:
ayran: a drink of yogurt and water.
bash'ara: to success.
bey'im: my Lords; sirs.
evit binbasham: yes, my general; certainly, my commander.
hydi geldim: here I am; Hi, I came.
hy hy hy' ya: The warriors' ululating cry in battle.
Imsak: first prayer of the Muslim day, at dawn.
ne var: what is it; what is happening?
saha teen each eleem: I drink to your health.
soos: hush; quiet.
Yesu boo yuke ter: Jesus is great; God is great.
Yesu gel: Come Jesus; God help us.

TRACKER'S DOGS

"They move away from the road, westward toward Samarkand and Khiva. They ride the donkey. His prints are deep. He'll tire."

The mounted men listened with respect to the old man, tracking on the ground. The leader nodded, understanding. "They're young and spry, but careless about leaving trails."

"We should catch them easily," the tough man replied.

A young man held the leash on two large kangals, who pulled impatiently, one toward the trail, the other toward the road. The young man spoke up hesitantly." The footprints of the woman end here. I wonder why she took to horse?"

The horsemen nodded and one spoke. "She was at the well and threw the gourd away. The man rode away, but here he returns walking."

Tracker pointed. "She was frightened there and here. There by the spirit of death, here by the murderers. They scuffled among themselves. See Murat, here and here. One may have desired or tried to kill her. She fled and the man came back with her, but wisely, did not follow. But we can."

The men turned at the sound of horses coming down the road. Two men came riding over the hill. At the sight of the five men they stopped, talked, and came on slowly.

"Is that you Atilla bey?" The leader's voice was friendly. "I heard you had returned from the East with treasure, but I've not seen you 'til now."

"Tewfik bey, you rascal, how are you serving your master today?" Atilla hastened up to embrace his friend. Kynan held back waiting while the group looked him over.

"You bring a foreigner to us? You know him well?" Kynan stood his horse and listened with care.

"I brought a friend to travel west with me. He's Turk, but nice enough. He can match you drink for drink of lion's milk and still ride circles around you." Atilla laughed loudly and thumped Tewfik's back affectionately.

"There are many strangers on the road. Our people suffer from their visits. We follow two on the road and three in the brush, hiding. We'll terminate the three, then investigate the two." Tewfik was still somewhat stiff and formal. "We pursue murderers, Atilla bey, the dog here was locked in the house, but he knows who killed his mistress. He has the scent".

"We'll have them before moon rise tonight." Murat shouted excitedly, still struggling with the dogs.

Tewfik's voice warmed and he squeezed his friend's arm. "Come now, you forget your manners, Your Turk has a name and people?" He walked his horse to Kynan's side while studying his face closely in the evening light.

Kynan spoke, "Kerim of the East Bulgars. My family and clan are small. We drive stock or do mercenary duty to maintain our family. I'm greatly honored to meet a sheriff, a friend of Atilla bey, my sponsor." Tewfik relaxed slowly, considering.

"Let us join your hunt, old friend. I'm a good shot you know. You'll let us in on the excitement, won't you?" Atilla was all fire to help.

Tewfik smiled for the first time. He laughed easily, looking over his men. "I'll take Murat with the dogs, Tracker, and one horseman to follow in the bush. Orhan's grandfather was a Turk, he can ride with you on the road to find the two strangers. Go with him until we catch up." The last sentence was directed to Orhan who nodded his agreement. Kynan masked his concern as the man continued.

"Welcome to my jurisdiction Kerim Bey, mercenary. I'm sure your aim is true and ability great. We'll meet again later." He ululated a war cry and the baying dogs plunged into the desert brush followed by the horses. Atilla's face was a study of disappointment. Orhan shrugged and moved onto the road ahead. He spoke philosophically.

"At least we'll get a look at the girl first."

> - - - - - - - >AT THE SHERIFF'S HUNT > - - - - - - - >

"The rock hill doesn't help does it Tracker? The dogs are of two minds again." Tewfik bey scanned the horizon.

"Too dark for details now, beyim. There's a bit of broken grass and scarred rock on this side. The donkey has gone to the right, I'm sure. Bitler seems to be uncertain, but the other dog is definite. The boys must be riding. They show no track, but on rock who can tell?"

The two horsemen sat uncertainly. Murat fell as both dogs plunged the same direction. Then Bitler moved sniffing to left and right seeking tracks while the other dog bayed and pulled Murat down again. Tracker hurried to help the boy.

Tewfik spoke. "We can backtrack if you're wrong. They can't be far ahead. Let's get it over with and get a meal and some rest. The relatives will be at the wake now."

The other man brought out a bag and squirted a liquid in his mouth. "It's only *ayran*, bey, but it's cool and fresh."

Tewfik took and squeezed the bag. He passed it down to Tracker and Murat. Last light was ebbing fast.

"What about the two strangers that Orhan and Atilla are seeking? You told him to wait for you."

Tewfik shrugged. "Orhan's a leach. He won't let go, even if I'm two days late." The men spurred their horses after the dogs.

"We'll wait for moon-rise if we hit another puzzle."

> - - - - - - - >REFUGEES HIGH IN THE TANRA DAH > - - - - - - - >

"The mountains shine above while we sit in shadow and nurse our tired feet." Seslee stopped rubbing her feet to gaze up at the

233

heights. Dahkool held the baby while Nooryouz stretched and fell back against the grass.

Manish spoke. "You have bathed, washed and become ladies before you're safe. You will also have more trouble passing in Islam where the only decent women are with their husbands and fathers."

Maril sadly nodded assent, but Seslee reacted. "Posh, Manish you can be Maril's brother and I can be married to Jon. Nooryouz is my married sister seeking her husband with the refugees. That gives us all a role."

"We have no resources nor are we warriors or merchants. If your beauty is noticed we'll suffer abuse and you'll be taken away from us. You'll be captive as surely as you've been with the Wigars. Manish's words worried them and they paused.

Nooryouz sat up asking. "What's to be done? Only one man knows now. Can he be trusted?" The party remembered the bold rider of the afternoon. His arrogant good humor aroused their interest.

"He is a herder, anxious to gain the admiration of other men as well as women. He may brag or tell stories. There are paid ears near the borders. Smugglers are rich and informers have their hands out." Manish's voice rose. "They work for the highest bidder or their masters."

"But your master has offered payment." Jon objected.

"For refugee herd boys, not valuable women."

"We'll be dirty and sweaty in three days." Seslee laughed. She held out her hands brushing the supposed dirt.

"You have combed and perfumed hair and have lost the smells and stains of sheep. You'll fool nobody."

As they talked the light faded, stars shone as the sounds of a horse drew near. Each checked their knives or other protection for the talk had revealed their danger. Several hid in the brush.

"*Hydi geldim*, I've come. Manish my friend, did you find your food and supplies? My apologies, they're intended for herder's use." He peered from his horse trying to see the people before him. Jon moved to hold the horse's bridle.

"What has happened in the village?" Manish asked.

"How did you know? Messengers came from the capitol. The missing women were described and great rewards were offered. But I kept your secret. How will you reward me?"

"What would satisfy you? More money?" Jon asked.
The horseman laughed. The horse cavorted and Jon let go.

"You can't beat the price offered in the village. No, I want one of the palace girls. I can't keep her, worse luck, but I want her for tonight." There was a long silence.

"I'm a palace girl and I'll pay his price." Dahkool spoke from the dark. There were several sounds of protest.

234

"I know what I'm doing. It's the only way to get help and satisfy his honor. You'll not hurt me? Give me your word. Swear by your love for your horses." There was a faint lisp in her voice. But he could not see her cleft lip.

"I swear by my love for all good things. Here, come take my hand. We'll ride to the loveliest spot on earth for the moon rise. Then we'll sleep till dawn." He reached out.

"You're a horse herder and have beautiful horseflesh to spare. I want to ride like a palace lady on a royal hunt. That way I can return to my friends."

He laughed again. "What is your rank lady? Your price is high, but I'm sure you're worth it. Ride with me now, I'll pick just the right horse later. Love of horses is another call to my heart, as clear as your voice, fair lady. Come." He reached.

"You may call me Princess, gallant warrior. I accept your conditions and promises. But I'll not kiss you. I must be able to say I've not been kissed by a man." She was swung up to sit behind him and he left in a rush.

"No kisses; agreed." His laughter faded away in the distance. A shocked silence held them.

Jon spoke to all. "She knows we leave at midnight and must be camped again before first light. Let's hope she gets the horse."

"What scandal, a promiscuous kitchen drudge daring to call herself a princess." Seslee's voice was high and hot.

"*Soos*, hush, she saved us. He might have chosen one of us and suffered rejection," Nooryouz spoke sharply.

"She's not loose! Not darkness but light! She was sold to the palace and abused as a girl. She had no choice then. Tonight she chose to give us another day and perhaps a horse." Manish was near tears as he confronted the group.

Maril exclaimed. "Someone had to go, Seslee. If not her then you or I, otherwise we've suffered these months for nothing."

"The reward would carry all else before it. Dahkool is a princess in my esteem, Seslee." Jon spoke firmly.

Seslee shrugged and no one could see her pout.

> - - - - - - - > KOKAND RUG FACTORY > - - - - - - - >

"Pigeons have just flown in with fresh news for us. Listen," Derk commanded. "Yeet is now living at the quarry where his friend has suffered injury. He and Sevman were hidden in the mines for some of the time. They earned money and hid from Ali bey, the chief of police. Now we hear that Erben bey, an heir to the Chipchak Khanate, has left with his daughter. They seem to be going west to the invading clans of their tribe. My Caliph desires him to come under His protection. I'm leaving to meet them before they

235

are intercepted by the troops of Onat bey. But I have important questions for you."

"Yes, Derk bey, you are good to tell me the news. In the factory we hear only gossip and rumor of the outside world. Now they talk of an invasion and war. Troubles never cease. What is your question, *beyim*?" The blind weaver continued knotting the threads of the rug.

Derk replied, "I think the Gray Wolf visited you here. What did his voice sound like? What did he ask you?"

She paused, "He asked about Yeet and Sevman: where they had gone. I was so afraid I'm not sure what he said. His voice held an accent, but perhaps it was intended. No one saw him come or go. I asked the others about strangers visiting the factory. Our manager does not normally allow it. But all maintain that no one came here."

He nodded, "Is that all he asked?"

She resumed work. "He wanted to know about Fatima." She smiled as she worked away. "Everyone wants to know about her."

"I want to know more, too. She's not in the grave, the remains are of an old woman's not a child, I got permission. It was witnessed by the Imam." Derk insisted. "You lied to me, to everybody. Why?"

"She became a prostitute: a shame to all the family. A homeless, old, neighbor lady came to visit us in the factory and was burned in the fire. Yeet was here to help, so we played like she was Fatima, burned and dead. I haven't seen her since then." Her face clouded. "She doesn't communicate with me anymore. She could be married or dead now for all I know. Yeet was always visiting me, but she hated the factory and left when she could. Some people thought she was possessed by a j*inn*. At times, I thought so too."

Derk watched her face closely but saw no change. He silently cursed this stubborn woman. He had to leave to protect Erben for the Caliph. He must ride west.

> - - - - - - - > SEARCH IN THE AMU RIVER VALLEY > - - - - - - - >
"We're back in the pasture behind the widow's house and there's the miserable creature we followed." Tewfik bey

236

pointed to the moonlit dark backside of the donkey. Murat easily managed the exhausted dogs while Tracker went to examine the animal. He grunted and turned to the mounted men shaking his head in wonder. Behind him from the house came the sound of people quietly talking at the wake.

"He's hardly sweating. They left him to go home. Probably on the rocks and we let them fool us."

Murat spoke. "The dogs are tired and need food. We can go to the house and eat." He motioned toward the house shining in the moonlight and lit with lamps and bonfires.

Tewfik spoke. "You all need food and sleep. Eat then, we'll meet after *Imsak* prayers. We'll search where the trail crosses the rocks." He swung away and the group watched him go.

"Why won't he come and socialize?" Murat asked the remaining horseman.

"Important men have come from all over the district to pay last respects. She was a rich widow and well liked. Would you like to admit a bunch of kids had thrown you off the trail? They weren't as dumb as we thought. Come on."

> - - - - - - - > AT THE BORDER EAST OF KOKAND > - - - - - - - >

"We welcome you in the name of the Caliph to the land of Islam. The Abbassids invite those who enter our land to embrace the true prophet and the one God, Allah. If so be, you may live and trade among us in the land of peace. Otherwise we wish you well as you pass through our territory to the lands of war. We've been advised of your coming. We invite you to go to the caravansary after you and your goods are registered. We tax metals and all commercial goods. We have prepared a dinner of welcome at the caravansary for you have suffered much under the hand of Idolaters. Welcome once again to the safety of Islam."

Sanjak replied for the group. "We thank you and your Caliph for the permission to pass to our own lands. We have come far and have few goods or metal. We long for home and safety. We plan for a speedy passage. We hope for help in food and transport from those who aid us."

Sanjak was wan and thin. The whole group looked tattered, like prisoners of war, though not as tormented as their leader. There were no Muslims among them. The few that had started had been allowed to press ahead without delay through Uigarland.

237

The troops came to attention before the customs building where the official presided. He motioned the refugees forward to the registrar, who started writing as the translators helped the families give the necessary information. They clustered around the table.

"You say you knew of our coming?" Sanjak inquired of the troop commander after dismissal. He laughed.

"General Valiman wrote to us through our embassy's secretary. We have traced your journey from the start. We support the general."

"*Shasher doom*, I'm astonished that he could help from so far. How wonderful" Sanjak's face glowed.

"We've been in touch with him because he needs help in his rivalry with the Tangs. We too, need help in our own plans and projects. So we cooperate. He recommends you. You have a future in our land."

The young officer looked at him shrewdly. He seemed to discern the struggle in his mind. "It is easy and profitable to convert. I was an Alani. We have all gone the way of Islam. Even in the old country, in the Caucasus." Sanjak nodded, he knew of them.

> - - - - - - - > ERBEN IN THE AMU VALLEY > - - - - - - - >

"We should stop and rest, my daughter; the moon is rising and the night half spent." Erben allowed his horse to flag and dropped back, but Leyla forced her horse forward.

"I wouldn't get a wink tonight. I can only sleep in the light now that I've seen him." She was still tense.

"We would make better time if the horses rested and ate. We've been traveling for weeks now and this day has been longer than they can endure. Let's stay in the next village."

Leyla shook her whole body in a shudder. "Better for us to sleep in the saddle and let them graze at dawn. The moon will help us advance. *Yesu gel*, Yesu help us, I can't possibly stop tonight."

Erben shrugged and brought his horse up to hers. He put his arm over her back. "Be sure of my understanding and love, dear one. Did I ever tell you how much you resemble your mother? When you were a growing girl I felt Tanra had returned my wife, but it was not custom to say so. I have saved it till now."

238

"*Tanram*, my God, I never knew!" She cried then, in great sobs as the horses plodded on. "I thought you hated me ..."

> - - - - - - - >ONAT BEY AT THE SEEPAGE SPRINGS > - - - - - - - >

"*Bashara*, to success, and a happy conclusion of our efforts." Onat bey raised his goblet high to his companion.

"*Saha teen each eleem*. I drink to your health, my Lord. This is a day to remember. You won it all without a fight. You have divided the tribe so they are powerless."

The Imperial camp was quiet. Onat bey laughed as he sat in the war tent with his second in command, Aslan bey.

"They divided themselves when their Khan failed to show up and they had to decide on their own future. Fearful, leaderless men will look to their own personal affairs and abandon the community's good. Rivalry terminates all unity."

His aide shook his head in wonder. "And now they are breaking camp and loading their carts to move west to take service with the Sultan. Our enemies become servants, praise Allah."

Then there was a noise outside the tent, the sound of a blow came and a grunt of pain.

SURPRISE ATTACK

239

"*Ne var*, what's happening?" Aslan moved to the tent opening. A man in flowing robes rushed in to strike at the aide, who raised his metal goblet to deflect the blow. The wounded Aslan pulled a dagger as he fell and struck the assassin above the heel, cutting the tendon.

Onat bey had time to reach his sword and behead the falling Arab as another rushed howling through the doorway holding aloft a blood smeared scimitar. Onat slashed just near the elbow causing the blow to go astray. His back stroke took the man's throat.

A third Arab, silent and swift, was on him as he shouted for his guards. He felt the knife in his side. The light chain-mail deflecting the point, he felt himself fall with the force of the blow. He slashed up with the point and the lamps came down with the wounded man.

There was a moment of silence in the tent, but outside all was shouting and running. Nearby some one moaned and a thrashing sounded on the rug. A heavy breathing and a sound of sawing cloth came from one side of the tent. Then, glimmers of light shown from moving torches outside as tent fabric was pushed to one side. Slowly the light was blocked out. The silhouette of a form crawling forward whispered.

"Abdullah, where are you? Did you avenge our dead commander on the Turk?" There was no answer. Then someone moved and tried to whisper, but it turned to a moan.

The caller spoke again. "Allah, Allah, are all dead? If you live, come quickly the troops are gathering. They've killed your cousins." No answers came. The figure slowly retreated and commented. "Praise Allah, you've had revenge for our commander, though it cost your life. Honor is satisfied." Against the light his thin face appeared to disappear again.

"Bring a torch, the tent is dark. Quick, light the lamps. Careful the rug is covered with bodies," Binbasha Onat ordered. A guard thrust in a flaming torch and all looked with astonishment.

"Don't stand there. Aslan bey is nearest the door. Get him out. He might be alive. He saved my life." Onat sat in a

240

corner, sword in hand. His face grim as he continued, "Give me a head count, Yuzbasha. How many killed?"

"Three killed and two wounded of ours. There are two dead Arabs here, one is wounded. They took us by surprise, they're our troops."

"Take these three assassins out. The first lost his head. If this one's alive I'll question him. I want to know how many were in on this plot." Onat painfully stood up.

"*Evet Binbasha*, yes commander." Guards were hustled into the tent to carry out the bodies. In the distance a cry arose, the scream of a camel in death agony.

"*Hy hy hy ya.*" the sound of ululating war cries filled the air. The Toozlu were attacking the camels and horses of the Arabs while the main camp was in an uproar.

KILLING CAMELS

241

PEOPLE, PLOTS & PLACES IN CHAPTER 20

Ahmed: delays and danger on the road takes a toll.
Atilla: finally gets excitement and adventure in the hunt.
Tayze: has trouble restraining her patient.
Ayden bey: brings a whole hunting party for the chase.
Dahkool: must ride to the border and lead the pursuit away.
Gerchen: can't resist hunting farmers to fight.
Hussein: hides in another quarry with an assumed name.
Jon: plans to hide by day and get over the border by night.
Kardesh: does not realize how damaged he has become.
Mahmut: backs his leader to the limit.
Manish: knows the mountain hiding places.
Maril: thinks that the serving girl's sacrifice is romantic.
Mehmet: finds more opposition than he expected.
Murat: the boy finds handling bloodhounds strenuous.
Nooryouz: must escape with the baby to save their lives.
Onat bey: sends troops after the Toozlu returning north.
Orhan: sent to search for two strangers on the west road.
Sanjak: persuaded by Derk, helps the situation of his tribe.
Seerden: had reasons to join the hunt for the criminals.
Seslee: regrets her lost comforts while feeling the cold.
Tracker: sets the hunt in motion from the donkey's trail.
Tewfik: loses part of his posse to chase dogs and thieves.
Umer: finds old tricks don't always work in new situations.
Umer the pretender: a change of name means acceptance.
Uncle: expects a brother's son to work for his keep.
Yeet: finds the task of nurse and housekeeper exhausting.

Glossary
Allah shu koor: Thank God; praises be.
ah man': oh; my gracious; damn it; my goodness.
beyim: gentlemen; sirs.
dee kot: attention; careful.
kanat: A tunnel connecting a source of water with a well.
kara koja: wife and husband; a married couple.
Nere day sin? : Where are you?
shim dee git: go now; go on, leave.

242

MURAT FALLS

"Did you see the foreigners when they rode by on the road?" Seerden asked conversationally. The men at the wake were drinking and speculating while the women prepared the body and cleaned the house of any sign of the angry dog.

"It was mid-day and everyone was working in the fields or eating a lunch. Merchants go by frequently. Reports say a man and a bare-faced woman passed, but from a distance you can't see much." The men shook their heads.

"They weren't very well off, the horses were ordinary. The clothes too, were worn and cheap, but the man had the look of a fighter and a woman with an open face isn't seen much outside the hill tribes."

"*Kara-Koja*, Husband and wife?" A smile went around the room. Some shrugged. One of the oldest spoke; "He was old enough to have grown ones, but if a man can afford it? A young wife is a trophy." Silence fell.

"Could they have been the ones who killed her?" Seerden put his question innocently.

The men paused. "There were foot prints all around the house, but they were different."

"Only the woman went to the well. The gourd was thrown off beyond the well as if she took fright."

243

"Somebody slept on the hillside."

"Made a fire."

"Left signs all over the place."

All agreed quietly. Goblets were passed again.

"No animals with them, they're on foot. They aren't good hunters."

"Town people don't know how to live off the land," one added.

"Besides, the murder happened early. She had just taken the dog in to feed him after guarding all night."

"That's right they track right up to the door. They must have been nice or she could have let the dog out on them." There was much shaking of the head and exchange of looks. The women in the next room started crying.

"She must have gone up to check the drying fruit or her treasure's hiding place." They all perked up.

"Rich people have to be careful, but I expect you know that *beyim*." They nodded to him amiably. Seerden smiled. "I would still like to meet the travellers."

"Tewfik bey will have them before tomorrow night." Several men broke into laughter and head wagging. "But he sure got taken in tonight by those city slickers."

Tracker came in to the mud-brick room with a goblet in his hand he looked round and nodded. "What are you doing here *beyim*? Come hunting for excitement?"

Seerden rose to put his hand on heart. "Could I join your party tomorrow? I'll help you."

"Tewfik bey will always accept you, my lord."

> - - - - - - - > A SMALL QUARRY SOUTH OF KOKAND > - - - - - - - >

"Yes Uncle, I'm Umer from the White Marble Quarry. Father said I should come to work for you. He'll send for me when he decides to forgive me. He was very angry. I know I've been disobedient and admit I'm guilty. I promise to obey your voice and work hard at the quarry. You'll suffer no problems with me."

"I just got notice of your coming. No preparations are made for your stay. I can get you work, but my family fills the house." The uncle was studying the boys' faces.

244

"My friend, Hussein here, came with me. We both know quarry work. We'll work hard." The indicated pretender, Hussein, nodded his agreement.

"I'll put you on a pallet for tonight and get you some work tomorrow, after that we'll see. But understand; I'll have obedience and no trouble from either of you."

"You can be sure of that, Uncle. We had our fill of trouble. We want a chance to live a quiet life."

The uncle stared at him steadily and nodded solemnly. He added. "You must take after your mother's side of the family. You don't really look at all like my brother, but you have come, as he said in the letter, so you are welcome to my house."

"Allah has ordained it, good Uncle," the false Umer smiled.

> - - - - - - - > REFUGEES HIGH IN THE TANRA DAH > - - - - - - - >

The distant sound of a running horse brought the walkers to a momentary halt. Then they scattered taking refuge out of the light of the moon, in dark shadows and clefts beside the mountain road. An exhausted, heaving horse came up to the spot and slowed.

"*Nere day sin*, Where are you? Can't you tell who I am?" Dahkool's voice was wild and thin. She slipped down from the saddle and stood beside the horse stroking its nose and calming it. She leaned her head against the strong neck and caught her breath. Then she led the animal to a low spot where the shadows fell and disguised their form.

A warm voice spoke. "We're here and glad you're safe, but don't know what to say." Nooryouz moved into the light toward her.

"Thank you is the most appropriate," she replied.

"Don't feel embarrassed with us, tell as much or as little as you wish." They hugged and cried some as the others came out of hiding. After greetings and thanks they sat around her waiting for her story.

"His herd was grazing at the high pasture. The scene was beautiful and he set out a spread of food for us. But I made him pick a horse first and to bridle her and put the reins under a stone so she couldn't wander. We ate and talked a lot and after a little while we lay back on the grass. He was as gentle as his promise."

Shy Maril exclaimed softly. "How wonderful and romantic!"

But Seslee protested. "In the grass with a herd of horses around you?"

Dahkool paused and then pressed by internal pressure added. "Later, he told me that he had let a word slip to his brother who

245

hinted until all the family started asking questions. He is afraid that money will be a lure stronger than just one member's love. I could tell he was sincere. I pretended to sleep and he left quietly, but the echo of his run sounded up to the meadow. I left before moon rise. I got a glimpse of you walking up the road." She paused.

"I have a plan." Jon spoke up, rising to his feet, facing the group. The moon lit his face, brightly. "I see that we will be sought by the horseman's family for reward. I think we should leave the road and hide in the mountain flanks by streams where the dense brush grows." Everyone stood and nodded agreement.

Dahkool, however, spoke again. "Yes, but it is Nooryouz that they want. Her person brings the big reward. The rest are simply to be punished as accessories. I must take her by horse as fast as wind to the border. When she passes all hope of a large reward dies."

There was a protest. "I would be a more suitable companion," Seslee cried. "All the harem girls are sought."

Jon spoke firmly, "Dahkool grew up in the saddle before she was sold, while none of you other girls ride." He turned to Nooryouz. "Take the baby and ride behind her. The border is beyond this mountain. God be with you." He suited action to his words and Dahkool was riding off as the others protested.

"Jon, how could you? We'll be caught now," Seslee pouted.

"Not if Manish hides us now and we go on later."

"I know a good place to wait, up there a way," Manish said.

"No way, we should follow now and go across the border."

"The horseman was nice to her. He won't betray us," Maril added hopefully.

Jon laughed and pointed down the valley road where lights were moving up the road and across the hill ahead of them.

They drew a sudden, shocked breath. Jon continued, "They will follow the sound and tracks of the horse. We'll hide safely. Our friends' only safety is speed."

> - - - - - - - >ONAT BEY AT THE SEEPAGE SPRINGS > - - - - - - - >

"The scouts report that the Toozlu tracks go on to split an hour's ride west. One continues on, but one part goes north. What are your orders, Binbasham?" The yuzbasha, Mehmet, reported.

"That can only mean that some have decided to return to tribal lands. The larger part and animals go on west?" Onat asked.

"Exactly commander, the party returning are fewer."

"The lure of wealth and promotion is proportionally the same in all men: a few with standards and loves, the many with desires and thirsts."

Mehmet waited his turn. "Shall we send troops after them?"

Onat bey looked out of the tent. His rug was being washed down by the spring. Farther away a group of disgruntled Arabs were working with wounded camels. Animals that died before they could be slaughtered ritually with its throat slit were dragged out for the vultures to eat. Others were cutting up the slaughtered camels and drying the meat in thin slivers on the tent surfaces and on the branches of shrubs near the water seep. They periodically broke into loud shouting.

The troops were angrily breaking camp. There would be two mutually exclusive burials that afternoon. Each group would seek their own ground, although of one faith. After that, there would be a return to garrisons.

Yuzbasha Mehmet watched and awaited his general's reaction.

"You see our condition. The Arabs would like to take vengeance for their camels, but they're no match without them. Our men are angry with the Arabs for killing their comrades in order to get me. So everyone is frustrated."

"Yes commander, but can you let the Toozlu go of their own volition. What will you report?"

"I'll say we came to an understanding. Some go west expecting to work for the Caliph. Others rejected Islam and return to the tribal areas. They are no longer a danger."

"But the attacks and assassination attempt? Aslan bey's injuries? The guards' deaths?" He ran out of breath.

"Those are internal troop problems. Every regiment has them in some degree. Why talk about such things?"

"Won't people wish to know? Your commander and Caliph expect a report." The yuzbasha was anxious for their reputation as well as his promotion.

Onat was annoyed. "They'll get everything. Your part is exemplary, so don't fuss. I underline the successful

247

policy. The Caliph's commanders know we'll have some problems between troops."

Onat was reluctant to start the writing that day. He looked out at the blood stained rug and gave orders to his new second. "Lead a troop to overtake the group going north. They won't fight if you're friendly. Treat them with respect. We have to decide to charge them or let them return to their people. It will be part of the report. We'll let the larger clan go and keep our distance if they behave themselves." After Mehmet left the tent, Onat stroked his bruised side and grimaced.

Mehmet was happy to leave the sour spirit of the camp. The Arabs looked up angrily as he rode by with the scouts. He heard some of them murmur the words: "cursed Turks."

> - - - - - - - > WHITE MARBLE QUARRY > - - - - - - - >

"Tayze, why can't you take off the cloth and let me see? I want to see Sevman and Yeet." Kardesh feebly asked.

"You can hear them, Praise God. Your face needs to heal and your eyes deserve a rest. You have broken bones. The swelling must go down and healing start. The bruises will lose their colour if you take care." She was firm.

"But really, just for a little while," he insisted.

"Eat your food and rest. In a few days we'll ask the doctor, but not now." Her face softened as he shrugged and sighed accepting her edicts as final.

Yeet entered. "How is our invalid today? The broth is good and I'm sampling it continually. There won't be any left in another hour if you don't get your part now."

"It hurts to eat, even drinking is difficult."
Tayze nodded sympathetically while Yeet stood wordless.

"That's why you get broth until the bones knit. Now don't chew, just swallow. Here try a spoonful."

"I'll feed him Tayze" Yeet offered and took the bowl to him.

"Sevman should come by in the cart soon."

"I hope he has the strength for driving all day."

Yeet grinned and fed Kardesh beneath his bandages.

248

"He did it in the mines and I know he'll be hungry tonight. He promised to eat, so I know he will." Tayze raised her eyebrows and smiled patronisingly. "Men are such idiots, ascetic fools, taking pride in self-abasement."

Yeet smiled back at her. "That's exactly what my sister Fatima says."

> - - - - - - -> QUARRY BOYS NEAR SAMARKAND > - - - - - - ->
"I wish I'd never listened to you. I get in more trouble every time I go along with your plans." Ahmed was trailing the other two, spouting his discontent.

"*Shim di git*. Go then. Why follow us? We're going to a city and enlist. We'll join the road ahead. No one will know us from other travellers." Umer's stubborn anger withered the self-pity of Ahmed. He fearfully followed the two unable to come to any plan of action for himself."

"The ridge of bare rock ends ahead. The moon will show us how to get on the road. There won't be many travellers now, but we heard some horses a while ago. It can't be far." Mahmut spoke to Umer, ignoring Ahmed with contempt. "Just so we don't hear the dogs behind us."

"Once on the road our scent and tracks will be defused and lost among the many. Now hush, get to the road." Umer forged ahead.

> - - - - - - -> SEARCHERS ON THE MAIN ROAD > - - - - - - ->
"This is the third inn we have visited without stopping to rest. You leave the horses at the gate and spend the time asking questions. Then we leave again. I can hardly finish one drink," Atilla complained. Orhan's only response was a grim smile and shrug.

Atilla did not let that deter him in the least. Continuing, he insisted. "We need to stop and have a chance to eat and have a drink. We're rushing round madly and finding nothing. We have no chance to have a round of drinks with the travellers and hear of their journeys and who they saw on the road. There's more to learn from many eyes than one pair can learn alone or, even, with a search party." Kynan listened quietly.

"It's Tewfik's manner of procedure." Orhan was smug. "He'll require it of me. He titles it diligence."

249

"*Delly* is a better word," Atilla affirmed. "It means crazy in Turkish. I can make a poem of it. I'll call it: Delly for Diligence or in my case,   Delly for Drink. I can always use another one."

Delly Daddy, dreads disorder;
Diligence will dig the dead.
Don't deny the dreaded drafts;
Deny the deed that drives the doubts.
Double deep and divot drivel;
Dries the drooling dodger's draft.
Devilish drenching due the dupes;
Dyes the deadly draught with drugs.
Dandies do die, destiny deals;
Drop the deaf digger's dumb drum.
Dream of drink and dire deliverance.
Deem the death that doodlers draw.
Damn the deal the delly's dread.
Drink the dram, don't drop the dish.
Darn the dry drapes drawn by dummies
Delay the doll that dwells and dives
Drop the driver that delivers dope.

> - - - - - - - > THE AMU VALLEY HUNT > - - - - - - - >

"You always start the best at the worst hour," Seerden complained to Tewfik bey as they stood waiting for Murat, Tracker and the dogs. It was just past first light and they faced east awaiting the sun.

"If you want the excitement of the chase you get there at the best hour. The men will be here shortly, they're bringing an extra dog." They heard deep baying of dogs.

"Here's Ayden bey riding up with his neighbours." Seerden observed. "We really have a hunting party now."

"The word has spread and the community is stirred up," Tewfik responded. "Mount up, let's start the chase."

"Ayden bey, you honour us with your presence," greeted Seerden.

"*Beyim*, I brought as many neighbours as volunteered last night at the wake. Others will wait for us on the road and follow the music of the dogs. That way we'll keep the guilty boxed." The other riders grouped around while the

250

dogs were taken out to the rocky ridge. The new dog stood wagging his tail, friendly, but confused. The other two seemed to recognise the place and old Bitler started left away from the donkey's trail. Murat shouted to Tewfik bey.

"Bitler is off his food, nervous and angry. Don't let any of the horses get too close to him. I'll keep the other two dogs away from him on the left." He wrapped the leashes on his wrists and shouted encouragement to the pack.

"Go ahead, we'll spread out and track on the side," Tewfik suited action to his words. The hunting party tracked on each side of the point of advance.

"Tewfik bey, you know this ridge crosses a road five hours ahead. There's a party on it, but shouldn't some of us move toward it beyond the ridge?" One man asked.

"*Evet*, yes, take half the group, Ayden Bey, cut between the desert and the river valley. Make sure the guilty don't get into the orchards or fields." Ayden led off.

At that moment the dogs detected a movement and scent in the brush and were off in pursuit. A small spotted cat-like form flashed into view an instant. The two dogs ran ahead, left to right behind Bitler who was moving ahead strongly. This pulled Murat ahead to the right and crossed his arms. He stumbled forward, twisted, flipped to his back. He was dragged after the two and lost the lead to old Bitler, who took off at a run along the ridge. Murat, obviously hurt, hung on to the two baying dogs. Men rushed to help. The new dog broke the leash and raced after the creature and was lost from sight. His detained comrade set up a howl, jumping and jerking the leash. Murat was screaming even louder.

Tracker grabbed the leash and jerked it with both hands throwing the dog off its feet while he cursed it roundly. "You son of a pie dog, scavenger of carrion; what have you done to my friend's arm? Hold, you rabid wolf."

"Murat boy, what hurts? Show me where." Tewfik bey was off his horse and leaning over the hunched body of the boy. Murat had become very still, but was crying and holding his shoulder. Other horsemen pursued the dogs in different paths. Ayden's group waited before continuing to their task.

"*Ahman*, Allah, aye, Allah, my shoulder, it's broken." He screamed again as Tewfik bey gently ran his fingers over the indicated area. Murat tried to move away from him.

"No, let me feel. I don't think it's broken. It seems to be out of joint. Be brave. Let me rotate it."

"Are you sure? Don't make it worse. Oh Allah, it hurts. If it will stop the pain." He gritted his teeth and straightened up. "*Tamom*, okay, I'm ready." There was a pop and a muffled moan. Murat felt his shoulder gingerly and moved it a bit. He looked up at Tewfik bey abashed. "I lost the dogs, sir. They're strong and I didn't expect them to bolt. I'm sorry."

Tewfik helped him up. "No one foresees the unexpected. Allah wills it. What can one do? Follow the old dog. I'll ride ahead. We'll meet at the caravansary." He motioned to Seerden and the two trotted off after the men following old Bitler.

> - - - - - - - > AT THE AMU RIVER INN > - - - - - - - >
"Umer look! In front of the inn. Three horses, the little man is holding their reins." Mahmut's voice quivered.

"Distract him. Admire the animals. Ask questions," Umer ordered.

"*Ta mom*, okay. Shall we wait for Ahmed?"

"Never, we'll grab and run. Now get going. The owners are not staying - maybe just a meal or a drink." Umer walked ahead as if he were going past the little man into the inn gate. While Mahmut stopped to admire the horses. The little man turned out to be a talkative hunchback, who earned his drinks with jokes and small duties around the inn.

"My, these are fine animals. Whose are they?"

"Atilla the merchant traveller owns the bay. Orhan owns the sorrel. He works with Tewfik bey, the Sheriff. The stranger rides the mare. She is good, but not top of the line. They are asking for two travellers, a man and a girl going by here last night, but no one saw them. They say the woman had no veil."

252

While he talked Umer returned quietly and stood behind them. Taking a knotted cord from his waist band he tensed it. The man turned at that moment. Umer smiled and dropped the cord to one hand. He then posed his question. "Did anyone see them pass?"

The little man nodded. "I wake during the night when there are sounds. They passed I'm sure. I heard two horses pass. I should have got up. I could have seen the girl." He sighed with regret. "The horsemen inside are talking to the others now. I'll tell them when they come out. People don't slip by me." He turned to look down the road. "Another stranger comes!"

"*Allah, shu koor*, thank God you stopped. My feet are hurting. I can't go on. Let's stay here and rest." Ahmed came limping up to the three. The little man watched him closely. Umer stretched his cord and flipped it over the man's head. The nervous groom jumped and fought strenuously. He thrashed and struck at them. Squeals and pants escaped him. Umer used his feet and elbows to buffet him and Mahmut tried to help.

Ahmed watched with open mouth. "What? Why are you doing that? Don't! No more. Stop!"

The twisting hunchback grabbed and bit the knotted fist. Umer howled and struck back with his elbow, but the cord had slipped and the man plunged away, kicking Mahmut in the stomach. He ran and disappeared inside the gateway yelling.

Umer cursed. "Mount up! Let's get away before they come out." With a leap they were in the saddle of the nearest horses.

Ahmed stared, stupefied by the turn of events. He hobbled toward the nervous horse that had broken free in the violence. The animal avoided the stranger and followed the other horses for a moment then came to a halt to look for pasture. Ahmed reached the horse and mounted, just as men came pouring out the gate of the inn. Behind them he heard the sound of dogs. He remembered hearing them the night before, so he urged his horse to a run. Someone had a bow and tried a long shot at him. He sobbed, letting the animal go where it would. The wind felt cold on his wet face despite the warmth of the rising sun. There was no sun in his heart.

> - - - - - - - >SANJAK ON THE ROAD> - - - - - - >

"Sanjak bey, will you please come with your people to Kokand. It's the closest large town. There are people who wish to meet you there." Sanjak looked the speaker over carefully. The young man was carefully dressed and tall.

"Tanra has not given me the privilege of meeting you before, so how do you know me?"

The man smiled grimly. "I'm Derk, the Caliph's servants have ordered me to meet you and convey you to Kokand." He looked about him. "You'll be more comfortable there and we need your help."

"What help could you possibly need from me?"

"You have been away. Much has changed among the tribes. I was on my way to protect a tribal leader from danger, but he flew the nest and is being chased – oh - ah... hunted by others. I was sent here to request your help."

Sanjak did not miss the slip. His reply was guarded.

"How can this poor traveller be of service to the Caliph? I have neither goods nor talents useful to rulers."

"You have knowledge and friendships that will help us to contact and persuade key people from your tribe. We have them trapped in the desert. Only one is still on the loose and another unaccounted for. But I'm ahead, let's start from the beginning."

Derk continued with his appeal. "Khorasan is the key area, the most important politically to the Baghdad Caliphate. The increasing role played by Turks and tribes is known to you. You nations of the north live in the lands of war without the peace of Islam. We hope by treaty for you to travel our land and to enjoy our commerce. Our merchants will be free to visit yours. We need an understanding with your natural leaders."

"The few leaders I know have not seen me for years. I'll have little influence on them. There's a new Khan now."

"Your father has led a large clan of Chipchaks to the south. They're in the scrubland. We want you to talk to him and to Setchkin, the Empress dowager of the old Khan."

The shock registered on Sanjak's face. He turned to study the forming column of people behind him then motioned to advance.

"Tell me what you expect me to do." Sanjak replied.

> - - - - - - - >REFUGEES HIGH IN THE TANRA DAH > - - - - - - - >

"It's getting light. We need to hide for the day." The horse was climbing slowly, tired by a night's work carrying double.

Nooryouz nodded drowsily behind Dahkool. "Aren't we near the border now? Can't we get across and rest there?"

Dahkool shook her head up negatively. "The area is patrolled and the guards will be riding over the hills. The horse must be released to wander and eat. He's too tired to run or get us across today." She pointed. "We have to get beyond this mountain. The river beyond runs into the Caliphate. It's called the Illi. It's the last cultivated valley on the frontier. To the north side lie the tribal territories."

Nooryouz was cleaning the baby. "We spend the day there? How can you hide on a hill of grass? Did Manish give you any help there?"

She smiled. "There are caves near the wadi used by the smugglers. We must find a small one. Guards don't poke in. They get paid not to notice them. We'll sleep and walk over tonight."

"We go up this wadi? If we let the horse go here they'll know where to look."

Dahkool replied. "I'll take the horse over that hill and leave him there. I'll walk up the next wadi then come back by another route. Find a cave. Toss a rock when you hear my bird whistle. Here take the dried food."

Nooryouz slid off the back of the plodding horse. Holding the baby with one hand and the sack of provisions with the other she picked her way up the wadi. The horse slowly climbed over the low hill.

> - - - - - - - > THE TOOZLU GOING HOME > - - - - - - - >

"You travel fast Twozan bey. It has taken two days and a night to catch up. We come in peace. Will you talk with us?" Mehmet's horse stood beside the tribal chief's fine animal. He noticed that the group he had overtaken was much larger than reported. His company was not larger than those he pursued. He couldn't intimidate them.

255

"We have few animals to nurture. We go home where we are free to follow our customs and beliefs," Twozan responded coldly.

Mehmet smiled. "The district Muktar wishes to honour you. The Caliph wishes good relations with the northern nations."

"My people are not diplomatic. No Khan has sent us with a commission. We are going home and have no time for entertainment." Twozan's people continued to move toward a steep hill with a sheer drop to a canyon. He turned to follow, but Mehmet rode beside him and took the reins.

"Wait, Onat bey wishes you to return by way of the Government post roads." Twozan knocked his hand away.

"We came as we chose; we'll go as we choose." He continued his trot back toward his group.

Mehmet sat watching them go. It was useless to try to bully them. An attack would be repulsed. Onat bey had said to be friendly. He must find someone the tribal leaders would respect enough to listen to. An attack would send them up the hill or into the canyon. He had them, but they had him, too. He called up a trooper to carry a message to the Muktar and his commander.

> - - - - - - - > RUNNING TOWARD BAGHDAD > - - - - - - - >

Gerchen called a halt and sat with the warriors while the drovers, herds, and wagons carrying the goods caught up. Two scouts came back to report.

"The valley ahead is small but irrigated. We can trade some animals for money or wheat, flour and salt. We can pick some of the fruit we need as we march and make it good later in the market when we deal with the mayor. They won't dare fuss too much."

Gerchen nodded. "The Caliph won't permit killing the gophers. They aren't on our lands. Are the men in the village?"

"They are working on a kanat – a tunnel on this side of the valley. They're not armed. They have only their tools for digging."

Gerchen smiled grimly. "Shall we have a little fun this day?" He turned as two men of the rearguard rode up in a cloud of dust.

"Any sign of the camels or horsemen tracking us?"

"None, my Khan, we left all pursuit behind, there are no eyes watching." Satisfaction was expressed by all.

256

"Lead on then, our fun with the gophers will clean the dust and sweat from us." The men were full of jokes and laughs as they rode on toward the villagers working on the water supply. The pleasant orchards and vineyards on every side were evidence of their abilities to make the desert bloom. The herded flocks broke into alfalfa fields to feed.

> - - - - - - - > NEAR THE BORDER VILLAGE > - - - - - - - >

"*De kot*, attention - look, on the hill. See, a horse and rider on the crest? Quick, move out, she is turning down toward the wadi." The command galvanised the riders into action. They raced their horses toward her position.

"*Do'er*, stop, don't run away! We'll help you. There's food in the village. We're not border guards. You will be safe with us." The headman's shouts went unheeded. Dahkool jumped off and ran. The horse was too exhausted to run. She was at the mouth of the wadi before they were in bow range. She plunged up the shallow stream and pools splashing recklessly over slick rocks and green growth. The older men stopped at the entrance to the canyon where the wadi issued. Watching the younger men run up the wadi in pursuit, one shouted.

"Enjoy it boys, but remember there's no reward for a dead body. Leave her alive for the judge." They laughed.

DAH KOOL SPOTTED

257

PEOPLE, PLOTS & PLACES IN CHAPTER 21

Ali bey: finds a way to avenge himself on Onat bey.
Atilla: gets adventure and a chance to show his skill.
Aziz: this smuggler has more expenses than profits.
Dahkool: leads the pursuit away from her mistress' path.
Doctor: finishes his work and wonders at what they do.
Emperor: gives an honor to one considered dishonorable.
Erben: finds travel with a frantic girl as hard as a battle.
Gerchen: loves a fight, but the enemy goes underground.
Kadir: guards his partners in the smuggler's cave.
Kardesh: wishes to be up and about, despite injuries.
Kemeer: finds his role increased and opposition greater.
Kynan: must compete with his friend and patron.
Leyla: frantic to get to the tribe for protection.
Manly: receives the royal honors his father covets.
Maril: tries to encourage her companions on the trek.
Nooryouz: finds it hard to care for a baby in hiding.
Sanjak: gets offers that exploit his weakness.
Seslee: complains about the difficulties of finding freedom.
Setchkin: starts to measure the true strength of others.
Sevman: will sing while his mentor, Kardesh, plays the lute.
Tayze: has a sick nephew; debts to settle and a move.
Tewfik: brings the posse into action.
Twozan: must get the clan back across the north border.
Yavuz: always suspects treachery from his partners.
Yeet: works to earn money and make a friend well.
Yusuf: wants to stay a while, but business calls him home.

GLOSSARY

Adonai: Lord; used by Jews in place of God's name.
dinars: gold coins; an ancient unit of money.
hoja: a man who completes the Mecca haj.
hookah: a water-pipe in which smoke is cooled and filtered.
huzla: hurry; move fast.
Nay ol lure: please; What's the harm?
Tanra eeyee'dir: God is good.

ARGUMENT IN THE CAVE

"I have a venture for you Sanjak bey. It will help pass the time and earn you honorable profit while you await your wife's arrival." The binbasha, commander of a thousand, waited for a reaction of interest or enthusiasm, but got neither. Sanjak stood dully before his captor. The binbasha persisted to smile condescendingly at the contemptible heathen. Still getting no response he hastened on sternly. "We need a man on the border far to the north near the Illi River and Issyk Kool Lake. Smugglers are rife and the silk and metals being smuggled out of China bring a fortune to those who catch the caravans. It's an opportunity for you. We have a detachment of Turkish converts who will need a firm hand. We have assigned a Mullah to go with them and continue their training in Islam and who will help you in anything you wish to know. He has our highest clearance and recommendation." Sanjak still made no reply as he listened.

"It is custom that we divide all confiscated material half and half. I shall have to make large contributions of gratitude to my superiors upward as you will have to do with your subordinates. I will give you a hundred silver dinars to pay your first expenses and soon you will be paying your own way." He paused a moment waiting for some response or show of gratitude. "You will leave tomorrow morning. My adjutant will fill you in on the details you will need to know. We expect your reports and success. May Allah grant it." There was no reply. The binbasha, his dignity, affronted, left haughtily.

The adjutant remained. "That was not very wise of you. He will work against you now," the young man stated bluntly.

"What does he expect? He moves me from my charges, those who came with me at such risk. He sends me to another border area, too far from our entrance into the Caliphate, where my wife might seek me, yet far enough from my own border to make escape improbable. He contributes half the silver given to other officers and demands half the goods before I pay my men their share. He does this with a smirk and religious words to salve over his greed and malice." Sanjak's pretended indifference flared into anger.

The adjutant stiffened. "I did not hear that. I do not recall what you said. I hope you will never repeat those words in any other man's hearing. You are already as good as dead and if I were not of your race you would be dead tomorrow, if not now" The adjutant stalked off tossing one phrase over his shoulder. "Seek me in the *hamom*, baths if you have questions. I could make your probation trials easier." He got no reply.

> - - - - - - - > HIGH IN THE TANRA DAH MOUNTAINS > - - - - - - - >

Nooryouz heard the rush of horses and the shouting beyond the hill, so she pressed forward up the steep side of the mountain always just below the brush level to hide her movements. Among the jumble of rock she sought a shelter. The baby was awake, but quiet, and seemed to be aware of the exertion and fear of his mother as she ran to exhaustion. Then, as she could go no further, Nooryouz crawled behind some tall bushes to rest and catch her breath. Her surroundings were quiet, but from a far distance she could hear sounds of pursuit. The baby started to fret, so she felt his padding and discovered it was indeed wet. Although it was still cool with a dawn wind she bared the baby and searched her bag for a clean cloth into which she had gathered clean dry grass. She doubled the surface of the cloth over the padding and, drew it between his legs. As the Baby laughed and struggled, she drew the skin bag close about his kicking body. They had a moment of play and she began to nurse him. They both nodded drowsily.

She woke to a distant scream and looking between the rocks saw movements below. Above on the mountain side she saw a dark opening. Reaching between the bushes. She investigated. She decided to crawl into it. She promptly entered, but stopped just past the entrance. She could stand and she could feel the empty space on every hand. She was afraid, but the light outside was increasing so she dared not leave. She heard the sound of a horse struggling up the slope and the light diminished for a moment. Then the sound grew faint. She sat with eyes on the contrast of the light from outside with the dark within. The baby again drew out his needs and soon fell asleep.

> - - - - - - - > TANRA DAH RAVINES > - - - - - - - >

Dahkool ran with determination. She must give the mistress time to hide and to get deep in the canyon. She must move up and to the right to lead away from any pass or ridge leading to the neighboring stream bed. She had toughened with the months of outdoor living and kept a steady pace. The noisy pursuit was below her at the mouth of the stream. She would continue to climb to the right up each bed that offered sufficient brush to hide her movements. She followed the trails made by the animals and sought the rough ground where she could lose the pack behind her. Suddenly as she turned in another dry stream bed, the cliffs rose before her. A narrow goat trail led off climbing up the mountain side.

She chose that way immediately. She was up and out of sight by the time the first of a pack of pursuers came to her tracks in the stream bed. Shouting they continued up the dry stream. However, two saw the goat trail and started up. Those below spread out and several started toward the descending stream bed on the left side of the canyon. They moved up toward the pass to the other watercourse. The one Nooryouz should be ascending.

Dakool noted this when she came to another cliff edge. She paused and suddenly screamed, kicking some rocks over the edge as she did so. She swayed as if she would fall and then recovering, moaned and moved out of sight. As a mother bird lures the hunter away from the nest, so she too appeared several times in close succession. Each time she showed signs of utter exhaustion and hysteria. All the men were on the goat trail by now.

Still higher she led, scrabbling and sliding on the treacherous rock path. Then she came to a wide shelf where rock and grass

261

mixed, the path seem to disappear. She searched frantically and discerned a set of perch like footholds on the sheer face. A fleet goat or mountain sheep could use these as jump spots, but could she? Behind her the two men were gaining the shelf. They both panted out calming words.

"We will not hurt you, bayan. We will take you to where it is safe. There is good food and rest at the foot of the mountain." Their faces were flushed and both were smiling, wolfishly; confidently waiting for her to collapse. Ready to laugh and shout their victory.

She blinked, opened her eyes wide with fear and leaped. She tottered, gained balance and leaped again. There was not a patch you could stop on, each motion called for another. She rounded a hillock and disappeared from sight.

The men were stunned. While one cursed their luck the other called to the climbing group below. "*Huzla*, hurry, pass a rope up. She's escaped. We must link up lest one fall." An answering shout came and they glumly awaited the arrival of the rope.

> - - - - - - - > LEYLA IN THE AMU VALLEY > - - - - - - - >

"Must you go now?" Leyla's voice was tense and quivering. Her father looked at her sternly.

"You go back to sleep. We rode all night and are short of supplies. I won't be long, the caravansary is only a short ride and our horses are too tired to go much farther today. We'll rest here and go on tomorrow." He turned away.

"Are we near the tribe now? Will we see them soon?" Leyla called after him. She lay back wearily; the blanket pulled up against the morning chill.

Erben smiled lovingly just for a moment as he mounted his weary horse. "They're about three days ride north of here. I'll get just a bit of oats for the horses to pep them up for the final push. I'll bring food and news. There might be a little early fruit in the orchards if you look later; when you've slept."

Leyla watched him go. There was a finality in the act that troubled her. She wanted to cry out and protest, but knew it would draw a rebuke. It's not fair, she thought, life is not what you choose, but what is imposed. I don't want to be alone; not now, not ever. She tried to call out, but her energy failed. Her eyelids weighed heavily and unwillingly she let them fall.

It was evening and the tea house was filled with talking groups of men enjoying a social time. This was one of the more important houses where the judges, men of the law and city leaders gathered. The Imam of the mosque rose from his corner bench and moved toward Ali bey who was chatting with a subordinate. He rose as the judge drew near. Both men bowed slightly and repeated the greetings required. Then the Imam asked. "You have heard of the destruction of the invading Toozlu Turks? That they are broken into fleeing parts?"

"Yes, but it is to wonder why they were allowed to come so far south," Ali bey responded critically.

"Can our defenses be so weak?"

Ali bey smiled. "The men who composed the invasion have been sent to the capitol and will serve the Caliph at Samara. But some are permitted to return to their lands."

The Imam was troubled, but Ali bey shrugged elaborately. "The governor has looked away while his men allow this breach of peace and it has caused some of the best Arab troops to protest. The affair was badly handled."

"Unbelievers are roaming our land, invaders using our resources. It can only be a measure of the lawlessness of our times."

Ali bey nodded understandingly and commented, "We all know the commander who has caused these disruptions and failed to honor the Sharia. This Seljuk so shamelessly affronts the leading families of Khorasan by his treatment of the camel corps."

"Action must be taken against Onat bey," declared the Imam.

"You would be the obvious man to lead it. First there is the escape of an enemy commander. Then, there is the defeat in the wild lands, and the slaughter of the camels," Ali bey enumerated.

"Something must be done," the Imam thoughtfully replied. His nose twitched with the sweet aromatic smell of the hookah. Ali bey was smoking. A *hoja* should protest the use of an opium mix in the *hookah*. He knew Ali bey was not a religious man, but his powers were pervasive. So, instead he nodded submissively and spoke in a whisper. "Help me to plan our next move."

> - - - - - - > THE WILD LANDS BETWEEN RIVERS> - - - - - - >

Setchkin sat watching the somber assembly eating, scarcely talking, contemplating their future; the cumulative effects of their recent choices. Twozan sat calm and resolute. He had passed from his emotional depression to his normal, positive state. Only a strong man would choose to ignore the tribal decision to go west and offer their services to the Caliph: a capitulation which implied a religious change of allegiance. Only a strong man would decide to return and submit to his enemies and await judgment by the Khan of the Chipchak Nation. Only a strong man could admit that his dream of union with the Khan's brother and a political act of confrontation failed. Everything lay in ruin. The strong man now had no words of recrimination or rebuke. He was now empty of self-pity and excuses. He sat quietly marking lines and dots in the sand of the cave bottom. His mind was deep in some calculation. The rest sat eating, resting, gathering strength for the moment it would be called on by their chief. The recent past was too painful to speak about. A few spoke of long past events while other men sharpened their weapons.

Twozan at last lifted his head and spoke quietly. "We will make faster time without the few animals. Those remaining with us will be slaughtered, everything except the extra horses. We'll ride north making speed our main objective. We'll disregard any pursuit unless it is evident that we'll be pressed to fight. They will likely be glad of our departure without more war."

Only Setchkin questioned him. Confidently, she attacked in anger. "You have offended by refusing to meet the Muktar of Samarkand. Such an affront will surely bring a pursuing force." Some of the women stirred nervously.

"To accept an invitation to enter a town would guarantee the success of the opposing force. A hundred men is nothing in Samarkand, but in the desert a hundred men is a formidable force. We are more than that number and our women and children will not be enslaved easily here. Will they expend gold to send thousands after us? Are we such a danger to them that we must be taken at such expense?" He lifted his head in the disdainful negative gesture.

"Then it is settled?" Setchkin looked at the men who were listening intently. Some shrugged, others spoke.

"The Binbasha is right."

"The commander knows."

Setchkin hid her smile of delight. She scooped her toddling child to her arms and held him up to laugh. She was surprised by the feeling of relief and delight in her.

> - - - - - - - >HUNT ON THE AMU VALLEY ROAD > - - - - - - - >

Ahmed found himself pursued by some men on foot from the caravansary. The arrows buzzed past the boy's head. The cry of discovery brought horsemen from an orchard down by the river. The sound of baying dogs reached his ears. He drove his horse desperately for a trail in the brush leading west, away from the main road. He must widen the lead before the mounted men arrived.

The men issuing from the caravansary had split into several groups. Some ran after the escaping riders. Most stood talking and gesturing excitedly and others ran into the stables to saddle horses. A group from the orchard was riding toward the saray. A baying dog on a leash burst on to the road followed by several men. They raced toward the crowd.

Soon the men afoot returned to the crowd while the horsemen from the stables and those from the country mingled and exchanged remarks. The horsemen with the dog arrived and took control of the mob. Tewfik bey rose in his stirrups and called commandingly. "Orhan, take the search team down the road. I'll lead the saray men here in pursuit. Come, Atilla and you others, we must have him now, in the foam-stone thornland we could lose him."

Kynan was mounted on a splendid black horse that was fed and rested, full of speed and enthusiasm for the chase. He and Atilla soon put the other men behind. The trail was fresh and obvious. They sighted the boy and then ate up the distance between. Both drew their bows and feathered arrows.

"I'll buy you that black horse if I get the shot," Atilla shouted, anxious to win the fame of the chase.

"Better let me send your arrow in that case," taunted Kynan to his friend. "You drank three times this morning."

Atilla laughed loudly and whipped his horse. "To put an edge on my shooting, watch me!" Taking the lead he loosed his shot as the boy turned to look at his pursuers. Ahmed flinched to one side as the arrow planted itself in his shoulder joint, spraying the horse's neck red with blood.

"Now watch me," Kynan whooped as his arrow launched straight for the boy's back. At that moment the tiring horse tripped. Ahmed flew over its head and the arrow took the falling horse in the abdomen. The men drew to each side of the thrashing animal giving him room for his deadly lashings. Then it lay as quietly as the rider. The men dismounted gingerly as the other pursuers drew up beside them.

> - - - - - - - > WITH REFUGEES IN KOKAND > - - - - - - - >

"These are the dividing roads I am offered, Yusuf bey. I wish help in my choosing," Sanjak pleaded. "One wishes me to go see my father who has led a part of the tribe south to meet the Khan's brother Erben. They want me to play the diplomat. The second wishes me to go to another section of the border to act the commander over new Turk converts and mercenaries of Islam. In the first case I will be hostage to any decision my father makes. My fortune will depend on his decisions and I know what a stubborn and capricious man he can be. In the second, I will be exploited while made responsible for the action of these so-called converts and their condition will reflect on my safety. Yet I know how lightly religious responsibility can rest on the heart of men blown by the wind into any profession that offers new chances to gain wealth and promotion. Which of two impossibilities do I choose? Here in Kokand I must decide. It seems I must leave the rest of you to make your ways alone to your ancestral homes. I will not be allowed to stay here for news." Sanjak's sober face told the anguish of the choice. Koolair sat cuddled close in his lap and Yusuf and his wife sat close by him sharing his sorrow.

Yusuf spoke. "I am close enough home to wait here for news of Maril and Nooryouz. I have means to stay in this humble house. We do business here, so I'll work with the agent. My people are in contact now and are eager to see us, but they'll understand any delay. The girls haven't been recaptured, so we'll hear more soon."

Koolair reached up to touch Sanjak's face. She spoke carefully. "*Tanra eeyeedir.* God is good and will help. He got us out of Tanglands he'll bring my sisters here." Sanjak buried his face in her hair.

> - - - - - - - > WHITE MARBLE QUARRY > - - - - - - - >

266

"Kardesh, brother, the doctor has come to take off the bandages." Sevman's voice was happy and Yeet's face glowed with excitement. Tayze hurried to the door to bow.

"Welcome to our humble house. Is there anything you need? The boy is impatient to be up and about."

"Nothing is needed now, thank *Adonai*. The healing has been good the deeper cuts are mending and the bruises are clear now. Only the eye needs to be tested. I think one will serve. We'll find out about that one now." Kardesh sat on the sleeping platform with pillows about him.

"*Nay ol lure*, please, can I get up and go outside now? I'm so tired of just lying here being waited on."

"Yes, perhaps about the house, and outside only after sundown. We don't want to expose your eyes to the sun yet. Nothing strenuous, the cuts might open." The doctor quickly removed the head bandage. He looked under the lid of each eye. He dipped a thin straw into a black liquid in a small glass vial and dropped a drop of it into each eye. The doctor waited.

"These drops from the digitalis plant will make the apple of your eye enlarge so I can see inside. There is seepage from the one eye, but the other may serve. You must avoid strong light and stay out of the sun."

"Doctor, my father and sister have left on important business. I must join them as soon as possible. Can't I travel now? We can move at night to avoid bright light." The doctor sat holding the boy's hands and wrist.

"Your pulse is strong, but I would counsel delay. You can move faster at any hour of the day if you wait."

"Sevman and Yeet have not paid off the horse and cart yet. We must wait out the fall." Tayze was firm.

"Do you see? You hold the lamp up, young man, as I look into his eyes. This one must see something." Yeet took the lamp.

"I see the light but no detail. Just with this one. I see nothing with the other."

The doctor sighed. "Yes, I thought as much. Inside the good eye there is something loose. It moves, but must be left to attach itself. I don't think you have kept your face up as I said."

"He won't lay still, Doctor. He won't listen."

"He can't move about then. That loose bit must settle on the back of the eye if he is to see more than light. The choice is yours son, limited sight is better than none, but to see you will have to remain quiet with your face up"

Kardesh's face filled with agony and indecision. "May I then practice the zither or lute?" The voice turned to pleading. "Will the music hurt my healing?"

"It will speed your recovery if you will rest, face up and not sing." The boy smiled.

"My voice is weak and breathy. Yeet does the singing after work. His voice is clear. I can only play." The doctor bandaged his eyes again and left with Tayze.

"Those floating particles are like a raft they will float with the slightest movement of his head. He must be still or be blind. Those are the two end results," he explained.

"For how long, Doctor? You know what boys are."

"In the fall after Rosh Hashanah, my new year, we will know more." He wondered if they would wait that long.

> - - - - - - - > IN THE UIGUR PALACE > - - - - - - - >

Manly, dressed in the silk robes of state, bowed low before the Emperor and the chief eunuch and then resumed his stand. The Emperor watched from his dais. His royal councillor beside him had the frayed, frustrated look of long sessions. The man being honoured was too popular to be destroyed and too able to be denied admission to the rank of the rulers of the nation. His family could not be suppressed; better they should be joined to their peers. The eunuch spoke reluctantly.

"I have been instructed that on the auspicious day chosen by the court astrologers, I shall convey to your house the Princess Manihan. The priests of Mani will perform the necessary rituals to bind your families and future as one. The Emperor of all the Uigurs assures you of the value we place on your worthy family and on yourself. With the marriage to the princess we elevate you, the fortunate groom, to become prince and member of the supreme council of the Uigur nation, with all the privileges and duties therewith."

The emperor smiled ever so faintly. His little mouse would marry into the troublesome family. He was placing a reliable informer into the inner workings of that devious clan. He watched the effects of the ceremony on his binbasha. The general bit his lip in anguish and humiliation, while Manly stood unblinking and cool to receive an abject bow from the eunuch who handed him a scroll delineating the genealogy of his promised bride and a gold-plated key, signifying free access to the palace. It was presented while the general boiled and the promised bride observed approvingly from the women's screened balcony.

> - - - - - - - > IN THE TANRA DAH MOUNTAINS > - - - - - - ->
"We'll freeze to death without fire." Seslee was shivering even with the wool cloak pulled tightly about her.

"If we were with the flocks still, we could squeeze in among the sheep and be warmed." Maril recalled longingly. "Like all the new herd boys will be doing now." The two girls huddled miserably together behind the sheltering rocks.

"Too many eyes on the mountains tonight; tomorrow we may be across." Manish was huddled with Jon in the cleft sharing warmth while they waited for the moon to rise.

"When we're walking it will be easier to stay awake. We'll sleep in the morning." Seslee shook her head. "I'd go back to the harem just to be warm. Finding a good husband is harder than I thought, you need more than looks to get the best."

Maril comforted her with a pat. "Daddy will help get the very best for you. He has lots of cousins and business friends. He says it just takes a bit of time and patience to get an ideal mate for a girl. He says it's a matter of family standards as well as her personal taste."

Seslee snickered and remarked. "Don't worry when we get free it'll be easy. I'll do my own sales pitch."

> - - - - - - - > WEST ROAD TOWARD IRAN > - - - - - - ->
Kemeer sat his horse looking at the village. The houses were empty and there was little of value to be found. Some articles had found their way to the nomad tents, but the village people remained underground and although their crops suffered they stayed well, though angry.

Gerchen was still angry as well. He longed for a battle that the farmers were unwilling to give him. However, they were ready to avenge themselves. They issued at night to kill some of the flock for meat and some of the herders for payback.

Kemeer's victory over the right hand wrestler had been a means of his promotion and the absence of Twozan catapulted him into a position of leadership of the left hand of the clan. Ayshe had persuaded him to move toward peace.

"Come now Gerchen, the Caliph will be angered if we stay and kill. They have taken to earth and we must turn gopher to dig them out. We gain little here."

Gerchen shook his head stubbornly. "They deserve to die. My anger does not retreat. They are not men. They refuse to fight outside their holes."

"So do badgers, but they can fight down a dog and break the leg of horses with their holes. Villagers are a danger to stay around. Take what you will and let us go."

"We should stay and make them fight."

"Forget them, the left hand Toozlu are breaking camp. We lost animals last night and have a good man wounded. Stay if you will, we are going to the Caliph; I can't afford to attack his villages."

Gerchen openly sneered at him. "You have become careful after giving up the great truths of our faith. Your wife teaches you to serve another master."

Kemeer rode away slowly and called over his back, "Judge you this: Which is the greater sin? To give up a great encompassing faith for a smaller earth-centered one or to cling to the greater, but not obey it?"

> - - - - - - - > IN A SMUGGLERS' MOUNTAIN CAVE > - - - - - - - >

The cave echoed with the sound of horses and yelling, angry men. Nooryouz woke to the din below her. It came from deeper inside the cave. She looked at the small hole where she had entered, crawling, and saw the increasing light of day. She moved down toward the new sounds and felt the floor of the cave descend, gradually at first, then more steeply. She was on a window like shelf where air and defused light entered the larger cave below. She leaned out to listen to the talk it was in the language of Sanjak, her lover.

"You fool of a guide you almost led us right into the herders. I thought you knew the mountains," barked one.

"Why did you hire a senile old man? I told you he had passed his usefulness. He's slow and stupid," a shrill voice accused. The old man about whom they directed their complaints paid no attention, but was busy unpacking the yaks while a small boy gathered the horses and led them to a pile of hay held in a wooden cradle against the wall. A fourth man stood with light behind his back at the entrance. He listened to the complaints, then with a disgusted shrug turned his back to face the light and drew his sword. He took up a position of watchful waiting. The light accented his straight black hair and broad shoulders. The big-fisted complainer shoved the wiry little man who challenged his every decision and leadership.

"I hired him. I've got a right to complain. You came along and got scared by the crowd. They would have ignored us for the price they get, but there may be agents about who get a share of the goods. Those are the ones to watch for." The big man walked over to help the old guide.

"Kadir, why are you standing guard? You know we pay their village not to poke about the caves." The big man continued to find fault and move the packed gear around, not allowing any to remain where the old guide had put them. The smaller man also moved everything again, glaring up at the leader.

The guide paid no attention to either and started to curry the Yak and instructed the boy to do the same with the horses.

"Kadir, damn you, answer! You can help stack these crates. We have to pack out the silk and brocades tonight. The spices will have to wait." The two men continued piling the goods about.

"Treachery pays too high a wage. There are always takers." Kadir turned to make his statement and turned again. The smaller man and the giant stopped to stare.

"Yavuz, did you hear that fool? He fears treachery. Does he know how much we pay these lazy villagers?" Yavuz opened his mouth to answer, but Kadir was faster.

"Aziz, you happy man, do you understand? They pay five times what you pay each year. Greed breeds treachery." Aziz looked even more unhappy as he rubbed his big head and squinted at little Yavuz.

"If it comes to that, why do you think one man on guard will make a difference? Would the village trust one or two to do the job? What fools these smugglers!" Aziz grinned, proud of his logic.

"I've told you we shouldn't let goods accumulate like this. We need to keep the cave with as little inventory as possible. We could pay the village more. Keep it to their best interest." Yavuz raved on while Aziz stacked packs.

Nooryouz listened as the smugglers bickered and worked. The sound was comforting. She dozed again. She woke in a fright as the baby started to cry.

BABY CRIES

271

PEOPLE, PLOTS & PLACES IN CHAPTER 22

Atilla: has the opportunity to glory in his achievement.
Ayden bey: in charge of men searching for the fugitives.
Aziz bey: wants to leave smuggling for a quiet retirement.
Bitler: the dog finds and stops the objects of his search.
Derk: continues his work for the Caliph, to save the Toozlu.
Erben: is discovered, past help, by a search party's arrival.
Fuat: must stand guard over a corpse until it is identified.
Gerchen: is always angry when he doesn't get his way.
Kadir: a guard and partner in the smuggler's enterprise.
Kaplan: this tiger eats his young for his own enrichment.
Karga: the crow is very careful when feeding the tiger.
Kerim: meets memories in the face of a dead man.
Korkmaz: a boy named Fearless, learning family business.
Kemeer: the leader of the left hand clan mercenaries.
Kynan: finds his disguise wearing thin and must escape.
Leyla: waits for her father, but is found by her enemy.
Mahmut: an enemy makes him pay for what he took.
Mother: finds new freedom and sight, but leaves mystery.
Nooryouz: hides and waits to cross the mountains.
Orhan: finds the dying body of an unknown man.
Sanjak: hopes to save his clan from destruction.
Tewfik: in one day loses dogs, horses, fugitives & travelers.
Umer: gains goods and girl, but loses friends in his flight.
Yavuz bey: a small, suspicious, complaining smuggler.

GLOSSARY:
beyler: gentlemen.
Bock ora da: Look over there.
ji had: great exertion or effort; holy war.
ordu eve: army headquarters; war camp.

KYNAN'S PRAYER

"We found her here this morning. She was slumped at the loom and staring at the door as if she could see. She looks surprised, but not afraid. She must have been killed during the night."

Ali bey stood with the rug factory owner and looked down at the covered form of the woman. He grunted knowingly. "Cut her throat and took her money. Did any one else miss things?"

The owner replied carefully. "Nothing whatever is missing, except this: the new silk prayer rug she was completing. She had no money to speak of." He pointed to the loom whose strings had been cut and the woven piece removed. The man continued. "The girls report her claim to have heard the Gray Wolf. It was several months ago. They say he wanted information."

Ali bey grimaced and nodded. He sighed as he turned to go. "I wanted some information too, but I believed her disclaimers and thought she knew nothing about her son's location or activities. She must have known more than she let on. Did she know how to write?"

The owner shrugged.

> - - - - - - - > IN THE CHIPCHAK HOMELAND > - - - - - - - >
"Well, have you news today?" Kaplan, the Tiger demanded. Karga bowed submissively, while his heart burned with humiliation and resentment. The Tiger is in a man-eating mood, he thought as he had

scarcely finished his greetings on arrival at the large yurt. His face was as smooth as the tiger's was sour.

He smiled deferentially, "My Lord, three pigeons flew in today. The news is good. Events are moving quite fast in the south. The old Khorasan Arab families that subdued the rebellion and have ruled the Caliphate are losing power to the Seljuks and other Turk related families. The Caliph surrounds himself with troops that have no loyalty to the older generation of supporters. He isolates himself from the people of Baghdad and is building again near Samara. The greatness of Harum El Rashid is forgotten. Our people gain more power."

"What is new in all this? Am I addled that I need to be told what is obvious? Get on with it." The Tiger spat patting his bulky chest.

"The Toozlu have split. Gerchen leads the tribe west. They go to work for the Caliph as promised." Karga continued, "Twozan returns with the Princess Setchkin and the child. The party is large enough to, perhaps, reach the border without capture."

The Tiger's face shifted to alertness, "It would be a pity to have to bring this matter to the Khan. It would prove much better if they all died on the way. We have the child of promise here among us still. It would divide us yet again if one returned to trouble our ploy. We would lose face before our whole nation."

The Crow bowed and paused to consider. "I think it can be arranged, but I hesitated to plot against your daughter."

KAAPLAN COMMANDS

274

Kaplan grumped nastily, "The bitch caused us enough trouble with her behavior before and after marriage. She doesn't appreciate or use her powers for us. She is expendable. I plan to keep the Khan's brother out of the inheritance; why not her as well?"

The Crow gulped, hesitated, then spoke, "I'm expecting to hear of Erben's ...er, demise any time now." He waited for the nod of approval and went on with the report. "Twozan's son has crossed the border leaving the Uigur lands. He waits for his bride, who was detained for the harem. Her escape has caused a scandal. Our cousins, the Uigurs, are angry, but they didn't keep the man. They hope his presence will draw her to that section of the border. The Caliph's men are sucking up to him and offering him various places of importance, if he'll convert."

The Tiger grinned and picked at his teeth with a small knife. "They'll have agents on both sides of the line waiting to pounce.
"Sanjak, as I remember him. He was a wild fool and I'm surprised he got over to the Tangs and back even if he didn't stay long. Things are still pretty hot in the East."

"The Christians among us are very distressed by the continued news of persecutions. They pray much and request that we protest to the Tang Emperor," snickered Karga.

Kaplan shrugged. "The Tang ignores us, unless we threaten their borders. We'll let it pass with comforting words to our Nestorians. Now, what was the third message? Is the best last in this case? Come, you've kept it long enough."

"Your son, Kynan, is still at large. His evasion of the army and police is causing a great stir among the most influential people. A reward is about to be offered."

"What a surprise! The boy may be worth something after all. It's most unlike him. I shall have to think on this, humm ... Shall we let the Seljuk command lose face? Sacrifice a potential gain for special favours from their key people? Collect the reward ourselves? Or has this hard experience changed the boy to something valuable? I would sacrifice to the spirits of the ancestors if I had one child who was worth his nurture. Yes, I'll have to think on this."

> - - - - - - - >AGENTS RIDE IN THE WILD LANDS > - - - - - - - >

"We have so far to go and so little time." Derk bey's voice was apprehensive. "Your Khan Erben will be joining the tribesmen in a few days. If he does, it could mean war among the Chipchak clans. If it starts in our land some will

275

think it is our policy. It will be a political embarrassment to our Caliph. We are not yet healed from the effects of our Civil Wars."

Derk bey rode furiously with Sanjak at his side. Each had had his choice made for him. Being compelled, they were again men of action.

"Why are you worried by a threat of rebellion among Chipchaks, a nation outside Islam?" Sanjak responded as they rode.

"The Seljuks are eyeing the growing weakness of the Arabs of Herat. The old families of the conquerors are worried lest they lose control of the situation and the Seljuk tribe's strength increases. The Caliph has had enough obligations and problems with Khorasan. Civil war in the north will further upset things. There are local factions that would like to destabilise the frontier. Some Imams would preach for a *jihad*, holy war." The horses strained up the mountain slope toward Tashkent.

Sanjak spoke grimly. "The Empire's effort to conquer Turkish land has been repulsed for over two hundred years. The promised thousand years of leadership to the Kayalar family is not yet half expended. They believe this promise and will always repulse your efforts. You will never conquer Turkish tribesmen. Fighting is their chief joy and pleasure."

They slowed their horses and dismounted to walk beside them, letting the animals rest as they descended the mountain side.

It was Derk's turn to observe, "The Caliph wins them over by letting Turkish tribesmen go to war for him. He pays well. They flock to him."

"He buys loyalty and avoids the hatreds formed among the Arabs in the recent Civil Wars. No wonder the palace guards are all of Turkish origin," observed Sanjak.

Derk smiled. "It makes opportunity for our promotion and our people too. We are enriched."

Sanjak frowned, "What does it do for those of us who are still Christian?"

Derk shrugged and observed. "Those who do convert can become rich, live well and secure. Otherwise you are enslaved."

"Punished if you don't; rich for a time if you do, but for all eternity?"

> - - - - - - - >A HUNT IN THE AMU VALLEY > - - - - - - - >

"Look there's a horse by that grove," Orhan shouted and pointed. His scattered ranks pulled in from each side of the road where they were searching for tracks. Orhan led from the road, but some of his men were closer and arrived before him. They sat their horses in a circle looking down at the man's body. No one moved. A warrior lay twitching with an arrow in his neck, above the hard leather breastplate. His exhausted horse, too tired to seek the sparse grass near the grove of thorn bush, stood head down, as if in mourning. The man had just been shot and was still dying.

"Who were the men searching on this side of the road?" demanded Orhan.

The men shook their heads in wonder. "We were all moving about."

"We looked for tracks."

"I didn't notice."

"Fuat and Ismail were with me."

"Jelal and I were by the river."

Each looked at the others and back at the man dying before them. Then one asked a key question. "Who is he?" Orhan shrugged. Ayden bey pointed.

The dying man was feebly starting to make the sign of the cross: forehead, chest, right shoulder and at the left, his hand dropped. His strength departed with his soul.

"Not Muslim."

"Ambushed."

"His horse is badly used."

"He has callused and damaged hands."

"He wears old garments."

"Why would such a man be killed?" Ayden turned to ask Orhan. "I hear you were searching for a traveller."

"This could be the man, but I don't know. I need to get back to Tewfik bey." Orhan turned his horse to go.

"What do we do with him? Do we go ahead with the

277

hunt?" Ayden bey called out. Orhan urged his horse into a run.

"Fuat, you stay here until he returns. Dig a grave!" Ayden ordered. "The rest of you get back to tracking." Ayden left the youth Fuat waiting.

> - - - - - - - > AMU VALLEY TAVERN > - - - - - - - >

"There we were, *beyler*, gentlemen, racing neck and neck ahead of the mob in pursuit. Both armed and ready to shoot. Kerim, the champion of the East Bulgars took the horse, but I took the rider." Atilla chuckled boastfully.

"You must confess that it was I who stopped them. You might have had to chase them more and missed these first drinks." Laughter greeted Kerim's response.

"Dead riders don't continue far," Atilla replied. "Shoot for the man, not the horse, Kerim bey. Am I right gentlemen?" Heads nodded and throats moistened on the bounty of the hunter.

Kerim moved purposefully among the group collecting the coins lost in the betting. Wagers made in the heat of the chase and given grudgingly until the second round of drinks had loosened their purse strings.

"Congratulations hunters. There are still two murderers on the loose with stolen horses so don't miss the excitement. Justice must be done, Allah forbid that we should neglect avenging the innocent." Tewfik bey's entrance had been unnoticed until he spoke. The men nodded assent again.

"Come, drink to our success," Atilla invited him.

"Tonight, we'll all celebrate our successes. Now we must ride. Kyn...Kerim... bey, I need your company now. Come."

Atilla looked annoyed, but said nothing. Kynan knew something important was afoot. Tewfik had stumbled on his assumed name. How much did they suspect? He was asked to leave the party Atilla had organised in his own honor, bragging about his killing shot and the fact that Kerim of the East Bulgars had only brought down the horse. Kynan knew the shot had not killed, but the fall had. He was glad to leave the party for he knew something

278

important would come of the ride down the valley. No word was spoken during the long ride.

"What do you think Kerim? Do you know this man?" Tewfik bey sat watching Kynan carefully, waiting the answer.

So this was it, a question of identity. Kynan let his mind recall the repeated dream he loved.

"I was a boy of nearly nine years when my father let me ride with him from our lands to the Chipchak *Ordu Eve*; the Central War Yurt, for a royal wedding. The younger twin of Khan Erdash, Erben, took a girl of great name and fortune in marriage. Warriors came from every nation and the beauty and dash of it all befuddled my eyes. The woman was so dazzling. I had never seen her equal, fragile and radiant in beauty and charm. I was won over and have never forgotten her. This man, dead here, seems old and worn compared to the groom that day, but it is the same man, Erben of the Chipchak."

Tewfik smiled knowingly and thanked him. "I thought as much, now we must find his companion. The man is clever. He rode well and is hard to track in the foam rock thorn bush. The horse is exhausted and we fed it and sent it to the stables, I hope it may live. Now you may consider yourself free, for the moment, to return to Atilla bey's party."

Dismissed, Kynan could not depart. He asked, "You will bury him today? Here?"

Tewfik nodded. "He is not Muslim. The cemetery is closed to him. We have no priest or shaman to say words over him."

"May I then stay for a time? His face brings old memories."

Tewfik scrutinised him carefully then assented. "You will stay as guard until relieved. Fuat has dug a grave by this thorn grove. We will return at sunset. Fuat, you come with me now. Bring the personal effects. The stolen horses entered the desert above near here, we must hurry." Tewfik rode away followed by a tired and dirty Fuat.

Kynan dismounted and walked to the body. Weapons and boots were robbed, taken as booty. The old worn breast plate of leather remained since Muslim chain mail was better. The cummerbund of frayed cheap material was also undisturbed. Kynan found a small dagger hidden under the back. Carefully he removed the breastplate and carried the corpse to the grave. There he lay the body and covered it with rock and dirt. He found some rocks at the side of a field to lay on the surface to discourage any animals digging. Then standing, he recited one of the prayers Father Agaz, the priest, had taught him and crossed himself. He then addressed a few impromptu words and left. He repeated the words again as he mounted the black, tracing the trail back out of the valley. "His travelling companion will be waiting, let me find her and be her guide to safety." It became his prayer.

> - - - - - - - > IN THE SMUGGLER'S CAVE > - - - - - - - >

Nooryouz blew gently on the baby's face and nuzzled him to her breast. His cry muffled and ceased. She pressed back into the shadow and waited quietly: there was a silent moment.

"What was that? It sounded like a baby!" The guard, Kadir, whirled from his stance. The bearded giant laughed.

"The fool hears babies in the cave of Aziz. It was but some varmint up by the vent. Something quieted or killed. What kind of a fool would hide a baby here?"

Suspicion marked the face of his little companion. Yavuz bey shouted in anger, dropping a bail of cloth. "It was a baby! Boy, climb up and see what's there. We can't trust you anymore. You're smuggling slaves now. I know some of the great families are acquiring concubines and wet nurses for service. Why have you failed to consult us? Don't partners count for anything?"

The guide and boy exchanged glances and shrugged. The boy started climbing.

"Stop fool, I'll have no nonsense. Come back Korkmaz. I've not hidden anything. All my operations are known to everyone. I pay my partners, the police, the officials and the army well. There's hardly any profit left for an honest smuggler. I'll have no more accusations."

Kadir spoke, drawing near the center. "My ears are not fooled. It was a child." He motioned toward the vent as the boy continued climbing.

"You'll not take us into any new ventures without prior agreement. Think you can treat us any way you please: you greedy know-it-all, boss-it-all, hog-it-all." The tiny Yavuz rudely pointed his finger in the offended man's face.

"For sixty years I've climbed these mountains and I wish to

280

make but one last journey and I make the mistake of bringing fools with me. No, not my mistake, you insisted on joining me, because you don't trust me. And now this! It's mutiny!" Aziz drew his weapon and waved it dramatically. Yavuz bey's shriek filled the cave as he too drew.

The boy paused just below the brink of the vent, looking down, he shouted. "Don't hurt grandfather, you dried-up worm."

"Devil's brood! How your vile nature shows in the spawn. He threatens me." The two men stood nose to nose.

"I heard a baby," Kadir insisted, turning back, pointedly ignoring the quarrellers, who stood poised, threats ready. The guide shifted a bail of cloth.

Aziz continued, "My ears are as sharp as anyone here. I'll not deceive you. I've no slaves to trade, or new girls to take to the army, my honor on it."

> - - - - - - - > AMU VALLEY THORN GROVE > - - - - - - - >

The day was passing, still her father had not returned. The pony was exhausted and unwilling to seek food, so she ventured out and walked to the river before dark, to bring water and grass. He failed to eat. Head down, wasted and shivering he stood waiting in weakness. She took the long knife Erben had left her into the crawl space under the thorn trees, in the heart of a grove for protection. There she had fitfully slept and wakened to the horse's moaning. Before sunset it died, her heart died with it.

The birds, already sailing high above, were seeking food. She left her shelter to overlook the valley from behind the thorn bushes. There were riders among the orchard trees, moving her direction, but none were of the shape so dear to her heart.

Running, she turned back to her camp. Rounding the trees, she saw two horses beside her dead pony. A man stood holding the reins as another crawled out of her sleeping bower. She braked violently, it was Umer! He snarled and straightened up. She turned to flee toward the riders in the valley.

A huge kangal, tongue out, eyes wild, came staggering toward her. His coat was flecked with the stain of dried foam and dirt. He held the touch of madness that marks some dogs in mourning. She froze. Umer laughed and moved forward, not seeing the dog hidden by brush. She jumped back into the thorns. Bitler seemed not to see her, but followed the scuffed marks of the horses' hooves.

Umer stopped, surprised. He didn't recognise the dog. Bitler continued doggedly to where the youth Mahmut stood. While everyone stared in disbelief he reared up, knocked him down and lunged for the throat. Mahmut shrieked and tried to ward off the attack. Umer, shouting, ran to the two and plunged his knife into the side of the struggling dog. The horses reared up free and escaped while Umer struck the dog again and again with knife and foot, but the animal would not release his hold on the bleeding Mahmut. He continued to shake him until, with a crack, the head dropped at a strange angle.

A shout called Leyla's attention and she saw a stranger on a black horse gaping in shock at the scene. Shouting he started forward. She jumped back, deeper into the embrace of the thorn trees. Umer, hearing the approach of the horse, freed his knife and ran after his horse. Old Bitler sank upon his prey still holding and shaking it like a rag doll; then, moaning, he died.

Kynan rode behind the running Umer. He rode to Orhan's great horse and gathered the reins. Umer managed to catch and mount Atilla's. The two men glared hatefully, at each other. One was marked for death if they met again, but they broke eye contact, each riding urgently in a different direction. One rode past the thorn bushes into the desert, the other hurried back to the scene of death.

Kynan returned to Leyla and dismounting sought to coax her out of the embracing thorns. She was unresponsive.

"I'm Kynan of the Chipchak. We are kin. We met one time.., when you were exiled. I've come to help. We must go before the enemy gets here."

She stared at the familiar old leather breast plate he wore. Then she looked into his anxious eyes. A trickle of blood came down her forehead and ran beside her nose like a tear. She saw his face in a red haze. She knew she had known him sometime, somewhere. She swayed forward and the smell of blood filled her senses. Pain came with motion.

Kynan found himself in the childhood dream. The moon

282

maiden stood before him distressed and in need. He didn't know what to do. He reached for her and pain met his hands and arms like dragon claws. Their eyes locked and he found himself drawn to fall into the depths of them. He couldn't breathe. Why couldn't he wake? The dream must end!

She slumped forward into his arms and he carefully drew her out of the embedded thorn branches. His hair rose on his neck as he felt the warm wet touch of blood as he carried her to his horse. He slid her over the saddle and quickly mounted. Leading the second horse he drew her up into an embrace. Like a baby he carried her and they turned into the desert of scrub and thorns to run among the foam stones. Droplets of their blood mingled and dried as they fled. The growing circle of wheeling birds marked the darkening place of vengeance and death.

BITLER ATTACKS

PEOPLE, PLOTS & PLACES IN CHAPTER 23

Ali bey: loses a man who could disrupt northern enemies.
Atilla: gets a hangover and questions, but misses the hunt.
Tayze & family: leave the quarry to everyone's great relief.
Aziz bey: finds opposition and suspicion on his last trip.
Bolben: is devastated by the turn of events in his life.
Dakool: fears capture and trial for the harem escape.
Derk: tries to keep on good terms with everyone.
Hussein: risks himself choosing a girl his friend rejects.
Kadir bey: the young man's belief in fate is confirmed.
Korkmaz: the brave grandson of Aziz, the smuggler.
Mehmet: makes the Toozlu stand-off seem his victory.
Nooryouz: finds mercy and sympathy when she needs it.
Sanjak: angered by offers in the army, visits his clan.
Tash: serves to inform, not to change events.
Tewfik: has only finished part of his many duties.
Umer, the pretender: likes the daughter of a fellow worker.
Umer the murderer: escapes dangers, but not his passions.
Yavuz bey: always reacts angrily to what his partners say.

GLOSSARY:
kafir: heathen; idolater; unbeliever.
sappuk: maniac; molester.
soos: hush; shut up; be quiet.

FUGITIVE FOUND

"The girl has stayed up there all night. Could she have
escaped?" Six men were roped together searching the rock and
crags where the girl, Dakool, had disappeared the day before. They
were inching along a small goat path that seemed to vanish from
time to time. The wispy, retreating snow line lay close above them
and fog pressed about the rock making visibility poor. The path
seemed to climb endlessly.

One man exclaimed. "The old smuggler's trail is beyond this
point. We are paid to stay away from that road."

The leader spoke. "The trail signs and footprints led here, but
now they seem to have ended. We need to back track at the foot of
the cliff. Since there are no prints in the snow we know that she
hasn't gotten here. Let's go up to the juncture and double back
below the cliff face and check the caves." The leader's words were
accepted immediately. It would be a relief to be off the cliff face
and down by the stream bed. Out of the wind they felt the chill of

their exhaustion. They removed the rope harness. Then the leader stopped suddenly and leaned over a ledge carefully.

"Look, she is there below." The others crowded round for a look. She had fallen into the canyon. She lay on a rock floor by the stream, one leg seemed twisted. They drew their breath sharply.

One boy whispered softly to Bolben, "Do you recognize her?"

Another caught his breath. "How lovely! Is she the Umayyad princess?"

> - - - - - - - > IN THE FOAM STONE DESERT > - - - - - - - >

Umer rode hard, but as the horse tired he dismounted and led the animal. Several times he detected distant groups of horses. He hid until all had passed on. They would add prints to the desert and make trails hard to follow. In the dark he walked up a rocky, dry stream bed. He was sure the wild Turk he had met would also be running from the authorities. He would wait until moonrise and see if he could cross his trail. The horse he had stolen from Atilla bey had food and drink loaded. The animal was strong. He would settle with these *kafirs*, infidels, before going to Samarkand. As he thought of the girl he again felt that strong desire to humble her. He longed to hear her cry for mercy. He shook himself from his fantasy. He must escape. He listened intently for pursuit and hearing none, hobbled the horse, lay down in the shelter of the embankment to eat and sleep deeply. He would waken at moon rise to sharpen his knife and prepare to hunt.

> - - - - - - - >WHITE MARBLE QUARRY DEPARTURE > - - - - - - - >

The cart was loaded with wooden chests and bundles of cloth. Food and kitchen-ware rode on top. Room was left for a bed where Kardesh rested. Sevman, with Tayze beside him, guided the team while Yeet rode the old horse.

A few neighbors observed the Kayalar's going with words of farewell and good wishes, but many were at work. For others the departure of the foreigners produced as much joy as sorrow.

"Allah be thanked, the barbarian family is taking their invalids and leaving. It about time, praise Allah"

"Allah save us from others like them."

"We must insist on the hiring of good Muslims at the quarry."

"Bold barefaced girls always cause rivalries and fights."

The families of the five escaped boys celebrated. Threats were murmured among the men who drank at the tea house. "We don't need such wanton flirts in our village."

"We must authorize the mosque to enforce the dress code for decency's sake," the men agreed.

The women, segregated in the kitchen and inner rooms, were echoing the same theme. "Religious police are needed to enforce the dress code and practices of Islam on the believers and barbarians."

"Civilization must come to the rough quarry village."

"We'll be able to bring back our poor, unfortunate boys."

"Justice will prevail now." The heads nodded together, true religion would save a God fearing community.

> - - - - - - - > CANYON FLOOR IN THE TANRA DAH > - - - - - - - >

"They have found me" Dakool murmured as the sound of the approaching men above came to her. She drew her small knife from the waist band. She rested her hands on her breast and prayed fervently. "Yesu of Light, I confess my failure to live as you have shown us in the elite and those who follow close to you. Have mercy on me and others who follow from afar and fail you. Yesu you know my pain from slavery till today. I admit that I loved my moments with the horseman. I confess my sin and ask for pardon. Take me to yourself or at least give me another life by incarnation to serve you better." The voices of the men came now from the valley bottom. She made a quick slicing motion with the knife and laid her bleeding wrist on her abdomen.

"Light is coming. Is it You?" Dakool smiled as she stared up at the mountains. She continued speaking as the red stain spread across her shalvar and robe.

"Why are you sad? My faith is small? You had something more for me to do? You would have been with me to save a village? But I was afraid, you know what these men would do to me... Oh... I didn't know, please forgive me. Yes, let's go." Her whispers ceased. The mist thickened.

"Look, blood, she's killed herself." The men stopped and took in the scene. Like a wounded bird she lay fluttering, scarlet blood spreading.

Bolben pressed forward. "She's still warm, can we stop it?" They shook their heads sadly.

"What a waste. Is she the one you loved?"

287

"I don't know. I would have to hear her speak. I never saw her face clearly. It was before moon rise."

"She's pretty even if she has a split lip. Let's see what the rest of her looks like." The man spread the top robe and started to pull down her blooded shalvar.

"Stop that. Don't you touch her," Bolben shouted angrily pushing the man away. As he fell the offending man drew his knife and gathered his feet under him to dive at Bolben's legs. He thrust up at his crotch. Bolben jumped back and kicked the hand away. He drew his own knife and moved forward.

"No fighting!" The search party stepped between them.

The knife-less man began to justify himself vigorously. "Your family's rich. They can get you a wife. When will I have enough money to marry? You had one of these yesterday. When do I get one? She's dead anyway. She can't object. Better dead than never!" He stood, still on guard.

"*Sappuk*, maniac! You're sick! Keep your hands off her or I'll--" The opponents continued to glare.

One of the older married men interrupted. "There's no reward if she's molested. The Khan would fine our village and punish the man. It's bad enough that she's bled on the shalvar. There'll be talk." He motioned to the opponents to move away. "Put your knives away, we have to carry her back."

However, both men paid no attention to the order. One picked up his fallen knife and started back down toward the foot of the mountain. Bolben climbed back up the tiny valley.

> - - - - - - - > TANRA DAH SMUGGLERS' CAVE > - - - - - - - >

"You keep your dirty old hands off my grandfather or I'll report you ..." The boy's voice trailed off. Who would he report them to? The police? He would be jailed with the grandfather. Complain to other smugglers? They would take over the goods and route. There was no higher authority in the illegal, but profitable trade he was being trained in. Both his father and mother had died in the 'trade'. An awkward silence ensued, followed by the chuckle of the others present. Tension died.

"Go on up son, I'll be alright. This little man has more bark than bite." Aziz smiled at his opponent, adding, "You see what kind of grandson I have, Yavuz bey, brave, all heart." He smirked and patted his stomach with pride.

"Get up there, I won't hurt the old goat," said the scowling Yavuz as he turned back to his fallen bale. Kadir paced the entrance and the old guide continued to pile bales. The hum of activity below masked the boy's efforts to reach the ledge.

"There's no one up here! Now, are you satisfied?"

Yavuz and Kadir looked thoughtfully at each other and spoke. "Tracks?"

288

"Trash or scat left behind?" A long silence followed.

"Old rags in the corner, no fire traces. Someone was here yesterday, maybe. Came in from the opening. No tracks near the vent. It couldn't have climbed down."

"So the cave's contents would still be a secret?"

"Naturally, stupid! Our secret," commented Aziz.

"Wait," commanded Kadir. "Pick up the rags and describe them to us." Again there was a long silence.

"An old herder's coat, ragged and stinky. I'm going outside a moment, but there's nothing more here."

"What would I do without Korkmaz? Fearless, like his name. That boy will make a top smuggler, one to be proud of in our village. I won't need fools and halfwits to work with when he's of age. You hear me Yavuz bey?" An angry reply restarted the feud.

> - - - - - - - > THE WILD LANDS BETWEEN RIVERS > - - - - - - - >

"Have you come from the Toozlu camp, Mehmet bey?" Sanjak and Derk rode up to the adjutant and his small troop where they were quenching their thirst and watering the horses. After the required preliminaries of greetings and acknowledgements were over, Derk asked his question again.

"We frightened them into high rugged country for defense," Mehmet bey replied. "They were so worried by our troopers that they would only talk at a distance. They are a day's easy travel from here, but they'll probably run all the way to the border. They've killed their stock and are riding their horses to death." He drew himself up proudly to state: "So Allah has again proved his love for his faithful with victory by scattering the unbelievers. May they all perish!"

"Not until we have carried out the Caliph's commands concerning them. Allah is merciful to the needy." Derk bey's reply was made with courtesy, but Sanjak could hardly keep anger from his face. He used the quirt on his horse rather than on the adjutant and rode off before the customary farewells.

The adjutant snorted and indicated the retreating figure. "How vile and rude these barbarians. I've heard that one of their khans was killed yesterday near Samarkand. Good riddance!" Derk's expression saddened then he sighed.

"Had I found him he would have lived." He smiled tolerantly as he said the words of farewell.

Mehmet put out a hand to detain the departure of the agent. "Why would a man of rank keep company with a kafir? You have the Caliph's seal, why such a rude companion?"

"I'm setting bait for a wolf and must stay alert, for he is treacherous and well hidden. I also, don't forget my origins; I'll not despise my own. The Koran states that the Christian may be the most faithful of friends. Give your commander, Onat bey, my greetings when you meet." Derk bowed dutifully and without further comment repeated the necessary words of farewell. Sanjak was out of sight when he rode away.

It took a half hour of hard riding to catch up with Sanjak; but Derk waited another equally long period before he spoke. When he did, it was of business.

"The village there ahead is where we will find our baggage animals waiting. They will need the supplies to reach their territory without great losses"

Sanjak was still angry. "I know you didn't believe those lies," he growled.

"There is much to learn even from these: rugged country and shouted conversations mean they're going to remain defiant and ride for the border. The killing of the herds confirms this. As for the great victory, where was their booty? No loot means no wins in our world. You shouldn't let fools annoy you so easily."

Sanjak shook his head. "I suppose they have their uses, but I hate their bragging ways."

They rode on and Derk made a face and looked closely at his companion. "I learned something else of interest. Our adjutant had another rumor to pass on." Sanjak showed no interest, but stared ahead. Derk continued, "Rumor has it that a barbarian Khan was killed yesterday. He was trying to join his army for the conquest of this land of two rivers. The people fear they're that close to death or domination by the Turkish tribes."

Sanjak's shock was clear. "Erben? Dead? Why did he delay so?"

"Those who killed him caused it. The Caliph wanted him alive. The Gray Wolf has had his victory. Your father will be the new target. Erdash's sons must be isolated and destroyed so the candidate of the Gray Wolf will rule."

> - - - - - - -> AT BLACK MOUNTAIN QUARRY > - - - - - - ->

"Look, here she comes now!" Umer, the pretender, nudged his friend, Big Hussein, as they sat at a tea house located at a juncture conveniently near the fountain where water flows for the households of the village. Interested young men can sit, and for a small sum, drink, and eye the girls they pretend to ignore. As long as you don't look directly at them, the religious police can only complain at the increase of customers at the precise hour that graceful girls fill and carry water jars home. Early morning and last light are the favored hours when the families send their women to the task. Water is a necessity, early and late. The tea house fills with men going to or coming from work.

"Watch her eyes when she looks at me," Umer whispered. They did, and her eyelids fluttered and then her green veil puffed where the lips are located. Did she blow a kiss? When she lifted down the jar from her head, a smooth black arm was revealed under the long sleeve. She filled the jar and hoisting it up hiked her ample hip showing a bit of black ankle above the sandaled foot. Umer sighed noisily, the girl giggled and then with head straight she walked gracefully by, again favoring him with a flutter and kicking him a pebble.

Umer whispered, "She's Brahui, her folks came north during a famine ten years ago. Her dad works in my quarry: a great guy!"

Hussein interrupted his friend's recitation vigorously. "You are promised to marry the granddaughter of our host. It was arranged between the brothers; by your supposed father. How are you going to get out of that?"

"Are you crazy? She's lame and old; must be nearing 18. Umer was always talking about the time he saw her: pale with washed out, thin, light hair, green-eyed like a cat. I'd rather tell everything; the truth, than marry her." Umer shuddered and took a deep breath.

291

Big Hussein hissed at him. "*Soos*, hush stupid, here she comes now." He elbowed the fake Umer and watched reverently as the tall, thin girl slowly approached. He stood as she came near and his height towered over her. He smiled at her and bowed slightly. Startled, she tripped, her foot turned under and she lurched forward. He caught the falling jar with one hand and her arm with the other. They stared at each other. She was too frightened to speak. Everyone stopped to look. The whole village would hear and talk. Big Hussein carried the jar to the fountain and filled it. He lifted it offering to place it on her head. She stood indecisive. Then, placing the head pad over her scarf, accepted her burden with a soft spoken thanks. It was the equivalent of a public proposal of marriage by the friend of the man who was supposed to marry her. Scandal! What would her father say?

> - - - - - - - > NEAR THE SMUGGLER'S CAVE > - - - - - - - >

Nooryouz ran up the narrow trail from the ledge that led to the cave where she had taken refuge. She dodged behind a rock and looked furtively back. The boy, whose loud voice had warned her, was crawling out from under the bush.

She waited for him to return to his friends, but instead he moved up the trail toward her. The baby hiccupped as he passed the rock. She automatically put him up to her shoulder to burp him.

Korkmaz whirled to face her. "So you were in the cave; this is your coat." He held up the garment.

She shrank back as if he would hit her. "We meant no harm. I didn't know it connected to your hide-away. Please don't hurt us."

He glared at her. "Then you're not a slave my grandfather hid there? You came by accident?"

Eyes wide, she nodded eagerly. "We were trying to cross the border. I'm lost." The baby chose that moment to burp again and hiccup.

"Why try with a baby? It could die on the journey."

"If they catch us he'll die anyway. Oh, save us."

The boy paused, troubled, then he looked at the baby again.

"I had a baby brother once. He and mother were ..." His voice failed him.

Nooryouz touched his arm carefully. "You will help us? I heard you say you leave at moonrise. I can follow?"

He looked doubtful. "Kadir is very sharp, not much gets by him. If you follow too close he'll see you. They'll be convinced that

292

we are smuggling slaves. I'll have to walk behind and bend a branch or line up two or three stones on the trail. You can't be closer than an hour behind us. He'd see any light for sure. So would the soldiers." He handed her the shepherd coat and took off his gloves for her. She impulsively kissed his hand.

He whirled around and set off up the trail. She followed. At last he spoke, his voice unsteady, "There's a cave up here where you can see the trail and leave after we've passed tonight. I can't help if they catch you. If you get to the village, stop at the crest where you can first see lights or village huts below. There's a small, roofed, rock shelter there. Go in there, sleep and wait till I bring food.

> - - - - - - - > THE AMU VALLEY CARAVANSARY > - - - - - - - >

"You have had a long wait Atilla bey. We have been very busy with the pursuit of the fugitives. But thank you for the information you gave us earlier. We have identified your friend, Kerim of the East Bulgars, as the escaped war prisoner, Kynan of the Chipchaks. He's left a trail of blood. We feel sure we will have him in a few days." Tewfik bey did not add 'dead or alive' to the statement.

Atilla's surly gaze did not change. "You have kept me detained in my room, deprived of the thrill of the chase to say that? Isn't there yet something more to add to it all? A fine? A charge?"

"God forbid that we should do you an injustice, but we did not realise how much you might know about the true identity of the escaped prisoner. You have been long gone to the Tang's empire and we did not know where your loyalties lay. We couldn't let you join our hunt, for those and other reasons". Tewfik smiled slyly. "You must admit we let you finish your drinking party."

Atilla grimaced. The headache had lingered and was still with him. Waking up to detention in the inn added insult to injury. Therefore, he responded sullenly. "You woke me with questions during the night. You accuse me of helping an enemy of the Caliph. I told you all I know. You keep me from the chase or travel today, yet think me ungrateful that you do not detain me longer. You do recognise the great deception I have suffered. Will you then, give me permission to continue my journey?"

Tewfik frowned and delayed, then smiled indulgently. "Normally we hold people for other inquiries, but since we were boys together, I'll let you go."

Atilla stood. "I'm leaving now! I won't stay here any longer! I can make a fair journey before sunset. I have supplies to carry me farther -- faster."

"Go with God, my friend." Tewfik's smile mocked him.

>------- > KOKAND POLICE STATION >-------->

Ali bey looked grimly at his sleeping charge. Then he shook the boy roughly with his foot. He gradually shifted his weight forward to press on the boy's elbow. He smiled as Tash cried out and moved hastily to relieve the pressure.

The boy moved up on his knees and bowed abjectly. "*Affet beni*, forgive me master, I slept. It was a long trip."

"Your report was unsatisfactory, so don't grow careless with assumed success or lazy with leisure. We have lost a man that could have tied up the north with internal wars and friction. We lost the man and the opportunity. I don't forgive that kind of failure."

"What could I have done? You said to watch and report. Everyone was watching the chase; no one saw the Khan's brother murdered or the girl escape."

Ali bey turned his back, his face changed to smiles. "Yes, the girl, where will she go? To the tribe? Where else! One is already with the tribe and this one remains to cross the border. Which holds the key?" He turned to push the cringing boy over with his foot, making him sprawl. "Take your rest today. Be ready to travel tomorrow."

> -------> AT THE SMUGGLERS' CAVE >------->

"You're the biggest idiot of them all, Yavuz bey," Aziz shouted. The argument was still heated when Korkmaz came in the main entrance to the cave.

Kadir looked him over carefully. "You said there was a ragged shepherd coat. What did you do with it?" Kadir stood across, blocking the path inside.

"I tossed the dirty old thing. You wouldn't have worn it." Korkmaz lifted his face to Kadir. They looked intently into each others eyes.

Kadir cocked his head quizzically and smirked as he replied. "Pfu, I could have told you who had, and where they had been. You know that, so why toss it?" The boy shrugged and looked past him.

"Don't they ever stop?" He indicated Aziz bey and his nemesis with a motion of his head.

Kadir grinned, "You know they don't." He returned to his pacing and let Korkmaz walk into the storeroom. He walked over to the silent guide and started helping sort the cargo.

"We shouldn't wait till moonrise, Aziz bey. Too much is visible, the moon's near full." The little man thrust up his face to Aziz, pugnaciously.

The big man sighed, disgusted. "Who are you protecting, Yavuz bey? Not our camels, they can't see in the dark. Not us, we make twice the time when the trail can be seen. Not our fuel supply, it saves oil to use Allah's light. Protecting us from the neighbours? Our money does that."

Yavuz hopped back and forth on tiptoe, nodding and gesturing. "We leave the cave before the light, so no one will see our hiding place."

Aziz, hand to head, shrugged and shouted. "Alright, I give up! We leave before moonrise, but only just before to be away from the cave. Fools I suffer!"

There was a chuckle of glee from Yavuz and a brief moment of silence.

GIVING COAT & GLOVES

295

PEOPLE, PLOTS & PLACES IN CHAPTER 24

Bolben: needs friends to find comfort over the tragedy.
Chichek: accompanies Peri hanum for an acquisition.
Dahkool: dooms the village that receives her.
Derk: ignores anything but his mission for the Caliph.
Erly: a Chipchak guard with the returning Toozlu clan.
Jon: must resort to violence to protect a friend.
Kaplan: continues his heedless pursuit of power.
Karga: has devious ways of dealing with every new need.
Manish: works a way toward freedom for his refugees.
Maril: cries for a dead friend.
Peri hanum: the old nurse knows her girl's weakness.
Sanjak: meditates on his mistakes after a quarrel.
Seerden: envisions new gains from two masters.
Seslee: is frantic to leave the dangerous mountains.
Setchkin: under duress and pain makes a romantic trip.
Twozan: a surprise visit brings an unforeseen departure.

GLOSSARY:
 Afet beni: Forgive me.
Arkadash: friend; one who guards your back.
Babam: my father; daddy.
dekot: be careful; attention.
hanum: lady; a title of respect.
hiyer : no; negative.
hanja: traitor.
janum benim: beloved; my life.
Kim gecher: Who's passing? Who's coming?
oloom: my son; my boy.
yoke: not so; negative.

LOVE SCORNED

The bag of gold reassured him. Seerden counted it again. The Gray Wolf always paid; bountifully and immediately for difficult tasks well done. Some hand unseen had laid it in his room at the caravansary; therefore, some news of the event had travelled to the local head of the society with power and riches to act. He wondered briefly if ever dishonesty tempted the messenger. Seerden thought the penalty would guarantee short enjoyment of any gain. Honesty thus backed by fear made for efficiency. But again and again came the question: where did the head lie? Was it within the empire or outside it? The culture source was obviously Turkish, but the local scene had always been filled with Persian tribes suffering invasions of Arabs from the west and Turks from the north. Both were powerful in local happenings and now especially in the empire. There had been time for the news to go and orders return. He had stayed to commiserate with Atilla bey; who was a valuable source of information on the situation in distant lands. Now Atilla had left. Several options were open: go to Perikanda or even the north frontier. In another day they would catch or lose the fugitives. Perhaps that was the best way to chose. Let the fugitives lead him?

There might be additional, local rewards or even more vital clues to find the Wolf's head.

> - - - - - - - > A VILLAGE BETWEEN THE RIVERS > - - - - - - - >

"How much for your cage of pigeons?" The tribal nomad wore no veil and spoke the local language poorly. The village seller looked carefully at the jeweled hand that gestured toward the cage. He shrugged disdainfully.

"They're sold. I'm waiting for a friend." He looked around the market as if hunting someone.

Old Peri insisted. "My mistress wishes a cage of pigeons to use as meat for her child. He is delicate." She made a gesture with her hand: two fingers pressed against the thumb with the outer fingers cocked-up forming ears.

Surprised he replied. "A thousand pardons, Bayan, they're yours." He quickly passed over the cage crowded with live birds. "Does the lady know that mules loaded with food are awaiting some government agent? They are ready to travel."

"You will have orders about what to do. Thank your master." The lady left with her cage to join her waiting companion, Chichek. She mounted her horse at the edge of the village market and left for their tribe. The Wolf would hear of the contact and know his plan's success.

> - - - - - - - > THE WILD LANDS BETWEEN RIVERS > - - - - - - - >

"Our orders are to hold intruders where we meet them and Twozan bey will come. Outsiders are not to enter our camp." Erly was emphatic.

"But I'm known to you," Sanjak retorted. "I'm of the tribe and nation and I've brought an emissary from the Caliph."

Erly nodded his agreement and continued to inspect the cargo of each mule. He memorized the number, size and content of each load.

"If we were home it would be different. Security is now the first consideration. No offence intended, Sir." The guard's glance included Derk in his response.

"How far to the camp?" Derk asked curiously.

"Only a short distance, very close." Erly made a vague sweeping motion behind him.

Derk refused the evasion. "You camp by the well then?"

The guard paused. "Water is necessary to every camp."

Derk looked away to hide his annoyance. There was a spring in the area also, but he knew now that he would not get the location easily. However, the older men were doing duty usually reserved for the younger. That would indicate the shortage of young warriors. They must be on the way to serve in the Caliph's forces. Mercenaries were always welcomed by the ruler of divided Arabs.

"Twozan bey has come." Erly announced and at that moment they saw horses coming on at a run. Then just out of earshot they came to an abrupt halt. Two older men sat calming their horses. Heads nodded silently. Time passed; then they slowly came ahead.

"*Babam*, my father, I've come." The cool tone matched the welcome.

"*Oloom*, my son, do you now return to the tribe and family?" The dust of the arriving party billowed in the evening air. Twozan Bey ignored the emissary and spoke only to his son. Sanjak looked away from his father to answer.

"My wife has escaped the Uigur Royal Harem, so I must wait until I have her with me to travel home."

"Who is this woman from a royal harem that you claim as wife?" His tone was sceptical, even caustic.

"She's the granddaughter of the former Umayyad ambassador and business man in Changan. I met her there," Sanjak replied stiffly.

"You marry outside the tribe, without our approval, to an enemy unbeliever whose troops try to conquer us. You refuse to fight free back to our nation with us? Is this your choice: betrayal?"

Derk intervened at this point. He held one hand up to quiet the rising anger. "The Caliph wishes peace with the northern nations. We offer trade and opportunity to your people." His words were ignored.

"I'm no traitor and the choice of wife is mine," Sanjak stated slowly. "She will be whatever I am. You need no extra warriors. Derk bey offers the Caliph's peace for your return home."

Twozan answered them both. "Free warriors need no guarantees."

CONFRUNTATION

299

Twozan sneered, "The Caliph has passed through two civil wars and cannot trust his troops. They are using peace to ready new conquests using the Turkish troopers whom they entice with wages and women. You, my son, show the same rebellious spirit of your youth. You broke your mother's heart and you resist the obedience due to me."

"Let us stay and talk at the camp," Derk pleaded.

"We need neither emissary nor deserter in the camp."

"You're the same stubborn old grouch I remember. I knew that you wouldn't agree with me or the Caliph. Go home then! Your attempt to make Erben khan has failed. Wherever he is, he's not here with you. Go home and face all the enemies you have made with your ambition. I'll not go with you." Sanjak reared his stallion and turned to gallop away.

Twozan watched his progress with anger. Derk however remained calm and resumed talking when the rider was out of sight.

"The Caliph has other offers to make concerning a common foe: the Gray Wolf. If you're interested let's go to camp."

Twozan sat silent for a time; then motioned with his hand and set out. Derk drew up to ride beside him.

> - - - - - - - > THE TOOZLU CAMP IN THE WILD LANDS > - - - - - - - >

"He's not coming to camp? You know it is Sanjak, but he went away? How could you let that happen?" Setchkin's voice was high, thin and hysterical. She glared angrily at Erly who gestured pleadingly.

"He would not come because they quarrelled. He had married an Umayyad lady and is seeking her in Abbassid lands. Twozan bey accused him of joining the enemy. He brought an emissary of the Sultan who has important news. The prince left in anger, but the emissary comes to our camp. I came to you first, but we must prepare now."

"Go then, prepare all. I'll not meet this foreigner. Tell Twozan bey his people can entertain him." She turned angrily to enter her yurt. Inside she caught her listening companion, Peri Hanum by the arms and whispered desperately. "You must cover for me while I ride after him. Prepare something for the road. I must be off while they are distracted with the guest. They must not see me go. You can show off the baby if they ask."

"Yes, my lady. The horse and provisions will be ready, go change." As Setchkin prepared, the old servant stepped out of the entrance to give orders for horse and food, she whispered to herself. 'Pigeons will carry the news and I might be rewarded. Poor mistress, she still believes in the love of a fool.'

"Damn them all. I'll make them pay. That smart bastard! Bragging about loving a harem girl."

Jon woke with a start. Below him he heard the sound of rock smashing rock. Cautiously he peered through the brush that grew about him. A man was sitting near the mountain stream throwing rocks across a small pool and fragments flew as each skipped and smashed into the rocky bank. He threw with all his strength and anger.

"What's that?" It was Seslee's complaining voice. She was lying half asleep in the warm morning sun, her shepherd's coat spread under her. Her bundle rested under her head, she basked in the scanty remains of her Uigur harem clothes. Jon turned cautiously and hissed. "*Soos*, hush!"

Manish was awake and moved silently beside him. Peering down they saw the youth had turned and was moving toward a place where he could climb the bank.

"*Dekot*, take care; hide!" Manish's shrill treble carried the warning to all, but Seslee was just sitting up when the intruder appeared and stared avidly down at her.

"Well look here. I got something better, and they won't know or share." She squealed and flipped over to run. He dived on her and flattened her to the ground. His right arm circled her neck to choke her. His hand tore at her clothes. Too late he felt the presence of Jon and Manish above him. Their knives plunged into his neck and back before he could scream.

Sanjak rode slowly as the night passed. His life had come before him and he was sad. He had made so many mistakes and foolish choices. Only two things stood out in his mind. He loved and needed Nooryouz and he would not be an easy convert to Islam. Yesu had warned his disciples of false prophets that would come after him. This religious system enslaves everyone, and especially those who did not conform. He had a year of grace, but neither promotion nor freedom would come meanwhile. He would be watched, and kept useful for the year. He sighed with vexation. His childhood playmate, Setchkin, was at least free and would return to the tribe and the freedom of the Tiger's daughter. Her position was assured; her future secure and positive. Continuing, he prayed for her happiness and his finding Nooryouz. Her discovery and capture was his chief worry as he rode north to the proffered post. He rode the trail alone, careless of consequences. He watched the last light of the sun fade. Solitude and sorrow filled his heart. His anger was forgotten. He recalled the young, happy days with nostalgia; and stopping to admire the last fading clouds, he sang.

#1   Days gone by, but dear to my heart,
                      With my friends I played long and hard.
                      We dreamed greatness: sang love songs;
                      Stayed up late; ate too much;
                      Thought we understood it all.
                      I remember our joy and pride,
                      Longed to glorify our names,
                      Little knowing the tears we'd cry.
                      Old, true friends from days gone by.

DAYS GONE BY

302

#2   Days gone by, but dear to my heart,
                     When we vied with words mean and sharp,
                     We wanted last hit: top wrestler;
                     First rider; best archer;
                     Last beer drinker on his feet.
                     I remember our grit and pride,
                     Sought to make it all our own,
                     Leaving ruin and wreck for some to cry.
                     Long gone friends from days gone by.

#3   Days gone by, but dear to my heart,
                     When we fought and thought we were smart.
                     We killed rivals; fought warriors;
                     Wooed girl friends; stole men's herds;
                     Hated all the other tribes.
                     I remember contempt and pride.
                     Sought to put all others down,
                     Leaving death and angry kin to thrive.
                     Long lost friends, from days gone by.

He remained thoughtful and prayed to the Tanra of his youth. A God who, he thought then, approved of adventure and brave deeds. He knew now the methods had not gained approval. With regret he turned again to the road. He had far to go. He coaxed his horse into a trot and then a run. A smile had returned to his face. There must be news from the East in the town where he had his appointment.

Sanjak slacked his speed and listened carefully. Night was coming and he had not taken care, someone was following him. He looked back, but saw nothing, yet in the distance where he had descended the hill at a run, there were now two tracks. Like thin lines on paper the one paralleled the other. He left the trail and circled behind a hill, gradually he came back to view his own trace. He dismounted and waited.

A rider came into view. Bundled against the night chill he rode a tough little mare with tribal harness and saddle. His eyes were fixed on the tracks and he did not see the observer. He knew or cared little for sound or protection, but rode boldly and hastily on. Sanjak rose and put his bow away. He had little to fear from such a rider. Perhaps he was a messenger sent from the camp. Sanjak walked to the trail.

"*Do'er*, stop friend. Why are you following me?"

The rider uttered a cry of surprise and turned toward him eagerly. Her voice carried tears. "*Janum benim*, beloved, I have found you at last." He stared: the one trailing him was Setchkin, his old flame. He had resolved never to see her again. Yet here she was! His proud, haughty, passionate, forbidden fruit, she was the source of his wanderings and pains. He was speechless.

She dismounted hastily. "Dearest, I have sought you so long. How could you leave me? I thought I would die. It has been three long, miserable years." She embraced him passionately and buried her head in his chest. Then raising her face, she stood on top of his foot, wrapped one leg behind his knee, an arm under his and behind his shoulder, she held his head with one hand and kissed him long and hard. Astonished, he tried to pull away. He stuttered as he struggled to push her away.

"S-sech-k-kin, Wh-what-er you d-doing?"

"I heard that they turned you away from the camp. I know how your father has always been jealous of you. He drove you out of the tribe. He envies my love for you. Your whole family was against us. They told lies around the camp. But now I've found you, we can leave here together. He will never separate us again." He held up his hands to protest against this torrent of accusations against his family, but was forced to fend her off.

"Hi-yer, no, n-not t-true. Your father and the Crow t-tried to kill me. They were bound to marry you to the old khan. They wanted power and they used you to get it. They t-tried to scare me away. I wanted to go. I needed time to think." He continued to keep her at a distance.

She cried, "We've won against all opposition in my family and yours. Tanra has brought us together again. We'll not be parted by any of them. We can go away, leave them all." She again tried to embrace him, but he was ready and held her off by her shoulders, shaking her a bit.

"I've never blamed you." he explained. "You were always treated harshly and wanted affection. You needed love and appreciation, especially when your brother was sent off to the Bulgars. You thought you had found it in me. We went riding together and I taught you what I knew of the steppes. I felt you were a kid still and I was just playing around. You had a crush on me and I took advantage of you. I got expelled from the seminary and caused a lot of talk. When I saw what the Tiger was up to, I cleared out."

She looked up at him indignantly, shook her head vigorously, and angrily stamped her foot.

"But he's your baby! I have your child. They thought he was early and was the Khan's, but he was yours. I know. It was always you I wanted. I love you!"

He continued to hold her off, shaking his head. "*Yoke*, never! You were thrilled when they offered you the chance to marry the Khan. You put your little nose in the air and let everyone know how important you were and how low they were. You were terrified lest I tell. Have you forgotten that you asked me to leave? You weren't pregnant when I left. Your father would have killed you if there had been any doubt on the legal succession. He's not my baby. My wife has my baby."

She twisted out of his grasp and stood sidewise to him crying. "You married a foreign girl? You expect her to be accepted by the tribe? Think she'll like our hard, simple life? I can accept it, she won't. You used to love me. Search your heart."

He sighed in despair. "My father's family has always been against Kaplan's search for power. It was like tweaking his whiskers to play with his daughter. It added zest to the fun of having you idolize me. It was a conquest to brag about to my friends. I know you'll never forgive me. It was a sin that I now regret. It has cost me dearly, but love was not a part of it"

She stood silent for a moment breathing hard, fumbling in her girdle. Then she whirled with a drawn knife and threw herself at him. "*Hinja*, deceiver! Devil's spawn, die," she screamed. He jumped to the right, pivoted on his right heel and swung his right hand to grab her wrist and carry it forward to his left. She tripped and screamed again as her momentum carried her to the ground and the dagger dropped from her pain-filled hand.

He released her wrist, left her sobbing in the dirt and walked to his horse. He mounted and leaned in her direction. He spoke softly, but with the voice of finality. "The past lives no more. I've confessed my sin and left it. Go home! Find happiness in God and forgiveness. It would mean death to follow me further." He rode away.

> - - - - - - - > IN THE TANRA DAH MOUNTAINS > - - - - - - - >

Under Jon's directions they had dragged the dead body higher into the mountains, staying beside the stream with its small waterfalls which sang merrily and covered their noise. They watched from the distance as a party of men descended from a gorge in the slope and carried their burden, a body on a contrived stretcher, in the direction of the village.

They sat in stunned silence. Then Maril started to cry and Jon spoke for them. "I'm sure it was only one body. It had to be Dakool." All nodded.

"At least she won't have to face the wrath of the Emperor," Seslee added.

"How did she die?" Maril crossed herself tearfully.

Manish spoke. "She would be worth more alive, surely they wouldn't kill her"

"Maybe they raped her like that man tried to do to me." Seslee's voice was high and hysterical. She continued to stand away from the man's dead body and would not look at it; as if not acknowledging its existence.

"We can go up that way and perhaps find out." Jon suggested.

"Never! I'm going up this one before it. I don't want to know how or where she died." Seslee walked off leaving the group as she had done earlier. The rest exchanged glances and took up the body, dragging him by his clothes into the shadow of the mountain valley where the stream issued. There, where the boulders piled one on another, they hid the body deep in a hole between the rocks. They kept only his coat and knife. Without a word they continued their climb into the heights. They looked for a grove to rest.

"It's still light we shouldn't be moving around much yet. There will be herders and travellers on the mountains." Jon was apprehensive.

"I want to get away from that body we dumped, I'm tired of hiding. Let's just get out of here." Seslee's voice reflected tension.

"Surely there would be no one up this steep wadi. There's brush and wilderness everywhere." Maril pushed through some thick foliage.

"The villagers are sharp-eyed and they know where people are supposed to be and where they shouldn't be. They're also curious and will investigate when things don't seem right. Let's stop at the source of the Wadi and wait for night." Manish, in the lead, underlined his advice by pointing above to the clearing just coming into sight a few hundred yards ahead. The steeper part of the climb was now behind them. The alpine grass covered shoulders of the mountains that stretched ahead.

"*Kim gecher*? Who goes there?" The challenging voice froze them into silence. Above them, on the edge of the meadow, someone was sitting, peering down into the brush that lined the watercourse. When no answer came, the figure of a man arose from the rocks and moved toward the brushy banks. He stretched his neck and peered over the scrub.

"Why Manish, is that you? Why do you come here?" His voice became angry and resentful. "It wasn't my fault. I didn't do anything to her. She killed herself when she broke her leg. If she had surrendered she would have been safe. I would have fought to keep them off her." Bolben's voice became choked and tearful. "I did fight one of them, the dirty bastard. Wish I'd killed him." He couldn't go on.

"*Arkadash*, Friend, we blame no one. We came seeking her. Tell us how it occurred and we will mourn together. What happened?"

They sat, forming a circle around him and Bolben told the story in broken bits and pieces, while the girls joined him with their tears.

> - - - - - - - > IN THE CHIPCHAK HOMELAND > - - - - - - - >

"So, now my precious little brood mare returns to the north with the rebel Toozlu. What shall I do with her?" Kaplan, the tiger, growled to Karga, but the 'crow' did not venture a reply. Kaplan sighed. "I had hoped that the Arabs would take her when they split the clan. Surely they would have taken some women. We must get more details of the battle. The baby makes a problem as the other is now accepted as the heir. The mother was always a problem. She will not play the part of the serene widow for long."

The Crow nodded vigorously and spoke. "If both were lost it would seem a judgement from Tanra."

Kaplan laughed and sat staring for a long minute. He nodded, agreeing. "The spirits bring both grief and healing of heart. You have promised to take action on this question Karga bey. I await your report. It must seem natural, an accident or sickness. Don't wait for her to waver or disobey me."

Karga nodded, "We got some pigeons into the Toozlu camp. We should be up on their news soon. We can time things more precisely now."

Kaplan stared, "It's about time, too. You are too cautious. And speaking of time, what ever has happened to our agent Seerden? He found Erben's hiding place, but there is no news about his visit to the quarry. What is our grey puppy doing now?"

"I expect news soon now. The man shows great promise."

"You are too easily impressed. I'll take his next pay out of your income." Kaplan smiled nastily and settled back.

Karga nodded dully. Then, after a pause, he spoke cautiously watching his master's face. "There is a rumor among the women. Some whisper that the Khan Erden's wife has at last conceived and is hiding the event."

Kaplan stared. "To make sure? Then they will make the stunning announcement? When might the birthing be?"

Karga nodded agreeably, relishing the moment. "They say early spring."

The Tiger's face was set and hard. "This must not be! It won't matter about the child or the widow of the old Khan Erdash. It annuls all we accomplished before to set the inheritance of power and position in my family. We got rid of Sevim in the racing accident. How can we stop this?"

"I have a friend among the queen's companions. She will think of a way to prevent her lady's fulfilling her term."

PEOPLE, PLOTS & PLACES IN CHAPTER 25

Chavush: the inquisitive sergeant is warned by his *Pasha*.
Cheechek: dances for a guest's pleasant diversion.
Derk bey: the Caliph's agent makes an agreement.
Kadir: the young partner of smugglers suspects a trick.
Kardesh: sure of his father's success sees conquest.
Korkmaz: slows things on purpose; to save a baby's life.
Onat bey: arrives from Kokand to his new assignment.
Seerden: makes a sudden decision to go north.
Tayze: fears for her brother-in-law and Leyla.
Tewfik bey: sends out scouts to scour for fugitives.
Twozan: goes to find the mother of the 'child of promise'.
Uigur Official: finds only one dead girl instead of four.
Uigur Yuzbasha: knows the border is cleared of guards.

GLOSSARY:
Bosh ooze too nay: As you ordered Sir; Immediately Sir.
dekot: attention; careful; caution.
Goo-lay, goo-lay, koo-la'nan: enjoy: when praising gifts.
hiyer: no; not at all.
keman: a small cello-like instrument with a high range.
Kurban bayram: a feast with an animal sacrifice.
Muktar: a district or town official in Islamic government.
ona bock: look at her.
Pasha: a commander in charge or military leader of rank.
tamom: alright; agreed; okay.
Yuzbasha: lieutenant; leader of a hundred men.

MOONLIT CLIMBERS

The smugglers' caravan was formed up and ready before moon rise. Kadir took the lead as guard, the guide held the bridle to the first animal, the leader of the string of beasts. Yavuz and Aziz circulated, leading and checking cargo fittings, while Korkmaz came at the rear. As they cleared the canyon that led to the cave the boy stopped and placed three large stones in the center of the trail. At every turn or wide spot the three stones were lined up to point the correct trail. He lingered to be able to do this when Kadir was out of sight. It was dangerous to lag because of the competition or bandits. Either could take the laggard. The mother would run the same danger. He couldn't abide the thought of her running the danger alone. But with the shepherds coat she might be taken for a mere wanderer. He prayed Allah that it would be so.

Higher and higher the trail wound out of the dark valleys and into the steep slopes. Each slope led to yet higher steeper slopes. Gradually the light intensified as a moon of blood rose behind them bringing a ghostly semblance to the landscape. No longer could Korkmaz seek out the larger stones and place them by hand. He resorted to small stones, fist size, that he could kick into the road and line up without stopping. Once he thought he saw someone behind them. He stopped to look, but saw nothing. He started again and saw Kadir riding back to him. He hurried to catch up to the last animal, a yak.

"Something worries you? Did you see anything? I notice you stop. What is it?" The boy was checking the bindings and the load on the Yak and did not look up at Kadir. He shrugged, kicked up a foot and the sandal flipped off. He caught it out of the air.

"Loose strap," he indicated. Kadir clicked his tongue, looked at him closely, then turned his horse and rode back to the lead. He passed Yavuz and Aziz, who were too busy arguing to notice. At the next sharp parting of the way, he took the steep, little travelled, short cut up a narrow track. The boy ran up the slope beside the yak and knocked a stone or two down so they rolled into the main trail; while both the warring owners complained of the change of route, berating their beasts and each other. Korkmaz knew that Kadir was suspicious and would hurry.

> - - - - - - - >IN THE AMU VALLEY CARAVANSARY > - - - - - - - >

"Tewfik bey, I have received an invitation from Onat bey to join him in their march up to the northern border. It seems that the supply agent needs the aid of one who knows the producers and handlers of provisions. I feel that I have done all I can at this point." Seerden bey's voice was suave and polite as he spoke to the harried Muktar.

"It's unlike you, bey, to desert an effort before it has come to its successful end; but since you have special status, you'll please yourself." The man's tone was cold and disapproving.

"No, I please the one who pays and protects me. I think this will be a government matter. They will give direct orders soon. Two murderers are brought to justice and the last will soon be caught. The Bulgar and the royal girl are running north to the tribe. He hopes for a reward no doubt, but the tribe is no danger. They have lost their Khan and have no further ambitions in the south."

Tewfik looked the speaker over carefully before answering, still cold and frowning. "This is an over-simplification of the matter and does not do you credit to say such a thing. We have heard of a possible expedition from the oasis city of Merv. It is common talk. We know how thick the blood is between those departed and those who move north. What happens when they

310

hear it? There are enemy spies among us who work for other interests. The Chipchak are the power of the north, only the Bulgars hold them in check. The eastern tribes attack the restored Tang to loot them. We are the natural prey of the northern tribes. This is why we must divide to conquer. If they ever combine we could be lost."

Seerden bowed humbly. "It is our purpose to see that it never happens. That is why I must travel north to the commander in the morning. I beg your pardon and permission."

A reluctant grunt was all he received.

> - - - - - - - > TOOZIU CAMP IN THE WILD LANDS > - - - - - - - >

"According to your desires you will leave our borders and return to your land this winter. I for my part will see that you are not molested nor interfered with on your journey. However, you must not raid the villages. The Caliph authorizes your passage with food provided by agents of the government. We consider you an ally now. We need your help with the common enemy." Derk sat before the fire with the older men of the tribe inside the yurt. The fire reflected from their stern faces. A murmur of approval arose round the circle of seated men.

Twozan spoke for them all in his reply. "We accept your Caliph's generosity and agree to watch for the agents of the hidden enemy, the Gray Wolf. We know there are men in our land and even among the Caliph's bodyguard that harbour connections with this enemy; but we will sniff them out." Bowls of kumiss were passed out to the men.

"Has the Princess Setchkin arranged for our entertainment?" asked Twozan of the boys who served.

After a moment of confusion one of the boys answered with downcast eyes. "Cheecek, has everything ready, she will come now." A boy with a lute entered as well as a drummer. Another set up a *keman* before him with the bow. The audience smiled in anticipation.

Twozan requested. "Have the princess come to accompany us as we listen."

The boy stuttered and seemed reluctant to reply. "Sh - she requests your p-pardon, she won't sit with you." He rushed on. "She'll remain in her yurt. The baby has a fever."

"Let Cheechek proceed." Twozan suggested frowning.

"Nothing seriously wrong, I hope," stated a smiling Derk.

311

"Just a sick child, the mother will care for him," he replied.

With the soft drum beat and whine of the *keman*, Cheechek entered dressed in her best silk shalvar, loose trousers, gathered at waist and ankles, under an open caftan. Her dance would be from the south lands, slow and flowing, but the lyrics were of the north lands of cold and long absences. She poised her right arm in the 'S' position of the snake. The other hand, with henna-stained palm, fluttered above her head. Her manicured nails were long, curved and a brilliant red. Moving in Hindu sign language she conveyed the idea of solitude, quiet devotion and humble waiting. Her head moved from side to side on her slender neck. Her hands and fingers floated slowly. The head of the snake, formed by the three top fingers opening and closing over the touching thumb and little finger, rotated. The head moved left and right, toward and away from her at eye level. The left hand above gyrated in slow circles, the fingers making signs borrowed, like the dance, from India. She moved her legs slowly in high prancing liquid motions that moved her only a pace or two from her starting position. Her feet too, bore henna stains. Sensuously, Cheechek swayed as grass in the wind, stretching and bending low. Her dance slowed and her song began. Now, her gestures matched the theme. Her fingers beckoned and soothed.

She began to sing in a slow hypnotic way. The words were precise and crisp, whispered and blown, cool yet passionate. She alone moved in the room full of fascinated men.

#1	Cold winter winds blow round my yurt; My heart grows colder too. I count the days since you depart; My tears flow just for you.
Chorus:	Summer's madness, summer's love. Warm sun shining from above; They warn us not of winter love.
#2	Cool wind sweeps o'er the grassy plains; I dream and count the hours. My eyes grow dim, the days grow long. Wake me with all your powers!
Chorus:	

#3   My wounded heart waits your return;
                    Like spring that's coming soon.
                    Come warm my lips, my heart, my all;
                    And take away my gloom.

Chorus:

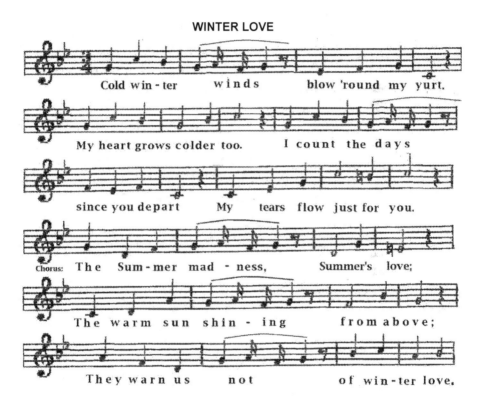

WINTER LOVE

Cold win-ter winds blow 'round my yurt. My heart grows colder too. I count the days since you depart My tears flow just for you.

Chorus: The Sum-mer mad - ness, Summer's love; The warm sun shin - ing from above; They warn us not of win-ter love.

    The yurt was silent except for a sigh of approval that followed the girl as she bowed, hands together under her chin, and slipped out of the assembly. Derk sat silent. He had touched his childhood roots and was moved. The men nodded to each other in approval. That was the life of the nomad. As the drinking started again, Derk, lost in thought, did not notice the departure of Twozan. The sound of a horse leaving at a gallop did not disturb them.

> - - - - - - - >KARDESH ON THE ROAD WEST OF KOKAND > - - - - - - - >

"My father should be joining the tribe now," Kardesh said as they bumped over the road to the west. "I can imagine him riding up to Twozan bey and embracing him. The men will all wish to kiss his hand and to pledge their lives to his cause."

Tayze looked worried. "I hope they have arrived on time to meet him. We could not get news from them once the plan was launched and the news here was scarce, especially after leaving Kokand."

Kardesh laughed spontaneously, "We heard enough to know everyone was talking and that the presence of an army of Turks fills everyone with fear. It will be easy to rule these sheep. I only wish we had not been held up by these bruises."

"When ambitious young men plan, they rarely admit there will be casualties."

"What could go wrong when it concerns loyal men like Twozan and his warriors. I only hope Sanjak was back from the East to get in on the action. Tanra, how I've missed them!"

She shook her head sagely. "Timing is more important than strength. Much can happen. Especially if an action divides rather than unites the tribe."

"My uncle, the Khan can break free of the Kaplan's bonds with the addition of larger lands to the south. We will cage the tiger and pick the crow's bones for all the misery they have caused."

Tayze shivered. "Don't mention Karga, its bad luck, even that way. I just wish we could know how it goes." They spoke no more as the cart bumped on westward.

> - - - - - - - >BORDER VILLAGE IN THE TANRA DAH > - - - - - - - >

The oldest of the search party, a married man led the way. The other four followed with the dead maid between them on the make-shift pallet they carried. The village awaited them in the afternoon light. A weary relative of the local governor had ridden in great haste to be present. The reported sighting and expected capture of the escapees excited everyone.

It was obvious even from a distance that they returned like a funeral procession; there was no joy in them. The children, boys and girls, ran to meet them and examine the cargo, which they solemnly conducted to the village, while the girls cried.

The authority waited, seated and drinking a refreshing beverage of wine from the irrigated valleys. The village had given its best acquisitions, expecting recompense. Gossip had raised the reward offered to a fantastic sum.

"She fell from the cliff above. Her leg was broken when we found her and she used her knife rather than be captured," the leader said to all the assembled villagers.

The authority rose from his seat to see. "Only one? There were four women and accomplices and you bring one dead? Where is the man that reported seeing all of them?"

The head man hastened to report the facts as the party drew near. "We sent two parties; Bolben was in the group that found this girl."

"Why is the man not here with you?"

The group leader spoke up now and the men lowered their burden. "He was sad and angry so he left. None of the others saw more than this one."

The shocked official spoke indignantly. "We understood you had them all under observation!" He turned to his lieutenant.

"Yuzbasha, did we call off the watch on the passes? Remember? When we heard that they were being captured here."

The military man spoke with reluctant care. "Yes my Lord, I saw to your command myself yesterday. Extra troops for the watches are cancelled. They will all have the notice by now. Some will return to barracks tomorrow."

The courtier's anger flared. He indignantly pointed at the dead girl placed just before him. "*Ona bock*, look at her! What have you done to her? She is all blood below! How can I report this to the Emperor? What will they say? How awful! I'll lose face as the bearer of evil tidings."

"So we found her, my lord. Just this way! See her hands. We did not do this." All the men affirmed their leader's statements.

DAHKOOL ARRIVES

315

The crowd murmured and looked indignant. Several of the younger women moved in to take the poles of the stretcher. They moved the body toward one of the houses. One of the mid-wives directed their activities as she raised her voice. "We will soon know the truth of all this. Go eat and rest till we return."

The official raised his voice to a shout. "See to it. I'll have to take a full report for the court. Send someone to bring in the missing man." He returned to his drink while the villagers whispered among themselves. A youth was dispatched to summon the missing villagers.

After nearly an hour the older woman returned to the village headman. She bowed and addressed them both. "We have the child ready for burial."

The official objected. "*Hiyer*, no, we take her with us. We'll not leave her here. Tell me what you found."

The woman blanched and kneeling, bowed at his feet. "The woman has a lover. Yesterday - recently they - only one, but not more."

The official glared at her and asked angrily. "How do you prove that? You lie for your village men."

She looked up with the experience of age and many births, shaking her head sagely, she explained. "The amount is consistent with one, not with many. Her body shows no sign of abuse, only the exertion of flight. The act of love came before the broken leg and suicide. Any trained woman can tell you."

"Yes, we will have to have another examiner. But you will come to town with us as a witness. If you have changed the evidence it will go hard with you. You, the group leader, you go too. Pick one other man. We will want the details of everything. The others are detained here, they must not escape. We go now; I'll not stay in a village such as this. Believe me: the Khan will repay all failure and lustfulness with the fire of his indignation." The stunned villagers gave no reply.

> - - - - - - - >THE VILLAGE AT THE WHITE MARBLE QUARRY > - - - - - - - >

The quarry was in mourning, two of their youth had been reported to them as killed. The details were uncertain and muddled. A horse fell on one and a dog attacked another. Their bodies were buried at the scene within twenty-four hours, as determined by Islam, so there were no bodies to bury in the worker's village.

Umer was reported to be working at a distant quarry and was in the process of acquiring a wife. It might take several years to work off the bride price, but if the girl was young it

316

wouldn't affect things much. Otherwise, they could go ahead and consummate the marriage by legal arrangement and the girl's parents live with the couple at his expense. A previous parentally arranged agreement had been by-passed, to the scandal of the local village. Another friend and companion of Umer had stepped in to take the rejected girl. Relatives decided to send gifts rather than make the arduous trip over for the celebrations.

There were reported raids and occupation of mountain valleys by restless tribal groups expanding their grazing rights. Some of the village youth had gone to join the army, for the excitement and booty promised. Therefore, work was abundant and workers fewer at the quarry, so openings were up. New families had come to take advantage of the opportunities offered. The houses were full. The Jewish doctor was kept busy with the normal problems of communal health, infections and diseases. The plaza and tea houses were filled by day with the idle, watching the girls come to carry water. By night the workers discussed prices and work in the same tea houses. There were new bully boys to take Umer's place. The mosque announced the five calls to prayer with resounding voice, reminding men of the demands of Allah for faith, prayer and right living. Little boys went to Koranic school to memorize the Koran in ancient Arabic and some learned to write in that language. The best would become scribes or Imams. Several little girls of poorer families were sent to be apprenticed to the rug factory in the Fergana valley at Kokand. They would have a skill to help earn their living with their husbands, when they were married off. Life in the village had returned to normal.

> - - - - - - - >FRONTIER ARMY BASE IN THE TANRA DAH > - - - - - - - >
"Binbasham, I put your goods in your quarters," reported the sergeant in the *Ordu-evee*. "I perched your eagle at the west window, I spread your prayer rug facing south-west toward Mecca."

"Sah ol, thanks, *Chavush*, you may resume your usual duties."

317

"Begging your pardon, *Pasha*, I noticed that the rug is new and has not been finished on the bottom edge. It needs a sewn edge. I can do that kind of work, Sir. It would be a pity to let it ravel away."

General Onat looked at him closely, then, signified his approval.

"I can clean it for you too. The bottom corner is stained, the dog is dyed darkish." He smiled anticipating his commander's approval.

"Yes, it got blood on it during the *Kurban Byram*, a lamb was sacrificed."

"The silk will clean quickly enough, but the wool will be harder, Sir. It's beautiful work I've never seen anything like it."

"A blind lady did it for me. Her husband was a soldier who died under my command. I once visited her to tell her the sad details. I would say she never forgot the visit or my voice. You noted the white turban and the red bar over the crossed Seljuk curved swords? That shows it's mine." The commander had turned friendly, and the sergeant was enjoying this moment of intimacy.

"*Evit, dough rue, Pasha*, the gray dogs face in toward a standing golden bear and rearing stallion, underneath the crossed swords. Why did she put them at the bottom of the rug? It would have made a worthy central medallion." The man had the *Pasha's* total attention now.

"Prayer opens the door to Paradise, so the central theme must be the door showing the garden beyond. You see the fruits and flowers shown in the upper design. She thought it was Yesu's garden. It even has two symbols in the upper corners, the letter called Tau in the Greek alphabet, a sign of peace and salvation." He stopped abruptly and then he continued deliberately. "The kangals guard the golden horse and bear under the control of the Seljuk protection." The *Pasha's* spirit had changed and the man felt a chill of disapproval and perhaps dislike, touch himself.

"*Goolay, goolay, koolanan*, enjoy it, Sir," he quickly finished.

"Do you read and write, Sergeant? *Pasha* queried.

318

"No Sir, I was born on the steppes north of here, my mother knotted rugs. I learned a bit from her. I learn from what I see."

"*Tamom*, our pleasures are for ourselves, and are not to be talked about carelessly. You may stitch up the bottom of my rug, but it is a treasure shared between us only." Both men nodded, agreed.

At that moment the adjutant arrived, "I trust your quarters are satisfactory, *Pasha*? Your troops are now fed and settled down."

"I'll inspect them shortly, Captain. We are on a frontier and good care of troops is essential to control the borders."

"Sir, we hope to supply our out stations now that colder weather is coming." The yuzbasha felt the *Pasha* appraise him coolly.

"I have a government man coming to help do just that. There is also a man from the tribes who comes as yuzbasha. He must be watched closely. I expect him to attract some very important people here. I understand the two villages here are related: ours on the plateau side and theirs in the valley, one people. I knew a man from Spain once, an Umayyad, he said: 'pueblo pequeño, infierno grande!' 'A little village is a great big hell.' It's true. There has been carelessness in past times. I will change that now." After a pause the *Pasha* continued. "I have been busy with travel and administration, my bird has lacked exercise. I wish to be out before first light to a high spot on the border to satisfy that need. Where is the closest border point to the village?"

CHEECHEK'S DANCE

319

PEOPLE, PLOTS & PLACES IN CHAPTER 26

Aziz bey: an old smuggler, tired and rich enough to retire.
Barmani: the Manichean leader takes a gift to the capital.
Cheechek: the young helper despairs of the heir's life.
Kadir: knows something is amiss, but is not sure what.
Kerim: intends to carry the moon maiden back to her tribe.
Korkmaz: has a promise to keep and a baby's life to save.
Kynan: travels all night to find a place to hide.
Leyla: wounded and unconscious is carried to safety.
Nooryouz is alone, yet never alone as she had feared.
Onat bey: his eagle spies out the weaknesses of his post.
Peri hanum: the old family nurse warns Setchkin of trouble.
Setchkin: finds love, returns to the tribe and saves a life.
Twozan: makes peace with his hostage for a push home.
Yavuz: always spies on his partners and adversaries.
Yusuf bey: leaves instructions as he starts for Baghdad.

Glossary:
ahman: for goodness sake; what next?
akul'suz: stupid; brainless; dummy.
ayran: yogurt and water mix; a popular drink.
bayan: lady; madam; a title of respect; precedes the name.
hanum: lady; madam; a title of respect; follows the name.
kemer: sash; cloth belt or cummerbund.
koozoo: a lamb.
koo'zoom: my lamb.
tamom: okay; I agree; alright.

HOPELESS GRIEF

The moon guided his steps. A faint glimmer showed two sets of tracks, not close enough to be travelling together, but evidently one followed the other. Twozan's thoughts were bitter as he followed the trail through the short thorny scrub and grass. He muttered his frustration, anger and observations to the uncaring world as he rode.

"They move to destruction regardless of all advice and warnings to the contrary. Why do we trust our parents until we reach the age of near maturity, then switch to our peers who know as little as we do? To show our longed for independence, we desert all early teaching and contradict all we have learned to be true; thinking the consequences will be minimal. The arrogance of thinking that nature and the world will permit such an affront to their rule and purpose. God in heaven, why should they be permitted to be the exception to all creation's obedience? Why this suicidal frenzy to have some imagined peak of passion or virility; surpassing all the rest? This competition is the height of ignorance and folly. When the blind lead the blind don't they know there will be pits before them? Yet, I do recall my own foolishness. We ennoble stupidity and brag away our shame and lack of prudence. When good sense does not prevail, we weep away our bruised and broken hearts, bodies and spirits; grieving that madness is not the way of the world or of God."

He rode more slowly now, observing the direction and lay of the land. Ahead below a hill there was something not right. One trail goes up, the second ends with a black lump where the faint show of a curve intersects. The trail goes back round the hill, an ambush then? A muffled sound comes from the black lump. Twozan sighs and feels wetness on his face. Now he must recover her and heal the damage done.

The moon is starting to rise and a pale glow lessens the darkness. He speaks, "Setchkin Hanem, come, I will take you back to your yurt and child." The dark blob only continued its sobs. He sits his horse awaiting a reply, but none comes. The silence hangs on him like a weight. "He was always a wild one, especially after his mother died. Come, you gain nothing here:" Still no reply or acknowledgement. Twozan searches his mind for some clue - some word of comfort. He finds only perplexity and anxiety. He clears his throat, walks the horse closer and sighs. He prays, but no answer comes. Finally he asks, "Are you hurt? Is there anything I can do?"

The crying takes on strength and the shadow moves away. He follows. Then, she screams, "How can you help me, up there on your horse? You khans and lords on your high horses; you help none but yourselves."

He reluctantly dismounts and leading the horse moves toward her again, hands open. "See, I'm here because I'm concerned. I don't want to see you hurt or unhappy. I know how..." He breaks off without finishing.

"How can you know? Have you ever ached for someone you loved?"

"Yes, I have - I do."

There is a moment of silence. She moves. "Help me, give me your hand." He stretches out his hand and she catches it with both hands, pulling herself up, but she releases him suddenly and would have fallen, but for his quickness. She is breathing heavily and her weight pulls him forward. She lies back down again, groaning. "Oh, I can't. It hurts so. What shall I do?"

He stands over her protectively, bending to comfort her. Moon glow is lighting the scene and he can see her hands pressing her breasts. She continues to cry.

"What's the trouble? Are you injured?" She leans back on the hill. Her face, full of pain, shows now in the increasing light.

"I need my baby. I hurt, there's too much milk. I can't bear it, what can I do?"

Twozan is surprised. He grins and can't resist a joke. "Every Chipchak girl knows how to milk. Get to it." He laughs, relieved that the hurt is that simple and basic.

She grimaces. "*Ahkul-suz*, stupid! You don't understand anything: men never do. At least you could be sympathetic. Sit down, stop lording it over me."

He sits reluctantly and pushes his sword and dagger aside to sit.

She laughs wearily and points at his armoury scornfully. "The hedgehog sleeps in his spines. Does your desire for safety and protection bring you to such a rest? Give me water, I thirst." He rises and goes to the horse to bring back two bags. He takes off his *Kemer* belt with the harness for sword and arrow quiver and ties them to the horse's saddle. He returns to sit beside her, lifts the bags and says, "Here is ayran and here is water. Which will you have?"

"I have enough milk, so give me the water. You can have the ayran, so help yourself."

He complies, helping her lift and squeeze the thin stream of liquid into her mouth, adding. "If we were with the flocks now, we would get you a new born lamb to wrap and feed. You would soon feel better."

Her voice trilled. "Aha - a, *koozoo*? A lamb? Yes, I've heard of that practice among the sheep people. But we're a horse tribe, so I've never seen it. Oh, now I'm oozing. What can I do?" Her face lifts to his and he feels himself blush. He knows he's out of his element. He wonders what his mother would do with her - this foolish, love sick girl, who was half his age.

"Why did you leave the baby? He is so cute now that he's walking. I should have thought it would appeal to Sanjak."

She looks at him with pity, as if he were bereft of his senses. Her face averts as she says: "He is not the father, he knows that. The heir could grow up with the women of the court, without me. We give him supplements from our goat and I thought I would dry up if I left off nursing. I hadn't any idea of the pain."

"Perhaps it will stop." He suggests.

She lifts her head in the negative gesture. She groans in answer and presses her breasts. "No, the fever starts here and spreads. Here, feel the heat. I saw it once; in three days she died." Her sobbing started.

"You're not going to die. You're going to come back to the camp and marry me in the traditional manner. We have received food and assurances of safety. I have always loved you. I will make you

323

happy, if you will trust me and obey, as our religion demands. We will not argue this matter. You will marry me on our return.

She starts to laugh through sobs. "Behold the man! He tries to solve everything with one declaration of intent. As if all the problems of the world could be solved by one statement of commitment. *Tamom*, okay, I accept your declaration and will do my part as well as I can. I don't promise miracles, but I will try." She continued, "You have been good to me in spite of my taunts and anger. Will you forgive me? I knew you loved me and I took advantage of you. You are truly good: for me and for the tribe. You do pardon me, don't you? You wouldn't have asked me if you hadn't. There, I feel so much better now that we've said it."

He nods his agreement and she puts a hand out to touch his hair and stroke it. She holds his head close and croons. "You are a mild man really, not angry like Gerchen. You're a lamb. You love me in spite of all my foolishness, don't you?" Again he nods his agreement and she continues with her thoughts as the moon rises.

"You are loyal to the ruling family and to the stronger twin of Erdash's family. I wonder why the messages stopped and he never came to direct the tribes activities. Your plan was good and you won through, but Erben never came. He would have come. Perhaps they're all dead? My baby is the only true heir left. Isn't that so?"

Twozan answers distractedly. "We can't be sure of anything yet, but time will tell."

She pauses and searches for the right words. Her crying is over and her face glows in the moonlight. She sighs and smiles.

KOOZOOM

324

"Oh my lamb, if you are the guardian of my baby he will inherit the throne someday. You would see it through."

He adds softly. "Your father, Kaplan is the main obstacle. He would have the throne himself. He counts me an enemy."

She clasps her hands around to lift his face and laughing in triumph, kisses him long and hard. "But when we are married he will have to protect the father with the grandchild. He would be regent and have what he seeks after."

"You forget, Erden is Khan, though he has no boy child."

She laughs. "Erden is soft clay in the hands of my father. Kynan too is weak and weird since his stay with the East Bulgars. Only you are strong my lamb, he knows that. You will make a fitting father to my child. Come, he'll make his peace with you, when we're married every thing will be right." She pulls at him to bring his face up to hers for a kiss, as she adjusts herself comfortably on the hillside. Her eyes are wide and dreamy as she repeats his name and croons. "Twozan, my lamb, my lamb, *koozoom, koo...zoom...*"

> - - - - - - - > SMUGGLERS' CARAVAN > - - - - - - - >

"I put you behind and you dawdle and linger. I put you in the lead and you wander, lose the trail and zigzag up the road. Are you dazed or deliberately slowing us down?" Kadir was angry and shouting. Aziz and Yavuz hurried up to calm them and confer with the others while the old servant checked the harness on the loaded animals.

Aziz protested. "The boy's tired. We've been pushing it. Besides this is not the regular trail. You left it hours ago. Why I can't imagine."

"You raised him on these trails and he knows them all. What are you up to boy?" Yavuz stormed. "Leading us on a merry goose chase, he is."

"If we delay any more the sun and the troops of the new commander will be upon us," Kadir warned. Korkmaz shrugged and started walking back to the servant also plucking at the harness. "That's another thing," continued Kadir. "He keeps checking and stopping to adjust the belts and straps. I never saw so much trouble with harness as we have this trip."

Aziz held out his hands dramatically. "Why do you think I want out of this business? Everything is wearing out. More trouble, less profit every year. Now we get a new officer at the army base."

Yavuz bristled. "You pocket the money I approve for new replacements and keep the old harness even if it's falling apart. But you can't fool me I know I'm being cheated."

325

"Start your own business and get out of mine." Aziz bellowed at his tiny opponent. "But you won't, you make too much gain in mine."

"Without my intervention you would be the poorest man in the village," Yavuz replied.

Aziz held his hands up to heaven and sighed. "*Aman*, Allah, and it would be worth it: poverty and peace."

> - - - - - - - >AKSU MONASTERY > - - - - - - >

Father Barmani looked at the message left at the monastery gatehouse. It was a summons to court. The royal house had been in turmoil since the escape of the servant and three harem-girls about a year ago. The expulsion of the Chinese empire exiles had brought disaffection among the minorities both pagan and Christian. New pressures were being felt from Tibet where there was drought and an exodus of herders to save their droves. They were Buddhist in theory, but they had no problem with killing those who opposed them. The army was in the north chasing the reports of the escapees. They were rewarded with more evidence of the missing girls. Now the troops were divided, part riding south where they would remain until the rains returned. Standing armies were draining the resources of the ruling house. The luxury of the harem was by-passed for security in the south.

"I ought to go walking, it will take two weeks, but the call is urgent and the time allowed is short. I must forgo merit and ride."

"Yes, my Lord Bishop," the Mother Superior replied in response. "Speed would be advisable. We'll miss your presence and guidance."

"What can I take for a gift to our preserver of the faith?"

"A serving girl to replace the one missing might be an appreciated gesture," she suggested. He smiled remembering little Koolair, such a lovely, innocent child. Surely he could find a child uncorrupted by time and the enticements of the flesh, to show gratitude and respect. True surrender is to give one's best. He would take the sister's advice. He nodded agreement.

"Look for such a girl among the orphans. Get one of the best, for the honor will be great and she will gain merit for her dead parents." They exchanged smiles of mutual satisfaction.

"She'll have so many opportunities and choices." The nun paused, she sobered "There will be great temptations at court."

"There are temptations even in a monastery."

"The flesh is everywhere the same and weak." She looked down, blushed and drew a sigh.

Father Barmani smiled understandingly. "For this reason we have the Jesus of light to show the way and to give example and help. Whether the little one, by virtue, becomes a servant to the

Queen Mother or a concubine of the head cook will depend largely on her choices. Worth and spirit are always noticed and promoted. It is God's way."

The bishop made ready to go. "I leave the details and choice to you. We leave tomorrow at first light."

"I'll send Maniette, She shows promise. She will be ready, my Lord Bishop, go well," she bowed.

"Stay well, blessed sister, in the care of all angels and emanations." In his mind he traced their journey.

>-------->LOST ON THE TANRA DAH >-------->

Once the moon had risen, Nooryouz could see the rocks in pairs and triplets left for her. But when they left the road for the rough high trail, they were hard to distinguish. Sometimes natural occurrences confused her as to the trail. Fortunately, the baby slept and it brought no danger by crying. The night wore on and she stopped to eat a few bites to keep her flagging steps on their uphill march. She had grown strong and country-wise as a shepherdess, but had not the experience that years in the field would have given.

She realised that she was lost; everything was scattered and random except the sky. Two stars had remained consistently before her; she tried to keep them there in the west where they were lowering; she could not stop. She prayed to Allah, but he seemed far away, remote and uncaring. She remembered the words of Maril, the story of the good shepherd that she loved to tell. They had learned to be shepherds too. He went seeking the lost sheep. Her heart went out to call the shepherd. Was He too far away? Would He hear? The guiding stars moved behind the looming mountain-side. She sat to recover her breath. She was numb from the cold, so tired, so sleepy.

>-------->TOOZLU CAMP IN THE WILD LAND >-------->

"Go to your yurt, your baby will need you, we'll talk to our priest, Mukades later. First light is upon us and we must hurry."

From the hill they could see the camp still resting, but in a short time it would be busy as the horses awoke and the mares were milked. Now, only the guards would be awake, waiting to be relieved.

Setchkin protested. "Let me come with you. I would sleep in your bed. Why should we wait?" Her voice pleaded, but he replied with calm confidence.

"We will do this by tradition. It is right that the bride-to-be make preparations with her women. It will please the tribe and, as I said, your child needs you." He pointed to her yurt and set off in another direction to ride the perimeter where guards would be alert to intruders or to a chance visit by their commander.

"The baby has been ill, my lady. We've not slept tonight. He has a fever. We have used the herbs and even baths to cool him." Cheechek's voice was shrill and nearly hysterical. The baby's cry filled the yurt. Setchkin hastened to pick up and comfort the child. After an unsuccessful moment she gave him the breast and it seemed to quiet him. She hummed an old song and went on feeding him while the women gave a sigh of relief.

JUST WHAT TO DO

#1   If your life blows up like bubbles,
        And you find yourself with troubles.
        Calm your mind and pray it through.
        Then you'll know just what to do.

#2   When your heart goes pity patter,
        If you see someone who matters.
        Calm your mind and pray it through.
        Then you'll know just what to do.

#3   When you feel the world's attractions
        Know the pull of many factions.
        Calm your mind and pray it through.
        Then you'll know just what to do.

#4 When in combat or distractions,
 Wounded, weak, uncertain actions:
 Calm your mind and pray it through.
 Then you'll know just what to do.

#5 If in marriage there's divisions:
 Acrid words and wild decisions,
 Calm your mind and pray it through.
 Then you'll know just what to do.

#6 Loss and suff'ring are not funny.
 Life's not easy, but it's sunny,
 Calm your mind and pray it through.
 Then you'll know just what to do.

Peri hanum, the old nurse seemed more composed and in an aside to her mistress commented, while Cheechek cooked near the fire. "So you decided to return. Was it for the sake of the child or the rejection of the man?"

Setchkin gave her a hot glance, but said smoothly. "I found I had followed a fool, but a real man rescued me and made me understand where my duty and future lie."

Peri hanum cackled knowingly. "He's been hot for you for a long time. I wondered if you would ever give in. A widower can be a real comfort to a deserted young thing, especially a good man prestigious and old enough to balance a cold, overbearing father." Peri hanum nodded and patted her mistress fondly.

"We'll see Mukades today about marriage. No one will object if I show myself happy and approving."

Peri hanum cocked her head and looked sly. "What will your father say? Have you considered what marriage to this man, an obstacle to his plans, would do? What does it make you, his supposedly loyal daughter?"

Setchkin listened, eyes downcast. The child started to cry again. Cheechek returned to bring a warm bowl of crushed bulgur and attempted to feed the child some more, while Setchkin changed out of her travel clothes.

Peri hanum rubbed butter on her many scuffs and bruises, massaging away the soreness, while she lay on the rolled out bed talking. "It has been over three years since the marriage my father made for me. I have been maid, widow, mother, and now I have a child that should be weaned. I have briefly known youthful betrayal, weakened lust, and finally I have found a mature man I'm not willing to give up. Can't my father understand that?"

Peri hanum stroked her firm young body. "Understand? Yes, but not approve. Think back. Have you ever been able to stand against his wishes? Not once, even when in love or sickened with dread. Has this long trip to the south changed you?"

"Yes, at first I admired an adversary and captor. Then I saw his character in contrast to others. Now I love my *koozoom*, I want to go to his yurt."

The old lady shook her head as she finished her work. "Go as much as you will, but if you marry, you put yourself beyond your families help and protection."

Setchkin sat up to dress. "Twozan is serious about the tribes traditions, he is a Christian in more than name. He will break it off, if I refuse the ceremony. He'll persuade me, I'll want him to."

Peri hanum shook her head thoughtfully. "Perhaps you have changed, grown up and have a love that will be your new family. "I'm glad for you. There are few enough who do find it, but your father will find out. He has a dozen eyes and ears in every camp."

Setchkin stared at Peri hanum, her nurse since she could remember. She had always disregarded her, taken her servile ministrations as normal to one of her standing: the daughter of a noble chieftain. "And you will tell him? You have always told him? You're his spy?"

A SPY'S CONFESSION

"I said a dozen eyes. If I don't tell him, another will and it will go hard for me. Cheechek or some one will send notice. He might not let me live to see my grandchildren or even hurt them for my not reporting. He punishes all those who fail him." Old Peri hanum was serious.

Setchkin cried an objection, "But you love me and take care of me."

The old woman patted her. "Always, little miss impudence, but I must live within the limits that Tanra allows me. No one will defend my life, rights or property. I will write the note with Cheechek's help and you may see it. But it must be sent by the next morning. We can't stretch it out beyond that. He is impatient with failure to be prompt."

Setchkin laughed mockingly. "How do you propose to do that? Where will you make contact?"

"We got fresh pigeons at the last village. Our contact is only one way, but he'll get through to us if he has any orders."

Setchkin was stunned and sat in silence a long moment. Then she looked at the boy who was now peacefully sleeping, his face smeared with the bulgur paste. "At least he will sleep a while. God give him strength for this day, poor darling, it will be busy."

"He will be well enough now, *Bayan*, but he would have been dead by tonight if you had not returned. The standing order since his birth has always been that the day you abandon the child, would be his last day."

Cheechek and the child's mother stared at her in horror. She pulled a thin bladder pouch from her shalvar waist and tossed it on the fire. A hiss of burning consumed it and a strange aromatic smell filled the yurt. Peri hanum continued smiling reassuringly. "We'll not need that, the odor is harmless. You both can have your sleep now; your decision has saved you and him."

> - - - - - - - >REFUGEES IN KOKAND CITY > - - - - - - - >

The Bowzhun family was ready to depart for home. The anticipation produced joy and worry. Reports of his family enterprises had not been encouraging. There were debts and unfilled orders. Management seemed slack from Baghdad. Leaving Kokand was a relief and others would report if Maril, his daughter, or the harem escapees were discovered. Koolair was with them, passing as a daughter, because she would be taken from them if it were discovered that she was orphaned.

They had wanted to take Mariette with them from Aksu, but Barmani would not let her depart with her friends. He would not let her live with Christians who did not obey Mani. Koolair was now talking in Turkish as well as Arabic and Chinese. She was eager to see their new home in Baghdad.

The caravan was ready and departed at the first light of day. Yusuf promised his purchasing agent that he would set everything in motion when he arrived home. His last orders concerned his missing servant, Jon, and the missing women was clear. They were to be sent directly to Baghdad without delay, whatever the expense.

All hearts were filled with happy anticipation and prayers as the caravan moved out for Baghdad.

> - - - - - - - > ESCAPEES IN THE THORN-LANDS > - - - - - - - >

He rode as fast as the horse could manage. The night was chilling and Leyla clung to him half sleeping; awaking to moan painfully and then to sleep again. Kynan in the same way woke to dream and wake again. She seemed as light as a feather and he felt her feverish body throb as the thorn points spread their venom through her thin frame. She shuddered frequently. He wondered if there were any way to alleviate her condition, but necessity drove them on. They must escape the danger that followed. There was no alternative to flight. At dawn they would rest and recover. He dreamed again of the Kayalar wedding that had so impressed him as a boy. Every detail of dress, music and words stood out in brilliant display.

Then, sequentially other emotional events came one by one to mind: a cold, but politically sensitive father who sent his son to be a guest/hostage to the Bulgars. He was full of advice, but showed very little affection. Kynan remembered the bullying and tricks of the hostile Bulgar neighbours and then the affectionate reception and high standards of the family of Kerim of the East Bulgars. This man's name had served to get him past the last greatest obstacles to escape and freedom. Gratitude mingled with details of his escape from prison came in these moments of remembrance.

He loved the face and form of the maiden and felt himself cuddle closer to the little form lying limp in his arms. The body so warm and the air so chill burned his consciousness. The scent of blood and female flesh

332

kept him alert between his drowsy spells. He must get her back to the tribe, her people and his. Yet, the contrary urge came to mind; run away with her and never seek their people again. "*Yesu gel*" he groaned when the turmoil surfaced. But he was guided north by the polar star; toward the tribe and homeland. He would have to travel by night and rest by day. Tewfik bey had identified him with questions. He had used him for his aims to identify Erben and detect the way to his wanted companion. There would be pursuit.

Moon rise came with lightened glory and he looked on her sweet face. It etched its lines into his tender consciousness and increased the inner throb of his heart. He had found his treasure. It was so simple, yet so complex. He was no longer free, but a sense of well-being filled the slave with delight. He laughed at his new found joy and mystery. He held his trophy close. She would be the living proof of the new man he was now becoming, but he wanted to keep, not share, his prize.

THE DREAM DISCOVERED

Adjutant: despairs of future gain under the austere *Pasha*.
Bolben: leads friends away from dangers of captivity.
Derk: completes his mission, but a puzzle intrigues him.
Jon: discovers new dangers for his group.
Manish: helping a friend, spots trouble from far off.
Maril: lame again, can only finish with the help of others.
Nooryouz: finds safety in impoverished conditions.
Onat bey: exercises his bird and sees new sights.
Sanjak: finds rest and restoration on his journey north.
Seslee: meets new circumstances to complain about.
Setchkin: full of joy and confidence, surprises everyone.
Twozan: ready for marriage and a safe trip home.
Uigur Official: condemns all sinners to a fiery perdition.
Yuzbasha: carries out an order: the death of the guilty.

GLOSSARY
ahtesh: fire.
bashlayin: let it start; begin it; start from the top.
bowskurt: gray wolf.
Bosh ooze too nay: As you command. It will be done.
dekot: careful; attention.
Isa: ee'sah, Arabic name for the Messiah Jesus.
kavalta: breakfast.
Meseheem: my messiah.
shimdi: now; right away; this instant.

IN THE EAGLE'S EYE

"We've climbed all night, Bolben, when will we get there?"
Seslee voiced her complaint from the rear of the straggling
band of climbers.

"We'll be there just about first light. I used to do this climb
for the village running goods, but then I had to stop. So it has
been a few years, but I remember still." Bolben's voice was
clear and confident.

"Are you sure none of the border patrols will be out this
early?" Jon inquired.

"Not in the old days or now according to one of our
steadies. They called off the heavies yesterday according to
some. But we still have to be extra careful. There are folks in
the village who hate us."

"Why is that?" Jon asked curiously.

Bolben shrugged. "Old grudges between villages, plus a
personal scrape I had a few years back. We still have some
friends here, but caution is the word."

Manish was helping Maril, who had developed a limp and
was trailing with Seslee. Suddenly he looked up and noticed a
movement above them. His voice came low and warning.
"*Dekot*, Careful, there's a man on the hill over there." He

gestured with a movement of his head. All turned to stare in fright.

They saw him clearly outlined against the moon. Hooded and robed against the cold, he held an eagle on his glove, clearly ready to exercise the bird in the dawn light. He stood like a statue without moving in the semidarkness. They could not tell if he saw them as they scurried away over a dip in the trail. Bolben's voice was no longer confident, he panicked. He stared over the edge of the hill as the figure resumed its movements again. The bird opened its wings against the rising currents of air in the pass and screeched passionately.

"It's the new commander of the garrison. He loves to hunt with birds, they say. He made peace; failed to destroy an army of Turks. The Merv people have been up in arms demanding his punishment. He's been sent here till they cool down. He's a stickler for discipline and effectiveness and many hate him already. A few smugglers have decided to quit; for reasons of health." Bolben laughed, shook his head in wonder.

"We'll have to carry Maril if you go faster." Manish said.

"The Muslim village is at the bottom of the hill. We go to the edge a friend has his house there."

Jon and Manish took Maril between them. She swung her foot forward to hop as they took part of her weight on their arms. In this way they arrived before the house as a cock crowed.

> - - - - - - - >AT THE TANRA DAH UIGUR VILLAGE > - - - - - - - >

"Is the village surrounded and secured?" The Uigur Official demanded. "The midwife, witnesses and body were dispatched?"

"All were sent off last evening, My Lord," the Yuzbasha responded. "We have left no avenue of escape."

FIERY PENALTY

336

"We have no need of any others, except the witness Bolben. We want no survivors to report this. Let the act speak for itself."

The Yuzbasha bowed his answer. "All is prepared for the punishment of the village as you ordered. We await your signal."

The Uigur Official smiled his pleasure. He strutted and folded his arms across his chest. "A member of the Royal Harem was assaulted and murdered here. Village men are guilty. Let the righteous judgment begin. Our Priests say at funerals: 'Dust to dust, ashes to ashes.' Make it so. *Bashlayin, shimdi*, let it start, now." The Official nodded to the Yuzbasha, who drew his bow sending a goose quill arrow shrilling up into the sky.

At the signal the troops brought their torches out of the large inverted wine jars which had directed their light downward. Each man, lighting the tender on the tip of his arrows, sent them into the farther houses, while closer buildings were fired by the torch bearing soldiers. Those who sent the fire arrows now, armed themselves with deadly infantry arrows and awaited those who would attempt to escape. Infantry waited behind them, pikes and sabers ready.

"Remember that you will be awarded by your arrow count at morning light. Let no man go free! All are condemned," said the Yuzbasha as the stick, mud brick and thatch buildings caught and blazed in a burst of heat. Cries from the awakening Uigur villagers and the twang of bows gave evidence of confusion and the carnage of massacre.

> - - - - - - - > ABOVE THE ABBASSID ARMY BASE > - - - - - - - >

"You saw what I saw." The Commander demanded as he exercised his eagle, letting it fly in circles on a tether. He pulled it to indicate a return. It came to rest, perched on his gloved hand. Onat bey's words were not a question but a statement.

The adjutant nodded, "smugglers."

The new commander grimly smiled as he exercised his bird. With one smooth motion he swept off its tether and launched it into the bluing sky. With a cry of freedom, the bird mounted on the air current and was immediately circling up to become a point in the sky. The commander followed its flight. Below him the distant shrill of a goose-quill arrow was scarcely heard. Fire flared as tiny pinpoints blossomed toward each other. The points of light spelled tragedy for the village.

His eyes focused again on the distant valley where a fire spread burning brightly in the dark. "*Atesh*, fire!" He nodded his head knowingly. "Justice! The Uigurs have burned the adder's nest; the babies will have escaped to plague us in our land. Have the troops out for a sweep of the village after breakfast. Many more will have arrived by night."

"*Bosh ooze too nay*, by your orders, Onat bey, I'll see to it now." The adjutant left the cold hill gladly, he wondered at the astuteness of his new commander. Alert and vigilant, Onat had detected the movement his men were paid to ignore. He sadly calculated how much his income would drop as the *Pasha* took the illegal caravans and smuggler's profits away. If the village in the valley were burned, would there ever be money again in the far north army post?

> - - - - - - - > ON THE NORTH ROAD TO THE ARMY BASE > - - - - - - - >
Sanjak greeted the dawn with relief, he had ridden all night with a repentant, searching heart. Now, in the first light of day, he had made all the decisions he deemed necessary. Now he could rest and be glad in his resolutions. It would not be easy. He would need Tanra's help to keep them. His heart flooded with an old song of his faith. He sang to the dawn and the eternal blue sky.

MESSIAH'S LOVE

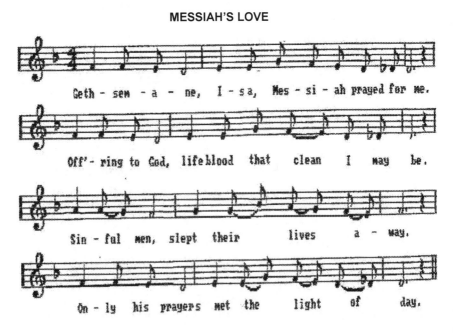

338

#1	Gethsemane, Isa Messiah prayed for me.
	Off'ring to God: lifeblood that clean I may be.
	Sinful men slept their lives away.
	Only His prayers met the light of day.

#2	Calvary, Isa Messiah died for me.
	Judged by God, for my sins He hung upon a tree.
	Innocent, He bears the guilt of all.
	That I be free, hearing God's sweet call.

#3	Glory and grace, Isa Messiah lives for me.
	Up from the tomb, guarded & buried, He's set free.
	Love calls to hearts, seeking His gracious own.
	Those who refuse keep their hearts of stone.

#4	*Meseheem,* Halleluya.
	Crown Him King, Halleluya.
	Coming again, Halleluya.
	Joyful He reigns, Halleluya.

Satisfaction and hope filled his heart. Now he could rest at the caravansary ahead and continue to the new military post, his assignment, later. He must trust and obey Tanra for his lost love's return to him in the future. Confidence led him.

> - - - - - - - >THE SMUGGLERS ON THE PLATEAU> - - - - - - - >

Kadir was furious as he rode back to the end of the column of burdened beasts. There a bale of cloth lay spilled on the rock and sand of the trail. The yak stood patiently waiting, two packs still balanced across its back. The third, top bale lay open on the trail. Korkmaz was calmly tying a rope to pull the bale together. Several pieces of rolled up cloth and clothes lay scattered from the fall.

"What now? How did this happen?" Kadir snapped, The boy shrugged, continuing to close the bale. "We've never had a trip like this. Why are you causing these delays? What are you up to?" He was off his horse now, his face close to the boy's.

Korkmaz straightened up and made a wide gesture. "Last trip, old gear, late start, taking a short, but rarely used, steep trail. Why is this trip filled with troubles? Bad judgment!"

"It was bad for not keeping a closer eye on you," retorted Kadir. He ground it out between clenched teeth. "I'll find and spoil your game, whatever it is." He reached down and picked up the bale placing it on his horse, securing it. He clicked his tongue and the yak moved down the trail toward the end of the column. The horse without its rider obediently followed. "Gather the scattered stuff and get down to the base cave. We'll deal with this question there. First light is here, there will be eyes open to see us."

"*Evit*, yes," was the only response that Korkmaz made. Kadir pondered this fact as he ran to catch up to his horse and lead it toward the head of the column. No defense or excuses meant a growing maturity in the child he had patronized before. His response to the questions hurled at him had been accurate. He had not fallen into the excuses and heat that his grandfather and his partner opponent used. Kadir felt respect grow, but determined to burn him a bit more at their depot. There had to be something more behind all this.

Korkmaz gathered the loose fabrics in a pile. He placed a black burka under a shalvar, embroidered blouse, and leaf green coat. He was careful to include a dark green blanket for the baby. He folded them over with the black and left them at the bottom of a sand pit under a plateau rock near the hut. She would need these and the canteen of water in the hiding place. He glanced down the slope to see if she were in sight. He prayed Allah's mercy, and left to face the chaffing he knew he would face when they unloaded the goods at the base cave.

> - - - - - - - >TOOZLU CAMP > - - - - - - - >

"You look beautiful Setchkin Hanum, but shouldn't you rest first, then, go?" Cheechek suggested to her mistress.

"Do you think I could sleep after a night like this one was? Full of life shaking events! I would drown in my joy if I lay down."

"What will you do now?" Peri Hanum inquired.

"Twozen will have relieved the guards and be dispatching our guest from the Caliph. You said his name is Derk bey? How strange. But they allow us passage home. That is surprisingly generous. I suppose it's because of Gerchen bey's agreement to serve the Caliph. I should put in an appearance there. Then, we can seek out Mookades our priest. He ought to be the first to know."

The serving ladies exchanged glances and agreed. "You are ready and we have ordered a fresh horse for you."

Should you wear Abbassid colors, my lady?" asked Cheechek.

"My heart is too full for black. The green coat will do." They helped her and she mounted and cantered away.

DERK'S SURPRISE

340

Derk bey was awake, but wishing he could sleep off the excess of kumiss from the night before. However, herders must always be up with their animals and there was no hope of sleep even when the animals were few. The camp was readying their departure. He was to have *kavalta*, breakfast with Twozan in the Khan's yurt.

He was surprised by the arrival of the princess, who had avoided him up to this point. Twozan bey smiled his approval and presented the lady. She was forthright and talkative as they ate.

Derk was astonished by her happy chatter. She explained that the baby was well and she thanked the Caliph for allowing them to return home. She seemed to sparkle and her face and voice radiated her joy. Derk wondered if this was the abducted woman and according to his sources: one they hoped to attract away from the Toozlu band. It was evident she was enjoying returning with them. Her affection for the leader was obvious. Why had she chosen to wear Umayyad colors? He wanted to stay longer and learn more, but Twozen bey reminded him that the road was long and the band needed time to depart for the north. He left reluctantly.

Already the change in Setchkin had been noticed and women exchanged nods and glances of understanding as she rode laughing beside Twozen to the yurt of Mookades, their priest. He became the last to know of her new found joy. She also realized that the traditional customs and preparations for marriage were full of joyful moments that she had never known previously. Love added a new dimension to life.

> - - - - - - - > ABOVE THE SMUGGLERS' VILLAGE > - - - - - - - >
"Allah, please do not destine me to die here, let my baby live." Nooryouz paused at the top of a rise to catch her breath and peer at the moonlit horizon. It seemed that a wider world opened around her, it was getting lighter for the mountain slopes were no longer steep, but rolled away into the horizon. The high mountain cold was intense and her fingers were stiff in the borrowed gloves Korkmaz had given her. Again her voice rose in her monologue with God and the light increased.

"Yesu, Messiah of my husband, save his child and let us be one, together again." She staggered forward and found herself sprawled in a low spot filled with blown sand. She looked down the slope in astonishment. She had climbed all night, now it went the wrong way. She climbed back up the ridge. Now in the increasing light she saw that the slope went two directions. Ahead was slightly down and behind it was steeply down. She paused in confusion, but the light meant danger. She moved slowly down the dry, sandy slope, sliding and staggering.

Then she saw it, between the high rocks and the sandy pits a trail of pressed earth threaded westward. Something moved off on the horizon like a procession of ants, each holding a load on its back. The moon was now resting in a blue sky. The light increased and the leading ant-like yak disappeared over the distant ridge. "That must be the smuggler's caravan I was following. Yes, they are going to their village in the land of Islam, where my family came from." She heard the distant clear call of a cock surely waking a village. A dog barked and the last ants vanished. She hurried wearily forward. She had braved the elements, now she must avoid men.

She saw a rocky mound beside the trail on the far left. Could that be the shepherd's hut? She wondered at the name, there was nothing for animals to eat here on the high passes. She paused a moment to catch her breath. The mountain air was thin and cold.

She saw a dark bundle that showed an edge of bright green. She gasped as she inventoried its contents. Gathering it together she staggered to the hut. The mound's opening faced south. She hurried to go in and pushed a flap of leather aside to enter. It held only enough room for three people to sit or a pair to lie down on packed earth. The flat surface of a rock near the door, a hand-span above the floor, served as a table. The flap of stiff, old leather served to close the opening as the sun rose over the barren hills and waking sounds came from the distant village below the ridges.

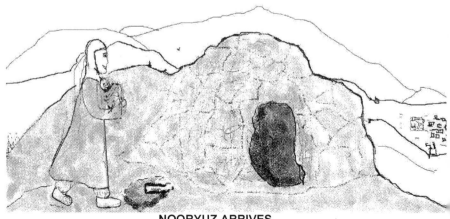

NOORYUZ ARRIVES

342

She laid her bundle of presents on the flat rock table. She would be properly dressed when the occasion demanded. She took the blanket and wrapped little Sanjer in it. She praised Allah again for the merciful boy. The hovel seemed like paradise; she was safely out of Uigur lands. The boy would bring food. Allah had delivered her back to the land of her ancestors. Generations before, they had departed Damascus, the capital of empire. They went to represent Umayyad interests in far China, where the Tangs ruled.

Endangered there, and among the Uigurs, she was now saved from their hands. Surly the heavenly shepherd had taken her to safety. She thought of a hymn she remembered from her husband's songs. Now it seemed natural and fitting. So she sang: of Gethsemane, Calvary, death and resurrection. Hope is born again. The music comforted her heart. "The Messiah Isa really is all they say," she murmured to herself reassuringly. With her face toward the covered door, she curled her tired body around the sleeping baby and slept. The dawn of a new day came with warming light over the barren ridges.

> - - - - - - - ->OUTSIDE THE ARMY BASE > - - - - - - - >

The Commander Onat smiled grimly as he watched his bird exercise while below the village burned. He knew his adjutant's preoccupation. He wondered if the fear of a new commander would out weigh the custom of payoff and if indeed the sweep would produce no more than a few, who were remiss on their regular payments for protection. He marvelled at how soon a soldier's sense of duty and right was replaced by corrupt seeking of bribes.

The Uigur commander, his equal across the border, had found fault with the village and burned it. The condemned village people there had forgotten Allah and turned every one to his own way. Now they suffered condemnation and death. Few would escape.

How easy to keep the external form of religion and lose the content and fall away from any truth it contained. This slackness was the hunting packs opportunity. *Bowzkurtlar*, gray wolves, were only a few predators among many grazers. Yet, they lived well by the packs persistence and co-operation to bring down large, powerful animals. The lesson is made obvious by their success.

The Seljuk migrants, like other Turkish tribes that were still in their homelands, considered the gray wolf to be an ancestor and totem of the tribe. Their human descendants were shifting the balance of power in the Islamic empire. They too, were purposefully killing an isolated few of the vast, but careless, human herds. The choice killing of one isolated rival Khan, Erben, and the innocent death of a blind Christian woman who knew too much, coupled with the conversion of a young Turkish leader, Gochen, put the political domination of the Arabs of Merv and Khorasan in the jaws of the pack's head. Those who thought they could control or prevent these events would soon be the new victims. Blood for the wolves needs was being sacrificially prepared. The head would command the feet and jaws. Let the hunt begin!

As the sun rose the commander gathered his bird and returned to the command post. He knew what he had to do.

He stopped, puzzled. He thought he heard singing. It was an old song of praise his old grandmother had sometimes sung. It was a beautiful, but sad song of betrayal and condemnation; yet somehow, victorious joy. His eyes swept the barren ridge, but nothing moved and the song soon ceased. Childhood days filled him with nostalgia. His mind traveled to the past and the choices now irrevocably made. A longing for an indefinable need pressed him. What did he lack? What reason was there to regret anything? Yet the moment lingered. His thoughts returned to his grandmother and childhood.

However, the new day must sweep away the old. He thought again of the wolf pack, as he directed his steps down the slope. The head would command him; the hunt would become intense.

Who could tell what a new day would bring forth? Only the Creator, the Tanra of the everlasting blue sky, knew, but kept it a secret to be revealed at a future moment.

READY FOR THE HUNT